The Doctrine Discovery

Paul Casella

The Doctrine Discovery
First published in Great Britain in 2022

Published by Paul Casella
Edited by Paul Casella
Cover Art by Sharon Rainsword

ISBN: 9798810384960
Imprint: Independently Published
www.pcasella.com

Tracy. Thank you for helping me grow into a better person, or whatever I am.

To explain all nature is too difficult a task for any one man or even for any one age. 'Tis much better to do a little with certainty, & leave the rest for others that come after you, than to explain all things by conjecture without making sure of any thing.

Isaac Newton

1

Elysia Martin looked down at her functional work shoes. She longed for the luxury that would soon be available to her. Manolo Blahnik, Christian Lacroix, Philipp Plein, the shoe world that would soon be hers. She smiled. It was a costume. No more, no less. It had taken years to create her persona. An instantly forgettable character who would soon be gone as if she had never existed.

She stood in the doorway and closed her eyes. Locating the corners of the industrial unit, she imagined a similar space half a millennium earlier. Fires, chimneys, athanors, and glass. Lots of glass. Glassblowing was a burgeoning enterprise. She smiled again. The Vauxhall Glassworks would have been just a mile or so away. Industries taken for granted now were developing at a rapid rate, and the cleverest men in history were leading the way. It was a golden age of innovation. Lives were improved daily by the latest invention or development, and yet so many of these wise men spent a seemingly excessive amount of time in pursuit of the solution to nature's greatest mystery. Some believed they had achieved the impossible. Maybe they had. It was of no interest. Her concern was locating the fruits of their labour.

"I have a delivery."

Lost in thought, Martin was startled by the noise. A delivery man wearing a brown shirt and shorts stood at her shoulder.

She signed for twelve boxes marked 'fragile'. The delivery man helpfully made four pallet-trolley trips, wheeling the boxes inside the space and placing them against a wall.

The shrink-wrapped packages included metal, plastic, and glass cylinders, bottles, tubes, and various other scientific components for which she did not know of or care for their purpose. It was not her task to put it together — the adept would do that. She checked her watch. He was scheduled to arrive in two hours.

She opened each box to check the stock against the manifest. She was pleased there were no breakages. Everything was there except one item. Her attention switched to the one item. She could have made alternative arrangements for the equipment delivery, but she wanted to be here for the desk. She *had* to be here for the desk. Too many people had entrusted her with bidding for it at auction to be absent for its arrival.

Martin waited outside the unit and stared at the gravel as she paced. It turned into a blur as she scraped her foot through the dust. After an interminable age, the rumble of a van's engine broke her mind drift. She looked up. At last. She waved her hand to declare her presence and waited for the driver to see her in his wing mirror. The van backed in front of the unit, beeping as it slowed to a stop. She watched as the tailgate lowered. The driver opened his cab door and walked around to the back.

"Unit twenty-five?"

"Yes, that's me."

He pushed the roller door upwards, revealing the space within. There was a single item inside. He climbed aboard the tailgate, pressed a red button on the side of the van, and raised the tailgate again. A colleague jumped from the passenger side and joined him inside the back without acknowledgement.

Bouncing on the spot, she peered into the space. "Careful with that. It cost a lot of money."

"Don't worry, love. We do this for a living."

"Yes, but not with nearly two-million dollars-worth of desk."

The two men walked to the edge of the van and looked down at Elysia Martin. She nodded slowly. They carried the desk onto the tailgate as if made of precious metal, rather than poorly carved, discoloured oak, with dents, scratches, and damage all over.

Martin thought the colour had drained from their faces when the driver handed over a clipboard for a signature. She handed the younger man a fifty-pound-note tip and thanked them without averting her gaze from the desk.

Once they had driven off, she walked back into the unit, closed the door, and locked it from the inside. She tentatively walked to the desk and dragged a hand across the surface, bumping fingers through the scrapes and blemishes, all the time considering the legendary work that had taken place upon its aged wood. She stepped around all sides before reaching for her backpack. She removed a long ruler and a black marker pen and headed back to the desk.

It took around forty minutes to draw the five-centimetre squares across the surface. She did not count. It did not matter. As long as the people in unit twenty-one were able to cut to her guidelines precisely. They had laughed at the strange request and asked for two hundred pounds. She handed them a thousand pounds in cash and told them she would give them a further thousand pounds if they returned the desk worktop's neatly cut squares, shrink-wrapped individually, and placed into packaging boxes. Only then would they be sent to the craftsman.

Three sharp taps and three more, with a short time space between, on the steel door, broke the silence.

Jason Price was not the healthiest looking character, nor was he the smartest-dressed, but he was fully appraised of his task and more equipped to follow the ancient instructions detailed by the greatest minds of the seventeenth century than anyone she had met.

Martin said, "I have taken delivery of the equipment you requested, and I have marked the desk where I would like it sawn, both on the surface and around the sides for thickness."

Price said, "I wonder what Sir Isaac would say if he saw you had drawn little squares all over his desk."

She did not respond to the comment but continued, "I would appreciate it if you could arrange for the people at unit twenty-one to collect the desk. They have been paid. What else? Yes, the steel work surfaces you have requested will be delivered this afternoon, which will give you a chance to start unpacking and setting up."

"What about incidentals?"

Martin walked to her backpack once again and withdrew her purse. She handed over a credit card. "This card does not have a limit, but please don't go booking a holiday to Brazil just yet. I will be fully aware of each transaction."

"I wouldn't—"

Without expression, Martin said, "No, I know you wouldn't, Mr Price."

She placed the ruler and pen back into her backpack and pulled out a small, padded envelope. She handed the package to Price and said, "One final thing, and again, I expect this does not need saying, but please guard this with your life," she leaned forward, and whispered, "It is, as you know, more valuable than your life," and then stepped back. "Once you have set everything up, I will return to check on your progress, and I will have at least one more for you."

Price took the padded envelope and carefully placed it in his jacket pocket. He was profoundly aware of its value to the project.

2

"Okay, let me get this right. The electrician is the roadie because he installs stuff and makes sure there's light and sound. The brickie is the bass player because it's the easiest instrument to play. Heating engineers, then. What am I, in your band analogy?"

"Oh, plumbers are like keyboard players. It's more technical than you think. There's pipework, bends, straights, welding, and central heating guidelines to follow. Showers can be even harder. Customers haven't got a clue what's behind the wall where their shower pipes run."

"Okay, so what's the chippy?"

"I'm a carpenter."

"If you say so. What's the chippy?"

"Lead guitarist. Obviously."

"How's that?"

"Well, the most visible second fix and centre of attention.

We've got skirting, architrave, staircases—"

The door to the garden opened.

"Heads up, here comes the lead singer."

Rob said, "All right, chaps? What are you jabbering about?"

Eddie replied, "Usual nonsense. Jamie reckons a team of trades is like a band."

"So, what am I then? Actually, don't answer that. I just came to tell you the owner will be on-site this afternoon. Something about the floorboards where you're running pipework jutting against some wood panelling. They haven't been touched for four-hundred odd years, and he wants to make sure there's no unnecessary damage."

"That's all I need," Eddie said.

"I never heard anything from him while we were doing the kitchen, but now we have removed the boarding from the upstairs floor he wants to be here. Anyway, that's all. Enjoy your lunch, and I'll see you tomorrow."

"Your hair looks nice today, Rob."

"Get stuffed, Jamie," Rob grinned and swished his long wavy hair as he walked away.

"See. Lead singer."

Eddie had not visited the top floor of the building. He knew the road was full of old buildings. A couple had been there for over six hundred years, but he was only interested in his part of the project — upgrading the heating and plumbing for the six bedrooms and bathrooms.

With the door removed for repair, he walked through the opening to a light-filled room. Two original feature windows dominated the space. To check for soft areas, he pressed his fingers to parts of the dark brown oak wainscot, oxidised by centuries of open-fire smoke and tobacco. It was as firm as it had ever been. The instruction was explicit — no repairs.

Something Jamie would be relieved about. He looked to his right. He saw a narrow staircase leading up to the bathroom, and thought, that will be fun with pipework. He consoled himself with the knowledge that he wouldn't have to attend to hundreds of rusty floorboard brads.

He heard the owner approach before he entered. He was not as Eddie expected. Wiry, athletic, and tall. Not as tall as Eddie's six foot two, but close enough. He was bald. Proper bald. No closely cropped areas above his ears. The red bow tie and brown duster coat were out of place on a building site. Perhaps he was playing a middle-aged country squire and had come straight from filming a cider commercial.

"Hello, mate. Eddie," he held out his hand. A name was not forthcoming, but the owner shook. His grip was firm. "There's nothing to worry about. Your joists run to the windows, but there are gaps. So, although I would ordinarily have to make notches for the pipework, I should be able to get away with using plastic and push-fits, which will allow for plenty of flexibility."

The owner nodded and looked towards the dark wood wall.

Eddie said, "I won't damage the panelling," and straightened his knee pads before grabbing a claw hammer. It was a quick process. As soon as he raised two long nails, he agitated the board free, which made it easy to elevate the adjacent three. The thick dust had a medicinal aroma. It always did. He had no idea why.

The owner peered over Eddie's shoulder. "Is there anything down there?"

"I wouldn't have thought so, but you never know, these boards haven't been lifted before. The ceilings below are probably only a hundred years old," Eddie swept his arm from one side of the room to the other, "but these four floorboards have been attached to the joists for centuries."

Eddie scanned the length of the revealed space before

14

reaching below the unexposed boards. More dust. He felt a need to fill the silence. "This shouldn't take long. I'll push some pipe around the joist nearest to the panelling to run it through to the next room. I'll then attach a ninety-degree push-fit and lay the pipe along the full width. I will add copper tails for the radiators."

The owner nodded but was still staring at the oak wood wall.

Eddie slowly pushed a length of pipe around the space by the wall panelling to avoid damaging the old joists. He walked to the other end and forced it through to the room next door. It hit an obstruction. "Would you mind looking below the end joist where it meets the panelling to see what's holding me up?"

Eddie was surprised to see the owner lay flat on the floor to peer below the panelling. He stretched his arm to reach in all directions, completely ignoring the years of accumulated dirt and debris.

"Try now."

Eddie pushed the pipe firmly. It moved freely. "Well done. What was it?"

Eddie thought he saw the man hesitate before he heard, "Nothing. Just some dirt."

As the owner lifted himself upright, Eddie saw he was covered in dust. "Sorry, mate. It looks like I've got you all messy."

The man looked down at his coat. "It's nothing, don't worry," he was halfway through the door when he added, "Sorry to have disturbed you."

Eddie stared at the empty entryway and said out loud, "That was weird."

He peered down the stairs to see the man disappear around the winder before he returned to the task at hand. Reserved for repurposing into a door, Eddie propped the four ancient lengths of wood against the wall. Jamie had pre-cut flat and straight replacements. He was impressed by the distressed finish and dark varnish his friend had applied.

He lowered the first into position and pulled it in place, careful not to damage the wainscoting. He felt a large gap. A chunk was missing from the support beam. He laid flat and moved his arm upwards behind the wall. A decorative panel fell outwards onto the floor. Eddie looked around. Did anyone hear that? He would have to fix it back on straight away. He gazed into the space to see the support strut was missing.

He knew he would be last on-site but called out anyway, "Jamie? Ahmet?"

No answer.

He found a length of wood in the corridor and two small steel straps in his toolbox. Fifteen minutes later, he threw his toys in the toolbox and made his way down the stairs. Four creaked. Jamie will need to see to these, he thought.

Eddie crossed the road to 'the country's tidiest work van'. The lads ribbed him, but he could always find his tools while they often rummaged as if at a jumble sale. The toolbox fit neatly in the wooden compartment he had built when kitting out the interior.

As he was closing the van door, Eddie heard a noise. He looked around to see two streetlamp illuminated figures moving quickly. He saw a punch connect with the side of the property owner's face.

"Oi!" Eddie raced between the parked cars, looking both ways at the otherwise empty road, and saw a second bald man turn and run in the opposite direction. His attention switched to the owner, now sprawled on the floor.

"Are you all right, mate?" Eddie grabbed the man's arm to lift him.

"Yes, yes, I'm fine. Don't worry. It was just a dispute," he spoke quickly. "I know him. Don't worry."

The dazed man thanked Eddie before he also hurried off. In the opposite direction to his attacker. Eddie stood there. "Well, that was weird." He watched as the man vanished around the corner and looked in all directions. Early evening drizzle glinted in the streetlamp light as it cast its lambent glow across the empty road — the only noise, distant traffic.

3

As Eddie pushed the door open, a familiar blast of malt and hops greeted him. A comforting aroma of the ages. From childhood memories of soggy beermats and smoke-filled saloon bars to teenage liaisons and adjusting tastes. He had been through an alcopops phase, a real ale phase, but now he just looked forward to a cold lager with his best mate.

"You wouldn't believe what I have just seen," Eddie grabbed a pint from the table and took a long glug before taking his seat. "The owner of our building just got smacked in the face outside. I checked to see if he was all right, but he just trotted off. Said he was fine. Thanks for the pint, by the way."

Jamie said, "I'm already on my second. How long does it take to pack your van away?"

"He looked okay. I thought it was worth mentioning but never mind. I'm late because the room I was preparing had a chunk missing from inside one of the wall panels. I had to repair it before I left. I think something must have been hidden in there at some stage, but there's nothing there now."

Jamie said, "You know what, in all the years I have been doing this, the only thing I've ever found on a job was half a dozen headless Action Man dolls, posed like a murder scene, behind an old wardrobe."

Although a regular, the pub was a beacon of unfamiliar familiarity in Eddie's world. Work, pint, chat, home. Everything else was fluff. "I wonder what was hidden there," he looked around as if for the first time. "It's like an Aladdin's cave of ephemera in here."

"Eddie, it's just junk."

"To you maybe, but all of the things Mark has on the shelves around the pub will have its own history. Who knows what? See that typewriter," Eddie pointed to a shelf behind Jamie. "It's probably about a hundred years old. Used by a secretary to a businessman, or accountant, or something. Who knows what might have been written with it?"

"Eddie, it is just junk," Jamie shouted over to the landlord, "Mark, where did you get all the stuff around the walls? I am running a serious risk of Eddie boring me to sleep. Tell him it's from a trade replica supplies company so I can get on with my pint in peace."

The landlord threw a cleaning cloth in the bar's sink and made his way around to their table. "Actually, it's not. That hotel down the road, along from where you're working. You know, next to the place that reckons it was where Portsmouth Football Club was founded," Mark paused for nods of acknowledgement. "When that was being renovated, a couple of house clearance workers came in and said their van was already full. They couldn't fit everything in. So they asked if I was interested in buying some antiques to decorate the pub. It happens now and then. Someone is always trying to make a few quid. Well, anyway, I had been thinking of changing it up in here and bought this stuff from them."

Eddie said, "So, it's all from that hotel down the road?"

"I don't know. Maybe. They just said they had a load of stuff, and I could have whatever I wanted from their van. I've always thought it looked nice, and some of it makes for a talking point. Which you two are proving."

Jamie said, "It wasn't me. Eddie has an active imagination. He thinks Miss Moneypenny owned that old typewriter, and he's just missed out on a box of gold that was once hidden behind a wall."

"Don't take any notice of him," Eddie said as he rose from his chair to take a closer look at the shelves. "You know what, Mark, I've always liked those old buckets. I reckon they must have come from a Victorian fire station."

"How much do you want to give me for them?"

Eddie laughed, "Why, are you redecorating again?"

"As you give me so much of your wages, I might as well tell you. I've sold up."

Jamie threw his hands in the air. "Oh, that's typical. You find a decent pub, settle in, and then it turns into some kiddie disco club."

Eddie said, "Jamie, it's not all about you. Mark, it will be sad to see you go. We almost got to like you."

The landlord laughed. "Thanks, mate. It's all got bit much, what with the wife's mum dying and all that. I think we're off to Torquay to be a bit nearer her dad."

Eddie did not want to pry further. Mark would tell them more in his own time. As he continued to peruse the shelving, he asked, "What's that?"

"What's what?"

"There's something wrapped in old cloth. Looks like sackcloth and old string."

"No idea. I just piled it all over the place when they brought it in. You know what, I agree with Jamie. It's just old junk."

Eddie picked up the package. He estimated it was around the size of a book. It was tightly tied with straw-like strands but bulged at the top. He placed it on the table. Mark and Jamie watched as Eddie retrieved the two fire buckets from their hooks. He deposited them on the floor next to the table before walking over to another shelf, where he picked up an old whisky branded water jug, three leather-bound books, and a pewter beer mug.

Mark looked at them as if examining a rare and delicate butterfly.

Eddie laughed. "It's not the Antiques Road Show, Mark. How much?"

"Fifty quid."

"No."

"Twenty quid."

Eddie laughed again. "I'm looking forward to meeting the new guvnor."

Eddie closed the front door and yelled, "Luce, you home?"

As he entered the living room, his fiancée emerged from the kitchen. She was wearing her class T-shirt and tracksuit bottoms. Heavy strands hung loosely from her dark hair.

"You're late. Long day?"

"Well, an interesting day. That's for sure. How was Chopsocky?"

"It was good. We had a new guy join today," Lucy kissed him on the lips while simultaneously prodding him in the stomach. "And as you well know, it's *Wing Chun*."

He smiled. "Another big bruise on your arm, I see. Are you going to wear a sleeveless wedding dress?"

"It's a tough sport, and never you mind what sort of dress I will wear to the wedding. You will see it on the day. And no bruises, promise. These arms are harder than Wolverine's,"

Lucy slapped a lumpy forearm. "And why was your day interesting?"

Eddie pulled out a dining chair. The smell of crisping onions prompted instant hunger. It was sausage night.

"Er, what are you doing? You can't sit down in those," Lucy pointed to his dust-covered trousers. "Give me your Dickies. I'll stick them in the washing machine."

"You want to do what with my Dickie?"

Lucy said, "Your trousers, dummy. Give them here."

Eddie placed the package on the table before removing his trousers and polo shirt. He handed them to Lucy and sat down in his boxers and socks. Lucy shook her head and raised her gaze to the ceiling. Ignoring Eddie's transparent attempt to play with her, she asked, "What's that?"

Eddie looked at the package on the dining table. "I have no idea. Why don't we find out?"

"Where did you get it?"

"I bought it off Mark at the pub. Along with some antique books and breweriana things. There's a couple of old fire buckets in the hall."

"Oh, good. More rubbish. Haven't you got enough in the garage?"

"I thought they would make good plant pots for the garden."

Eddie grabbed a T-shirt, and tracksuit bottoms from the clotheshorse, turned his attention away from the package and explained the day's events. After he told her of the strange behaviour of the owner and the attack, Lucy rose from her seat. "Well, I'm pleased he was okay," she emptied the change from Eddie's trouser pocket and walked into the kitchen before dropping it in the wedding fund tin. "The buckets are nice," she added while simultaneously pushing onions around the pan and turning down the bubbling potato-filled saucepan.

Eddie began to unwrap the parcel. The string was stiff, but

a slightly firmer tug, and the knot untied. He gently lifted the aged cloth apart to reveal a brown coloured, dusty, but smooth-edged stone. Beneath was a thin book.

The book had the title *Mutus Liber* printed at the top. Below was a drawing of a piper climbing a ladder, surrounded by a ring of foliage. Eddie gently prised open the delicate pale, yellow-edged pages to reveal an illustration on each page. Fifteen in total. There were no words.

"It appears to be some sort of ancient kid's book. It's just drawings."

Lucy walked over and replied, "This must be Latin. Or whatever they spoke back then."

Eddie creased his eyebrows. "Keep up, Luce. The writing below is in French," he said as he retrieved his laptop from the sofa and typed *Mutus Liber.* The information page appeared at the top. He read "Hermetic Philosophical works - *Mutus Liber* (Mute Book). Latin: Silent Book. First published in La Rochelle, France, 1677 by Pierre Savouret. Important literature related to Alchemy. Includes illustrated plates detailing alchemical paths to enlightenment, although interpretation is often considered controversial and contradictory in alchemical fields. Twelve original copies are known to exist — first reprint in 1702," he sat back and puffed his cheeks, "Well, I don't know what that's all about, but it carries on. He scanned the page with his finger. "Oh, here you go. It says alchemy is 'speculative thinking looking for the spiritual equilibrium whose metaphorical form would be the philosopher's stone'."

Lucy said, "So, it's an old Harry Potter book?"

Eddie snorted, "No. It appears this is a seventeenth century book about alchemy. You know, turning metal into gold. That sort of thing."

"I suppose they believed that stuff back then," Lucy gently turned the book towards her. "If only a few dozen copies were printed, it must be valuable. Some rare books can be worth a small fortune."

He stared at Lucy and grinned. Lucy raised her eyebrows and shook her head. Eddie said he would take the book to a dealer in Portsmouth to see if it was worth anything.

They ate dinner, spoke about the mundanities of work, and packed the dishwasher. Lucy turned on the television, but Eddie wasn't paying attention. He was staring at the book. Something was niggling him, and it wasn't the potential value. He grabbed his laptop and walked over to the dining table.

Lucy asked, "Don't you want to watch?"

"No, it's not that. I want to check something."

Ten minutes later, Eddie slumped back in his seat and breathed out loudly.

"What's up?"

"While I was in the pub, I noticed some old photos of the surrounding area. Not just the Victorian and Edwardian street scenes, but more recent ones. There was one of the Queen's Silver Jubilee street party from 1977 and one of the Christmas lights being turned on a couple of years ago. I also saw one of the opening of the hotel along the road from the property I'm working on."

"What the green one, next to where you told me, ever so interestingly, Portsmouth Football Club was founded. I think my mum said she had been in there for a drink."

"I will ignore some of that, but yes, that's the one. Some of the items Mark said he had around the pub might have come from there when it was being renovated."

"Might have?"

"Yes, but he also said it could just be general house clearance stuff. The thing is, in the photo of the hotel opening — it didn't register at first — but I recognised someone. I wanted to check with the local newspaper archive online."

"And?"

"It was the owner of the place I am working on."

"That sounds like a coincidence. Didn't you know he owned both properties?"

"No. I didn't. He must be worth a few quid. I also know he doesn't own the other place now because I found a press cutting about its sale."

Lucy recognised a facial contortion from Eddie's range of distant expressions. "It's not that, though, is it?"

"No, I was thinking about the book. I don't know, Luce. It's been sat on a shelf for a few years, with no one knowing what was wrapped up. It seemed to me the owner was looking for something today. He was then attacked outside."

"Maybe he was looking for some old fire buckets to use in his back garden."

"Or, maybe he was looking for an old book that would have fitted in the space I found. Maybe it is scarce and worth a fortune. Maybe he was attacked outside by someone else that wanted it."

Lucy laughed, "You have a very active imagination, Eddie Hill."

Eddie knew he had an active imagination but was also sure the man had been looking for something, and was attacked for something else. Or, possibly, the same thing.

4

Eddie turned for the umpteenth time. He peered at the clock with one eyelid open. 03:47. He squeezed his eyes shut, knowing time was marked only by those glowing red numbers. He looked again. 03:53. He blinked away the red dots of the drifting imagery from his focus, but sleep would not come. He pulled the covers to one side and shuffled out of bed as quietly as he could.

He gently closed the bedroom door and walked to the bathroom. He pressed the light switch and stared at his reflection. His dark hair was showing a touch of grey at the sides. He wiped a gripped hand across his stubble as he yawned. After showering and brushing his teeth, he dressed in the back bedroom before creeping downstairs.

He retrieved the package and placed it on the kitchen worktop. His gaze barely averted while he reached for the steaming kettle.

He was still staring at the package when he set it on the passenger seat of his van. He gently turned the key. The engine came to life. First time every time. He pressed a knob and watched as the windscreen wipers shuddered across the glass to clear the autumnal dew.

Fifteen minutes later, Eddie was parked in between the worksite and the green hotel, which he could see was called *Ye Spotted Dogge*.

He reached into his console tray and turned some loose change over in his hand. Why was the owner so keen to be present? Did he think the book was there? What is so special about it? Was he attacked over it? Why would someone attack him for it? Was the owner being watched? He looked over his shoulder and at the view from his mirror. *Was he being watched?*

Just as it was when he left work the previous evening, the road was dimly lit, and everything was quiet. As the main thoroughfare away from the seafront, it would not be long before the road's activity began in earnest.

He stared at the building across the road. He had seen it many times but had never taken any particular notice. He had not even known what it was called. It was split into two halves — two buildings joined as one, like non-identical twins. One section, a child's imagination of a house with six large split panel sash windows. The other, separated by an offset front door. This part of the property looked like a standalone home, with a former doorway converted to a window, two arched panes, and two more shed dormers on a gambrel roof. It was an attractive and characterful building, the sort used in a romantic comedy film about a wealthy advertising executive and a local news reporter who fall in love before moving into their dream home — except in Portsmouth rather than New York.

Eddie's attention returned to the package. Why was he so bothered? Could it be because a man was attacked over it, and he could not prevent it? Or was it because the man knew it had been hidden for centuries, and he wanted to know why?

A tap on the window woke him. His neck was stiff. Eddie wiped saliva from the corner of his mouth before looking outside. Jamie was standing next to his van with two coffees. It was his turn.

Eddie opened the door. His friend had that stupid hat on again, 'J Stuart – Carpenter Extraordinaire'.

"I wondered when Lucy would come to her senses and kick you out," Jamie handed him his steamless coffee. "It was only a matter of time before you were sleeping in your van."

"I just got here a bit early and nodded off."

Jamie directed his gaze to the package on Eddie's passenger seat. "Is that the thing you got from the pub yesterday?"

Eddie took a sip of the tepid drink as he gathered his senses. The priority was asking Rob to call the owner so he could find out more about the package. "Interesting story. I opened it when I got home—"

"Did you clean your toolbox first?"

Eddie frowned, "Yes, of course. I have wet wipes in the glove box."

"Really?"

"No—"

Eddie saw a car pull into the space next to his van. "It looks like Rob's finally turned up. I'll tell you later."

Rob reversed into the space behind Eddie as two other workers walked along the road. The sparks.

"All right, chaps," Ahmet said.

Eddie and Jamie nodded in unison.

Rob closed his car door and hurried towards them. "I've got some bad news, I'm afraid, boys. The job's on hold. We've got to close up the site."

Eddie asked, "What's up, mate?"

"The police have just called. They have asked me to go down to the station. It seemed the owner didn't have a wallet on him, and they couldn't get into his phone. All they had was my business card."

"What are you on about?" Jamie asked.

He tried again. "The owner, Mr Prior, is dead. I think he was murdered."

Eddie could see Rob was agitated, so he calmly asked, "Did they explain what happened?"

"They don't tend to answer questions. I suppose I will learn more when I get there. They did ask if I had been paid on time and how the job was going, though. I thought they were accusing me, but they claimed they were just following all leads, and mine was the only route to identification Mr Prior had on his person."

Eddie thought his boss needed a coffee. He handed him his.

"Thanks. I said everything was fine with the job. I was getting the money in instalments upfront, and it was a good job. I asked what was going on."

Sergei and Ahmet glanced at each other. Eddie and Jamie stared at their boss, who corrected himself, "Well, they didn't say that it was a murder exactly. They described it as a suspicious death."

Eddie said, "I think that just means they don't know the cause of death."

He wondered whether the property owner was attacked for the package in his car rather than his wallet.

Rob looked at Eddie. "He was attacked here. Outside the property."

Eddie said, "That's a bit odd, I was—"

"You were the last one to leave, Eddie. The police said a witness saw a commotion. Did you see anything?"

"Well, I was going to say—"

"If he was murdered, there would have been noise. The

killer must have been after something. What did you see?"

Eddie replied, "I didn't see anything. I must have still been inside, or I had left when whatever happened, happened."

Ahmet said, "Hang on. He couldn't have been killed here. The police would still be here now, and this would be a crime scene. It would be surrounded by black and yellow tape," he looked around the group and smiled. "I like cop shows."

Rob said, "I didn't think of that. They said he was attacked here, and it was a suspicious death."

Jamie said, "You were just putting two and five together. It's no surprise. I'm sure it was a bit of a shock."

Sergei and Ahmet had a short conversation in Romanian before Ahmet said, "It could mean anything. They haven't discovered how he died yet. There are medical examination results and whatever other procedures they follow before they can officially declare what has happened."

Rob said, "Well, all I know is I am going to have to make a few phone calls to see what happens next. We will have to stop work until I can find out about the job. There's no point in carrying on if we aren't getting paid."

Rob then turned and walked back to his car. Holding the door open, he said, "Look, I'm sorry, chaps, but I'll give you all a call later, once I know what's going on."

He drove away and left the four men standing together.

Jamie looked around the group and said, "He seemed to be in a bit of shock. The bloke probably just had a heart attack or something."

Sergei said, "He is a good boss. I think he is just worried about the project."

Eddie shrugged his shoulders. "It's the first time I've worked for him."

Jamie said, "I've only done one other job for him, but I think Sergei is right. We're not going to get paid, so what's the point of carrying on?"

Eddie looked at the electricians and said, "I haven't got anything lined up. This job was supposed to run for a few weeks, and I have a wedding to save for. What about you two?"

Ahmet glanced at Sergei and then back to Eddie. "Sergei knows everyone. His mates will always have something going on. We should be all right by tomorrow."

Jamie said, "It comes in handy speaking Romanian."

Ahmet replied, "Romanian and Eastern European Studies at Uni."

Eddie laughed, "My history degree isn't much help in my job."

The three men turned their gaze to Jamie.

"Don't look at me."

The electricians walked back to Sergei's van. Ahmet said, "If anything comes up, I will let you know, but I am sure we will be back on site again in a day or two."

Jamie said, "It's fine. I could do with a day off."

Eddie and Jamie watched as the electricians drove away.

Eddie stared at Jamie, "Let's go. I've got something to show you."

5

Detective Constable Ian Gale draped his jacket over the back of the chair and sat. He adjusted the pneumatic pump to its highest bracket and got as comfortable as he could. He was new to the role, and hot-desking was the best he could hope for. He retrieved his notebook from his pocket and thumbed through to the page that detailed the telephone call's content. He needed to join dots between what he knew and what he could guess?

Mr Prior left his property – attacked outside.
One anon call witness to attack.
Tall man, well-built, dark jacket, dark hair. Nothing else.
Witness also saw work van drive away shortly after.
Partial plate. GY07.
Later died on lower ground floor car park Gunwharf

Quays. Awaiting report.
Prior sustained injuries to face and blunt force trauma
to back of head. Blood evident by railing.
Area cordoned off for further.

Gale leaned back. The man was attacked twice. Once
outside the property, and then again in the car park. Where he
either hit his head or was assaulted once again. Maybe he
wasn't attacked a second time. Maybe he was concussed after
the first attack. But how did he hit the back of his head and not
the front as he fell? People tend to fall forwards, not backwards
— unless pushed. No. Someone did this, and whoever it was,
did not get what they wanted the first time, so they had another
go somewhere quiet. The car park would have been quiet at
that time of night, he thought.

He looked back to his notebook. 'One anon call witness'.
Who was the tall man? Was he a worker? Was he the attacker?
Gale turned the page of his notebook and then turned his
attention to a sticky note on his desk.

The partial plate was good enough to identify a single
Portsmouth resident. The worker's name was Edward Hill. He
typed his name into the desktop computer. A file popped up
immediately. "Okay, I need to talk to this guy," he said out
loud. He looked around. No one was paying him any attention.

Owen Garvan walked up the steps and over the blue road
bridge to its centre. He vacantly watched as the cars drove by.
The railings vibrated as each vehicle passed below. Fast.
Everything moved so fast. He set off for the other side of the
bridge and paced outside a carpet shop. He climbed back up
the steps and repeated the process. Why was he here? What
could he do? It was an accident. He only grabbed his coat.
How could he have known he would hit his head as he fell?

He didn't have it anyway. There was nothing in his pockets

except his wallet. And that stupid red tie. Who wears a bow tie these days? It wasn't in his car either. He had checked everywhere. Surely the police would not have it? How could they have found it if he couldn't?

He stopped pacing and stared at the nondescript red brick rectangular building. He considered the consequences of a visit to the police station. What would happen? He could hardly tell them he had an argument with Ken Prior in the afternoon and punched him in the face. Neither could he tell them that he followed Prior's car to the car park later in the evening, where he confronted him again before he fell and cracked his head open.

Oh yes, that sounds like an accident. Stupid. *Stupid*.

He had one job. Watch to see if anything suspicious occurred at the building site and look out for irregular behaviour. Approach and question anyone acting out of character. Have casual chats any time. It was not the first time they had spoken to each other. No one said anything about hurting anyone. Certainly nothing about killing them. But it was an accident. Not that anyone would care about that. Not the police. Not his friend.

It was dark when Garvan returned to his car, but he knew he needed to drive back to the property for a thorough look around.

He pulled into a space in front of the pub along from the latest potential building. The lights were on, but no one could see him through the old-fashioned glass windows. He heard muffled noises. A couple walked by, laughing, holding hands. He waited for them to round the corner at the end of the street before he left the car, gently closed the door, and walked to the front of the property. He looked along the kerb and under the single parked car in the road. There was nothing other than a lone chocolate bar wrapper nudging along in the wind.

He walked back to his car, climbed in, and sat in silence.

He looked through Prior's wallet. Driving licence, work pass, some bank cards, an Oyster Card, a couple of restaurant business cards. There was nothing of any interest in there.

The man that chased him off. *Why did I run? I'm trained.* But the man was big. He could not gather his thoughts. He squinted in concentration. What had he seen? The work van was white but unmemorable. He shouted over the road to me. Plastic piping. Yes. The man put thin plastic tubes into his van.

He was the plumber.

What if he had it?

He knew he would need to find out who the man was. Garvan turned the key to start the engine. Once he knew who the man was, he would take it.

Former Sergeant Major and Warrant Officer Class One William 'Billy' Gray looked down at the belt stretching across his undress uniform. It was getting a bit tight. Not that Lou-Lou would help with his waistline issues. His wife thought food should accompany all conversations. And she liked talking.

Gray's colleague, also a former Sergeant Major and WO1, John Jackson, walked in. He closed the large wooden door behind him and entered their shared office, "I have some bad news."

Gray looked up from his keyboard.

"Ken Prior is dead."

"What, in Portsmouth?" Gray felt instant dizziness. "I asked him to go down there. I was only working on his rota this morning."

"I took the call at your house. I was having a cup of tea with Lou-Lou. Your wife has been wonderful to me since Dorothy died. You haven't taken your phone off redirect."

Gray fumbled with the phone. New technology. It was so much easier with dial telephones. "What did he die of?"

"That's just the thing. According to the policeman I spoke to, he was attacked late afternoon and then again that evening. He died in a car park."

Gray sat back in his chair. His arms dropped to the outside of the armrests. "Poor Sam. Ken and his wife are so nice. He was only young. I think mid-fifties. He looked after himself. Fit as a fiddle. Carried himself much younger than his age."

Jackson nodded.

Gray stretched his blue uniform coat down once again, "And always so smartly dressed. He did his twenty-two years and came here just a few weeks later. I will have to visit with Sam."

Jackson said, "As soon as I left Lou-Lou, I went straight to their house. They live two doors down from me. Sam is obviously in a bit of a state, but I think her sister is with her now."

Gray said, "We will do all we can for her," he rapped a pen against the desk. "This can only mean one thing. The building was bought speculatively because it was on that road. Unlikely, I know, but just in case there was something there."

Jackson asked, "What are you suggesting?"

"Well, we don't know if anything was, but it seems a bit coincidental that Ken would be attacked twice on the same day. Surely it can only mean one thing."

Jackson wrinkled his eyebrows in confusion.

Gray said, "I am going to see Samantha. This is so, so sad. I don't know what I am going to say to her. So sad. Poor Ken."

Gray pulled on his hat, smoothed the red rosette to the front, and lifted himself from his chair. He opened the door to leave. "When I get back, we need to have a chat."

6

Eddie and Jamie walked through the historic barracks to a café within one of the Hotwalls arches. They entered and sank into two sumptuous leather armchairs near the door. As Jamie picked up a menu from the decorative rope wheel table a waitress quickly appeared.

Eddie said, "Two flat whites please."

As she walked away, Jamie said, "I hadn't chosen what I wanted."

"Don't worry about that. I want to tell you what happened yesterday."

Jamie sat back in his chair and steepled his fingers. It was his best contemplative professor. "I thought you had told me what happened yesterday, but go on."

Eddie shook his head. "Well. You know I had to sort the boards out by the panelling?"

"Yes. I hope you didn't damage them. Were the

replacements adequate, sir?"

"Yes, thank you," Eddie said equally formally. He moved his backpack closer to his leg.

"The owner, Mr Prior, was at my shoulder getting on my nerves. I asked him to see what was holding up the piping I was threading through. The next thing I know, he was spread on the floor as if it was the most important thing in the world to get his clothes dirty, just to help me out."

"I know you think he was looking for something, but I will admit, that is a bit odd."

"That's what I said. Not as odd as what happened outside, though."

The coffees arrived. Eddie waited for the young woman to walk away before continuing, "As I said yesterday, I was packing away my van—"

"After using your wet wipes?"

"Yes, after I sanitised everything—"

Jamie thought he knew where Eddie was going with this and leaned forward. "So, you did see a murder?"

"No, nothing like that. I shouted, and a bald man ran off. Mr Prior had a cut lip but said he was fine and walked off in the other direction."

"That's strange."

"That's what I said. It then got stranger," Eddie reached down to his bag and pulled out the cloth-wrapped package. He carefully unwrapped the package and placed the small rock to one side before turning the book towards Jamie. He leafed through the pages to show his friend the diagrams. "It's some sort of antique book about turning metal into gold."

"Do you think it's worth a few quid?"

"There must be something important or valuable about it if someone died over it."

"What are you on about?"

"The man that owns the property we are doing up was also

something to do with the green hotel along the road. I think this came from the hotel when it was being renovated. The way he was rooting around seemed strange at the time. I am going to say he was looking for this."

"Why that? It could have been anything. It's a bit of a leap to presume he was looking for an antique book that might have been hidden somewhere else. Then found years ago by house clearance guys."

"I know. But I had a good look around the pub, and there wasn't much else it could be."

Jamie asked, "Why didn't you mention it earlier when we saw Rob?"

"He had more important things to deal with. The police called him. He seemed to be in shock, and he wasn't making sense. As Ahmet said, if Mr Prior was killed outside the site, the police would have been there with yellow tape and stuff."

"Maybe the man had a heart attack. I don't suppose it's connected."

"It could be something to do with him getting knocked down. Concussion or something. Who knows? I brought this back to ask Mr Prior about it, and then Rob was going on about whether I saw something."

"Yes, but that can't have anything to do with this package. It's been in the pub for years. I don't suppose Rob meant anything by it."

"I know, but when the attack happened, I looked around and was sure I was the only person there. I know it's usually busy, but the road was completely silent," Eddie fidgeted in his chair. "I just wanted to see what you thought before I said anything to anyone."

Jamie raised his hands to surrender. "I wouldn't have a clue, but I would get rid of that book, just in case. Maybe you could take it to a book dealer and try to flog it. It might be worth enough to buy me a pint for a change."

"The problem is, the owner is now dead, and I have his antique book."

"So, what are you saying?"

"If I tell anyone I have this, it might look like I had something to do with his death."

"I didn't think of that."

"I did. As soon as Rob started asking me if I had seen anything. I realised that's what the police might want to know. I might have been the last person who saw him alive before he was killed."

The sun had drifted around to shine through the large glass arch, and caught the edge of the table. Eddie moved his chair away from the direct glare and saw a faint red light bouncing off the flower vase in the centre. The colour came from the small rock resting on the woven cloth.

He had not paid attention to it before. He thought it was just a medium-sized pebble or stone, but instead, it was a thumb-sized, dull red glass-like misshapen ball with smooth indentations. He picked it up, rubbed the dirtiest side, and plopped his finger in the flower vase before wiping the dirt away with the dripping water. He studied the object and turned it around. He then sat up in his chair. "I may have been barking up the wrong tree."

"What is it?"

"I think I will have to pay a visit to Lucy's mum. I don't know if it's about this book at all."

"What do you mean?"

Eddie held the object to the sun. "I think this might be a ruby. A large ruby."

A bell rang as Eddie pushed the door open. A woman looked up from a glass counter filled with rings and shiny things. He had told himself she was too young for glamorous, and too old for sexy, but Eddie thought she was as attractive as any over fifties model he had seen in a magazine. She was only twenty years older than Lucy, who was like a younger version. Not that he paid that much attention, of course.

"Oh, Eddie. Hello. What are you doing here?"

"That's a nice way to greet your future son-in-law, Jean."

Jean Brisley stepped around the corner of the counter and headed over to Eddie. She stretched her toned arms and hugged him. "Oh, you know I don't mean that. You just caught me by surprise. Where's Lucy?"

She always smelled different. She must have a house full of perfumes, he thought. And shoes. And clothes. He smiled. "She's at work."

"She does work hard, that girl. If she's not in the office, she's teaching one of her classes," Eddie's future mother-in-law added, "Not the same for you, I see," she lifted an eyebrow. "Skiving?"

Eddie thought Jean Brisley had a wonderful way of not saying what she meant by saying exactly what she meant.

"No. We're waiting for materials, so I have the afternoon off, and I thought I should come and say hello to my favourite future mother-in-law."

She placed one hand on a hip and cocked her head to one side. "Future."

Yes, she had a way of not saying just what she meant by saying it. Eddie changed the subject. "I found something at the site and wondered if you could tell me what it was," he said as he placed the red glass object on the counter.

"What do you think it is?" Jean asked.

"That's what I was hoping you could tell me."

She grabbed a loupe from below the counter and looked closely at the stone. After turning it a few times and holding it up to the light, she said, "Well, unfortunately, it's not a ruby. It's not bright enough. It seems a bit dull, maybe like garnet," she tapped a sharp tool against the surface, "No, it's too hard for garnet. You get red sapphires and even diamonds, but I don't think it's anything like that."

"What do you think, then?" Eddie asked.

"Well, there's beryl, spinel, sunstone. There are a few red stones, but we only really sell rubies and maybe garnet. I'm not an expert," she frowned. "I'm not sure. It might just be a red glass rock or perhaps a tourmaline like rubellite, but I don't recall seeing some of those different gemstones up close. Certainly not any time recently. Sorry."

"Oh well. It doesn't look like I'm getting a bonus for the wedding fund, then."

Jean said, "You should be close to having enough by now. You've already got the suit. You know, that nice one you take on all those holidays."

Just what she wants to say by saying it. Eddie leaned over and gave her a peck on the cheek. "Must run. I'm waiting for my boss to call to say the materials are on their way," he closed the door with a smile and a wave, and wondered why he felt the need to lie to her?

Eddie paced his living room and spoke out loud, "Okay, so it's not a ruby. So, why was it with the book? Why wrap a small gemstone up with a book? It's shiny glass. Maybe they didn't have shiny coloured glass," he shook his head. Of course, they had coloured glass. "They must be connected. The book and the glass stone."

He sat at the dining table and placed the glass stone close to his eye. He tried to look through it and at the diagrams as he flipped through the pages of the book. Nothing. He asked himself, "What did you think? A mysterious code would show through the red glass? Dummy."

He placed the book in front of him, the packaging next to it, and furthest from him, the glass object.

He started with the packaging. After looking closely at the

string, he examined the cloth. Nothing there. He looked at the glass object once more. No. He then studied each page of the book carefully. A sun. Two men. A raindrop-looking thing with people inside. Pebbles around a Neptune-type figure. A couple in a field with some sort of sieve. He turned each page and carefully studied until he got to the back before returning it to the table, reverse side up.

It was no good. The most logical thing to do would be to take it to someone that knew about alchemy and what the drawings in the book might mean.

Indentations on the back page of the book caught his eye. He had presumed it was part of the text, but it was faint and faded. Not printed. Maybe a formerly dark colour of ink. It was writing. He drew himself closer and read out loud.

"One: Thomas to Elias Collecti. . ."

"That might be an 'o' and 'n' missing."

"Two: The Cross is the Touchstone of Fai. . ."

"Faith, perhaps."

"Three: Hooke's Folly."

There were more numbered phrases. Some faded, some easier to read. He retrieved his laptop from the sofa and flipped the lid. The cursor blinked along the search line before he typed, 'Thomas to Elias Collection'. Nothing of any possible relevance appeared. Perhaps it was two names or people.

He tried again. 'The Cross is the Touchstone of Faith'.

The first search result was an advertisement for a book. There were additional pages for the same book. Too new. Oh, hang on, what's this? *The 1662 Prayer Book: The Touchstone of Faith*. He read the page but failed to gain inspiration. He typed, 'Touchstone'. The search revealed it was a 'Stone used to identify precious metals'. Promising.

Half an hour later, he was no further forward.

He clicked on the images section. Crosses. Books. No, none of that.

He opened up a photo of a fireplace mantle. A passage of writing accompanied the picture. 'House of Villiers Fireback. Fidei coticula crux — The Cross is the Touchstone of Faith. A large and heavy cast iron fireback bearing the arms of George Villiers Duke of Buckingham — French late century'.

He had three different books about the French Revolution on the go. Lucy teased him about his waste-of-a-degree, but no, he would not be better off reading about magnafilters and the latest basin taps. He loved reading history and his years at Sussex University were the best of his life.

He immediately got stuck in and typed, 'George Villiers Duke of Buckingham'. The first entry provided brief details. He read that the Duke was stabbed to death in 1628 at *The Greyhound* pub in Portsmouth. His killer was named John Felton, an army officer injured in battle and passed over for promotion by the Duke.

He wanted to read on but knew he had found what he was looking for. He typed, '*Greyhound Pub. Ye Spotted Dogge*, Portsmouth'. The pictures popped up straight away. It was the building along from where he was currently working. *The Greyhound* was the establishment's previous name. It was also known as Buckingham House. He sat back in his chair. He had learned something interesting. The book belonged to George Villiers, Duke of Buckingham, and 'The Cross is the Touchstone of Faith' was his family motto.

His excitement quickly turned to confusion. He knew, or at least thought he knew, who owned the book, but what did those words and phrases mean? What was the red stone?

He did have the answer to one question. Mr Prior had still been looking for the package before he died in suspicious circumstances. And it had been sat on a shelf in a pub since another of his properties was renovated.

He also knew the answer to another question. Who had the package Mr Prior was looking for, and died over?

7

"DC Gale, I would like a word," Detective Inspector Alan Spears beckoned his young colleague.

"Yes, sir?" Gale studied his superior as he strode towards him. He did not look happy. His red cheeks appeared more florid than usual.

"I know you were only just assigned to this car park case, but we already have some good news. We may be ready to make an arrest."

Gale asked, "Great, we have new evidence?"

"I am happy with the call we received this morning. The witness described the attacker," Spears said, looking down at his notepad. "It has been confirmed by his boss that the worker left at around the same time as Mr Prior. His van was spotted leaving the scene shortly after the attack outside his property."

"Yes, I have that, but the new evidence, is it the car park? I knew someone must have seen something. There are always people around in that car park.

Continuing to look at his notepad, DI Spears said, "No witnesses have come forward as yet, but I have a couple of officers canvassing the car park. I am sure that by the time we have brought Mr Hill in, we will have someone that saw him attack Mr Prior a second time."

Gale shifted where he stood. "Does this mean we do not have additional witnesses, sir?"

Spears glared directly at Gale, who felt his face flush. "The importance of a quick resolution has escalated. It appears Mr Prior was a Yeoman Warder at the Tower of London, and Regal Portfolio Properties are the owners. We know Hill was involved, so I would appreciate it if you could bring him in for questioning, please, DC Gale."

Spears closed his notepad, removed his glasses, and walked towards his office.

Owen Garvan stood at the window staring between two apartment blocks to a slither of the Southsea beachfront. Sunshine bounced off the corridor of glass and steel before the gloom returned. He was not picked because he possessed a unique set of skills — he was local — that was all. With the chain draped over his fingers, he looked at the gold cross in his hand. He touched the red rose in the centre and placed it in a dish by his television. He would not wear it again until he had retrieved the item he was looking for.

He was shaken from the diversion by the sound of his telephone ringing. Good. Instructions.

The other end of the phone said, "I have spoken to our people, and we believe you should lay low for a while."

"It was an accident. I thought I had been seen, which is why I ran."

"That's okay. The investigation will list it as an accidental death. Mr Prior fell and cracked his head on a railing after a concussion received earlier in the day when an attacker stole his wallet."

"You can do that?"

"There are many people that believe in our project. We also have an attacker."

"The plumber?"

"Yes, the plumber."

Garvan said, "I think he has what we are looking for, and I would like to make amends and retrieve it?"

"That's not very clever. He will recognise you."

"He won't see me. I will gain entrance to his house or his car and remove it."

"You have put me in a difficult position. In your haste, you have created an inconvenient situation. I am, however, aware that the best way of resolving this is to conclude it quickly. We do not have long."

"I will not make any mistakes, and I don't intend for it to take long."

There was another pause. Garvan thought it was the end of the conversation, but he learned the person he was looking for was named Eddie Hill, and was provided with an address.

Gale flicked a remaining jalapeno around the sandwich wrapper on his passenger seat. The report confirming the cause of death was not ready, so why the urgency? What could Prior have done to cause this plumber to attack him not just once but twice and in two different locations? It could not possibly be for a wallet. It did not make sense, especially on the evidence of one unnamed telephone witness. Questioning was one thing, but Spears appeared to be intimating an *actual* arrest. It wasn't just misrepresentative instructions. Why else would he want Hill's presence at the station?

He pressed the search button on the radio. He heard strings and swooping drumbeat noises as it stopped at a classical music channel. Why not? It might be relaxing.

Gale looked back towards Eddie Hill's house through his windscreen. He was parked six doors down. He would wait until Mr Hill returned home to begin his own enquiries.

Owen Garvan had read *Theatrum Chimicum Britannicum* several times. It was heavy going, but the words meant little. It was the incredible potential that captured him. He would certainly do everything he could to help. If he retrieved one of these objects, it would lead to the greatest gift he could ever imagine.

Garvan thumbed through Elias Ashmole's famous book once more as he stared unblinkingly at both the new car along the road with the man eating his lunch. And at Eddie Hill's front door.

His attention diverted to the single lane road that ran along the side of Hill's garden. He might need to create a distraction for the man in the car, and this was his most reliable access point. Garvan watched as a cat raced over the fence, slipping on a mossy shiplap board as he went. He would be more careful.

He could wait.

8

Eddie boiled the kettle and pondered what he had learned. As he swirled the bag around with a teaspoon, he decided to break it down into research topics to see what else he could determine before Lucy returned home. He dropped the teabag into the small dish and watched as brown droplets bounced onto the worktop surface.

He resumed his laptop studies with the original starting point, *Mutus Liber*. It did not take long to discover the immediate contradiction with his initial celebrations. The book was published in 1677, and George Villiers was murdered at *The Greyhound* pub in 1628.

He typed 'George Villiers' once again. That's interesting, he thought. There was a second Duke of Buckingham called George Villiers. His son. He looked at his watch. He had an hour before Lucy got home from work. That should be plenty of time to learn about this new Duke of Buckingham.

It felt like just a few minutes when he heard the front door close.

"Eddie?" Lucy entered the living room. "I didn't think you were home. Where's the van?"

Eddie saw perspiration glimmer on her forehead. Running in work clothes again, and with the usual disregard to dry cleaning bills. "It's in the garage. I won't need it for a few days, so I thought I would keep it off the drive."

"Why won't you need it for a few days?"

"Come upstairs to the front bedroom."

"A bit early for pillow talk, isn't it?"

Eddie puffed his chest out and made guns with his arms, "You should be so lucky."

Lucy laughed. "You are an idiot. You do know that don't you?"

"Of course. It's my most endearing quality," he grabbed Lucy's hand and repeated his request.

Eddie pulled the bedroom curtain aside slightly. "Someone knocked while I was in the bathroom earlier, and I was too slow to get to the door. Well, you see that white hatchback along the road? There has been a bloke sat in there all afternoon. I think it might be the police waiting for me to come home."

Lucy turned to look directly at him. "What are you talking about?"

"I think my boss told the police that I was the last on-site when the owner left yesterday."

"Isn't that exactly what he should have told them?"

"Yes, but I was the only witness to the attack, and the man died later that day. I don't know when or where he died, but they will want to talk to me as a witness. We have seen plenty of crime shows where the only witness is the chief suspect."

"That's paranoia. He may have died in his wife's arms, for all you know."

"He wasn't, but that's not the point. Don't forget I have the package."

"They probably just want a witness statement. Give the book to the police. Tell them where you got it from, and that you were going to talk to the owner about it today. You can tell them to ask your boss."

"You're probably right," Eddie took her hand again, "Come back downstairs. I learned some interesting stuff today. Let me show you."

Lucy enjoyed how excited her fiancé was. He loved getting stuck into a project. She listened as he told her the book belonged to the second Duke of Buckingham, who was brought up in the seventeenth century, as a brother to the future King Charles II, after his father's murder.

"It's rumoured that George's dad and Charles' grandad James I were lovers."

"What, the previous king?"

"Yes. Anyway, again, that's not the issue. I looked for a connection between the book, George, and the king. It didn't take long. Back then, most people in the scientific community were into one thing," Eddie paused for dramatic effect. Lucy cocked an eyebrow. "Alchemy."

"What, the metal to gold thing?"

"Sort of. It's complicated and related to early medicinal practices, but it all relates to the philosopher's stone."

"And?"

"Well, I visited your mum this morning."

"Oh, that's nice. It would be great if you got closer to mum. How is she? I've been too busy to speak to her this week."

"I don't think she thinks I'm good enough for you."

"Well, you're not. Obviously."

Eddie smiled and pulled an object from his pocket. He held it up so she could see it clearly in the light of the ceiling bulbs.

"At first, I thought this was a ruby, but your mum told me it wasn't. Nor is it a different type of precious stone."

"Glass? Where did it come from?"

"I think you know what it is, Lucy."

She wrinkled her eyebrows.

"It's the stone that was packed with the book," Eddie looked into her pale blue eyes. "I think it's the philosopher's stone."

Lucy slumped on the sofa. Eddie tried to assess her mood in the silence. Almost as quickly as she sat, she stood again. He watched as she walked towards the kitchen.

She looked around as if studying for an examination in observation techniques. Eddie had left a teabag half on the worktop instead of in the little dish — again. The wall cupboard door groaned as she opened it. He still hasn't fixed this. He said it would only take five minutes.

Eddie followed her.

Lucy glared at Eddie and raised her arms. "So, what do you do? Rub it against metal, and it turns it into gold? Should we try the kettle? It is your favourite thing in the world, after all."

Eddie knew he had to intervene before a dark cloud descended. He grabbed her waist and drew her close. "I don't think it's quite as simple as that. I think we might need to talk to an expert to learn more."

She pulled away. "Hang on a second. You were giving this to the police a minute ago."

"I am sure you can appreciate my immediate reluctance."

"What do you mean?"

Eddie walked back into the dining room. "The attack. The death. The only witness thing. And now, an antique book and the philosopher's stone."

Lucy followed him and placed a mug on the table. Firmly. He said, "You forgot to put tea in it."

"Eddie, I know you," she placed her hands on the back of a

chair, "What else?"

"I had hoped we would get there more calmly."

Lucy frowned.

"Okay. As I see it, the owner bought the house because he thought this package might be there. He could not have known for certain."

"That seems speculative."

"I know but bear with me. He was only interested in the areas of the property that had remained untouched for centuries. So, you talk about speculative. I think that's exactly what it was. He was hoping something was there. Maybe not even the package. He looked eccentric. Perhaps he buys these old properties in the hope he can find historic valuables," Eddie could see Lucy was unconvinced, so continued, "Whatever his reasons, they are not as important as the minor detail of a man waiting for him and attacking him."

"Yes, but what for?"

"That's easy. One of two things. Either, whatever he may have found — which would suggest he is some sort of rival artefact collector. Mr Prior did say he knew him. That would mean it could be anything. They might not even care. If old, it could be valuable. Of more concern is if it's for the second thing."

"What's that?"

Eddie moved the book towards her and placed the stone on top.

"A package containing a book about alchemy, which the richest man in the country owned. Who, along with most scientists of the day, was on a lifetime quest for the philosopher's stone. The problem is that Mr Prior died in what might be suspicious circumstances while I had the package in my possession. If I give it to the police, it could implicate me in his death," his volume rose, "There could be third parties involved who were watching the house, one of whom attacked him. And someone may even have seen me," Eddie pushed himself up from the table. "Oh, and what else? Someone is also watching outside *our* house. A house that you live in. Which might put you in danger," he was now speaking loudly. "And that is the only bloody thing I care about."

Lucy walked over to hug him. "Yes, but it was not found in the property you are working on. And there is no proof it was found in the hotel."

"It doesn't matter where it was found. What matters is the man that was attacked and died owns or works for a company that owns the property I am working on. And at some stage, he might have had something to do with the hotel," Eddie stared into her eyes. "I'm not having anything happen again. I mean, I'm not having anything bad happen to you."

She held him tightly. "I know."

Eddie kissed Lucy on the lips. "Thank you. I'm fine. I am not concerned about myself. You know why I worry about you."

He hated letting his guard down in front of Lucy.

Lucy knew she had to ease Eddie's concerns while dealing with her own. "I do, but I don't think we're near to that yet. Let's deal with this one thing at a time."

"I agree. It's probably best to avoid the police for a couple of days. Maybe we can go away?"

Eddie grabbed Lucy's hand and led her back to the table. He gestured for her to take a seat and flipped the book over. He pointed to the writing on the reverse. Lucy shook her head with confusion, so he explained his theory.

She read down the list, "They do look like clues, don't they?"

"Clues to what, I can't say, but I think your idea about going away for a couple of days is a good one. It's Friday, so I can't see how a weekend break would raise suspicions, especially if no one knows where we have gone. It will also give the police time to find the person they should be looking for."

Lucy said, "Don't forget, your involvement only stretches as far as seeing someone getting hit in the face and helping him to his feet. He was fine when he left you. While his death was tragic, it didn't happen then, so why should it affect your plans? If it came to the police, anyway? And don't forget, no one knows about this book. You are speculating that someone might work that out."

"That doesn't sound particularly empathetic, but when you put it that way, it's hard to disagree."

"Put bluntly, it is quite brutal, but you have no reason not to carry on with your everyday life, and that includes going away with your fiancée for the weekend."

"You are forgetting something about this book and stone. If the man was looking for it and someone attacked him over it, it doesn't matter how long it sat on a shelf in a pub without anyone knowing. Someone is looking for it."

"Okay, fair enough. So, where shall we go?"

With composure returned, Eddie explained why he had pointed out the writing on the book. He knew precisely where they should go.

"Go on," Lucy said.

"How about outlet shopping at Bicester Village, near Oxford?"

"That sounds like a good idea, but what's the ulterior motive?"

Eddie shrugged his shoulders.

Lucy smiled and raised an eyebrow.

"Okay. In Oxford, there's a museum called the Ashmolean. While I was researching, I learned that it was founded in the seventeenth century by a man named Elias Ashmole. It was to house his collection of curiosities and ephemera. He was also in with the science and alchemy crowd. He even wrote books on the subject. Hopefully, there will be an expert that could shed light on this."

"Will I get a new coat?"

"I think it is vital that you get new a new coat. I saw a square inch of floor in the spare bedroom that hasn't got piles of your clothes on it."

Lucy laughed before asking, "Why that museum?"

Eddie looked up from the book and drew her gaze towards it with his finger. He pointed at the first numbered sentence, 'Thomas to Elias Collecti. . .'

Lucy disappeared upstairs to pack a weekend bag, which gave Eddie time to immerse himself in further study into Elias Ashmole. He also wanted to avoid thinking about the police. Half an hour later he heard her descend the stairs.

Lucy said, "We need to work out a strategy. We can't let anyone know about the book or the stone while we are at the museum."

"We also need to know a bit more about what the philosopher's stone is. I think the best approach would be to tag onto a tour. That will supplement anything the internet throws up."

"What have you learned so far?"

Eddie replied, "Ashmole was a bit of a rogue. His acquirement of antiquities was not without controversy."

"That's not connected to what we're trying to learn."

"True, but like many of that period, he was an interesting character."

She said, "There are two more things we need to do before we leave. Sort accommodation out and work out how to get you out of here without the policeman or whoever is in that car, knowing."

Eddie suppressed a grin and said, "I have found accommodation, but I hadn't considered the second issue. So, thank you for that. We make a good team. I think you will make a more than adequate sidekick on this adventure."

"Sidekick?"

"Robin to my Batman."

"Surely you mean Brains to Muppetman."

"Prove it. How should I escape the police?"

"Way ahead of you. Go upstairs, pack a bag, and I will drive around the corner. You can jump over Jim next door's fence — they are on holiday. That way, no one will know, and I can pick you up down the road."

Eddie nodded, "Good thinking, Brains. You never know, you may even usurp the kettle in importance one day."

After he received the obligatory punch on the arm, Eddie performed a similar packing ritual to Lucy, who had made it easier with a pre-packed toiletry bag. Before leaving the room, he twitched the curtain. The white car was still there.

Lucy called a gym colleague, who agreed to take her spin class the following morning. That would cost her a favour. She closed the front door, and her hand trembled as she clicked the fob to unlock her car.

At the same time, Eddie threw his overnight backpack over his garden fence before grasping the top and slipping over quietly from one supporting step. He peered above his neighbour's fence before repeating his slow climb. He brushed the moist moss from his hand before leaping down. As he landed, Lucy rounded the corner. She checked her rear-view mirror to see the white car was parked in the opposite direction. It did not follow.

Owen Garvan saw someone drop to the pavement side of the fence as a black hatchback pulled alongside him. Before climbing into the front passenger seat, a man opened the rear door and threw a bag onto the back seat. He recognised him instantly. It was the man that saw him confronting Ken Prior.

He started his engine, turned into the same road, and fell behind at a discrete distance. He thought quickly. Why would Hill climb over his fence to get into a car? Who was he avoiding? He would change his plan. If the package was in Hill's home, he could retrieve it later. He would follow them wherever they were going. If they knew the value of the package, they would keep it with them. He did not want to harm Hill, but after the previous day's events, if he had the item with him, he would retrieve it. Whatever it took.

9

Billy Gray answered the phone call on the second ring. "Hello, Mike. What do you have for me?"

Michael Foster and Gray had sat together to fill out their Yeoman Warder application forms. Foster's went in the bin as soon as he read the list of requirements, which included a Long Service and Good Conduct medal. His background was not quite as unblemished as Gray's. They had been friends for many years, but the disciplinary entries on his record precluded its award. Gray never judged Foster for it. After meeting them just once, he knew how challenging living with his parents must have been. While Gray went to work at the Tower of London, Foster had worked as a part-time private investigator since leaving the army.

Foster replied, "I have just left the police station after speaking to a Detective Inspector Spears. It seems they are about to call a suspect in for questioning. They believe the man responsible was the heating engineer, Mr Edward Hill. DI Spears said that an eyewitness saw him attack Ken Prior outside the property. Mr Prior was then found dead in a car park at the local shopping centre, after a second attack, later that night."

"We have to presume this will be over the stone. Have the police recovered anything?"

"I asked if anything was missing, and Spears said, just his wallet."

"I can't believe anyone would attack someone over their wallet twice in one day in two different locations. Is the DI competent?"

Foster replied, "I have no doubt he is, but I did notice he seemed a little flustered when I explained my interest in the case. I suppose he could have felt a bit intimidated after I mentioned who owned the property. Plus, of course, Ken Prior's job."

"If Ken's wallet was missing, how did they know to contact us in the first place?"

"An eyewitness provided a name, and Mr Prior was wearing a bow tie with your Tower logo on."

"That wouldn't be much to go on."

"And socks, Bill."

"Not incompetent, then. Mr Hill may or may not be involved, but I am saying this with regret — I think we need to leave the police to investigate Ken's death. We should concentrate on recovering the stone. If that is what this is about. Let me think," Gray paused. "Okay, the first attack did not achieve Mr Hill or whoever's objectives. Which we will have to presume are the same as ours. You will need to speak to the witness from the car park assault that led to Ken's death."

"Bill."

"Yes."

"The police do not have a witness. I believe DI Spears may have rushed his decision."

"I see. In that case, would you be kind enough to visit Mr Hill to see if you can learn what he knows? With your background, you don't need me to tell you how to do your job, but it goes without saying that if he has the stone, we will need it. Oh, and thank you for doing this Michael, I wanted to make sure someone local could get on it straight away."

"It's no problem, Bill. I'm only in Southampton. It's good to be doing something constructive with my retirement. I think I've just done the last lawn cut of the year. And I know Ken Prior was a friend of yours."

Gray finished the call, "Thank you anyway. And yes, Ken was part of our family here."

Michael Foster checked his watch. The lights were off, but it was not twenty-two hundred hours yet. He tried the doorbell. There was no answer. He gently pushed the handle downwards. It never ceased to amaze him how few people understood a failure to push the handle upwards after closing, left it on its latch. He forced a pocket knife into the rubber seal and pressed. It opened with ease. He shook his head. The public should get anti-burglary lessons.

He knocked on the inside of the front door. No one was home. The living room curtains were closed, so he pressed the light switch. It was a through lounge. He looked around the room. There was not a stone with a label attached declaring, *here I am*. He tried the kitchen. He looked in the drawers and cupboards, ensuring he left everything as he found it. Foster walked up the stairs and followed a similar procedure in each room, including the bathroom. Nothing. Except for some clothes strewn over the floor on what he presumed was the wife's side of the bedroom. He descended the stairs to check the laptop he had seen earlier. He thought he saw a napkin alongside it. Instead, it was an old, ragged piece of cloth. He lifted the lid, and the computer came to life. There were open pages, but he only needed to see the first one. He looked around the room and paced throughout the ground floor. He needed to leave Mr Hill a message that ensured he spoke to Billy Gray as a matter of urgency. He would visit again if Bill asked him to.

Ian Gale woke with a start. He was disoriented for a few seconds before the fog cleared, and he realised he was in his car. He looked outside. Clouds the colour of soot and ash blanketed the sky. He checked the time on his phone. It was gone midnight.

He recalled feeling a little sleepy at around seven-thirty when Ms Brisley drove away, but had decided to wait as Mr Hill was not in the car. He also remembered listening to the radio. He decided it must have been after nine when he fell asleep.

It was now pitch-black outside, the last wisp of grey cloud consumed by a bigger, angrier version. There was no moonlight, the streetlamp nearest his car was out, and Mr Hill's van was still absent from the drive. It made little sense to stay. It was clear that Hill would not be returning tonight. He said out loud, "Unless he was already home, and he came back on a ten-ton truck that I couldn't hear because I was fast-a-bloody-sleep."

He stretched his arms to touch the roof to see off the stiffness, pressing until his wrists turned white. As he went to turn the ignition key, he saw movement in front of Hill's house. Despite the darkness, he could see a man. It was not Mr Hill — he was tall. This man was stocky and of average height. He estimated around five-foot-eight. As the man walked nearer, he could see he was balding with bushy eyebrows. Gale stared out of the side window as the man passed. He was holding a Christmas sweets tub. Gale presumed the man must have been a guest, but looking back at the house, he saw there were no lights on. That's strange, he thought. He set his alarm for six and reclined his seat. He would make sure he spoke to Eddie Hill first thing in the morning before returning to the station, where he would undoubtedly be allocated another case.

10

"What do you mean you're not telling me?" Lucy asked.

"We're nearly there. You will see it in a few minutes. It was a late offer, so we've got a good deal. I think you'll laugh."

"It had better not be one of your famous budget options."

"I have no idea what you are talking about," Eddie turned and smiled at Lucy in the darkness of the car. "One time. Just one cheap holiday in Sardinia."

A few minutes later, the satellite navigation on Eddie's phone told them to turn right onto a cobbled area of road. On their right was a building, lights pointing to the heavens, casting shadows through the façade.

"This is it," Eddie said.

"What, a castle?"

"Not exactly. I will read what it says about it here. 'Housed in a former prison, the rooms in our Oxford hotel are rather

more spacious than your average jail cell and come complete
with luxurious beds, super-fast Wi-Fi and power showers'."

"A prison?" Lucy asked.

"Originally, it was Oxford Castle, but it was turned into a
prison. The Malmaison hotel chain bought it in the 1990s and
changed it into accommodation. I thought it might be ironic."

Lucy punched Eddie on the arm.

They parked up and entered the reception area. Eddie
looked around the airy space as Lucy took care of the check-in
procedure. She paid for the parking with no intention of
revealing the cost to Eddie. They collected their key cards and
walked along 'A-Wing', both staring in all directions at the
unique renovation. Their accommodation was originally three
cells converted into one luxurious room. There was an iron
door, vaulted ceiling, extra-thick walls, and the carpet even had
had a 'how many days' pattern with four lines and a fifth
crossed through it.

"Oh, look Eddie, a roll-top bath," she winked. "Brilliant.
You're going to love this. The toiletries have 'The best you
will ever steal' printed on the containers," she poked her head
out of the bathroom. Eddie was lying on the sumptuous bed
with his eyes closed. Ready for lights out.

They were scheduled to meet their tour guide James
McAllister, outside the museum at the Victorian Gothic
monument and set off for the short walk from their hotel. They
agreed it was 'turning a bit nippy' and wrapped up warm.

They were not the first to arrive. Eddie took a quick
headcount. There were nine other people in their group, which
surprised him. He wondered why they couldn't just visit a
museum without a guide, before remembering there were
additional parts of the city and its history added onto the tour.
Additional parts he had no interest in.

They did not have to wait long before McAllister arrived in

a whirl of swaying trench-coat, swirling briefcase, and potentially hazardous umbrella action — which was too long for his small stature. He was roughly Lucy's height. His balding head featured some unkempt blond tufts, and his forehead seemed a little large for his narrow chin and lips.

McAllister rushed the group past large black doors and through the entrance. Eddie and Lucy took in their surroundings while McAllister told a story of three sixteenth century martyrs.

"Please, just one moment," McAllister said as he walked to a security guard and handed him his coat, bag, and umbrella. Eddie watched as the security guard raised his gaze to the ceiling when McAllister walked away.

McAllister addressed the group, "Although I am an independent guide, they allow me to keep a small office."

Eddie doubted the veracity of this. Lucy thought he said it with a certain amount of 'puffery', as her dad would say. She smiled. She missed her dad. Eddie nodded towards Lucy. She edged away from the group as if looking at the Conservation Area while he followed McAllister through to the Ashmolean Story Gallery.

McAllister said, "Elias Ashmole was a royalist, lawyer, antiquarian, scholar, and collector," he theatrically swept his arm across the large room. "He donated his collection to the University of Oxford in 1677. The intention was for the museum collection to aid with the advancement of knowledge."

It was standard tour guide stuff. Eddie looked to make sure Lucy had left them as he walked behind two 'overly made-up for-the-time-of-the-morning', as his mum would say, American women. He nodded to himself. He needed to call his mum more often.

McAllister continued, "The original Ashmolean Museum was constructed near the Bodleian Library. It was a repository for rare materials and a centre for research and learning."

Eddie knew it was also the hub for the most advanced scientific practitioners of the time. He tsked as the American women thought it appropriate to provide assistant commentary to McAllister's ramblings.

The guide made a fleeting mention of the Tradescant family before gaily skipping along to the basement area, which contained a "state-of-the-art chemical laboratory."

Eddie's ears pricked. While the group stopped to peruse the display pieces, he took the opportunity to approach the guide. "Hello, James. I read a little bit before I came, and it seemed to me that Ashmole might have just ripped all this stuff off the Tradescant family."

McAllister inflated his cheeks and blew air. Eddie could see he was affronted.

"Oh goodness no. John Tradescant the Elder and Elias were close friends. But John was just a gardener, Elias catalogued the collection for him, and then Tradescant's son gifted Elias the collection for this wonderful museum."

Eddie knew John Tradescant the Elder was a bit more than 'just a gardener'. He was a botanical adviser to King James I. Eddie also knew Ashmole befriended the Elder after the collection grew so large it had become known as 'The Ark'. He was also aware that the son and his wife fell out with Elias Ashmole after the father died. "Didn't Ashmole cut a wall into the Tradescant home next door and pretty much walk in and steal everything?"

By now, Edddie knew this vague account would rile the tour guide.

"Oh no, certainly not. *That* is all historical mudslinging. Elias had legal agreements with the Tradescants."

McAllister walked away from Eddie and stretched his arms to gather his flock. "It appears my guests are ready to continue the tour," he half-turned to Eddie, who thought he saw a scowl.

The walk-and-talk continued with the guide providing his version of history. He was in his element but immediately regretted asking, "Does anyone have any questions?"

Eddie took the opportunity, "Did Ashmole murder Hester Tradescant for this collection?"

Eddie thought McAllister's face managed to choose an expression somewhere between anger and astonishment. He suppressed a laugh as McAllister answered, "No, no. Of course not. You are, of course, talking of Mrs Tradescant's unfortunate death," the flustered guide looked towards his tour party. "She drowned in her back garden. I can assure you it had absolutely nothing to do with Elias Ashmole, who, as I have already informed this gentleman," he pointed in Eddie's direction, "had a legal agreement with the Tradescants."

Eddie was having fun now. "Ashmole's wife was much older than him, and widowed. What was it, three times? She was rolling in it. To paraphrase one of my mum's sayings, I think old Elias may have been a bit of a gold-digger."

McAllister looked around for some help. The security guard from earlier was close by. McAllister glared at the guard and sharply turned his gaze to Eddie. "The," he hesitated, "family disputes and other background issues are for another tour. This tour is of his marvellous collection and the exhibits of the Ashmolean. As you appear to be on the wrong tour, it might be better if you left."

As the security guard approached, Eddie shouted, "But I paid for this tour."

Everyone in the vicinity was now looking towards Eddie. The security guard said, "Disrupting the tour is not fair on the other guests, sir."

McAllister said, "I am sure the tour company will refund you in full."

McAllister ushered his group in the opposite direction, leaving Eddie with the security guard. Eddie looked around to see if he could see Lucy. The guard placed a hand on his elbow before guiding Eddie to the same black doors he had earlier gained admission through.

Eddie paced outside the building while shaking his head. The purpose of the visit was to learn something new, but he had sabotaged any opportunity of gaining additional knowledge simply because he found his tour guide annoying and preferred to run his mouth off.

He checked his watch. It had not been long, but he felt the wait was never-ending. He circled the martyr statue for another few minutes and watched as pigeons pecked at the floor around him. He looked up just in time to see Lucy jog over.

She stopped abruptly and said, "I can't believe what I just did."

Eddie was not listening. "Sorry, darling. I just wasted the whole trip. I managed to wind the drippy little tour guide up sufficiently to get thrown out of the museum before I learned anything useful."

Lucy grinned. "Let's just take a minute to catch our breath, and we can go for a coffee to work out what to do next."

Eddie stared at her. "I have just told you I was thrown out when it was my job to find something helpful among the exhibits," he held up his backpack, "in the hope that we could find something that would help with what is in this bag, and you suggest we have a chat over a coffee."

The Randolph Hotel was just a few paces from the statue. A queue had formed below the bus shelter by its entrance. In the line, Owen Garvan watched a couple deep in conversation. A dark-haired man, who he knew to be Eddie Hill, lifted a backpack.

He was in the right place, and he now knew what he was looking for was in that bag.

11

As they walked, Lucy said, "Well, your tolerance for pomposity appears to have sunk to a new low, Eddie."

Eddie loved Lucy's smile. The way one side lifted slightly higher than the other, while creases sprung open at the corners of her blue eyes. She knew something. "Okay, out with it."

"Well, while you were supposed to find an association with the book, or stone, among the exhibits, it was my job to find an expert to talk to."

Eddie stopped and folded his arms with mock impatience. He knew what they were supposed to be doing.

"Well, I have a confession to make. I didn't find an expert. When I left the tour group, I felt like I was acting suspiciously, even though I could have just gone up to anyone and asked. I don't think I would be very good at covert operations."

"Yes, but you still found something out, didn't you?"

"I did."

"Are you going to tell me?"

"I am, and we will need to stop for a stronger drink than coffee because I'm shaking," Lucy held out a trembling hand. "I think I have worked out what this is about."

The nearest pub was on the next corner they turned around. Lucy was sat at a table with her coat on the back of her chair before Eddie had closed the etched-glass door. She nodded her head towards the bar. "Half."

When Eddie returned with a pint and a half of lager, he saw she was tapping her foot. "Excited much?"

Lucy looked around to ensure no one was listening. "Oh, yes, you're going to love this. I watched the security guard take the tour guide's coat and organiser thing into an office. I saw him look both ways when he came out, which I thought was odd. Anyway, I looked to see if anyone in there could help. I hoped it might be a tour guide office or something," she took a sip of her beer before continuing, "I knocked on the door, but there was no answer, so I pushed it open. It was not an office. It was a large cupboard. I looked around the door and was half-in-half-out when I heard footsteps. As I said, for some reason, I thought I was acting suspiciously, so I went back inside and closed the door."

"What was it, a store-room?"

"More like a staff cloakroom, I would guess. All that was in there was a filing cabinet, a chair, and a coat stand. I don't think he has an office. Why would he? He doesn't work for the museum. Anyway, the tour guide's coat was on the rack, and his book was on top of a set of filing drawers. I tried them, but they were locked."

"What did you think you would find?"

"I don't know. I don't even know why I went into the cupboard. Anyway, I opened his organiser, and a small key fell out."

"And?"

"Well, what do you think?"

"Bloody hell Lucy, get on with it."

Lucy beckoned with her hands as if wafting Eddie's impatience like a spritz to her face. "The key was obviously for the drawers. I opened the top drawer. Empty. So were the next two drawers. But in the bottom drawer, there was a large piece of cotton wool at the bottom. On it, all neatly placed, were these. . ."

Lucy scrolled to the gallery on her phone and showed Eddie the photo. He saw a small jar with a cork stopper. Inside were what looked like red shards of glass. There was another similarly sized vase, also with a cork stopper, but with a sand-like substance inside. He enlarged the photo to take a closer look at a third item — a red stone. It was smaller and more ragged edged than the one they had, but a similar colour.

Lucy provided space for Eddie to stare before adding, "And there's more. As I was locking the drawers, I heard something outside. I ducked down by the side of the filing cabinet and hoped no one would come in. I heard a man's voice ask, 'Who was that horrible man?' I think they must have been talking about you," she leaned back and laughed before continuing, "I heard them walk away, so I thought I had better stay there for a while, and I looked through McAllister's organiser. There was some writing on the first few pages and some phone numbers at the back. Nothing else, which seemed a bit odd for an address book cum diary. I took photos just in case it was helpful."

Eddie asked, "Did you read the notes?"

"No. Another group of people were talking outside. I didn't know whether to walk out as if I worked there or stay and wait."

"What did you do?"

"Nothing. I just stood there like a lemon. I kept opening the door slightly ajar to see if anyone was around. Eventually, after what seemed like an eternity, I managed to see that no one was, and I came straight out to you."

Eddie enlarged the writing and looked up at her, "You say you didn't read the notes?"

"No, do they mean something?"

"Yes, they do. I think they might help. I think they might help a lot."

Eddie unrolled a napkin from its knife and fork, smoothed it out, and placed it in front of him. He removed the antique book from his backpack and set it down, reverse side up. "I didn't say anything earlier because, well, to be honest, I didn't have a clue whether my hunch was right, but what you have found proves it."

Lucy looked closely at the writing on the book cover and then to Eddie, "Are we going clothes shopping now?"

Eddie laughed, "Do you know what this means?"

"Of course. We have solved the first clue on the back of the book."

"Not just that. You might have solved three of the clues in one go. One of those three items in that drawer is the solution to the top clue on this book."

"Explain."

"The philosopher's stone is not necessarily a stone. It was the conclusion of years of experimentation. Alchemists were trying to create the philosopher's stone, but the second word is misleading," Eddie pointed at the photograph. "It could just as easily have been the powder-like substance or the broken glass looking stuff."

Lucy wrinkled her eyebrows in confusion. Eddie put the book back in his bag and said, "What we now know is McAllister is collecting philosopher's stones. Maybe even the same ones as us. This means we need to leave and continue this somewhere a bit more private," Eddie rose from his seat. "Come on, we need to take a closer look at those photos."

Owen Garvan wiped grime away from the wavy glass to create a space to look through. He saw a thin book on the table but could not tell if the stone accompanied it. As Eddie Hill stood, Garvan turned his back to the window, and waited for the couple to emerge.

He crossed the road and turned as if assessing his direction options. After a pause, he scanned around. They were strolling along the pavement away from him. He crossed back over and walked a few metres behind, stopping regularly to look in shop windows, and it seemed, home windows, as a woman angrily pulled her curtains shut while he appeared to be staring inside.

He decided to continue following and wait for the right opportunity. He inserted his hands in his pockets. One rested on loose change, the other on his pocket knife. He fumbled with the knife and withdrew his hand. It was the last resort.

12

Lucy gazed around the solid walls of their hotel room. "I don't think we'll be overheard," she said as she opened the photo of the notebook's first page on her phone. Eddie joined her on the bed, as she read out loud, "Found hidden during renovations before relocation of the collection."

Eddie opened the browser on his phone. "The Ashmolean and its artefacts and papers have changed a lot. The museum has been altered several times over the years, and many of the documents and books are at the Bodleian."

"That's no surprise. Someone could have found the stone at any time over the years. Perhaps it was its discovery that started this."

Lucy swiped to her next photo. The explanation was in note form over two pages. It was Eddie's turn to read, "Charles got this from Edmund Dickinson, who got it from Theodore Mundanus in 1679. He gave it to Barbara Villiers, who was first cousin to Elizabeth Hamilton, first Countess of Orkney and mistress of William III, whose brother was Edward Villiers, first Earl of Jersey, who was father to William Villiers, second Earl of Jersey, known as Viscount Villiers, who was father to William Villiers, third Earl of Jersey, who was father to," he paused to look at Lucy, before taking an exaggerated breath, "George Bussey Villiers, fourth Earl of Jersey, who was father to Charlotte Villiers, who was married to Lord William Russell, who was murdered while a member of Parliament in 1840. It was a botched robbery blamed on his valet. Some items were hidden in his house."

They looked at each other and shrugged their shoulders.

Eddie typed in the first name from the note. "It says Edmund Dickinson, born 1624, died 1707, was an English royal physician and alchemist."

Lucy said, "Okay, there's the connection to King Charles. That was easy. Next."

Eddie typed 'Theodore Mundanus'. "That's brought up Edmund Dickinson again. It says it was around this time he met a man named Theodore Mundanus, who was an adept in alchemy, but it doesn't seem much else is known about him. It does, however, say Mundanus inspired him to devote his attention to chemistry. There is a quote from John Evelyn, who recorded a visit: 'I went to see Dr Dickinson, the famous chemist. We had a long conversation about the philosopher's elixir, which he believed attainable and had seen projection himself by one who went under the name of Mundanus, who sometimes came among the adepts, but was unknown as to his country or abode; of this, the doctor has written a treatise in Latin, full of very astonishing relations'. Evelyn also associated Dickinson with the Interregnum Oxford group of virtuosi that partly constituted the subsequent Royal Society."

Lucy said, "Right, we have a few connections there, starting with alchemy. We have Dickinson and Mundanus, and even John Evelyn was writing about them. So, what's the connection with the king?"

"Oh, this is good. Charles appointed Dickinson as one of his physicians in 1677. It says Charles took him into special favour and had a laboratory built at Whitehall Palace where, and get this — the King would retire with George Villiers, second Duke of Buckingham to conduct chemical experiments."

Lucy hovered an outstretched arm and opened a clenched fist to motion a mike drop.

Eddie said, "Don't do that. Okay, this is all related stuff here. We have alchemy, chemical experiments, George and King Charles."

She added, "And Barbara Villiers is related to George, so it looks like the stone was handed down through the family."

"Barbara Villiers was King Charles' unofficial Queen. I know about her. He had a Queen, I can't remember her name, but Barbara lived with him as if she was his wife. They even had a few children together. I don't know how she was related to George."

"Clever boy. It says she was George's cousin. No, half-brother's daughter. Wow, this is complicated stuff. It seems they were all related to each other somehow."

Eddie laughed. "Yes, chinless wonders. That's the top of British society for you. Just look at Parliament. They all went to school together, or are related to judges, media executives, big business leaders, whatever. I also know about Lord William Russell, by the way."

"Go on."

"I will have to research it a bit more, but if I remember rightly, he was an MP who died in mysterious circumstances in about 1850."

"You have literally just read that it was 1840, but go on."

"Oh, yes. Anyway, it was the original 'the butler did it'. He had a French valet who staged a robbery, cut the MP's throat, and hid the valuables around the house, which he planned to sneak out later."

"Swiss, but near enough. So, what do you reckon? Does this relate to one of those items in the drawer?"

"We won't ever know whether the stone was included in the goodies. The whole trial was controversial because it was circumstantial. But let's assume it was. You can easily see how it's gone from that period in history to the filing cabinet in the museum."

"Can you?"

"Well, no, but it could be a cover-up, a conspiracy, a secret society. Who knows? What we do know is these are the tour guide's notes, and they must relate to the stones in the drawer."

"Fair enough."

Eddie scrolled to the next page. "This one's very easy. It says, 'Boyle donation — Cliveden'."

Lucy typed in 'Boyle Ashmole'. Then said, "This is Robert Boyle."

"You know who he is, don't you?"

"No."

Eddie smiled.

Lucy shook her head, and curled her lip into a smirk. "Go on then, darling."

"Another chemist. Very famous. In fact, I think he was considered the father of modern chemistry. He was one of the founders of the Royal Society. Boyle's Law or something."

Lucy asked, "What was that?"

"I can't remember, but he was another alchemist."

They both read about Robert Boyle on their phones before their research moved back to George Villiers. The energy drained from their batteries simultaneously.

Lucy said, "Did you know that George wore a coat that would be worth £30,000 today at King Charles' coronation?"

"Isn't that what your coat cost from Regent Street in the January sales?" Eddie plugged his phone into the charger, as he said, "Yes, I had just read that myself."

Lucy said, "I think we might be duplicating ourselves. We need to separate our research and tell each other our findings to save time."

"Perhaps we should go for an evening stroll around Oxford, grab something to eat, and have an early night."

Lucy paced the room. "I think that makes sense. What now?"

"We should probably think about what we know and what we should do next," Eddie grabbed a fluffy white robe. "I want to have a shower. If you call room service for a quick pre-dinner sandwich or something, we can have a chat about it."

As Lucy pulled the hotel information book from the drawer, Eddie gently closed the bathroom door. He undressed and turned on the water. Once the correct temperature had taken hold, he stretched his hands to lean against the wall and allowed the water to cascade down his back. The steam rose to cloud the room. He hummed a few bars of his latest earworm and mumbled, "This has been fun, but if other people are collecting these stones, they could be following the same clues," he wiped shampoo from his eyes. He could not work out how this was possible. At least one stone described in McAllister's organiser did not match up with the clues on the back of the *Mutus Liber* book, but he would have to tell Lucy her involvement was over if he was to pursue their next clue. His fingers began to wrinkle. She would not take it well, but he could not allow anything to happen. Not again. Not to her. He dried himself in the steam-filled room and pulled the robe over his shoulders — time to face the music.

As Eddie closed the bathroom door behind him, Lucy said, "I know what you are thinking."

He saw a tray of sandwiches and a pot of tea on the table

next to her.

"You have been gone for nearly half an hour. You are going to tell me to go home, and you will follow up the next clue on your own."

He stood still. *How the hell did she know that?*

"I know you, Eddie Hill. You want to protect me like some Victorian patriarch. You might be big, but—"

Eddie looked down the robe towards his groin before looking up and smiling.

"You wish. You know I can take care of myself. I'm pretty sure I could take you as well."

Eddie cocked his head sideways. "I know you have skills, but if I charged you, I would flatten you before you got off a punch, GI Jane."

Eddie reached for a sandwich, and Lucy moved her arm to block. He reached with the other hand, and she blocked again. He turned and walked away before twisting quickly and diving at her. They laughed as they landed on the bed.

He said, "No, it's not that. We need to split up. You need to go home and do some more research because I think we might be playing catch up against people who are also chasing these clues. You can confirm what we already know and learn more about our new friend George Villiers," he took a bite of a ham and mustard sandwich, "I need to go to Kew Gardens and then follow up with the next clue."

"You want to look at flowers?"

"No, the National Archives are there. I will be able to learn more than we can find on our phones. I doubt everything we are reading is completely accurate. It is the internet, don't forget."

Eddie dressed and checked the timetable. "The first train into London is at ten to four, so I will need you to drop me at the nearest night tube before you drive home."

"Why so early?"

"I can put the bags in the car right now, so we're ready as soon as we wake up."

"Eddie, why so early?"

"I want to get home by lunchtime if I can. London is impossible to get around quickly. Especially if I'm going to the archives as well as solving the next clue."

Lucy picked up the book and turned it over. She looked up, "The Cross is the Touchstone of Faith."

"Yes. That's the one."

As Lucy began to pack her bag, Eddie sent a text to Jamie, explaining what he needed him to bring and where to meet.

13

Owen Garvan sat on one of the black stone balls operating as a driveway guide to the hotel's front entrance. People busied themselves with bicycles as he hid in the shadows of an information board.

He was reading *Die warhhaffte und volkommene Bereitung des Philosophischen Steins der Bruderschaft aus dem Orden des Gulden-und-Rosen-Creutzes*. It was a gift from a museum curator. He had used a translation dictionary to learn it was called *The True and Complete Preparation of the Philosopher's Stone by the Brotherhood from the Order of the Golden and Rosy Cross*. He had used the same dictionary to translate every word into English underneath.

He looked up to see Eddie Hill emerge with the woman he saw earlier that day, who he now presumed was Hill's wife. He closed the book and placed it in his inside pocket before walking at a watchful distance beside some decorative foliage.

As the couple approached their car, he increased his pace while maintaining a position equidistant from the couple but with his back against a towering red-brick turreted building. He saw them reach the black car and ducked below the side-window of the vehicle, three cars along, before edging around the front to remain obscured. Guests wheeled noisy suitcases to the hotel entrance, but no one paid attention as he crept towards the vehicle.

He saw the woman lift the boot door and took the opportunity to squeeze past a balustrade. Garvan ignored the transparency of the glass and quietly opened the passenger door, leaving it unhooked from its locking mechanism, but closed to a view from the rear. He watched as they placed their bags inside. He did not care if someone saw him. He would not run again. As the woman closed the boot door, he nudged his way to the front. He heard the woman's key fob beep.

Garvan waited until the car park was deserted before he moved back to the side of the vehicle. He pushed firmly on the passenger door. The stiff thud caused the buttons to shoot up. He opened the door and leaned across to the driver's side, and pulled the boot lever. He then walked to the rear of the car, lifted the boot door, and pulled a small suitcase towards him. He rummaged through before turning his attention to a backpack as if leaving dessert until last. He saw the book, *Mutus Liber*. He had seen a copy before, but this was not what he was looking for. He removed clothes and rifled through personal items.

The stone was not there.

James McAllister was unsettled. He liked order and organisation and was not sure his day was ordinary and organised enough. He wanted reassurance and made the call.

"Hello, Mr McAllister, how can I help?"

McAllister got straight to the point. "I am somewhat

concerned by my day's events and would like some advice."

"Please continue."

"I had a rather strange and annoying man visit this morning. He seemed very confident in his abuse of Elias Ashmole. Some may argue he was right about several things, but it was out of character for the type of tour constituent I usually guide."

"You have a delicate way with words, Mr McAllister. May I ask why you are calling?"

"It seemed somewhat odd that I had the most frightful tour guest at the same time someone accessed my personal effects."

"Please explain, Mr McAllister. I haven't got time for wordplay and guessing games."

"Yes, of course. Well, while this awful person was on my tour, I believe someone entered an office I use. I have taken possession of a key to a filing cabinet within which I keep the three additional stones I have collected," there was a silence at the other end of the line, which McAllister felt he should fill. Quickly. "I keep the key in my diary, but it was not in its place when I returned. It was inside the pages rather than the credit card sleeve."

"I do not believe I need to remind you of the value of these items. I think it would be in your interest to deliver them straight away."

McAllister opened his mouth to speak but heard a click at the other end of the line. The call had ended.

Owen Garvan stared blankly through his windscreen and then to a dull arrow of fading light slowly moving across his dashboard. He needed to get his thoughts together, but his mind kept drifting to the past. It always went there at times of crisis.

He was standing on a metaphorical precipice. Flashbacks of war. A little boy dying in his mother's arms. The same nightmares were repeating. Tripping on a leg and landing face-first on a decapitated head. Anxiety from crowded places. Diarrhoea and heart palpitations. He would walk for miles, often finding himself calling his wife to pick him up from where, he did not know. She had tried. She had supported him through the early days, but they had a young son. It could not continue. He closed his eyes to squeeze the pain away.

It had been three years since he had met the people who would put him on an unexpected road to recovery. It was a long journey, but the recurring memories decreased as he learned more while slowly allowing the group to become his emotional support network.

Then the news came that would turn his world upside down once again. Six months ago. The same people gave him renewed hope for the future. Not just for him, but his son.

His knuckles began to throb. He let go of the steering wheel and breathed slowly. In, out. In, out. He concentrated on his mantra. Breaths. Deep and long. In. Out.

He paid another visit to the past. A more positive experience this time. This was the memory that set him on his road to somewhere — anywhere but the unrelenting visions of death.

It was a dream job that he knew he had little chance of getting. The post-traumatic stress would always be an obstacle, but he had to try. He was despondent when he left the interview but not devastated.

He was approached as he walked through the iron gates. He recalled his first impressions. The woman was short, rotund, and wearing a floral dress. Trendy though, with Dr Martens boots and an orange quiff in her brown hair.

He remembered her smiling as she said, "I am sorry to bother you, I saw you leave the office, and you appeared upset."

He recalled the conversation vividly. Why wouldn't he? It

changed his life. "Oh, no, that's my normal look," he had said returning a smile, but he knew the creases at the corner of his eyes hid an underlying sadness. His wife had told him many times.

"Bad interview?"

"Not really. I have the right credentials, but I suffer from stress, which had to be revealed during my application. I think they went through the motions. An army thing. But it's okay. I fancied a day out. And who knows, they may have taken pity on me and given me a chance."

The nice lady nodded and earnestly said, "May I ask if you have heard of Rosicrucianism?"

"No, I'm afraid not. Is it a religion?"

"Oh, goodness no, it has been described as a belief system, but not a religious movement. I have a book here," the woman rummaged in her oversized bag. "Take it away, have a read. Feel free to do some additional research, and if it's something that might be of interest, my number is on the back. Give me a call. You would be more than welcome at a meeting," she turned to walk away before adding, "I think it might help."

He recalled folding the booklet and slotting it into the inside pocket of his jacket. It was the last thing on his mind when he returned home to see the red light flashing on the answer machine.

It was his most lucid memory. Every detail was finely etched in his mind as if it were the previous day. He pressed the message button, and heard the quivering voice of his estranged wife and the urgent return call he was asked to make.

The next three months flashed by. The additional tests and examinations revealed his four-year-old son had an incurable cancer called Adrenocortical Carcinoma. The prognosis was not good. At best, his lovely little boy had just five years to live. There was nothing anyone could do except make his remaining time as enjoyable, and comfortable as possible.

A tear weaved a path down his craggy face as he recalled his failures as a father. His condition had become a wicked intruder. It took over his whole persona. It was no surprise when, after physically pushing an unhelpful shop assistant in front of his wife and son, his wife told him it would be better for everyone if he dealt with his issues before spending further time at home.

A few weeks after the 'incident' as it became known in his family, he went to hang his jacket in the wardrobe when the booklet fell to the floor.

It was called *Mystic Wisdom by The Rosicrucian Order.* It was the book the nice lady in London had given him.

Although initially reticent, mild curiosity quickly became an all-consuming passion. He devoured the subject in book form and visited branch meetings in South London, where he learned about esoteric truths in nature, the universe, and spirituality. He read countless books on related subjects by authors such as Arthur Waite, Daniel Cramer, Ralph Lewis, and Max Hendel. He had even translated ancient books in foreign languages by people like John Dee and Johann Valentin Andreae.

His studies became his coping mechanism. He developed self-defined cognitive behavioural therapy by finding spiritual comfort and guidance when it was most needed. He learned everyone has wisdom and knowledge that regular teachings and philosophies do not encourage. People have an in-built ability for expression and emotion that modern society never develops — a capacity to appreciate and evolve independently of traditional thought and teachings. He studied how to cope with his life's demands through compassion and friendship. Most importantly, he learned how to deal with his condition and to support his son through the remainder of his short life.

As much as he appreciated the help and encouragement his new friends had provided, he had overlooked an area of

Rosicrucianism that offered little comfort and practical knowledge for his needs. He was aware that many of the adepts and scientists of the early days of Rosicrucianism practised alchemy, but it merely provided additional background noise to his studies.

It was not until he had missed a few meetings after his son's diagnosis that his life turned on its head once again. The phone call came out of the blue. He had spoken to the man a few times at meetings, but they did not know each other outside of their shared interest. The conversation put everything he had read, learned, and practised into focus.

Could it possibly be true? Were the philosopher's stone and the Alkahest one and the same? Was Paracelsus right? Was there a cure for his son's illness?

He shook the thoughts from his mind to concentrate on the present. Eddie Hill must have the stone with him. He should just take it from him, but what would they say? He had been instructed to go about his business in the shadows. Draw no attention, and avoid any risk of a repeat of the actions that led to the death of the Beefeater.

This was a delicate operation that had been years in the planning, but he was within touching distance of the solution. He had to maintain the discipline of his training. Now, at the worst time of his life, patience was everything.

Garvan opened his eyes. Tranquillity had returned. His group had been an incredible help, and the reward was more than he could ever have dreamed of, but he was no further forward.

He had a new challenge. As much as he wanted to do as he had been told, his son had to be his priority.

14

Owen Garvan was angry with himself. He should have followed Eddie Hill instead of worrying about the bags — of course he would keep it on him. Why would he leave it in his backpack? Stupid. *Stupid.*

He entered the large glass door of the hotel and walked to the counter. A cheerful young man looked up as he approached. "Excuse me. I wonder if you could help?"

"Of course, sir."

"I would like to leave a message for Mr Hill."

"Do you have a room number, sir?"

"No, sorry, I do not."

The cheerful young man typed at his computer, "That's okay, sir, I have found him. I can write the message down for you."

Garvan patted his front pockets and then his jacket pocket. "I have it written down already. It looks like I have left it in the car. I will be right back."

The young man smiled, and turned his attention to another guest. Garvan knew Hill had not checked out, and decided to return early in the morning.

The hotel was silent. The only other person they saw was an older man dozing behind the front desk. The man nodded in appreciation that he did not have to move as they placed their room key in the self-checkout box.

As they exited into the dark, cold air greeted them. Lucy lifted the car boot door to throw their washbags in. She shook her head. Both bags were open, and some clothes were hanging out. He's always forgetting something, she thought.

As Lucy drove, Eddie slept. He was nudged awake a couple of times. "If I can't sleep. . ." Lucy let him be for the last few miles before pulling in front of Hounslow West Underground Station. Just along from Heathrow, but easy enough to rejoin the motorway.

Eddie kissed her before getting out. He held the door open and said, "If the police call, just say I left my phone at home, and you're not happy about it, or whatever, because you want to get hold of me. Add that after a weekend break in Oxford, I am meeting Jamie in London to watch Portsmouth on Sunday afternoon. They are away to Charlton Athletic."

"That might delay speaking to them, but you can't put it off forever."

"I know. I'll talk to them when I get back, but I can't help thinking putting a bit of time in between events might change things anyway. Surely, they will have an autopsy or medical exam, or whatever they do, to ascertain the cause of death. And if they find it has nothing to do with the attack in the afternoon, I am hoping they won't need to talk to me at all."

"That makes sense. After all, if the poor guy can't say anything," Lucy tailed off as Eddie closed the door. She watched Eddie use his Oyster card to go through the barriers before driving away.

The sky progressively brightened as Lucy's mood darkened. She pulled off at the Milford slip road, a place she had passed many times but did not recognise the name of. She found a café by the train station. She needed to see inside the boot. Even if he had forgotten something, surely Eddie would not have left everything strewn around.

Lucy saw the antique book leaning against the side of her suitcase. He certainly would not have left *this* unprotected by clothes. Someone had been in there. But how? The only kind of person capable of gaining access to a car would be someone who had a key or the right equipment. Unease crept up from her stomach.

The café lights were on, and a genial-looking woman unlocked the door. "Eager."

"Thanks. I didn't think you would be open on a Sunday."

"There's a bike race coming through today. I thought I'd make an early start."

Lucy took a seat by the window and asked for a mug of coffee and scrambled eggs on wholemeal toast. She stared at the bushes across the road through the condensation coated window and fought for an explanation. Her first concern was Eddie. She called. No answer. He must still be on the Underground, she thought.

The tour guide at the Ashmolean had three philosopher's stones. The search engine provided an instant response. 'The philosopher's stone is a celebrated, sometimes mythical, alchemical substance said to be capable of turning base metals into precious metals such as gold or silver. It is also dubbed the elixir of life, beneficial for rejuvenation, medical purposes, and even for achieving immortality. It was the most sought-after goal in alchemy for several centuries'.

Lucy decided she needed more than that. She knew there

was a connection between the funny little man in Oxford, the stones, and that period of history, but what it could be, she needed to learn. She had eaten the eggs and finished two mugs of coffee before she had skimmed the surface of philosopher's stone information. Additional research would have to wait until she got home.

Her attention switched back to the car, and her thoughts raced. Who would want to do that? They must have been looking for something, but why would they leave an antique book? They must have been looking for the stone. There had been an attack, and a death — which was possibly murder, over one of these stones. Someone had broken into her car. A tour guide even has a secret stash of these things. She winced, attempting to push the notion that Eddie could be heading into trouble from her mind. It must be him — the little man at the museum. He must be following us, or he has sent someone to follow us.

Her heart rate accelerated and her stomached heaved. It wasn't the eggs.

Ian Gale's watch read seven-thirty. That's not an unreasonable time, he thought, and rang the doorbell.

No answer.

He knew he should have gone home. His back was sore, and his teeth were sticky. He also knew he had to face DI Spears and explain that he was unable to locate Mr Hill.

Gale had wanted to be a detective ever since his first and only crime. He smirked at the memory of the kiss from little Dawn Kelly. He didn't think he would recover her new Parker pen, but he promised he would find it in exchange for a kiss, in full knowledge that he would steal his dad's pen and give it to her. He put a show on and asked his classmates if they had seen it or accidentally put it in one of their pencil cases. His foot caught on the inside leg of the desk and rolled forward onto something underneath. It was resting on the pen. Nobody saw him pick it up, but Dawn was suitably impressed when he handed it to her after break. A stolen kiss — his first and only crime. He smiled at himself in the rearview mirror and ran a thumb across the small scar on his forehead. This is why he tried his hand at any dangerous sport on offer — anything to avoid his light-fingered father from calling him names.

He decided to leave Eddie Hill's street. A street where he had memorised half the car number plates and could recall the colour of each vehicle from the start of the road with his eyes closed. He would have a shower and change his clothes before going in to work. He wrote his mobile number on the back of a business card and opened the letterbox, but then reconsidered. No, he needed to talk to Hill.

15

Eddie had not been to Embankment Underground Station before. He saw the moonlight bounce sparkles on the river to his right and a road he knew to be Villiers Street to his left. He nodded to himself — it was obvious which way he would turn. He walked past some temporary green netting, within which work was taking place to restore an area of aged stonework.

Victoria Embankment Gardens opened up in front of him. He could see statues, fenced garden areas, and curved benches ideal for office worker lunch breaks. York Gate was to his left. Sharp, stone edges no longer existed, but the worn façade was still well preserved.

As he approached a small, railed area that cut the public off from the historic monument his phone rang. "Hello babe, home safe and sound?"

Lucy had decided not to mention the break-in yet. "Yes, back home. It was an easy drive. There are hardly any cars at this time of the day. Are you there?"

Eddie wiped moisture from a park bench opposite the stone arch. "Yes, I am looking at York Gate now. What have you learned?"

"As soon as I got home, I dived in, and I think I have found out how this all began."

Eddie placed a used newspaper between him and the cold bench. "I'm all ears."

"Right. Let's look at what we know. George's dad was murdered outside a pub that is now a posh hotel. Reading between the lines, the first George Villiers, was James I's lover, or certainly sufficiently close for his son, the next king, Charles I, to raise George and his brother Francis as his own children, along with the future Charles II and James II. Francis was a bit younger, but they were all similar ages, and Charles and George were closest among the four. Their friendship was helped along by the big thing of the day — alchemy. Now, this is where it all gets a bit complicated."

Eddie stood. His backside was cold. He narrowed his gaze to watch his breathing dissipate. "Hang on a minute, can we walk and talk. It's a bit chilly, and I still can't work out where this clue leads," he wiped the dew from a large bronze plaque revealing the history of York Gate. "It isn't just turning metals into gold, is it?"

"No. I would go as far as saying, the 'transmutation of metals' as they might describe it was just a small part of this. I think it was more spiritual. They believed a universal remedy type cure-all, or even an elixir to everlasting life, was possible. Don't forget, it wasn't long after they thought the world was flat, so science was still in its infancy. Having said that, illnesses were better understood, and science was moving on in leaps and bounds. So, the idea that they could create a medicine to cure everything would have been highly plausible at that time."

"My mum thinks that's called a hot bath."

"I must admit, I went off on a tangent to Isaac Newton at that point. Despite being one of the most highly regarded scientists in history, I found out he spent much of his life's studies researching and practising alchemy, and he wasn't alone. It seems most of the scientific community were at it. Robert Boyle, Thomas Henshaw, James Price, Thomas Vaughan, loads of them. Anyway, getting back to George and Charles — they had more resources than anyone, and they spent a fair amount of their formative years in quest of the philosopher's stone. Somewhere along the line, they drifted apart. There appears to be conflicting theories why."

"Historians often fill gaps when historical accounts and letters aren't available, so don't worry."

Lucy replied, "Okay. Well, this is how I see it. Charles was going to be king, and his best mate and brother George — who felt he had a better claim to the throne than Charles — was not, but that's another story. They had very different responsibilities. A king back then pretty much ran the country. At fourteen, Charles led the English forces in the Civil War, while George and Francis went off to University. Although, to be fair, they did join the fight against Cromwell. Fairly unsuccessfully, it should be said. They had their possessions confiscated and moved to Europe. They lived in Florence and Rome, where 'debauched behaviour blossomed' according to the books."

Eddie read the plaque while Lucy was talking. He had seen the same image on the internet, so it did not provide new information. His attention reverted to York Gate. He walked around and studied the stonework, all originally carved by hand. The paving slabs aligned neatly, and although they looked more modern, he could see nothing that wanted to give up the solution to his clue.

Lucy checked her notes. "Here it is. In 1645, aged just

seventeen, he met up with Charles in Paris. Let me read you a quote from Bishop Burnett, who was travelling with Charles. He is talking about when George popped up in Paris.

Having already got into all the impieties and vices of the age, [Buckingham] set out to corrupt the future King by possessing the young Prince with very ill principles both as to religion and morality, but with a very mean opinion of his father, whose stiffness was with him a perpetual subject of raillery. And to compleat the matter, Hobbs was brought to him [Charles] under the pretence of instructing him with mathematicks; and he laid before him his schemes both as to religion and politicks, which made a deep and lasting impression on the King's mind so that the main blame of the King's ill principles and bad morals was owing to The Duke of Buckingham.

To cut a long story short, George was a corrupting influence in an age of extreme faith, but he and Charles were still trying to achieve the philosopher's stone. George certainly put a few of the elders backs up, not least because he and Charles lived extravagant lives and quickly ran short of funds. They still fell out, though."

"Friends and brothers do that," said Eddie, as he listened intently at his fiancée's enthusiasm. It was infectious. He shook off his smile as it dawned on him that he was wasting his time in the gardens. As he came to terms with the disappointment, he said, "I do know a bit about that time. After Cromwell killed Charles' dad, Charles was still proclaimed King during his exile. I knew lots of older political advisers surrounded him, so I can't say I'm surprised that he and George grew close again."

Lucy continued, "George and Charles didn't just play around with a crucible and some liquids. They employed alchemists while they were in France. The info is a bit sketchy, but I think one was a man named Claude Duval. It's books and films that make us think the philosopher's stone was something you found. The verb they used was 'achieved'. It was something they made. I won't go into detail, but I think Duval was the original gentleman highwayman."

Eddie asked, "As in Adam and the Ants?"

"Well, possibly. It would take a lot more reading, but most importantly, he is on the list of French alchemists of that time, along with a few Germans who may have crossed paths with the king. I even found a website listing Dutch paintings of alchemists from that period. In a nutshell, if you are a bored king without a kingdom, but with a hobby you share with your best mate, it's not outside the realms of possibility that they may have struck lucky."

Eddie interrupted, "Actually, can I call you back once I've checked into the hotel. It's freezing here."

They said their goodbyes, and Eddie took one last look at York Gate before he left the park and headed for the pier. It was still early on a Sunday morning, but there were already lots of people around. It would be even busier during a work morning. Too busy to access the solution to the clue.

A clue he had solved while Lucy was talking.

He had found the Touchstone of Faith, but he knew this was the end of his journey and wanted to come to terms with it before he told her.

As he boarded, Eddie read the side of the *Thames Clipper,* 'making life easier'. He laughed out loud. What was he doing? As the boat skimmed the surface of the Thames to its destination, Eddie considered his motives. To exonerate? Of course. Certainly, after an inquisition by the police during another time of his life. A tragic time. To forget and move on? It didn't matter now. For the adventure? Possibly. He liked to stick his nose in where it didn't belong, as a broken arm at primary school once proved.

He knew he would have to dismantle part of an ancient building to access a solution that might not exist. And what if he had it completely wrong? What then?

Ominous clouds darkened the sky as the boat pulled into Greenwich. He deboarded and walked past the *Cutty Sark*, newly renovated after the tragic fire. He had toured HMS *Victory* in Portsmouth and was now looking at the tea clipper upon which the more modern vessel he had just left had been monikered. He often considered what life would have been like on those ships of the past.

He made his way past the pubs and shops along a cobbled walkway towards his budget hotel. It was a quarter of the price of his previous night's stay.

Eddie found his room and sat on the bed to make his call. Lucy answered straight away. "In your room?"

"Yes. Not quite as luxurious as the last one, but similarly prison-like."

Lucy laughed. "Okay, I have been doing some more reading. Ready?"

He was ready. Whatever happened next, he wanted Lucy to enjoy whatever was left of this journey with him. "Yes, tell me more about George and Charles. Any beheadings I should know about?"

"No, nothing like that, and all of what I know so far was fairly easy to learn. The search engine had a couple of book links, but it gets a bit more complicated during the exile period of Charles II's life because there was not as much documentation."

"I don't suppose Samuel Pepys followed him around France to let us know what was going on."

"Exactly. But I have joined a few dots and come up with

nine, as it were."

"You have learned how historians do it, then. So, was the falling out over a stone?"

Lucy replied, "I am not sure how involved Charles is with this. I think this is all about George Villiers. He sounds like a real character of his day. He was a great raconteur and was well-known for doing impressions of high society people."

"That must have made him popular."

"I don't think he cared. He also dressed up as a peasant to get out and about. He called himself Jack Pudding."

"Jack Pudding?"

"I'm filling a few gaps here, but during this period in France, he went back to England disguised as Jack Pudding to give his sister some secret documents. His sister Mall, the Duchess of Richmond, was a prisoner — more Parliament stuff. Anyway, she was being transferred to Windsor when a jester stopped her coach. Because of the social unrest and the crowds, she had no choice but to listen to this jester ridicule her. After the performance, the jester asked her guards to present copies of his songs to the duchess. They agreed, and when he got closer, she saw it was her brother in disguise. He then handed her these secret documents."

"Do you think he gave her a stone?"

"No idea, but there were intense negotiations, plans, and schemes going on to get Charles back on his throne, including a deal with the Scots. There was also a lot of religious politics around at that time. It was extremely complicated, and it was this deal with the Scots that led to their issues. They wanted Charles to sign documents confessing his sins and those of his father."

"Religious cranks, then?"

"Most were at that time, but it was all very political. On the other hand, George was running low on funds and didn't care too much about the religious stuff. He just wanted Charles to return as King and for himself to be his main political adviser."

"So, much the same as their fathers?"

Lucy replied, "Charles I was king, and the first George Villiers was the country's most powerful political figure before proper Parliament came into being. So, yes, very similar. I don't know how much of that relates to his love for his friend or how much was about getting his riches back, but their first big row came after Charles stopped him taking charge of royalist forces."

Eddie had his own decision to make, and Lucy would not like it. He did not enjoy keeping things from her, especially when they were as important as this.

Lucy continued, "To be frank, I skimmed over most of this stuff to look for the alchemy angle. Suffice it to say, it was all politics, back-stabbing, and gossiping about George among Charles' advisers, which was added to by George constantly moaning about Charles' decision not to put him in charge of military forces. Anyway, to cut a long story short, they drifted apart, both trying to regain their own version of influence and power without each other."

Eddie asked, "How near is this to Charles' return to England?"

"I will get to that now. A couple of years before The Restoration, when Charles returned to the throne proper, George returned to England to make peace with the parliamentarians under Cromwell. It was probably a dodgy game to play, as he appeared to be betraying Charles."

"Was he?"

"Not exactly. Well, I don't think so. It seems to me, he was just taking care of himself and playing the angles."

Eddie wondered whether that was what he was contemplating. Playing the angles.

Lucy paused. "I just came in and sat down to read. I'm just going to stick the kettle on."

Eddie interrupted, "No, you're not. Carry on. I need to know what happened next."

"Okay, okay. So, skim reading is not the best way of researching, so I got a bit confused about what happened next. There was a General Fairfax, who was a Royalist, who Cromwell granted George's estate."

"So, a traitor?"

"No, he was a principled man who showed loyalty to the head of state — that sort of thing. Anyway, that's not the point. When George learned Fairfax had been given his wealth, he looked for a way to turn it to his advantage. So, he ditched Charles and turned up at Fairfax's door. Not long later, George married his daughter."

"Just like that?"

"Pretty much. They were related somehow, but after ingratiating himself with his big personality, it wasn't long before George tried it on with the daughter. I made a note. You will like this. She was described as a 'little round crumpled woman'."

"Not a looker, then?" Eddie asked.

"Let's just repeat, George was playing the angles, and although politics was still going on in the background, it wasn't long before Cromwell caught up with him and slung him in the Tower of London."

Eddie asked, "Hang on, when was this?"

"Correct question. It was 1659."

"Just a few months before Charles got his throne back?"

"Yes, and to summarise, I have a quote from George. 'I was then close prisoner in the Tower, with a couple of guards lying always in my chamber and a sentinel at my door. I confess I was not a little delighted with the noise of the great guns, for I presently knew what it meant, and if Oliver had lived for three more days longer, I had certainly been put to death'."

"Interesting."

"Yes, and here is another from around the same time, from a George biographer called Brian Fairfax, who I think was another cousin, 'This life of regularity and domesticity — No courtships but to his own wife, not so much as to his after beloved and costly mistress, the philosopher's stone'."

"Bloody hell, this is like Eastenders meets Dynasty."

"That's not the half of it. Cromwell had emptied the coffers warring, so when his son Richard took over, he lasted about five minutes before Parliament took control, and not long after that, Charles was coronated, King."

"So, what about him and George?"

"With Fairfax's help and influence, George was fairly instrumental in getting the monarchy returned, so it wasn't long before him, and Charles kissed and made up."

Eddie asked, "Where did we get to with the stones?"

"Well. Things could not possibly be the same again, with one as King and one still scheming to get his riches back, but the most interesting thing is they opened a laboratory together, and George had at least one separate lab of his own."

Eddie knew his conversation with Lucy would clarify his thoughts one way or another. He had made his decision. He would text Jamie to get there earlier than originally planned.

Lucy was looking out of the window as she spoke, "I'm going to have to call you back, someone has just rung the doorbell," she moved the curtain to one side, "and I think he has just got out of a white car at the end of our drive. It looks like it could be the police."

"Call me back once you have spoken to them."

Lucy said, "Of course. Oh, and while I'm gone, look up George Starkey."

16

Ian Gale presumed Mr Hill's partner had not been home for long. Her coat was on the couch, and although her laptop was open, she was still wearing her running shoes, despite her slippers occupying a space next to the adjacent table. "Can I ask when Mr Hill will be back? I need to speak to him urgently about a serious matter."

Lucy asked, "Is it about that poor man dying?"

"Yes. We need to get some background information on events, and we believe Mr Hill may have been a witness."

"He saw the man getting hit and another man running off, but nothing else."

Gale looked up from his notepad. "A man ran off?"

"Yes, Eddie said he saw a bald man attack the man who owned the property he was working on, and as he went over to help, the bald man ran off. I think they were both bald. But anyway, the one that did the hitting ran off."

"Did he see anything else?"

"No, that was about it. You really should talk to Eddie about it. He will tell you in more detail. I didn't ask. It didn't sound that serious until we heard that someone had died in a car park, and it turned out to be the same man."

"May I ask when Mr Hill will be home?"

"Oh, he's gone to football in London today. He's staying overnight in Greenwich and coming back in the morning."

Gale stood, "Portsmouth fan?"

"Yes, at Charlton, I think."

"I'm a Pompey fan. Fingers crossed. I would appreciate it if you could get Mr Hill to call me on this number when he returns," Gale said as he handed Lucy his card.

Lucy escorted Gale to the front door. "Of course. I am sure he will do all he can to help."

She was pleased with herself when the door closed. No nerves at all. She felt a pain in her hand and unclenched. She looked at the fingernail imprints in her palm. Well, maybe a few nerves.

Owen Garvan sat in his car outside his apartment, staring at a lone magpie going about its morning food hunting business. Magpies come in pairs, but this one was alone. He perceived an affinity with the bird — he had never felt as alone. Even though he had a simple job to do, he had not completed the task. One man was dead, and another was marauding around the country with the answer to his prayers.

He could telephone the curator directly to apologise, but what good would that do? His contact and mentor had advised him to call upon his armed forces experience and the efficiency of an organisation if members understood hierarchical procedure. What good would it do to aggravate the buffer between him and the curator? And what would he say, anyway? I know who has the stone, but I can't get it because you told me not to draw attention to myself?

Although it had only been a few days, he knew Eddie Hill was a suspect and was concerned that if arrested, the stone could enter evidence? Expediency was required. Did they not appreciate this? Not just for his son, but for the people that had made promises to him.

He needed to get his head clear. He retrieved a photocopied book from the holdall on his back seat. *Religio Medici* by Sir Thomas Browne was a seventeenth century best-seller. He could not afford a real copy, but the text was clearly printed, and he needed spiritual comfort.

Before he opened a page, he looked at his reflection in the overhead mirror. A round, puffy face stared back. It bore the scars of constant worry and anxiety. All the lines pointed down. There were no laughter lines.

He placed the book on the passenger's seat. He would return to Hill's house and explain the situation in the friendliest terms possible.

But what if that failed?

He would take the stone anyway.

He kissed two fingers and placed them on the dashboard photo of his son.

Ian Gale approached his desk as quietly as possible. He saw DI Spears pacing around his office and wanted to avoid him. The wheel of his chair squeaked as he pushed it aside to reach below the drawers to retrieve his kitbag.

Spears opened the door and said, "DC Gale, can you join me, please?"

Gale grimaced. "Yes, of course, sir."

Gale closed the door behind him, placed his holdall on the floor, and stood in front of his superior.

Spears looked at the kitbag.

"It's my football gear, sir. I forgot to take it yesterday. I play Sunday football."

Spears looked up and said nothing for a long enough period for Gale to ask, "How can I help, sir?"

"Have you found to Mr Hill yet?"

"Not yet, sir. He has gone away for the weekend."

"Well, make it a priority tomorrow, please."

"Yes, of course, sir," Gale picked up his kitbag and closed the door behind him. He muttered, "I only came in for my gear."

Eddie swiped the green answer icon on his phone, "You have been gone ages. What did the police say?"

"I took a long shower and then put some washing on. They would like to talk to you. I have a card from a Detective Constable Ian Gale."

"Oh, I see, you wanted me to stew for a while. I know I have avoided it for a couple of days. I will call tomorrow. More importantly, what made you get to George Starkey?"

"*More importantly*. I said the police, not the marmalade delivery, driver."

"Do they deliver marmalade, then?"

"Eddie."

"Okay, okay, I said I would call them tomorrow. I'm not bothered. They will just be following up. It's understandable, and I am sure they have found another witness by now," Eddie was bothered but quickly added, "So. George Starkey?"

Lucy was not happy but carried on with the conversation, "Okay, fine. And yes, Starkey. It was a hunch more than anything. While I was reading about George and alchemy, I came across Eirenaeus Philalethes, a pseudonym of Starkey's. I read he was one of the main alchemists of the time and wondered whether he might have hooked up with Charles or George somewhere along the line."

Eddie said, "Well, I'm not sure about that, but I did learn

he was born in Bermuda and went to Harvard at fifteen. He left for England in 1650, five years after he allegedly achieved the philosopher's stone at the age of just twenty-three."

Lucy said, "I thought he might have, because he seemed to have become involved with the scientific community very quickly after his arrival."

"Yes, you're right. Robert Boyle, John Locke, and Isaac Newton were all said to have been influenced by him. There was something called the Hartlib Circle around the time he came to England, which was the forerunner to the Royal Society."

"The question that nagged at me was, how he gained influence so quickly?"

"Well, this is one of those times where letters and records prove unreliable. Reports suggested that this Eirenaeus Philalethes was his mate."

"Huh?"

"I know. Starkey was one of these early influential chemists, but it appears he wrote his alchemical works under that Latin pseudonym. I'm not sure which of the names became friendly with the other chemists, but I am conjuring Starkey chatting to the other scientists as a sort of editor for this strange and mystical genius, and all these wise men nodding sagely at him while laughing behind his back agreeing that they knew it was him. One of the main reasons he came to England was because he built ovens for alchemical experimentation and could not acquire equipment of sufficient quality in America. So, I think you've got this impressive young guy that has already achieved the philosopher's stone, who also designs and makes these furnaces, which were called athanors."

"Okay, so let's assume that Starkey was the main equipment supplier to the big-name alchemists, slash scientists, of the day. Where do we go from there?"

Eddie paused before replying, "I think the best bet is for

you to carry on with George and Charles, and I will continue along with Starkey to see where it leads me, and we should catch up before bedtime."

It was nine-thirty when Lucy heard her phone ping. It was a message from Eddie. 'Eyes have packed in after staring at a tiny screen on my phone all day. I may have found a possible link between the Duke of Buckingham and Starkey. Find out what you can about the Vauxhall Glassworks, and I will call you in the morning. I'm meeting Jamie at four-thirty.'

A second ping.

'Love you'.

Lucy replied, 'Will do, and love you too'.

Only when she placed her phone on the bedside cabinet did Lucy wonder why Eddie and Jamie were meeting so early.

Eddie considered his paradoxical tiredness competing with his belief that sleep was a forlorn hope. How could he sleep with the knowledge of his intentions for the following morning? What if he was caught? What if it was not there? *What if he was caught?*

17

Apart from the noise of a distant street sweeper's motorised brushes, and the gentle eddy of the water drifting along the Thames, the early morning quiet proffered a calming serenity. Now that he had a plan, Eddie was surprisingly relaxed with what they had to do, and was watching his breath once again when Jamie arrived.

Jamie jumped out of his van, quickly took in his surroundings, and lifted his arms to appeal for an explanation. Eddie ignored him, and in a hushed tone, asked, "Have you brought everything?"

Jamie said, "I have," he looked around at the stone arch. "What are we doing here at this godforsaken hour?"

"The plan is, we will put the green fencing up around the garden to make it look like it's part of the general works going on around here. It will look like we are official workers. I presume you have the hard hats and high viz vests because that will give it the full health and safety worker look."

Jamie walked around the edifice, studying the three arches and intricate columns that supported two lions, separated by a coat of arms crest and an upright oyster shell above the central entrance.

"Oh yes," said Eddie. "See that crest? We're going to chisel around the edges, scrape the mortar away and slide it out."

Jamie turned his gaze to Eddie. "Are you mad?"

Eddie laughed. "Okay, you know that stone I showed you in the coffee shop?"

"Go on."

"I think there's another one hidden behind that crest."

Jamie looked back up at the emblem. "What makes you think that?"

Eddie swiped through to a photo of the back of the *Mutus Liber* book. He enlarged the image with his thumb and forefinger before pointing at the clue and said, "The Cross is the Touchstone of Faith," he waved Jamie over to the large brass plaque to the left of the façade. "Take a look at this," he pointed to the exact phrase written within the inscribed passage.

Jamie looked back at York Gate. "What is this, then?"

"This was the entrance to a mansion called York House, owned by The Duke of Buckingham. And this was the waterway access point they travelled to by boat. It was called York Watergate. These three steps, plus a few more at that time, led into the water."

Jamie looked down and back towards the Thames, glinting back in the moonlight.

Eddie added, "The Thames went up as far as here, but the Victorians built sewers along the Embankment. That is what I think is under us. Back in the day, this was mostly marshland."

Jamie frowned. "Right, thanks for that. Very good. But are

you saying we are going to hack that coat of arms off a historic monument?"

"No, of course not. I would even go as far as saying we will improve it. That mortar up there is not original. I would guess it was bodged up a long time ago. We are going to do a better job of it, and no one would even know we had been here," Eddie said as he walked over to Jamie's van to retrieve ladders from the roof.

Within a few minutes, they had removed most of the loose and aged mortar around the central part of the coat of arms. Eddie was able to grip the cross in the centre and began to prise it free.

"Morning, chaps. What's going on here?"

Eddie's ladders shook as he recoiled at the sudden interruption of concentration. Although the early morning traffic had begun to increase, only a few people had walked past. He saw a policeman looking up from the edge of the perimeter fencing.

"Vandals. Friday night."

The policeman looked up at the two workmen on adjacent ladders at the front of the structure. "Much damage?"

"There was some white paint on the arch here, and I think they were trying to scrape this crest out judging by the screwdriver marks."

Jamie did not take his eyes off Eddie as he stood like an accompanying statue to the stonework.

"Well, the arch looks cleaner than the rest of it, so you're doing a good job. How much longer are you going to be? Only you can't park your van there."

"We got here early and were hoping to have finished by now, but this is an ancient building, and we need to be extra careful that we don't damage anything while we repair it. I think we will be about another half an hour, but I can move the van if you want."

"Well, I'm just on my way to work. I was passing and wondered what was going on. I wouldn't hang around too long though, bikes will start using that lane soon, and you won't want them on your case."

"Cyclists," Eddie said, shrugging his shoulders.

The policeman raised his head in acknowledgement before turning and walking away.

Jamie had not realised he had been holding his breath. He looked at Eddie, "That was close."

Eddie was still wriggling the crest from its orifice. "We are in the middle of London. I was expecting a newspaper delivery man, or a road sweeper, or something, but I was always going to say that."

"Well, you convinced me."

"Grab the other side of this, mate."

Eddie lifted the bottom half of the crest loose from its housing. They walked down the steps, each with one hand holding onto their ladders and the other sharing the crest. The bottom half of the shield and the central and bottom vertical section of the cross was lighter than a building block, but they were vigilant about potential damage. They placed it gently on the weather-beaten entrance floor before climbing the ladders again.

They peered into the revealed crevice at the same time. Eddie placed his hand in the square hole and retrieved a small shape. He lifted a roughly wrapped piece of cloth from the stonework — it was folded over, not tied — and looked at Jamie. He quickly put the object in his pocket and said, "Right, we need to mix up some mortar and put all this back."

They said nothing more until they had repaired the stonework, packed the van away, and pulled into the now congested road.

"I need to call Lucy. I'll put it on speaker," Eddie said.

Lucy answered on the first ring, "Hi babe, what have you

113

learned?"

"Hi, Lucy," Jamie said.

"Jamie. I can't believe he's got you mixed up in this."

"Well, it appears I'm not working, and I'll do anything for my boo-boo," Jamie stretched his hand over from the steering wheel and rubbed Eddie's stubble.

Eddie raised his gaze to the roof. "Don't take any notice of him. What have you learned?"

"Loads more about George and Charles and as much as I could about alchemy. How did your reading up on George Starkey go?"

Eddie said, "So, who's a clever girl, then?"

"I thought he might be involved somewhere."

Eddie retrieved the stone from his pocket and turned it over. It was a similar colour to the other stone but with jagged edges. Pebble sized. He looked closer. "There's a crudely inscribed etching on the stone. It says 'Philatheles'."

"You found it, then. Where was it?"

Eddie thought the safest explanation was the longest explanation. He told Lucy the whole story.

"The policeman wasn't at all suspicious, then?" Lucy asked.

"No, he was as good as gold. He was more concerned about where Jamie had parked the van than what we were doing?"

"You had no idea where it was before you got there, then?"

Eddie raised three fingers and crossed his pinkie to his thumb. "Scout's honour."

"I'm not entirely buying it, but as long as you are both safe."

"Yes, both safe, and looking forward to breakfast."

Lucy said, "It would be hard to etch. They didn't have diamond-tipped instruments like my mum uses at the jewellers."

Eddie breathed a sigh of relief. His night in the doghouse was deferred once again. "That confirms the story then."

Jamie looked over to Eddie. "How does it confirm what story?"

"It's very roughly etched, which probably means it *was* by a diamond. Rich people had diamonds," Eddie shifted in his seat to get comfortable. "Okay, kids, ready? I will tell you what happened, but before I start, can you confirm something, Luce? Did York Gate have a significant meaning to George?"

"Yes, it did. After his brother Francis died in battle, the Duke personally took him through the arch by boat."

Eddie said, "Okay. That explains why the stone was where it was. Now, I can't say when or how our friend George met Starkey, but the elite of their time was a small community, so he would have bumped into him at some stage. Probably several times. As fellow alchemists, there was a shared interest."

Lucy asked, "Is that what you are going to try to find out at the archives?"

Eddie did not tell Lucy he was never going to visit the National Archives. He knew she would not have agreed to him desecrating a historic monument. "I'm not going now. I'm coming straight home. We have the stone, so I don't need to know more about him. I'm just speculating about how it got there. Tell me about Vauxhall Glassworks?"

"George opened the Vauxhall Glassworks shortly after The Restoration saw Charles get his kingdom back. He employed a team of Venetian glassmakers to make blown plate glass. He also persuaded Charles to ban the importation of specialised glass, which gave him a nationwide monopoly."

Eddie asked, "Have you found anything about an alchemy lab or furnaces? Or who installed them?"

"I'm afraid not. There isn't much info on the internet, but I can see where you're going with this."

Jamie asked, "This George Starkey?"

Eddie replied, "Yes. This George Starkey. It would certainly make sense. Pure speculation, of course, but it's not a great stretch of the imagination to surmise the country's foremost alchemy athanor builder—"

"Athanor?" Jamie asked.

"That's what they called their alchemy furnaces. So, we have the country's foremost expert, and the country's richest man wanted a furnace—"

"Well, go on then. What do you reckon?" Lucy asked.

"Well, there is a bit of time divergence, but to summarise, Starkey went to debtor's prison. He came out and mostly did proper medicine and then died of the plague."

"But if he was part of the in-crowd, how did that happen?" Jamie asked.

"From what I can make out, he stretched himself a little too thinly with his chemical projects. He made medicines and perfumes — and trying to achieve the philosopher's stone was an expensive business. He lost the support of the Hartlib Circle and went to debtor's prison in 1653 for a year."

"What happened next?" Lucy asked.

"He spent the rest of his life looking for the Alkahest — a universal solvent and medicine, which was what he started out doing. It was described as a medicinal solvent similar in purpose to theriac, which was considered history's wonder drug. It was an antidotal compound that was consumed to preserve health and prevent illness."

Lucy asked, "The elixir of life?"

"Sort of. I have his recipe written down here," Eddie picked his phone up from the dashboard and scrolled to a new page.

Jamie looked over, "What, the recipe for everlasting life?"

Eddie laughed, "Yes, something like that. Starkey's Sulphic Mercury was an amalgam of antimony, silver, and mercury, which, once dissolved, would produce a mixture they called the philosopher's stone. Swiss philosopher, chemist, and Rosicrucian, Paracelsus believed the Alkahest and philosopher's stone were the same thing. His recipe was caustic lime, carbonate of potash, and alcohol, which would create a similar chemical compound."

"Not the best description, Eddie," Lucy said.

"No, probably not, but that's the gist of the theories of the time. There will be variations and alternative compounds and ingredients, but it was all experimentation. I was tired last night. I seem to be getting up at silly o'clock now."

"I was up at two for this barmy adventure," Jamie said, adding, "Just because we're not working, and you want something to do. Jamie was not happy when I turned the light on."

Eddie affected a harsh tone, "I will have you know, there is a murder involved here, and I am trying to clear my name. And why do you two still call yourselves the same name? It's very confusing."

"Cobblers. You have a hero complex. And for your information, Jamie thinks it's cute."

Lucy laughed, "Now, now you two. You don't want to make me jealous."

Eddie said, "Okay. Back to the story. George bought, stole, or conned the stone out of Starkey."

"Is that it?" Lucy asked.

"I'm afraid so, yes. I couldn't find a direct connection, but this is Starkey's stone, so I can't think of any other way of George getting it. Starkey would have been penniless when he left debtor's prison and might have needed a sponsor of some description."

"I suppose. But how did it get in the stonework of York Gate?"

"No idea, but the answer to the clue was pretty obvious to

me, and that is where it led. I didn't know where exactly, but I was sure it was there somewhere."

"Yes, but how did it get put up there? It said on the plaque that the house was built in the 1620s," Jamie asked.

Eddie replied, "It's impossible to say for sure. Perhaps there were repairs at some stage. If I had to guess I would say it was hidden during the Great Fire of London. It was a year after Starkey died, so a convenient time for George to acquire the stone and also a convenient time for a rich man to get a stonemason to do some work on his house. In the end, it doesn't really matter how it got up there. The clue led to the stone, and we have it."

Lucy asked, "What now?"

"We are coming home, and I am going to give Jamie this stone to look after. We need to separate the two we have. I will call the police, and then we will tackle the next clue."

"You don't need to. I know where the next stone is hidden."

Eddie glanced at Jamie and then at his phone. There was silence. "Well, go on then."

Lucy laughed, "Hooke's Folly, right?"

"Yes. Go on."

"It took about thirty seconds to find out Hooke's Folly is actually Hooke's Telescope."

"Which is where?"

"Which is what?" Lucy replied before adding, "It is The Monument."

"What, as in The Monument to the Fire of London at Bank?"

"Yes, that's the one."

Jamie said, "We could go straight there."

Eddie remained silent for a short. "No. I think we will come home. I want to look at the rest of the clues and plan. I will come back to London tomorrow."

18

The number was visible. Billy Gray picked up the phone. "Hello Michael, do you have news for us?"

"Yes, Bill," said Michael Foster. "I have just had a chat with a friend at the Service Bureau in Portsmouth, and Detective Inspector Spears is a former Scots Guardsman."

"That would explain his discomfort when you spoke to him. He would have been thoroughly aware of the seriousness of Ken's case."

"Bill?"

"Charles the First."

Foster knew the Scots Guards were formed in the seventeenth century to combat the Irish rebellion and were personal bodyguards to Charles I during the English Civil War. They are also the oldest regiment in the British Army. "Yes, of course. Much the same job as yours. You are right. I wasn't thinking."

Gray asked, "What did the Detective Inspector say when you spoke to him this morning?"

"He was very understanding. He knows this could be a delicate situation and fully respects Ken Prior's family's wishes. He is confident that it was an accident."

"Are you confident that it was an accident, Michael?"

"Not exactly. Spears explained that an autopsy had been completed, as is the case with murder victims, but all this told them was blunt force trauma was the cause. I think he may be concerned about the Regal Portfolio aspect of the issue and would prefer an easy life."

"That would follow our working theory that Ken hit his head as he fell."

"Yes, but while that would indicate it was possibly an accident, I do think there was someone else present at the time."

"This Hill character?"

"No, I don't think so. I have been watching, and I think it may have been someone else."

Gray said, "So, did we make a mistake?"

"No. I think we have taken the right precautions. Mr Hill will come to you and let you know what he saw in the first instance, which will, in turn, provide a description of the person responsible."

"I can see how that would help the police, but how will that help us?"

Foster replied, "If Mr Prior was approached and attacked twice, I think it reasonable to presume it was for the reason we suspect. Now, I know I haven't been working on this for long, but I am pretty sure that between us, we could collate a list of likely suspects to identify him from quickly. We know someone else is looking."

Gray laughed, "I have no doubt. You are a good investigator, Mike. Is there anything else I should know?"

"I left a message, and the tin I retrieved from Mr Hill's house has been forwarded as instructed. It was too heavy to send in the post, so I changed the money up at the bank and placed a draft in there for the sum of £13,358.76."

"I can't say I'm thrilled that you took the money. I am sure the note would have sufficed, but I don't want to second-guess your tactics. Hopefully, Mr Hill will call as soon as he gets the message and will understand how urgent this is. I appreciate your help with this, even if I don't completely approve of how you sometimes go about things."

Foster laughed. "I wouldn't worry about it. The note will do the trick. I'm sure Hill will be in touch soon."

As Billy Gray placed the phone back on its receiver, he wondered whether he should have questioned Michael Foster's approach to all things in his life more often. Maybe he would still be married and perhaps even working alongside him at the Tower.

DI Spears beckoned Ian Gale, palm out, two fingers pulling towards him. "Close the door, would you, Gale."

The Venetian blind shuddered against the glass as Gale complied. Spears took his seat. "Have you spoken to Mr Hill yet?"

"No, sir, but I have spoken to his fiancée. She said Mr Hill was in London overnight for the Portsmouth match yesterday."

"I see. There is no further requirement for you to talk to Mr Hill."

"Oh, have we made an arrest, sir? I didn't know."

Spears looked up from his desk. His face was expressionless. "No. It was an accident."

"Sir?"

"The autopsy described blunt force trauma. Mr Prior hit his head as he fell."

He shuffled some papers and lifted his hand in the direction of the door. "That will be all, Gale. I believe you have other casework. Please close the door."

Forty minutes later, Gale was parked along from Eddie Hill's house. The black car was on the drive, but Hill's van was still nowhere to be seen. He immersed in his speculation to pass the time, Why was DI Spears so keen to close the case after initially being so eager to speak to Hill? He knew he could not sit in the office reviewing other cases after that nonsense, even if it did mean wasting his day sitting outside someone's house waiting for them to return home.

Gale screwed up a sandwich wrapper and threw it on the back seat with the others. How could they possibly know blunt force trauma was caused by hitting his head rather than being whacked? Spears would know this. Why does he want to shut the case down? It did not make sense. Perhaps assumptions that arrest figures related to budgets were true. He was new to his role and was yet to learn the politics of it all. Nevertheless, this could be a murder case.

And who is that man watching Eddie Hill's house? It was the second time he had seen him sitting in his car along the same road. He needed to speak to Eddie Hill, and it appeared someone else wanted to as well.

"It's Lucy again," Eddie said to Jamie as he watched the Spinnaker draw closer on their approach to Portsmouth. He pressed the speakerphone icon.

"Hi, Luce, what's up?"

"We have a problem."

Eddie heard Lucy's voice quiver as she spoke. "I'm nearly home now. What's wrong?"

"Don't come to the front door. Come around the back the same way you left. I don't know what's going on, but the wedding tin is missing."

Eddie pressed the tips of his fingers firmly at the sides of his phone. "What do you mean? Have we been burgled?"

"Not exactly, I don't think so, but the tin is missing."

Her voice cracked, and Eddie could hear the start of a sob. She added, "The house was as we left it. It's as if someone knew it was here and took the wedding tin but nothing else. I didn't notice until I went to drop my change in. I checked around the house, and the only difference from when we left was a couple of drawers were left slightly open in the bedroom."

Jamie interjected, "Was the one underneath opened further than the one above?"

"Yes, what does that mean?"

"It's the way burglars save time. It happened to my gran. They open from the bottom upwards, so they don't waste time closing them again."

"And there's something else. I was going to tell you when you got home because I wasn't that worried at first, but I am now."

Eddie asked, "What is it, Luce?"

"Well, did you forget something in the boot and open the bags up before we left Oxford?"

"No, I never went back to the car after we put the bags in."

"Well, in that case, the boot was broken into as well. Nothing was taken, but the book and some clothes were out of the bags and strewn around."

Eddie glanced at Jamie before adding, "It must be something to do with the tour guide from Oxford."

"That's what I thought."

"I will be home in a few minutes," Eddie adopted a smooth and quiet tone he was not completely comfortable with. "It looks like someone is targetting us. If the book was left it must be about the stone," he hoped that would help Lucy but was suppressing his panic.

Eddie placed his phone on the dashboard and said to Jamie, "Drop me at the guy along the road's house. Steve's. I need to talk to Lucy, and I'll give you a call later."

Jamie nodded, and they sat in silence until they pulled into Eddie's road. They passed parked cars on both sides, and Eddie pointed towards a drive a few doors away from his house. Jamie pulled in, Eddie handed him the stone, and they said their goodbyes.

Eddie closed the van door and made his way to the road that bisected his before clambering over his neighbour's fence and into the garden. He repeated the climb on his fence and walked through the damp grass to his sliding doors.

Owen Garvan sat in semi-contemplativeness while staring out of his side window and drumming his fingers on the steering wheel. He considered the decision he knew he had to make.

The telephone call was answered on the second ring. "Do you have the stone?"

The abrupt question caught him off guard. "No, I'm sorry, I don't have it yet. I was calling to ask what I should do next. I followed Hill to Oxford. He went to the Ashmolean Museum and then went to a pub, before—"

"The Ashmolean?"

"Yes. I know he has the stone. I followed him to his hotel. I managed to gain access to his wife's car, but the stone wasn't there. I did see a copy of *Mutus Liber*. It's an old book—"

"I know what *Mutus Liber* is. Did he go back to the museum?"

"No, they left Oxford early. The problem is, Hill's wife went home, but he didn't."

There was a pause on the other end of the line. "Okay, don't worry about it. I don't think you need to worry about the stone for a while."

Garvan looked up as a van pulled into a drive five doors along from Eddie Hill's house. He saw Hill get out of the passenger's side and hand something to the driver. "This is good timing. Hill has arrived. I will go straight to his house and get the stone."

The voice at the other end shouted, "No. You do not need the stone. Stay near and follow Hill at a distance. I would like to know where he goes and when. Do you understand?"

Garvan acknowledged the instruction, pressed the green phone icon to end the call, and placed it on the passenger seat. He bashed his fist against the steering wheel. He had an agreement — an understanding. What would make their needs more important than his own?

Eddie Hill climbed over the fence he had seen him land from just two days earlier. He thought there must be a reason he did not use his front door, but his attention was already elsewhere.

19

Watching in his rear-view mirror, Ian Gale saw Eddie Hill climb from the van's passenger side of the van. The vehicle then backed off the driveway. The silver sedan Gale had also been watching, pulled away and began to follow. It was now clear the driver was surveilling Eddie Hill's house.

Gale smiled when Hill clambered over his neighbour's fence. Is someone trying to avoid me? With Hill now home, he turned the ignition key. He would return after he had followed the two vehicles to see where they were going.

"What the hell?" Lucy asked. Rhetorically.

"We need to talk this through, but first, would you mind sticking the kettle on while I have a shower?"

Eddie was relieved to see her but now needed to gather his thoughts. Lucy wanted to keep her nerves in check and was calmed by Eddie's tone.

"I've got some bacon in the fridge. Would you like a sandwich?"

"That sounds perfect. I won't be long."

He made for the stairs before Lucy said, "Have a look out of the bedroom window. That policeman is back. I think he's waiting for you. I was going to go and tell him about the wedding tin, but I thought I should wait for you first."

Eddie took two steps at a time and headed straight for the bedroom. He gently slit an opening at the side of the curtains before peering out. He then lifted the curtain completely before shouting downstairs, "No, not there now."

"White hatchback?"

"Yes."

"No. Must have gone."

After he had showered, Eddie was pleased to see his sandwich on the table. He squirted both brown and red sauce on the side of his plate. Lucy gently shook her head as he looked up.

"Okay," Eddie said, mouth half full. "You say where you think we are, and then I will add my view."

"It's very simple. You found an antique book that turned out to belong to a man that is now dead. You have two philosopher's stones, which people want because they turn metal into gold and cure people of all illnesses. We have had our wedding money stolen. Someone has broken into the car. Oh, and the police are following us. How's that?"

Eddie looked up from his half-eaten bacon sandwich and smiled. "Well, that's one interpretation."

Lucy did not return the smile.

Eddie took a sip of tea before composing himself. "The writing on the back of the book is a list of clues to the hiding places of these stones. They don't have mystical powers. That's nonsense. But I do think some cranks believe they might have," he drained his tea before adding, "The only reason the police want to talk to me is to get a description of the attacker. They don't know anything about the stones or the book. Why would they? A man has died, and they understandably want to gather whatever evidence relating to that as they can. I will call them later."

"What about the wedding money?"

Eddie thought he saw her eyes begin to well and wanted to ease her concerns. "To be honest, I wasn't bothered about the stones, except when I thought the first one was a ruby. I thought the clues made for a nice chase. A bit of an adventure. A bit of a game."

"Seriously?" Lucy said loudly.

"Okay, not a game, but something to do while I'm not working. I'm not bothered about the wedding money. In fact, I'm quite pleased."

"Are you off your bloody rocker?" Lucy folded her arms.

Eddie instantly regretted his comment and tried again. "Look, the wedding money tin is just a sweets tin. No one could have known what was inside unless they opened it. It's at the back of the kitchen worktop. Why would they bother opening a sweets tin and not, say, the coffee canister? Someone either knew it was there, or they went through everything else in the house before they found it. It could just be a coincidence. Maybe he fancied a chocolate. No one knows we have a wedding savings tin. I think someone took it in the hope I would go to them to get it back."

Eddie was winging it, fully aware they may have just been looking for the stone and thought they would take a big pile of cash, as it was sitting there.

"So, who's got it?"

"No idea. It could be the little man from Oxford, but I reckon it might be the meathead who attacked the owner of the house."

"He sounds dangerous," Lucy said.

"He's just a big bloke. I am bigger. And you could easily take him. I'll keep you close as my muscle."

"This is serious, Eddie."

"I don't think it's that serious. Someone wants these stones, and they are welcome to them. I am sure they will gladly give us the wedding money back in return."

"So, what should we do?"

"The easiest way of making sure whoever they are comes to us is to carry on following the clues and find the other stones."

Lucy was not convinced. Neither was Eddie. He stretched his hand across. She folded her arms. Again.

Lucy said, "I don't think we can be sure we are not in danger. Someone is following us. Why else would they know where our car was in Oxford? I don't even know how they can break into a car without damaging it. And now, I feel violated. They have been in our house, Eddie. I am more angry than scared. This is not good."

"I know. And I'm sorry this seems to have escalated so quickly," Eddie chose his following words carefully. "I have tried to look at all this as if we were not involved. And to anyone, while we think the philosopher's stone thing is bunk, the people who believe differently are going to extreme lengths by anyone's measure. It is certainly a bit strange that they have taken our wedding tin without leaving a note or message."

He had not chosen his words carefully enough.

Lucy said, "*A bit strange?* Someone who knows how to break into cars and houses has broken into ours and stolen our savings."

"I know, and I don't mean to trivialise it, but we appear to be in this now. Whatever this is. Maybe we only get our money back if someone knocks at the door and tells us what they want. Maybe they will, but at this stage, all we can do is carry on solving the clues and hope it unfolds as we go along."

"And the police?"

"They will catch up with me at some stage. Hopefully, when this is resolved."

"You said you would call them."

"And you said they were outside. If they were there when I arrived, I would have been seen climbing over next door's fence, but they have gone, so they can't be too bothered. Look, I know I haven't done anything wrong. You know I haven't done anything wrong—"

"Apart from defacing a national monument, you mean?"

"I used the right materials — which reminds me, I owe Jamie some money — to improve upon what was there. A conservationist would have been happy with our work."

"This is no longer a laughing matter, Eddie."

"Right, I'll tell you what we'll do. We will have a read through the clues on the back of the book. Watch a bit of telly. Go to bed. And if the police still haven't knocked or called before morning, can we accept it's just a routine enquiry, and they are not that interested?"

Lucy turned her back to Eddie and walked towards the kitchen, before returning. "Fair enough. It does seem that someone is willing to do criminal things, but has not come after us directly, which I admit, is strange," Lucy looked up at Eddie. "Maybe they want us to carry on looking."

Eddie said, "Looking for what? They can't possibly know about the stone Jamie has."

"Good point. So, they think there is just one stone at the minute."

Lucy turned to leave for the kitchen, again. "I am struggling to get my head around this, but I think you're right. It's been a bit of a whirlwind. Maybe we should try to get on with our day and wait to see what happens. I don't know."

"I don't know what the best thing to do is either. If we haven't got anywhere further in a couple of days, we will report the wedding tin."

"Okay. Two days."

The drive did not take Ian Gale long. Just a few turns on residential streets before the van pulled onto a driveway. The silver car slipped into a vacant parking space two doors along. Gale looked around to find another gap. He pulled into a space a few doors further down the road.

He did not see the driver get out of his van.

Gale turned his ignition key but looked up rapidly when he caught a view of the second man running at pace from his car towards the drive. He fumbled with his seatbelt as he saw two men crash through the front door of the house. Gale slammed his door and ran towards the unfolding events. He was too slow. A bald man emerged from the front door and ran back towards his car, which was the opposite side of Gale's approach to the property.

Gale reached the drive and saw a man sprawled in the doorway. His head was at a strange angle against the newel post of the hallway stairs. In the other direction, the bald man was nearing his car. Gale quickly considered his options. Chase or help.

He looked again at the hallway inside the house. The man inside was not moving.

20

Eddie's leg was cold. He pulled at the duvet but was tangled. He could not find sleep and drifted in and out of the box-set they had been watching. Women in prison. Orange boiler suits. All wearing giant rings on their fingers with massive red stones. He lifted his arms from beneath the covers and laced his fingers under his head. He glared at the ceiling, waiting for it to make its move. And then at Lucy's lips and their gentle, rhythmic vibrations. She turned, and he stared at the back of her head. He would do anything to make her happy. He focussed on the ceiling once again before closing his eyes. He tried to mimic Lucy's slow, deep breaths. He tossed and turned a few more times before relenting. He moved the cover aside, climbed out of bed, and walked to the door.

He stepped down the stairs and ambled to the living room window. It was silent and dark outside. The streetlamp along the road was still out. He went to the dresser by the dining table and removed a small, framed photograph from the drawer. He pulled out its support stand and sat it on the table.

He stared vacantly and tried to push away the memories. The empty bottle kept clinking against the metal seat slider. If he hadn't used his back seat as a rubbish dump, it would never have happened. He was only distracted for a fraction of a second when he looked down. It was just enough to turn the steering wheel slightly. It was also just enough to hit the kerb and flip his car onto its side. The metal crushed his wife's rib cage at the same time he landed on her. She died instantly. He was cushioned from the splintering metal and broken glass.

"You really should put that on the shelf."

Eddie looked up with a start. Lucy sat down and took the picture from him. "She was beautiful. Wasn't she?"

"She was."

"You are entitled to love her. I do not feel threatened. I know you love me," Lucy smiled and added, "You certainly have a type."

Eddie hesitated, "She had red hair. Yours is black."

"Dark brown, but thanks for noticing," Lucy gestured towards the dresser shelf. "Put it up there."

"What do you mean, a type?"

"Fit birds."

Eddie returned the smile and rose before pulling the drawer open and placing the photograph on some papers before gently closing it. "It was my fault."

"Eddie, we have spoken about this before. Everyone has momentary lapses of concentration. You cannot continually blame yourself for something that could have happened to anyone. You went through the court process and took your punishment. A punishment based on law, not guilt."

He sat and looked down. "I know. Maybe I need to remind myself now and then. I didn't think I could ever be happy again."

She rose from her chair and pulled his head to her chest. She stood still until she felt Eddie's grip loosen and said, "I'll make a cup of tea."

"It's three in the morning."

"Yes, but it's not as if we're going to get to sleep, is it?"

Lucy returned a few minutes later and placed a steaming cup in front of him. "Is this why you are doing this?"

"What?"

"Chasing these stones."

"I know what you think. I am in a rush to move on and am constantly looking for new things to do to create new memories."

Lucy raised her gaze. "Within a fortnight of Rachel's funeral, you had joined my *Wing Chun* class."

"Are you saying I moved on too quickly?"

"Oh no, it took you months to get the courage to ask me out, but once you did, you stopped coming. The next thing I knew, we were learning to SCUBA dive at Southsea."

Eddie smiled. "And don't forget, we have sailed around the world."

In their five years together, Eddie and Lucy had taken two cruise holidays a year. After a three-day taster out of Southampton for Lucy's birthday, they had sailed from Southampton to Barcelona, from Barcelona to Dubai through the Suez Canal, and Dubai to Singapore. Going the other way, they had sailed from Southampton to Miami, Miami to San Diego through the Panama Canal, and San Diego to Hawaii. The remaining trip, and the one that put their wedding back a year — Hawaii to Singapore via Sydney.

"Well, that leads neatly to where we are now. We are missing the final leg of that journey, aren't we, Eddie?"

"Are you are talking about the wedding fund tin again?"

The final leg was supposed to be their honeymoon.

Lucy rested her hand on top of his across the table and said,

"I get it. I do. In the years we have known each other, we've already had a lifetime of fun, but this is serious."

"I know," he gazed into her eyes, "which is why I think you should go to your mum's place for a few days. I will call Jamie in the morning and—"

"Are you kidding me?"

"I, I just think it would be safer—"

"Have you not been paying attention to this conversation? I am more than capable of looking after myself. And you, for the fact of it. We have got to see it through now. It's our problem, and you can't keep involving Jamie. They are talking about having a kid."

"I didn't know that."

"That's because you don't listen hard enough. But make sure you listen up now, matey. We are going to go back to London, and we are going to get to the bottom of this."

"I love it when you're assertive."

Lucy curled her fingers into a fist and bumped them on his flattened hand.

"That hurt."

"Good. Now, I am going to have a shower. You can make breakfast. We might as well leave early."

Lucy moved her chair out and left the room. As she walked up the stairs, she said, "And we'll take your van just in case we need tools again."

Ian Gale pushed through the door. The room had two beds. One was empty. He saw the melamine covering the table extending across the bed was lifting at the seams. A clipboard without notes was attached at the end. There were no bedclothes. The other bed had a blue curtain pulled around on two sides. A section hung loose, detached from its ring. He pulled the drape aside and entered next to a large window traversing the two bed areas.

James Stuart was still unconscious. He had hit his head hard, and although the doctor said he would be revived, he was not sure when that would be. There were wires, machinery, and beeping noises. He was hooked up to the desk outside. Someone would know if he woke. Gale pulled the chair away from the wall and sat down. He rested his elbows on the wooden arms and waited.

He had called Mr Stuart's partner, who was on the way down from a business trip to Birmingham. He had tried to contact Mr Hill again, but there was no answer. He considered what he knew and the new person of interest. Maybe Eddie Hill was avoiding talking to the police about the assault he witnessed because he was guilty of something. He was not concerned. He would find out. His primary concern now was the bald man he saw rush at Mr Stuart before racing off. He decided to wait for Mr Stuart to wake so he could ask some questions. Better than returning to the office, anyway. He removed his phone from his inside pocket and dialled a number.

Three rings later, "Hi Suzanne, it's Ian Gale. Can you run a number plate for me, please?"

21

"Hello, this is James McAllister. How can I help?"

"It's me. We have a problem."

"Yes, I think we do."

"What is that supposed to mean?"

McAllister replied authoritatively, "Let me know the reason for your call, and I will tell you of my problems in return."

"The watcher we sent to the Portsmouth property has become volatile. I am not sure we can continue to rely on him to retrieve the Buckingham House stone."

"I see."

"What do you mean, I see?"

McAllister said, "Are you sure you do not have the stone yourself?"

"You what?"

"Well, the other stones have been fairly easy to retrieve,

but this one has caused no end of trouble. We are all aware of the value of these stones. I had three at the museum until this morning. I was not comfortable keeping them here, especially as it appears that we now have to eject visitors."

"What do you mean, eject visitors?"

McAllister sat upright in his chair and replied, "I had a funny man, as in he thought he was a comedian, ask rather rude questions about Elias just a couple of days ago. I may be growing paranoid, I am aware of that, but his line of questioning made me feel uncomfortable, so I had him thrown out."

"What did he look like?"

"It was not your watcher if that is what you mean."

James McAllister then provided an accurate description of Eddie.

The conversation wrapped up quickly, leaving McAllister looking at the phone as if watching the oddly abrupt end to the conversation rather than listening to it.

Eddie said, "There's a bag on a hook behind your seat. You can put it in there."

Lucy stretched her seatbelt and leaned around to place the wrapper in the bag. She turned back to Eddie and smiled before placing her hand on his leg. She knew only too well why Eddie's was the world's tidiest work van.

"Okay, go on, you know you want to tell me," Eddie said.

Lucy moved in her seat to get comfortable and finished her mouthful. "Okay, here goes. You know how Christopher Wren is credited with redesigning and building half of London after the Great Fire?"

"Yes."

"Well, he didn't. It's a myth. There was a lot of damage, and he would have been drawing his fingers to the bone if he had been solely responsible for everything historians claim.

There were lots of collaborators, whether just in idea or complete design of buildings. The Monument was no different. Robert Hooke was Surveyor of the City of London after the Fire, and while Christopher Wren was once again largely credited, it was mostly designed by Hooke. The weird thing is that there was a monument to the Fire at all. It wasn't a commemorative monument to the dead but just a reminder of the tragedy. A bit like putting blue plaques up wherever murderers lived."

He laughed. "It's not really, is it?"

Lucy grinned. "Well, no, but Hooke designed it to have a dual purpose. The secondary, or I should say, primary purpose, was as an observatory. It was a giant telescope. Which indirectly leads to the clue on the back of the book. Hooke also helped design the Royal Observatory in Greenwich and built the first reflecting telescope, so that all ties in."

"Okay, I get it. The Monument was a giant telescope, but what has that got to do with our stone hunt?"

"Hooke had a laboratory in the basement."

"That doesn't exactly answer my question."

"No, but the fact that he had a basement lab would suggest this is where we start looking. Admittedly it could be anywhere if it's there at all, but I think that's the first place to look."

"So, tell me this. If Hooke was into telescopes, stars, and the night sky, as it were, how does this relate to alchemy? And besides, I thought all that astronomy business was illegal back then."

"Well, Mr Hill, you do have a good memory, don't you?" Lucy said before adding, "People like Hooke were advancing scientific research into the field of astronomy. It would take a lot more reading and doesn't completely relate to what we are doing, so I skipped it. In a nutshell, there was a blurring of the lines between astrology and astronomy, and you could get your head chopped off if you created a horoscope for the king."

Eddie looked away from the road for a short while, "Really?"

"I don't know if it happened, but there was a law that decreed it punishable by death. As I said, it doesn't directly relate, so I was only really interested in working out how someone in that field came to be involved in alchemy, and then I ended up making stuff up again."

"What do you mean?"

"Well, it was hard to work out, but there was one relationship in Hooke's past that intrigued me. It turns out he was a nemesis of Isaac Newton."

Eddie looked at Lucy and held up a finger. "Hold that thought," he said as he pulled off the Old Kent Road and into a residential area.

"Where are you parking? We're nowhere near The Monument."

"This is the road I parked on when I went to Millwall for the football. The ground is over there. We can get a train from South Bermondsey station to London Bridge and walk. There wouldn't be a cat in hell's chance of parking anywhere near London Bridge."

He was unsure where he was going and kept his head down when the walk took longer than anticipated. After the two-stop train journey, he felt Lucy's amused glare burning into the back of his head as they got lost in London Bridge station.

Forty minutes after they left South Bermondsey, they stood beside The Monument.

Eddie read the explainer tablet stuck to the tower's base and made it all the way through before laughing at the phrase, 'Doric column'. Lucy was disappointed in herself. She found it just as funny. Although dwarfed by most buildings in the locality, they agreed it was still a magnificent effort for the seventeenth century, before they started laughing once again and acknowledged how childish they were.

They walked around the base and admired the sculpture depicting the devastation the Fire caused and stopped to look at the images of Charles II and his brother James, offering protection to the stricken city, and freedom to its citizens, while surrounded by allegorical carvings of liberty, architecture, and science.

Eddie said, "We should go over the road to that craft beer place and work out a game-plan. And you can tell me more about Isaac Newton and Robert Hooke."

Owen Garvan placed the dark red object on his table alongside a blue zippered carry case. He moved a cloth placemat beneath the stone and a margarine tub lid between them. The multitool kit was equipped with a nineteen-piece engraving toolset. He inserted the small grinding-stone instrument, paused, and took a deep breath.

Garvan had learned the properties of these stones were imagined and created over the crucible through decades of research by the greatest scientific minds of the seventeenth century. Men that began the journey all medical practitioners travel today. They were the greatest thinkers that ever lived, and they had created a cure for his son's degenerative illness.

The deal was simple. He followed and watched — that is all. His training provided him with investigative skills and patience, and they had promised he did not need to find a stone to receive his reward. They had plenty of people looking and if one was found, he would receive a share sufficient enough to cure his son. He had visited museums, former homes of scientists, churches, graveyards, but the reaction of the Regal Portfolio Properties guardian was unnatural. Perhaps he had recognised him from a previous stone hunt, but it was still a surprise to see him emerge in such a manner. Furtive. Guilty almost. He looked disappointed, but that had to be an act. Garvan had been sure Ken Prior had a stone.

His mentor, and Eddie Hill, were blocks in his road, but that was over now. As were the promises. He no longer trusted their word. Garvan pressed the blue button on top to activate the tool. The wheel rotated at pace, and the buzzing quickly accelerated. He gripped the stone firmly and gently placed the wheel against the side. A few seconds later, he removed the tool, switched it off and placed it next to the tub lid. He withdrew the stone and peered into the lid. There were shavings.

This was it.

This was the cure.

He pushed his chair out and raced into his bathroom, nearly sliding on the bathmat in the process. He grabbed an empty contact lens pot and squirted some saline inside before returning to the table. He gently poured the small quantity of stone debris into the solution and screwed the lid on the pot. He placed the pot on the table and stared down. At first, to the small container and then his stack of enlightenment books piled behind it.

A tear rolled down his face.

22

Eddie placed their drinks on the table. Lucy did not wait for him to pull out a chair before she began. "It was an interesting turn of events and obviously where the link comes in. It would take a lot more research, but although Hooke specialised in astronomy and telescopes, he was a far greater contributor to the development of the sciences during that period than credited with. He is largely overlooked by history because his relationship with Isaac Newton blurred his lines."

"What do you mean?"

"Well, it's complicated, but he was right up there with the best of them. Hang on," Lucy reached down for her bag and retrieved her purse. She removed a piece of paper. "I wrote some notes. He was Robert Boyle's assistant, and it was suggested that he may have contributed more to Boyle's work than was appreciated. He was a founder of the Royal Society and named Curator of Experiments. He also coined the word 'cell'.

"Cell?" Eddie asked.

"Yes, the word that describes individual units. Like in Biology. He was considered a polymath, and much of his work related to complicated mathematics and the workings of springs, telescopes and, well, loads of stuff."

"So, what about Isaac Newton?"

"Well, I suppose the best way of describing it is Newton thought he was the cleverest scientist in the village, and he accused Hooke of over-egging his puddings."

Eddie laughed. "Having fun with metaphors, Luce?" before adding, "I presume this means Newton thought Hooke was a bit generous about his personal contribution to scientific study."

"Pretty much. I am sure there will be many reasons, but essentially, it appears Hooke was experimenting and theorising about gravitation during the same period that Newton was recognised as the greatest scientist in history for writing *Newton's Law of Universal Gravitation*." Lucy considered her thoughts. "Unlike his contemporaries, it doesn't seem as though Hooke specialised. Instead, he was remarkable in all fields. This led to suspicions about him working with other scientists' ideas and theories. It might have been that Hooke was the greatest scientific thinker in history, but he died a quarter of a century before Newton, who took over the Royal Society, burned the only known portrait of Hooke, and generally rubbished him for a couple of decades."

Eddie sat quietly for a short period while Lucy stared across at him. "How does alchemy fit into this?"

"I don't know if it does. I couldn't find anything that confirmed Hooke was an avid alchemist. I'm sure he dabbled, but don't forget this is about George's clue. It says 'Hooke's Folly'. So, we have no option but to start there and look for a stone. For all I know, Hooke may have stolen one from Isaac

Newton."

"I wouldn't have thought so. Would you?"

"I was using that as an example. I think it's simpler than that. George was effectively King Charles II's top man. He was the richest person in the country and an alchemist. He would have known everyone at the top of society, including, I would presume, Hooke. But this may not even be about Hooke. The Monument was abandoned as a telescope project when vibrations caused by outside traffic created inaccurate readings, and the Royal Observatory provided clearer skies when it was completed. Which is why, I presume, George described it as a folly, and he would have had access any time he wanted. He may even have had something to do with the project. Maybe he objected to it. Who knows? What we do know is we need to get over there and go on a stone hunt."

With that, Lucy finished her drink, placed the glass down and stood with intention.

They looked once again at what Lucy explained was a basso-relievo of Charles II. This drew a predictable yawn from Eddie. She ignored his mockery and grabbed his hand. They walked around the other three sides and read the Latin translation plaques. Lucy nudged him when they saw the heraldic shield. Eddie shook his head.

They approached a redheaded man wearing a blue windbreaker, leaning against the door frame of the entrance. Eddie asked, "Hello. I wonder if you could answer a question for me?"

The man turned to open a small door. Eddie described it as a half Dutch-door. It was Lucy's turn to yawn as the man took his place behind a small ticket counter. A single bulb above his head shone a narrow line of illumination through his hair and onto his pale face. "Yes, of course. Will it be two adults?"

Eddie paid for the tickets by contactless card. "Thank you,

but no. We were hoping you could help with something else."

"I will try."

"We want to climb the stairs, but what we're really interested in is the lab."

"That's right under my feet," he opened the half-Dutch-door once again and moved his swivel chair out of the way. The black straps and bolt on the floor were well worn. Perhaps too worn for a swivel chair and a ticket booth in the not too distant future. "I am afraid the public can't go down there. I can show you what it looks like, though."

He pushed the door to one side and walked a few steps to move an advertising board away from the base of the stairs leading to the top of the tower. Eddie looked up at the number of steps and turned to Lucy with a grimace.

There was a light under a metal grate. They could see down to what was once Hooke's laboratory area, but which was now just stone walls and the base of the metal spiral staircase.

The man said, "That's pretty much it. You're not missing anything. It's about three metres by three metres, and I have to duck to get around down there.

Eddie and Lucy thanked him and shrugged their shoulders at each other. Nothing to learn there.

It is 311 steps to the viewing platform at the top of The Monument. Eddie was fine for the first 200 or so cantilevered steps, but when he started inspecting the mortar work a little too closely, Lucy was not going to allow the opportunity to pass. "Struggling, old fella?"

"No, just admiring the quality of the restoration project."

"Of course you are. Would you like a hand?"

"No, I am fine, thank you, darling. Please go ahead. I am formulating a plan."

Lucy took the last bite of a nutrition bar, scrunched up the wrapper, and shook her head while continuing to climb the winding staircase. Eddie was, however, thinking over a plan.

Knowing there was no way a loose block or secret crevice could have escaped the detailed and forensic restoration project of 2008, a different approach to locating the stone would be necessary. Not that he held out much hope of retrieving anything, even if it was there in the first place.

They emerged onto the viewing platform, and Lucy grabbed Eddie's hand. The Monument once hosted a copper urn from which flames, symbolising the Great Fire of London, were drawn to the sky. Eddie was impressed by the new gold leaf encased flaming orb, which graced the top. At 202 feet, they agreed the view could not be as impressive as it was before skyscrapers and imposing office blocks were added to the skyline, but it was still the distance between the site in Pudding Lane — where the Fire was said to have started, and what was once a towering edifice. Eddie scowled. He was disappointed to see how the modern buildings surrounding The Monument diminished its presence. He also knew he had to maintain Lucy's newfound enthusiasm because there was no way a stone would be there.

They circled the space and chose a position north of the Thames to avoid the biting wind. Eddie took a couple of breaths, and in his best I'm-not-out-of-puff voice said, "You know, we didn't need to come here at all."

"What?"

"Well, I mean to say, it's confirmed what I thought. The restoration of this would have taken care of the stone. That is, if there was one. The Monument has been looked after very well over the centuries. Modern tooling and technology would suggest that if there was anything left behind anywhere, the contractors would have found it during the most recent restoration project."

"So, where does that leave us?"

"Specialist stone cleaners would have used something like the Jos System to tidy up the decorative areas, and stonemasons would have carried out the repairs. The people that deal with these heritage buildings are usually very experienced at what they do. I know someone in that line of work. I'll make a call."

After descending, Lucy scrolled through a few messages while Eddie dodged office workers as he paced up and down the pavement while speaking on his phone. Ten minutes later, he said, "I called Ally Edwards, a guy I know from Chichester, who used to work for one of these firms. It sounds as though the mob that did some of the work here went bust. He said he would phone someone he knew that worked for them and would text me if he found anything out."

As they walked across London Bridge to the station, they stopped to look back at The Monument peaking over the top of the buildings, The Shard in the background, and across the vista of the Tower of London, Tower Bridge and HMS *Belfast*, docked along a pedestrianised towpath, fully loaded with restaurants and bars. Although now enveloped in the grey of dull light, they agreed there could not be a more historic view in the world.

Eddie's phone pinged. He read the message and said to Lucy, "Ally knows a personal assistant that worked for the boss of one of the firms I was talking about. He says she will be happy to talk. They owed her money when they went belly up."

They discussed anything and everything, apart from the journey they had unexpectedly embarked upon during their return to the car in South Bermondsey, but as soon as the return trip began, Lucy resumed the reading on her phone. Eddie welcomed the silence. He needed some time with his thoughts.

The drive took just over two hours before they pulled into a narrow street in Chichester. Eddie slowed to find the correct door number. It was a charming little cottage with whitewashed walls, a battleship grey front door, and chrome door furniture.

Eddie parked in a space out front and said, "I think this is going to take a bit of the old Eddie Hill magic. So, wait here, and I'll knock."

"Okay, Prince Charming, what do you have in mind?"

He raised his brows and lowered his eyelids while wobbling his head in self-satisfaction.

Lucy rolled her eyes. "Okay, I will wait here and marvel at the success of your plan when you return."

Lucy watched as a tall, slim, blonde woman in hot pants and a tight vest opened the door. When Eddie stretched his hand out, she saw the woman take it gently and smile before swishing her hair as they entered her home. It's too cold for that get up, Lucy thought.

Eddie returned nineteen minutes later. Not that Lucy was watching the time on her phone. He opened the door and climbed into the driver's seat with a smile stretched across his face. Lucy's expression was emotionless, and her arms were folded.

"What?"

"She was pretty, wasn't she?"

"Yes, she had a cute little devil tattoo on her lower back, as well."

"And how come you saw that, Eddie?"

"I spotted it when she opened the curtain to see you in the car. Didn't you notice?"

"No."

"Nice bum as well," he paused, but not for long before adding, "It was part of my story."

"Would you like to tell me your story, Eddie Hill?"

He laughed. "You can unfold your arms now. I explained that a few years ago, I planned to propose to my childhood sweetheart on The Monument's viewing platform, so I had gone up there to hide a ring in the stonework, where no one else could find it."

"Go on."

"She thought this was very romantic, so I doubled down. I explained that we split up when a work opportunity came up that my girlfriend couldn't turn down. I then pulled the sad face."

Eddie pulled his sad face. Lucy remained inscrutable.

"I then told her that I had left the ring there and forgot about it, but we had got back together to rekindle our teenage romance, and I went back with you yesterday to try to propose again."

Lucy's expression finally softened. Eddie laughed again. "But we do have a problem. I explained that it wasn't there, and I had learned The Monument had been renovated. I said Ally had told me she had worked for the firm before they went bankrupt and was hoping she could tell me who worked in the basement area."

"No dice?"

"Nothing certain, but she knew her stuff about construction and said while all the main visible areas were built using Portland Stone, the underground area was a cheaper mix of aggregate, Reigate Stone, broken Tudor brickwork, and even York Stone. She knew that the area wasn't intended for use as a public space when originally built, so cheaper materials were used. I was quite impressed."

"Yes, you looked impressed."

"Anyway, while specialist stonemasons worked on the visible areas, her firm brought in a couple of sub-contractors to work on the sections no one would see."

"Did she recall who?"

"Not exactly, but she did remember one of the guys was named Danny McDowell.

"Good memory."

"Well, apparently, he asked her out, but she turned him down."

"Still a good memory. I don't remember the names of all the men that ask me out. I can barely remember yours."

"What jogged her memory was he said he had found something that day and wanted to show her."

"His etchings?"

"That's what she said when she turned him down."

"I don't suppose she knew how to get hold of him?"

"No, that's where our leads dry up. She just knew he was a brickie that worked with his dad."

"At least we tried," Lucy said.

"I know. It's a bit disappointing, but look, I'm a bit worn out. It's been a long day. We'll go home and give it some thought. Maybe move on to the next clue and write this one-off. I want to catch up with Jamie anyway."

23

Eddie placed the handset back in its cradle. "No answer at Jamie's. I'll try his mobile."

"No point. Other Jamie is back from that big work trip, and they are going out for dinner tonight."

Eddie was restless. He paced the lounge, rounded the dining table and back again several times before Lucy interceded. "We need to find that guy's dad's firm and pay him a surprise visit. We don't need an elaborate plan."

"You're right," Eddie said as he flipped up the lid of his laptop. He typed, 'McDowell and Son, Bricklayers, Chichester'.

A few seconds later, Eddie laughed and shouted to the kitchen, "Luce, come and look at this."

Lucy walked into the room, stood at his shoulder, and read. 'McDowell & Son'. With the tag line, 'Bricklaying / Blockwork. We can do bricklaying, masonry and blockwork, no job too big or small. Extensions, refurbishments. . .'

Eddie researched the family business a little more. It did not take long before he had a home address for the McDowells.

Lucy had not seen Eddie wearing a suit since their last cruise. "So, is this your wedding look?"

"Oh, this old thing," he smiled. "I should hope I could stretch to a new suit for the wedding."

They shared a solemn glance. Eddie knew he needed to maintain a level of calm over the wedding fund situation to prevent Lucy from losing it. Lucy knew Eddie was pretending to be calm about the wedding fund situation to prevent her from losing it. She brushed her work suit down, took a final look in the hallway mirror, and nodded at herself.

The house was in a small hamlet between Portsmouth and Chichester on the outskirts of Westbourne. It was chalet style with a decorative stone pillar separating a front door from two similarly sized windows. The type a builder might have erected in the 1980s. Their tyres crunched on the gravel as Lucy pulled onto the driveway. Eddie thought the noise must have operated like an early warning system, as a man opened the front door and greeted them on the porch steps. He was wearing work boots and had building dust on the front of his trousers and fleece.

Eddie said in his most professional tone, "Thank you for coming back from work to see us, Mr McDowell."

Danny McDowell said, "I was coming home for lunch anyway. It's not a problem. Please come in. You said something about The Monument. I'm not sure what I can tell you. That job was a long time ago now."

"Yes, as I said on the phone, some documents were found in records at the Archive Centre that indicated an item was hidden within the walls of Dr Robert Hooke's laboratory."

"I'm sorry. I don't know how I can help."

As the man folded his arms, Eddie recognised a defensiveness he wanted to disarm, and said, "Oh, I am dreadfully sorry, I don't think I explained myself properly. There was a red piece of glass. It would have looked just like part of the rubble or stonework used at that time. I am sure someone would have discarded it during the repairs."

Lucy turned her head — it was all she could do to avoid sniggering, after which she would have also said, 'Oh, I am dreadfully sorry'. She curled her lips inwards and bit down.

McDowell asked, "The Heritage Society, did you say?"

Eddie replied, "British Heritage Properties Department."

"Oh, right, yes. Sorry, mate, but I'm afraid I can't help. Although it was a tiny space, there was all sorts of rubbish in there — wood, different stone and blockwork, straw, old paper."

"Paper?" Eddie asked.

McDowell glanced to the side and said hesitantly, "Yes. I think I kept some string and old paper that I found as a souvenir. Is that a problem?"

Eddie smiled, "Oh, goodness no. Of course not. It was junk. I don't suppose you still have it, do you? I do love anything old."

McDowell instantly appeared more at ease. "I think I have it in a drawer in the kitchen somewhere. I'll go and find it."

Lucy, who had remained silent throughout this exchange, whispered in her most qualified voice, "Oh, goodness gracious," she giggled, "I think he just slipped up."

Eddie grinned as she slowly walked around the room. It looked dated and not quite right for someone of Danny McDowell's age. The carpets were dark pink with indented swirls. There was well varnished dark wood shelving and an equally old-fashioned rustic stone fireplace with an integrated tropical fish tank complete with fish munching on the surface oxygen.

McDowell returned and said quickly and loudly, "I have found the paper. I kept it because it seemed old. There may have been writing on it at some stage. Maybe a letter, but it's too faded to read," he motioned with his head to attract their attention to the piece of old parchment he placed on the table.

"Nice fireplace," Lucy said as she approached the table.

"Oh, that's coming out. It's all coming out. This is my mum and dad's old house. They've given it to me. I'm helping them build a new bungalow in the next village."

Eddie did not hear the exchange. He was concentrating on the piece of paper, which had two creases and wax flecks remaining in the centre of two edges. It was a letter. Or, it had been a letter. "Would you mind if we took this with us? I think our forensic analysts may be able to use their technology to learn what the writing says and test to see if this document has significance."

McDowell hesitated, so Eddie filled the gap, "It will be returned to you unless it does have some historical significance. In which case, I would guess the usual fee would apply."

McDowell's face brightened quickly. "Fee?"

"Oh, yes. I don't know how much it is, it's not my department, but I believe it will be between one and ten thousand pounds for as useful a document as this may be."

Within five minutes, Eddie and Lucy were in their car on Danny McDowell's drive.

"Twice in two days, Eddie. I didn't know you were such a good liar."

"What did I say I did for a job when we first met?"

"Oh, yes, I remember. Deep-sea diver, wasn't it?"

"It worked, though."

"You don't think I bought that old nonsense, do you? I

knew who you were when you joined my class. You fitted a boiler for my Aunt Kathy."

"Of course I did. I forgot about that. Still, we got the letter that was obviously with the stone, even if we didn't get the stone itself."

Although there were no cars about, Lucy instinctively pressed her indicator. *Tick, Tick, Tick.* She looked away from the steering wheel to Eddie, "We didn't get the stone, but I know where it is if we want to collect it later."

"Where? . . What are you talking about?"

Lucy looked straight ahead. The gravel crunched once again as she steered through the driveway gates.

"It's in his fish tank."

Eddie gently unfolded the letter as if handling gossamer before delicately pressing it flat on the dining table.

Lucy said, "You can barely make out the writing. It's very faded. It will take a month of Sundays to work out what each word says."

Eddie remained transfixed for a short while before replying, "I have an idea. I need to go to the garage to find a torch."

Lucy stared as he left the room but said nothing.

When Eddie returned, he had his camera bag, a tripod, and a torch. He fixed the camera to the tripod and opened a flap to insert a shutter release cable, and without extending the legs, he set the tripod on the table, pointing down at the letter. "I am going to focus on this in three parts so I can get it as large in the viewfinder as possible. It's a 105mm Macro so it will increase the size of the writing."

Lucy nodded but didn't know what he was talking about. She just knew that it was her job to hold his camera bag while he took umpteen shots at umpteen angles of anything and everything while they were on holiday. Lucy regularly brought up the dead fish on the Antiguan beach incident in conversation.

Eddie focused on the sheet of paper before standing back and flicking his torch to the UV setting and pointing it directly at the top third section. As the plum coloured beam threw light on proceedings, he pressed the shutter release. He repeated this process several more times, while moving the page beneath the viewfinder for each shot. Without speaking, he then took the equipment apart, removed the SD card from the camera's side flap, and slotted it into the front of the laptop. He transferred the images to the pre-loaded editing software before returning the SD card home and stashing the camera gear back into the bag.

Lucy finally asked, "What are you doing?"

"I'm just going to transfer these RAW images, enhance the darkness, and then alter the white balance and contrast, to see what we have. I'm then going to transfer it to my photo software before fiddling about with the brightness and contrast some more to see if we can make out the words."

"Sorry I asked."

"I told you I know stuff," Eddie replied with a smile.

Twenty minutes later, the words were readable. Not clearly, but with effort and time, they transcribed the letter to a notepad.

Sir

I would like to expresse my sincerest gratitude for the purest glasse I have seen. The Duke of Buckingham has enhanced our practice and experiments in the greatest measure with welcome financial tribute.

My successe thus far was in such small scale, to make certaine whereby the practicall part of opticks might be promoted. This prospective first try was to make light of my owne conjecture.

The Instrument is but six Inches in Length. It has a one inch apperture, and a plano convex eye glasse as received and addressed. It magnifies, I should say, forty times in diameter which as you attested with me, is more than any six foote Tube can doe. I will pursue further study, the experiments for which I will atteste ye. In forward time I have sent instructions and example to Mr Cox at the Royall Societie, for a four foot contrivance. I truste your esteeme will be observed with proposal of suche to same.

Your encouragement and pursuance of my trevails over the crucible in exchange, I returne with greatest gratitude a gift of my latest and beste attempts.

I do not believe my discoveries likely possible in advancement of time, without your gracious advisemente on matters. I repeat my earlier pronouncement, I stand upon the shoulders of giants.

Your much obliged servitor,

I Newton

Lucy looked at Eddie and said, "This alters historical reference. There have been several letter exchanges between these two published, but nothing like this. As I said, they became mortal enemies, but this suggests they were more than collaborators at one stage. They were friendly enough to exchange gifts."

"I have heard that quote before," Eddie said.

"It is one of Isaac Newton's most famous quotes. 'If I have seen a little further, it is by standing on the shoulders of giants'. It appeared in a published letter from Newton to Hooke, and there has been a historical debate about whether he was being offensive about Hooke's small stature."

Eddie said, "Well, this clears that one up. He sounds in awe of Hooke."

Lucy moved the document to the corner of the table, retrieved the *Mutus Liber* book from the sofa and placed it alongside. She positioned the Buckingham House stone next to that. "We also know where the Newton stone is if we want to retrieve it."

"And don't forget, we have George Starkey's Stone, which would slot in here," Eddie pointed twice to represent the two additional stones in the space towards the book and letter. "That reminds me, I must phone Jamie. I have a couple of missed calls."

Lucy walked a circle around the table. She picked up each item and studied it before placing it back down. She turned the book, clues facing up, looked across at Eddie and said, "Can you look up 'Isaac Newton letters' on the internet?"

"Okay. Why?"

"Call one up and let me see."

Eddie quickly tapped at the keys, hit the images tab and found a .pdf straight away.

"I thought so. Look at George Villiers' writing on the back of the book, then at Isaac Newton's letter on the computer, and then our letter, here," she said, pointing at the parchment on the table.

"Oh."

"Yes. It's a forgery. Well, not a forgery, but a fake. George Villiers wrote that pretending to be Isaac Newton."

"What on earth for?"

"No idea."

Eddie sat down on a dining chair. Lucy paced the room. A few minutes later, Eddie said, "How about this? George has a chance meeting with Christopher Wren and Robert Hooke, where he learned about The Monument slash telescope that did not work. Also, Hooke's new feud with Isaac Newton, which he decides to manipulate. Maybe he did it in person dressed as Jack Pudding, bearing a letter from Newton."

"To what end? And I'm not sure the feud had started at that stage."

"All we have to go on is George's vanity, by mentioning himself in the letter, and the clue on the book, 'Hooke's Folly'."

Lucy scrunched her mouth to the side. "It doesn't matter. It's like the last stone, we can hypothesise, but it's not important. Maybe George was playing games with other society people. Maybe he just wanted somewhere not many people had access to, to hide a stone. It's not relevant. We have the stone."

"We don't."

"No, but as I said, we can get it if we want."

They stared at each other and nodded in acknowledgement.

Eddie's phone vibrated on the table.

"All right, mate?" Eddie placed his hand over the receiver, "It's Jamie."

"Is this Mr Hill?" asked the voice at the other end.

Eddie replied slowly, "Yes, who is this? A friend's name came up on my phone."

"I have had to access Mr Stuart's mobile to find contacts."

"And why is that?"

"I am afraid there has been an incident involving Mr Stuart. I am with him at the hospital. He is heavily sedated after a nasty head injury."

"Who is this?"

"This is Detective Constable Gale. I met with your partner the other day."

"St. Mary's?"

"Yes, that's correct."

"We will be right there."

Eddie pressed the icon and looked straight at Lucy, "We need to go."

24

James McAllister twitched nervously in his seat. He had
completed the task asked of him and was here to collect. He
felt cold air rush through as the door swung open. A short
woman in a knee-length floral dress walked in. She was also
wearing what appeared to be work boots and did not have a
coat, despite the chilly temperature outside.

His chair squealed as it scraped along the floor as he stood.
"Miss Martin, it is good to see you."

"I am sure it is," Elysia Martin said as she took his hand
with the tips of three fingers and a thumb. She placed her bag
on the rustic wooden table. "Do you have them?"

McAllister removed a cardboard box the depth and
otherwise dimensions of two shoebox lids from his briefcase.
He separated the two sections by peeling sticky tape from one
side to reveal a bubble-wrapped lining. Safely nestled within
the bubble-wrap was a cotton wool covered vase, a similarly-

sized container, and a red stone, which Martin estimated was between one and two inches in size. McAllister glanced around. The pub was busy, but no one was looking in their direction. He closed the lid and slid the box across the table. He then removed an envelope from his pocket and placed it on top of the package. "Full historical reference and provenance for the stones."

"Thank you, Mr McAllister."

Martin then removed an envelope of her own from her oversized bag and deposited it on the table before placing the box and McAllister's envelope into the bag. "Now, tell me of your complications."

He shifted in his seat once again and decided to say it quickly, "I think there is another stone. A heating engineer from Portsmouth called Edward Hill has it. If he has not already sold it."

Martin studied the museum guide. He had been useful in their quest, but his manner bothered her. It may have been the furtive glances when he thought she was not looking. It could have been the affected accent and language. He was, after all, the son of a Barnsley milkman. "Who could he have sold it to, Mr McAllister? It is just red glass."

"No, of course. I don't know."

"Unless your Mr Hill knows of the value of these stones," she cocked her head. "Mr Hill does not know of the value of these stones, does he, Mr McAllister?"

He felt blood rush to his face. "I can't see how. He wouldn't—"

"I would appreciate it if you could ensure the man you have looking for this other stone understands its importance. Remind me, how many more do you think could become available to us?"

McAllister regretted his earlier bravado. "Yes, of course. My emissary has explained that his agent is hot on the trail. I have no doubt the stone will be with us shortly."

"How many, Mr McAllister?"

"I cannot say for sure, but a close watch of Mr Hill's movements suggests he may have found information we have not been privy to. Information which could lead to additional unaccounted for stones," he fumbled with a card coaster, "that I may have been slightly reticent to procure in advance of additional data."

She raised her head and looked down her stubby nose at the part-time tour guide, and the person she had entrusted to organise recovery of the stones. It was not his place to arrange tactics.

McAllister said, "I think there could be at least another three, maybe more. It depends on Newton and Boyle's contribution to the cause."

"You know of the importance of provenance. I have no interest in stones achieved by any old Tom, Dick or Harry."

She rose and made for the door. As she took the handle to pull, she said, "I will see you at the venue next week, unless you can inform me that you have acquired additional stones in the meantime," she lowered her head and looked through her brow. "And please ensure you have Mr Hill's stone with you. The Indians have said they would like to process one themselves."

McAllister watched as the door closed before he turned back to his orange juice. He emptied the glass and reached for the envelope on the table. He waited for his hands to stop shaking before carefully removing the gum seal from the bottom flap. He prised the envelope apart to see a folded A4 sheet of paper. He opened the print-out. It detailed a deposit to his off-shore account, with a transfer sum of three million pounds. He fumbled with his phone, first trying his fingerprint to access and then the code, which he failed with twice before calming sufficiently. He removed a slip of paper from his wallet and typed the instructions. The bank account concurred with the print-out.

He glanced around once more before replacing the envelope flap and inserting it inside his jacket pocket.

Eddie burst through the door to see Jamie lying propped upright in his bed. His bright blue eyes were closed. His dusty blond hair was taped across and around his face to keep a respirator mask attached. His breathing was soft and shallow.

Lucy gasped and placed a hand on the guide rail of the bed. Eddie approached slowly.

A man rose from the chair next to the bed and stretched out a hand. "Mr Hill?"

Eddie snapped his head towards the man as if emerging from a trance. "Yes. Detective Gale, is it?"

"Yes, that's right. I know this is not the best timing, but would you mind if I ask a few questions?"

Eddie stared straight at Gale. "What's wrong with him?"

"Oh, yes, of course. I don't know for sure, but I think it looks worse than it is. The doctor was concerned about a brain injury because he was out cold when I found him, and the swelling was already large. She sedated him to allow the swelling to settle. They checked back in a while ago and said he would be awake by morning."

"So, he's going to be okay?"

"Yes, they ran some tests. I am sure they can tell you more, but the doctor said he will be fine. They were monitoring the swelling," Gale glanced around the room at nothing in particular. "We should probably have a chat outside. I don't think they like too many visitors."

Eddie looked over at Lucy. She pulled out a chair and sat before taking Jamie's hand in hers. "I'll stay here until Other Jamie arrives."

Gale said, "About an hour."

Lucy thanked the policeman as he opened the door for Eddie.

They took chairs in the corridor before Gale said, "So, where shall we begin?"

Eddie replied, "Let me help you. I witnessed an assault, but as no one else saw it, and the victim later died, I became a suspect because somebody said they saw someone that matched my description in the vicinity. I then decided to have a weekend break in Oxford until you found the person that did it. And now, it appears you have."

Gale laughed, "Yes, something like that. You went to Oxford?"

Eddie hesitated momentarily. "Yes, Lucy wanted to go shopping at the Bicester Outlets, and I wanted to stay in a prison."

Eddie maintained a deadpan expression as Gale paused. The penny dropped. "Malmaison?"

"Yes. We had a very nice stay. Oxford is a lively city. And now you know who committed the crime that leads us here."

"How do you know it was the same man?"

"Big bald man?"

"Well, yes."

Eddie said, "So, can I ask you a question?"

"Of course."

"How come it was you that found Jamie?"

"Well, you were right to access your property by the fence because the bald man was waiting in his car for you to return."

They both attempted to conceal smiles.

Gale added, "He saw you hand something to Mr Stuart and chose to follow him instead. I thought it could be important, so I followed them both. Unfortunately, I was too slow to get to Mr Stuart before he was attacked."

"I see."

"Yes, so what was it?"

Paul Casella

"What was what?"

"What did you hand Mr Stuart? Why was your friend attacked? What is this about Eddie?"

Eddie paused before replying, "A stone."

"A stone?"

"Yes. A philosopher's stone."

Gale's eyebrows wrinkled. "As in turning lead into gold?"

"Not exactly. I have no idea who the attacker was, but the owner of the building I am working on said he knew him when I lifted him up from the floor. I thought he was looking for something. I then found out the same man once owned the hotel down the road. I was in the pub and found some stuff that was cleared out of it when it was being renovated. If the owner was looking for something, I think it was the package from the first property, not the second property. I had no idea what it was at first, but a bit of research revealed it was probably hidden around the time people were trying to make these philosopher's stones. I was going to talk to the owner the following day but learned he had died."

The chair creaked as Gale pulled it forward. "What is a philosopher's stone, Eddie?"

"A good question. I think it's a load of old nonsense, but back then, they thought it was the Alkahest — a soluble substance that could dissolve base metals. Including gold. But also a universal remedy. Or elixir of life."

"What, live forever?"

"Yes, something like that. Maybe just something that would cure sufficient illnesses that people could live their longest life. Anyway, I think the bald man is some sort of fruitcake that thinks it will work."

The chair's plastic padding breathed air as Gale settled on his seat.

Eddie filled the void. "You didn't think I carried out the attack, did you?"

"I was put on the case to find that out, but it was closed fairly quickly. Forensics declared it an accidental death, and my superiors shut down the investigation."

"You don't sound convinced."

Gale frowned. "I don't suppose I do. As events have unfolded, it appeared to me, if not to my superiors, there was more to this than the unexplained death of an eccentric looking man wearing a bow tie. Something didn't sound right, which is why I wanted a chat with you on my own time."

"And?" Eddie asked.

"Well, I certainly didn't think this was all about ancient superstitions, but neither am I convinced you've told me everything."

Eddie hunched his shoulders and turned his mouth down. "That's pretty much it. I haven't got anything more to report."

"Okay, I'll tell you what, make sure your friend is okay. Do whatever you are going to do next. You have my card. Call me if you need any help," Gale was fully aware that Eddie had no intention of speaking to him again, so added, "I don't think the bald man will come after any of you again. He seems to have what he wanted. I'm going to visit him tomorrow."

"You know where he lives?"

"I ran his number plate," Gale got up and made to leave. "Keep in touch. As I said, if you need any help, let me know."

So much for not intending to speak to the police again, Eddie thought.

25

"Did you sleep?" Lucy asked.

Eddie was lying on his back, arms folded behind his head in what seemed like an early morning ritualistic pose, these days. "I think I might have drifted off for a while, but not for long."

"I think I should go back to work today."

"I thought you might."

"I agree that we should see where all this goes, but following the clues on that book. Well, it's now come at a cost, hasn't it?"

Eddie turned on his pillow to face her, his gaze drifting to a lone floating feather. "Yes, it has."

In unnecessary justification, Lucy added, "I'm not comfortable just taking time away from work. Maybe we should have another look at the weekend."

Eddie turned back the bed covers and headed towards the

door. "I'm going to have a shower."

"Eddie."

He stopped and turned to look at Lucy in the dark — the red glow of the clock numbers providing the only light. "I agree. Jamie's my closest friend, and is like family to both of us. It was just a bit of fun until I saw him in hospital."

Eddie and Lucy drifted around each other in the kitchen, preparing breakfast and making tea. Eddie eventually broke the silence. "It's the waiting."

She placed her hand on his arm. "I know, but someone will call soon. They said he would be awake this morning."

The microwave pinged. Eddie removed his steaming porridge and walked to the dining table. As he pulled out his chair, the phone rang.

Lucy emerged from the kitchen. "Jamie?"

Eddie picked the phone up and mouthed silently, "Other Jamie."

"Hi Jamie, is he awake?"

Lucy watched. There was nodding, and the call was brief. Eddie sat back down.

"Well?"

"Jamie is fine. He's awake and angry. He has a big lump on his head and isn't happy that they shaved some of his hair off for the stitches."

"He's worried about his hair? That sounds like Jamie."

"Actually, no, it's not that. Other Jamie said, and to quote, 'A big bald bloke jumped me. He's nicked the stone. Go and get it back and get Lucy to beat the crap out of him for me'."

Lucy could see the relief wash over Eddie's face as he straightened in his seat.

"You two are like a couple of big kids. What about Other Jamie?"

"Fine. Just happy Jamie is okay. I don't think the full story has been told. So, are you still going to work?"

She paused before picking up her handbag and heading for the hallway to retrieve her coat. "Yes. I haven't thrown a sickie in years, and I can't see any urgency now the bald man has the stone. We will want to visit Jamie anyway, so let's leave it until the weekend."

Eddie grinned. "I told you what Other Jamie said. What if I need some muscle?"

"Eddie, I am going to work. You need to work out what to do about the wedding money, and you need to get back to work as well. Why don't you make some phone calls?"

"Okay. We will visit Jamie tonight, and I will hit the phone. It makes sense to pick this back up at the weekend."

Lucy opened the front door and said, "I mean it."

As she closed the door behind her, Eddie found himself nodding in agreement.

Eddie counted out 117 steps. He walked from the front door through to the kitchen, into the dining area, and then the lounge part of his through-lounge. He counted, and added on additional steps for the furniture obstacles and then walked the route again. He sat. He got back up and repeated the process a further four times. He sat back down again and picked up his phone. The card was in the slip of the phone cover.

"Detective Gale, this is Eddie Hill."

"Hello, Eddie. How are you? And how is Mr Stuart?"

"Jamie is awake. He will be fine. Thanks for asking," Eddie paused before adding, "You know you said if there was anything you could help with?"

"Yes, what can I do for you?"

Eddie asked bluntly, "Have you found the bald man yet?"

"Let me call you back. I have just pulled up outside Mr Garvan's flat."

The call ended, and Eddie began pacing once again. *Mr Garvan.* They had a name and address. Good, that solves one issue. He watched the dew run down his patio door window pane and realised he hadn't mentioned the wedding fund tin, which was the reason for his call.

Ten minutes later, his phone rang. Eddie grabbed it from the table and quickly pressed the icon. "Hello, Detective Gale."

"Hello, Eddie. He wasn't in. It's still early, but he might have gone to work," Gale heard Eddie go to say something and then stop. "Don't worry. We will track him down. He assaulted someone, so there will be an official investigation."

Eddie replied, "I know, but I wasn't thinking about that. It was something else."

"Oh?"

"Well, as you said you were willing to help," Eddie stopped himself again to consider his words carefully. "Mr Garvan stole something from my house."

There was a pause at Gale's end this time. "Detective Gale?"

Gale replied, "Yes. Sorry. Was it by any chance an old Christmas sweets tin?"

Eddie stammered, "How did you know?"

"Well, Garvan didn't take it. I was waiting for you to come home, while you were, where was it? Oxford?"

"Yes. At the weekend."

"That's right. Well, I saw someone leave your house with a Quality Street tin. I presumed at the time that he was a guest, but I'm afraid it wasn't Garvan. It was an older gentleman, and he had hair. He was balding, but he had dark hair."

Eddie felt a surge from his stomach. "There was over thirteen thousand pounds in that tin. I wasn't worried about it at first because I presumed it was all to do with this stone thing. I thought it must be the bald man, and we would get it back, but it now seems we've been burgled. What am I supposed to say to Lucy?"

"Calm down, Eddie. Don't worry. I think it's probably

connected. I think it is *all* connected. The ownership of the property, the stone you describe, this Garvan character."

"The ownership of the house?"

"I think it's something to do with Regal Portfolio Properties, but never mind that for now. I will catch up with Garvan as soon as I can and get back in touch."

Eddie was not reassured, but Gale filled the silence once again. "Although the assault issue with Mr Stuart and Mr Garvan is official business, I was not happy with how Mr Prior's death was closed down without what I thought was a full investigation. It all seems just a bit too convenient to me, which is why I have been following up in my own time. We will get to the bottom of it, and it's Ian, by the way."

"Ian?"

"Call me Ian. I don't think my boss would be too pleased to learn I am still on this, so give me a few days, and I will let you know how I get on with Garvan when I catch up with him. I will then get on to your sweets tin. Unless you want to call it in and report it as a burglary."

"Thanks, Ian. No, I will leave it with you for now. I've got to get back to work anyway, so I appreciate your help."

Eddie paced again. He shook his head. He needed to gain control of both his anger and concern. He eventually calmed but knew he needed to keep occupied. Research into the next clue on the back of the *Mutus Liber* book was the response.

Eddie's phone pinged. It was a text message from Lucy.

'Give my mum a call. She has something to tell you'.

"That's interesting. Jean's finally going to tell me I'm not good enough for her daughter," he said to no one.

Perhaps she was right. It was his decision to change the coins and smaller notes into fifty-pound notes. It was his decision to ignore Lucy's advice and keep all the money in one place. It was his decision to keep it in the kitchen rather than a bank.

He dialled the number, "Is that my mother-in-law?"

"Future mother-in-law, Eddie."

He knew it was coming. "I understand you would like a chat."

"Tell me, did you sell that stone you brought in?"

"No. Why?"

"Well, someone came in with a very similar stone earlier today. He said there was a big scratch and wanted it buffed out."

Eddie smiled. "Is that right?"

"Yes, but it wasn't just a scratch. It was more like a crevice. I told him I could smooth it out, but it would still have a groove and would change the shape of the stone completely."

"Was he a bald man?"

"Yes, he was. Do you know him?"

"Sort of. So, did you polish the stone?"

"No, he mumbled something about how it was his fault or something and left. Is there a collection of these stones?"

"Yes, you could say that. A few of these decorative stones have come up recently. They are part of a set of display items. I will explain more when I see you. So did you have a chat with Lucy?"

He immediately wished he hadn't asked.

"She said there was going to be a delay to the wedding."

"No. No delay. It's still taking place next summer. I must go. There's someone at the door."

"Oh, okay, a customer has just come in anyway. Bye, Eddie."

He was relieved when the call ended and quickly phoned Ian Gale with the news about his suspect's recent whereabouts.

Fifty minutes later, Eddie was standing on the platform of Portsmouth and Southsea train station. He had never thought about its history before, and he didn't intend to now, but he did take in the Victorian surroundings and considered the historical reference that had invaded his life. He watched gulls fluttering through the rafters. A fluffy brown infant screeched after its mother. What was he doing? He looked at his ticket — almost forty quid for a day trip to London to visit a place where the clue led him. But also a place where a stone could not possibly be found.

He boarded the train and took his seat. He had seen a website that sold scatter cushions made from the geometric patterned cloth of British train company seats. Lucy liked them. The journey soothed his discomfort. He knew he had to keep moving. Keep following the clues. Complete this project. He always needed to complete a task before moving on. He recalled his mum's face when she looked at the half-finished pond in her back garden after his dad's accident. 'I will have to get this filled in'. Eddie had never seen his mother look so sad.

He looked through the window. Buildings, trees, and more buildings and trees rattled by. The odd streak of water trickled down the outside of the window at an angle in the wind. His mind wandered throughout the remainder of the journey. Football. What games to go to with Jamie when he came out of hospital? How long would they put him on pills before he could have a drink? Shelving in the garage. What about that company that does a pack for £99.99? Anything but the stones.

Eddie left Vauxhall Underground station and turned around to get his bearings. He looked back at the train station name and was momentarily lost before figuring out where he was and why he was standing there. He shrugged his shoulders and headed across the road to the short tunnel below the train line. He opened the map icon on his phone to ensure the blue dot was flashing in the right direction. He passed the *Royal Vauxhall Tavern* on his right and the arches on his left towards the park's entrance.

'Invisible above myne owne crucible'.

Of all the clues, this was the most obvious to Eddie.

It was also the one clue on the list that revealed the clues were a treasure hunt. He also knew he would not find what was 'invisible'.

He walked through the park entrance, which was effectively two trees, and into the wide-open space. The wind howled through the grass, bending it in a singular direction. He zipped his jacket to the top and removed a sheet of folded paper with a print-out downloaded from the internet from his back pocket. The map was from 1747 and marked the position of the Vauxhall Glassworks in relation to the one time commercially owned Pleasure Gardens. He turned onto Glasshouse Walk, considering it to be as likely as any place. On his right, he saw the Vauxhall Gardens Community Centre. He stopped to think over enquiring about further historical references before realising this would be as needless as his trip to London. He continued back through the railway arches and paused at the end. He strolled past a grocery store before stopping at a petrol garage on Albert Embankment. He looked once again at his map.

'Invisible above myne owne crucible'.

Eddie turned a full 360 degrees to take in his surroundings. This part of London had changed many times over the centuries. Even the past few decades. He nodded his head in acknowledgement. The crucible would have been here somewhere, maybe where the speed camera was, below which he stood. The stone would have been here as well. At some stage. A very long time ago.

He turned back towards the station. His visit was never really about the clue, the wedding money, or Jamie. He needed to reconcile his past with his future before he lost everything and everyone.

26

Eddie closed the front door and walked into the living room.

"Where have you been? I was about to call," Lucy asked.

"London."

Lucy walked from the kitchen to join him. "London?"

"Yes. You know the clue after the next one?"

"You skipped one."

"Yes. 'Invisible above myne owne crucible'. That one."

"Go on."

"I realised this was the easiest clue once we knew who it was all about. The book belonged to George Villiers, the Second Duke of Buckingham, yes?"

"Yes," Lucy said as she threw a tea towel over her shoulder.

"Well, it was a matter of working out where his crucible was."

Lucy interjected, "The crucible being where he attempted

to achieve the philosopher's stone?"

"Correct. I am going to guess that George had more than one lab, and it was at least a bit portable, but, and this is a big but, as soon as I saw the clue, I realised two things."

Lucy opened her eyes wide and raised her hands, palms up, in a gesture of impatience.

"The first was who the clue was for."

"For goodness sake, this is like getting blood out of a stone. Get on with it."

"This whole thing is a treasure hunt by George for his friend Charles, and the clues lead to philosopher's stones that were made or created by the great scientists of the time."

Her mouth opened to say something, but she gently nodded her head instead, as Eddie added, "It was just a case of working out where George would be able to place a stone in plain sight."

"It said it was invisible."

"It seemed pretty obvious that the best place to hide a lump of glass would be in a glass factory."

Realisation struck. "The Vauxhall Glassworks, which we know George owned."

"To be frank, I think it could be as simple as the stone was in a red jar on a shelf above his crucible, and even if he had more labs and more crucibles, the period we think this all occurred works well. I think if the clues were for Charles, the place where George most likely carried out his experiments makes sense."

"We don't know he carried out any experiments anywhere."

"You are right, we don't, but in the end, none of the places where George may or may not have had a lab, oven, crucible, whatever, exist. So that was my best guess at solving the clue," Eddie trudged from one side of the lounge to the other as if wading through a peat bog. "Luce, you'd better sit down. I

177

have something else to tell you."

Lucy frowned and slowly pulled out a chair.

"I spoke to Detective Gale this morning. The bald man that put Jamie in hospital did not steal the wedding tin. It was someone else."

Lucy sat quietly for a moment before haltingly said. "Does he know who?"

"No, but he's on the case."

"Eddie, that is all of our savings."

"I know. I did think this would all unravel, and we would get the tin back. I even thought it could be as simple as swapping it for the stone, but it appears there's a lot more to all of this than we know."

"What do you mean?"

"Well, talking to Ian Gale, it seems that he has been watching our house and saw who took it, so he has a description of the person that broke in."

"But what does that mean?"

"Gale only knows about the first stone. I haven't told him about the book, the clues or what we have been doing. What he does know is he was taken off the case when Mr Prior died, and there is more to this than we are aware of."

"How does that help get our wedding money back?"

"Fair question, and I can't answer that yet, but I think my best bet is to be as helpful to Gale as I need to be."

"And what does that mean?"

A coaster rattled as Lucy dropped her hands on the table.

Eddie said, "I'm not ready to tell him about the book or the stone hunt yet, but he knows the name of the bald man, and he thinks there is something suspicious about Mr Prior's death. He was only looking into this because he thought it was odd that his boss took him off the case before it was solved. He thinks there might be a connection with the ownership of the Portsmouth property. Whatever is going on, Ian Gale is all over this and wants to help. I am hoping we can solve the remaining clues while he gets our wedding money back and solves whatever crime is associated with all this."

Eddie saw he had not reassured Lucy, so added something that helped even less, "Oh, and Owen Garvan went in to see your mum today."

"Who is Owen Garvan, and what has this got to do with my mum?"

"This is where I think Ian Gale's investigation will lead. Owen Garvan is the bald bloke. Gale got his details from a number plate search. And the reason he went to see your mum is because he took the stone in to buff out what she described as 'a crevice'. So, he's damaged the stone after stealing it from Jamie, and it was all urgent enough for him to immediately take it to a jeweller to get fixed."

"So that's why my mum wanted to talk to you this morning?"

"Oh no. She just wanted to tell me how grateful she was that I was marrying her lovely daughter."

"Well, it doesn't look like anyone is marrying anyone without any wedding money, does it?" Lucy stared unblinkingly into his eyes.

Eddie stretched his hand out to place it on top of Lucy's. "You know what, Luce, I feel a bit better about the wedding tin now than I did earlier today. I think we will get it back. There is more to this than we realise, and we now have a team."

The power of positive thinking.

"A team?"

"Ian Gale seems like a nice guy, and he thinks there's a connection between all of these seemingly associated issues. He will track down this Owen Garvan, which could help solve the wedding tin issue. That leaves us to complete the other half of the puzzle."

Lucy stood and walked to the kitchen doorway. "Okay,

now that's all quite a lot to be chewing over, so I'll tell you what we'll do. We will make dinner. Watch the rest of that box-set. Have an early night and get up while it's still dark to find the next stone."

"What about work?"

"I'm not going in. I caught up on my casework today, so I will take a day's leave. It doesn't seem like I'm going to be able to concentrate properly until this is all over."

Ian Gale slumped in his chair at the desk. He had run through the database checking for whatever background information he could find on Owen Garvan, certain there would be a record. He had his name, two addresses, and a photograph, and although he had most recently assaulted two people — one of which led to a death, the other to hospitalisation — there was no criminal record.

Garvan's marriage information was easy to find. He wrote down the two Southsea addresses, both in joint names with Garvan's wife. He moved closer to the screen as if the information was shrinking, demanding closer scrutiny. It was Owen Garvan's employment history. Operation Granby, Operation Telic, Battle of Norfolk in the first Gulf War. Bosnia, Kosovo War. Garvan was in the Seventh Army Brigade, also known as the Desert Rats. Before leaving the army with post traumatic stress disorder, he also had a short period as a Regimental Motor Transport Warrant Officer.

Gale blew out his cheeks. Garvan was a war hero.

He looked over to his superior's office. He tentatively rose and headed towards the door. He knocked on the glass. DI Spears looked up and beckoned him in.

"I have been looking into this ABH case, sir. It appears that Mr Garvan is an Iraq and Kosovo veteran."

Gale knew Spears had also served during the Iraq War.

Spears placed his pen down and joined his fingers above

his desk. "Yes."

"I thought I should keep you updated, sir. He may have separated from his wife. I have two addresses."

"It would be nice if you could bring him in, DC Gale. Take DC Newman with you."

Gale closed the glass door behind him. He did not know why he felt uneasy telling his boss about Garvan's service record. He did, however, know he wanted to speak to Owen Garvan without the help of anyone else.

27

Lucy followed Eddie downstairs and watched as he put the kettle on. "We should visit Jamie before we leave."

"I know. I should have gone yesterday, but I'm feeling guilty. I got him into this."

"I don't think Jamie looks at it that way. We'll have some breakfast and go to the hospital. I've already packed for the trip."

"Packing my clothes now. Just like an old married couple."

"Eddie. The tin."

"I know. I know."

He did know. He knew only too well how important it was to their future. He also knew he needed to trivialise it as much as possible — for both their sakes.

Jamie looked up from his bed when they walked in. He said, "I'm pleased you're here. Can you pass me my phone?"

Jamie pointed at the side table.

Eddie said, "No, oh, good to see you?"

"I told Jamie I would call to say how I was, but the nurse put my phone over there and said I needed to rest. That's all I've done. I'm bored out of my skull."

"I think I can see it creeping out of your baldy head," Eddie replied.

"Is it that bad?"

Lucy knew this could go on all day. "It's nothing a 1970s footballer comb-over won't take care of, and it will grow back in a couple of weeks. It's only a small patch. And you're obviously feeling better."

"I don't even know what I'm doing here. It's only a little lump. I'd be better off at home."

Eddie stared. It wasn't just a little lump. He asked, "Any idea when that will be?"

"This afternoon or tomorrow, they said. Depending on some tests, blah, blah," Jamie slapped his arms on the bed covers. "So bored."

Eddie and Lucy laughed in unison.

"Anyway. What's going on? Give me an update."

Eddie provided a quick run-down of events before asking for Jamie's impressions of Ian Gale.

"He seems like a nice guy. He didn't seem too bothered about the stone. I don't think he knew what I was on about. He did say the bald man had committed assault, so it would be investigated, but he seemed to be more bothered about the original crime that kicked all this off."

Eddie said, "That's good. I spoke to him, as well. He has already found out the man's name. Owen Garvan. And he's tracking him down. He also thinks there's more to this case than we know. I get the impression he thinks it's organised crime."

"Well, that would tally."

"Tally with what?" Lucy asked.

"I was clearly knocked out when I hit my head on the stairs, but when I woke up this morning, I had a phrase going through my mind. I remember the man say, 'The cure'."

Eddie and Lucy looked at each other. Lucy raised her shoulders.

"Is that it?" Eddie asked.

"Yes. I remember him going into my pocket, taking the stone out and saying, 'The cure'. I must have blacked out after that."

Ian Gale guessed she was in her late forties. Of average height and weight, but with pinched features. Her glasses were not positioned evenly across her nose, and her shoulder-length, brown hair was untidy. She looked like someone who saw herself as less attractive than others would. A woman lost to the rigours of an unconventional life in the service of her country by association.

She held the front door open.

"Hello, Mrs Garvan?"

"Yes."

"I am DC Gale. May I ask if your husband is home?"

"He doesn't live here anymore. What has he done?" Mrs Garvan asked bluntly and without emotion.

"Oh, I see. I have visited his apartment, but unfortunately, he wasn't in. I was hoping I could find him here."

"No. Not here."

"May I ask if you have seen him recently?"

"No. I have not."

Gale gave Mrs Garvan his card and asked her to call when she next heard from her husband. She nodded her head and quickly closed the door.

Gale returned to his car. He moved the seat back and pressed the recline paddle. He knew he could be in for a long wait, so thought he might as well get comfortable. He did not believe Mrs Garvan's story — he saw a man's flat cap hanging in the hallway.

"The police have been around, Owen."

"Did they say what they wanted?"

"I have no idea. I said I hadn't seen you. The man gave me his card. It says his name is Detective Constable Gale," she turned the card over in her fingers. "Is it something to do with that little bottle of liquid you made Steven drink yesterday?"

"I told you, it was just water with a herbal remedy. It is supposed to help. Surely anything is worth a try."

"Yes, anything is worth a try, but are you sure it's nothing to do with that religious nonsense you have been obsessing about?"

"It is not a religion. I have explained this to you."

Mrs Garvan snapped back, "I don't care what it is, and I know you are just trying to do your best for Steven, but I do not want the police knocking at my door. Deal with it."

Garvan watched as the telephone symbol disappeared on his mobile.

After concluding their visit with a promise to see Jamie at home when they returned, Eddie and Lucy made their way to the car. They agreed neither knew what the comment had meant, but Eddie had an idea.

He typed 'Taplow' and the postcode into the navigation system and chose the quickest route.

"You didn't say how you worked out the clue," Lucy said.

"It was easy. I just typed it in, 'For Anna Maria – The Sceptical Chymist', and 'George Villiers', and it came up about half a dozen listings down. Once I read the history, it was obvious. I don't think George intended this to be too hard for Charles to work out. I don't know why."

They drove away from the hospital, and Eddie opened the internet browser on his phone. Shortly after, he said, "Bit of a problem. We can't stay there. The cheapest room at Cliveden House is nearly five hundred quid a night."

Lucy momentarily looked away from the road, "This little adventure is certainly turning out to be expensive, isn't it?"

"I thought it was just another one of those country hotels. I didn't think it would be that expensive. I will look for a pub or bed and breakfast nearby."

"Yes, I think you had better."

A few minutes later, Eddie said, "This will do. It's in Maidenhead, which is the next town. Ninety quid. Looks very nice."

"Yes, wherever, as long as we can go along and solve the clue, it doesn't matter."

It did matter. They were both acutely aware of their financial issues.

Ian Gale pulled himself upright. He grimaced as he squeezed the stiffness out. He had spent too long sitting in his car seat recently.

Mrs Garvan closed her front door and then the front gate behind her. Gale saw she was holding a boy's hand. He looked small for almost any age, and this was accentuated by the oversized man's cap stretched over his ears. He guessed it must have been the little boy's dad's cap, which blew his theory that Garvan still lived there, out of the water. He sighed. He would need to return to the other address.

28

Eddie asked the taxi driver to drop them off at the long drive
leading to the stately home. He had been researching and
wanted to give Lucy a quick run-down before their arrival. He
explained George Villiers built Cliveden as a hideaway for his
trysts with Anna Maria, Lady Shrewsbury, over whom George
had a dual. With her husband, no less. The husband died,
which caused a great scandal — not surprising, given that
George was also married while brazenly public with the affair.

"That certainly fits with the character we have been
learning about," Lucy said.

"It does. Although we hadn't heard of it, it's probably one
of the country's most famous stately homes. While ownership
was with the Royal family, it burned down. Charles Barry, the
man responsible for redeveloping the Palace of Westminster
after its fire, was in charge of rebuilding it. It became famous
when Waldorf and Nancy Astor bought it in the late nineteenth

century. Parties, famous people. Everyone from Gandhi to Roosevelt and Chaplin to Churchill stayed here. The Astor's gave it to the National Trust just before the Second World War."

"We wouldn't be able to afford to give our garden shed to the neighbour," Lucy said.

"Remember the Profumo Affair?"

"The 1960s scandal that nearly brought down the government?"

"Yes. That happened here. I'm looking forward to the tour. I think it will be fascinating to learn some more detailed history about the place."

Lucy feigned a bored face. "You would."

"The most famous recent guest was Meghan Markle, who stayed here with her mum the night before she married Prince Harry."

"I don't suppose she had to worry about the room rates."

"Now, now. At least you won't have your pictures all over the paper tomorrow after pitching up to dinner wearing flip-flops."

Lucy gently slapped Eddie on the arm, "I didn't know it was going to be this fancy. And they do have sparkly bits on. Are you saying I don't look nice?"

"You look beautiful. To be honest, it's a bit of a deflection. I should have put a suit on instead of just a shirt and trousers."

A few short hours later, they were getting ready for bed but still excited. Dinner was a blur, but Eddie recalled his Wagyu starter, and Lucy was still excited about how much she enjoyed her rock oysters. According to Lucy, the roe deer Wellington they shared was "Amazing. Probably the best meal I've ever had."

Eddie said, "I could have done with not being charged a tenner for some extra vegetables."

"Yes, but wasn't it incredible?"

"It was. The main restaurant was the right call. It was a great setting. I have never been to a restaurant with real antique chandeliers before. Shame we couldn't see what we went there for, though," Lucy said.

"I knew we wouldn't see the terrace. They shut the tours off at four. It's too dark to see anything at this time of year."

Lucy stared at Eddie with a quizzical expression.

"After the past few days, I thought we needed a treat. I looked it up and thought we had earned a special night out. And it really was the best place I've ever eaten."

Lucy walked over and embraced him. "Me too. Thanks. After the past few days, we needed that."

The morning tour informed them George Villiers levelled the hilltop to create the decorative gardens and Palladian terrace of twenty-seven symmetrical arches before starting on the construction of the house itself. Disappointed expressions greeted the news that three mansions succeeded Villiers' structure. Hopes were momentarily raised when they learned the south terrace remained from Villiers' days, but they knew the game was up when told the fire they had already learned about led to a complete restoration project in the mid-1850s. A combination of faulty drainage, which led to stone damage, and general decay, had seen alterations and repairs throughout its history. The extensive renovation project of 2012, which included the removal and repair of terrace flagstones, and refurbishment of the defective drainage system, provided some, if limited, hope.

The tour group left for the gardens, but Eddie and Lucy remained. If this was the only remaining section from George's time, it was also the only part that concerned them. Eddie's gaze was stuck on the central arch and the shield above it.

A voice from behind said, "Can't get enough of the old

place?"

Eddie and Lucy turned to see a dishevelled man in a paradoxically nice suit. He was Eddie's height but slimmer. His hair featured thinning spikes and a long nose topped a matching mousy coloured moustache.

"I was wandering the grounds yesterday evening and spotted a beautiful young couple arrive for dinner. You must be guests?"

"He called you young, Luce," Eddie said, returning the man's agreeable approach. "Do you work here?"

"Oh, I wish. No. I just love this place. I come along regularly. Sometimes every day. I enjoy speaking to anyone that has an interest in this great building and its gardens."

Lucy knew the answer before she asked, "What does your wife make of that?"

The man looked to the floor. "Oh, I lost Flo last year. This gives me something to do."

Lucy said, "I am sorry to hear that. It's nice that you have found an interest."

"You also seem to be enjoying the grounds. It's always wonderful to meet fellow enthusiasts. I'm Malcolm, by the way."

Malcolm gently took Lucy's outstretched hand in his curled fingers for a half shake.

"Lucy," she replied, feeling the strange need to curtsy before just stopping herself.

Eddie held out a hand. "Eddie. I'm afraid we're not guests. We could stretch to dinner, but sadly not the room. We did want to come back for the tour, though, and were admiring the terrace. It's the only original feature, isn't it?"

Lucy heard Eddie had affected his posh voice.

Malcolm was quick to animation. "Oh yes, jolly good. Well done. It's the last surviving feature from The Duke of Buckingham's original home."

"Fires?" Eddie asked with his, top lip curled.

"Yes, just so. It is sad, but I am sure you will agree, what has evolved over the centuries is the most splendid of properties."

Eddie sub-consciously, or consciously, he wasn't quite sure, began mimicking Malcolm's enthusiasm. "And such incredible scandal," Eddie said. Lucy grinned.

"Yes, indeed, but mostly, it's just a wonderful place to contemplate history. Question where we come from. And where we're going."

Eddie said, "Yes. It was both enlightening and fascinating. But you know what, Malcolm, for all the historical stories, I still find myself drawn to the stonework and façade of this incredible terrace," Eddie was in his stride now. He ran his fingers across the blockwork. Flecks of chippings crumbled to the touch.

Malcolm replied, "It has changed over the years, but it's still a remarkable introduction to the property."

"I am in the building trade. I'm always fascinated to see repairs that have taken place using different materials from different centuries to these historic buildings," Eddie said, wiping his hands on his jeans.

"Well, that's not something I have ever heard before."

"There will be five-hundred-year-old hay, small stones, and material that today would be worth more if not hidden, like marble. All sorts. Even small precious stones."

Malcolm nodded vigorously. "You are so right. I have a letter in my archive that suggests something interesting was found over a century ago when repairs were taking place. If you're not in a hurry, I would be happy to show it to you. You certainly seem to know your stuff. My little cottage is just down the road. Why don't you come back for a cup of tea, and I'll show you what I have? I think you will be pleasantly surprised."

Eddie said, "Oh, we couldn't possibly."

"It really would be my pleasure."

Lucy shrugged her shoulders in Eddie's direction. "Why not? That would be lovely."

The walk through the gardens to the main entrance took longer than Eddie and Lucy expected. Malcolm enthusiastically told them of the flora and visiting fauna. He could never tire of the experience. It was his favourite place in the world. Lucy placed a comforting hand on his arm at one stage of his reflections of the times he walked the same route with his late wife.

The cottage was built from similar stone to other buildings in the area. The garden looked as if it was well cared for but was now fading with the seasonal change. The light blue wooden door creaked as Malcolm pushed it open.

Eddie and Lucy took seats on the other side of the desk in a tidy but small office that included random furniture items. Eddie presumed it was a former dining room. Many of the antiquities, an expression of past endeavours when tooling and equipment, were not nearly as advanced as today. Malcolm rifled through a filing drawer in his aged desk as they looked around at the antiques. Time had stood still, but from what decade or century, neither could tell. The modern phone was undoubtedly out of place.

"Ah, here it is," Malcolm said. He placed a yellowing letter with faded writing on the desk. It was enveloped within a plastic archive sleeve. "I believe it is dated sometime in the 1850s. It's mostly a bit too faded to read, but that timeline would match up with the extensive renovations that took place around that time," he turned his attention to the body of writing. "What can be made out, says something along the lines of, 'My Dearest Louisa, I write to say that I should be expected to return home to you my love, in three short weeks'." Malcolm looked up, "I'm not sure what it says from there, but there is a mention of. . . ah yes, here it is. 'While repairing the crumbling terrace, a small section came away in one of the men's hands. Behind was a small hole, and inside the hole was a glass bottle with red coloured sand inside. I was standing nearby, and the chap called me quick smart'. As you will see, the bottom third of the page beneath the fold is completely unreadable. I know this was a letter to a loved one, but whoever owned it before me did not take the greatest care with it. I am sad to say it is not the only item in my collection with a shoddy appearance."

Eddie nudged forward. "Is there anything overleaf?"

"Oh, yes," Malcolm turned the letter over, ". . .glass container was inscribed 'Boyle'. I had little clue to the meaning, so I asked a friend at the Ashmolean Museum to investigate," Malcolm looked up once again and added, "The letter continues with some flowery love poetry, but as soon as you expressed your interest in the building materials, I was reminded of this letter. It is the romance that I so adore. Not just its age, but the feelings expressed at a different time in history."

"Well, it's very kind of you to show us," Eddie said while nudging Lucy with the back of his hand below the desk, out of Malcolm's sightline.

"I do so like to share the history of Cliveden. It's of such importance to our country. I have no idea what the letter means. It's just one of the many stories that the place throws up. Even that chair," Malcolm pointed to the corner and an ornate piece of furniture, "was one of many that were sat upon during the first performance of 'Rule Britannia' in 1740. I have acquired a few items in auction over the years," Malcolm was momentarily absent before gently shaking his head. "Oh, look at me. What a frightful bore. There were you, minding your own business, and I drag you in here to listen to me prattle on about nothing in particular."

Lucy replied quickly, "It's a privilege. It is fascinating," she winked at Malcolm, "and most definitely the best part of the tour."

Eddie stood and held out a hand. "Malcolm. Not only was it an absolute pleasure to meet you, but I would imagine it's only the enthusiasm of people like you that sustains the success of these wonderful National Trust properties."

Malcolm's face flushed, and he nodded his head in a slight bow. "Oh, thank you so much," he rose to lead them to the front door. "I know you have to retrieve your car, but before you go, please stop for a drink at the bar. You will not regret a short period overlooking the wonderful parterre."

As Eddie walked away from the cottage, he nudged Lucy on the leg. She nudged him back. They looked at each other, both with raised eyebrows.

On their return to Cliveden, Eddie and Lucy entered another high-ceilinged room that looked like a museum unto itself. They sat in matching wing-backed chairs by a small round table beside elaborate drapes that provided an elegantly framed window to the terrace and parterre below.

A friendly young barman with a hipster beard and slightly disappointing moustache laughed and said he knew Malcolm very well. Addressing Eddie, he added, "You must be his latest victims."

"He suggested we visit the bar. He's a very interesting man."

The friendly barman laughed again. "Yes, he is. Likes to talk. I think he tries to get converts to his religion. Did he preach to you?"

Lucy said, "No. What religion is that?"

"Rosicru-something-or-other. I don't pay attention. Anyway, what can I get you?"

Lucy said, "I'm driving, so I'd better just have a lime and soda water, please."

As she was finishing her sentence, the barman raised his gaze from the napkins he was placing for their drinks. "Hang on a minute, do you like Champagne?"

Eddie and Lucy gently nodded in unison.

"An American couple ordered a bottle with their lunch."

The barman walked over to his station and returned with a moisture encased ice bucket with an open bottle of Champagne leaning inside. The label read, 'Louis Roederer Cristal Vinotheque'. "He only had one glass, and she didn't have any. I gave him the bill, which was over twelve hundred quid, and he signed without batting an eyelid. He suggested I offer it to the 'next happy couple that walked in'. You're more than welcome to it if you like."

A cartoon grin spread across Eddie's face, "Yes, please." He turned to Lucy, while still smiling.

She said, "Well, I could have one, I suppose."

They closed their car doors at the same time and stared at each other.

Lucy said, "Very nice Champagne," she saw Eddie's eyelids were a little heavier than usual for a midweek afternoon. "You certainly enjoyed it."

"Yes. I'm not used to drinking during the day, but I wasn't going to pass that up. You do know it was the most expensive thing we will ever drink, don't you?"

"I will be drinking that every day with my next husband on our yacht. Don't worry about that."

"I am going to be your next husband."

"Oh, yes. I meant my husband after the next one."

"You do know what all that was about, don't you?" Eddie asked.

"Of course. Over friendly, Malcolm wanted to know if we

195

knew anything about the stones. He even asked his friend, the barman, to see if we knew about Rosicrucianism."

"I wonder how often he goes through that routine?"

Lucy turned her key, and the engine sparked to life. She looked over her shoulder and began to back out of the parking space. "You even managed to play along without giving anything away. Even about Malcolm's acquaintance with our tour guide friend from Oxford."

Lucy asked Eddie what he thought was going on, but he was asleep before they hit the main road.

29

"I am just calling in to say another young couple visited today who were curious about the terracing at Cliveden. Sadly, I don't think they are who you are looking for," Malcolm Finlayson said.

"How do you know this?"

"He was a builder. He was interested in history, but they had no idea about Rosicrucianism, even when they stopped for a drink. I quizzed a friend quite extensively about their expressions and behaviour, and they did not react at all. At first, it seemed odd that they would visit twice, and then the chap had quite an interest in the building materials. He even mentioned the possibility of precious stones being used."

"Really?"

"Yes, I was most curious about the two visits, but it seemed they just couldn't afford the hotel rates. They are costly, you know."

The conversation gap he created was closed quickly, "Go on."

"He had very rough hands, so I believe he was a builder. I even showed him the letter."

"And the response?"

"None, I am afraid," Finlayson was keen to bring an end to the call. "I said I would alert you as soon as anything remotely suspicious occurred, but unfortunately, I'm afraid these visitors were of no relevance to you."

"That is most unfortunate."

Finlayson added, "I have forwarded my cheque and look forward to seeing you at the weekend."

The call had already ended.

Owen Garvan sought solace in words as he once again read the *Chymical Wedding of Christian Rosenkreuz*. The Rosicrucian manifesto was first published in English in 1690 and was largely considered the third of the great early works in the field.

Garvan considered the romantic journey through seven days of Passover to be an allegorical tale he could identify with. Like Christian Rosenkreuz, he, too, had been invited to a wonderful castle of miracles. He had been called upon to assist in the cure of his son. Just as Christian was called upon to assist in the chymical wedding of a husband and bride. Also, like Christian, Garvan felt he had been on a journey of transformation. He read the phrase, 'I patiently took up my cross, got up onto my feet' and like Christian, he also rose. He walked to his small square dining table and stared at the open toolkit and the red stone. He took a seat to consider his options.

He could deliver the stone as promised but was concerned about the damage. They would notice. He turned the stone to see the marks he had made. They would know. Of course, they would know. He was only involved in this to get a vial for his son. They knew this as well. He could not fight away the doubts. The demons. What if one vial was not enough? He would have to deliver the stone. Who knows what could happen if he did not? If they figured he had caused the damage, he would not get the vial he was promised. What if one vial was not enough? He looked at the tool kit. He did not know if he was completing the process correctly. *What if one vial was not enough?*

He arranged the tools once more. He needed the stone more than them. This was about saving his son. He closed his eyes. He had made his decision.

Garvan's thoughts were interrupted by a knock at the door. He moved the curtain aside to see who it was.

The man standing outside was tall but looked half Garvan's weight. He had his hair in one of those man-buns and was casually dressed. Garvan thought he was scruffy, certainly not the kind of person that would have served his country. He had appeared far more respectable when they first met at the meeting. His presence turned his stomach. He was once an inspiration but was now an obstacle.

Garvan gathered the tools, opened a door in the alcove unit next to his fireplace, and shoved them inside. He grabbed the stone and swept the table with his free hand. He placed the stone in a small bowl on the fireplace mantle.

Another knock. Three raps this time.

Garvan opened the door. "Sorry, I was in the toilet. I didn't hear you."

"If you didn't hear me, how did you know I had knocked?"

Garvan stammered, "I heard, but I was finishing up. You know what I mean."

The man brushed past Garvan into the small living room. "It has come to my attention that you assaulted a man in his house. Is this correct?"

Garvan stuttered a reply, "Yes. Yes, but it was to retrieve

the stone."

How did he know?

"And did you?"

"Yes. I have it here," Garvan walked to the small bowl on the mantle to retrieve the stone. He handed it to his visitor.

"When were you going to come to me with this?"

"Today. I was going to take it directly. That is why I did not call you. Sorry."

"That's okay, Owen. But I should remind you that I am your contact. It is my responsibility to ensure integrity and process. Do you understand this?"

Garvan felt relief wash over him. "Yes, of course. I suppose I was excited. It has been a bit of a trial retrieving this stone, and I certainly didn't mean to hurt anybody. I just knew how important it was that I completed my job."

"For your sick son?"

"Yes, for my son."

Garvan squeezed his eyes together and turned his head to ensure his mentor could not see his emotions. He turned back to see the man rotate the stone in his hand.

"This is the first one I have seen. I did not know if it would be chippings or powder. It looks attractive as a stone," he examined the ragged edges more closely. "You would think it would have either smooth edges or rough edges, but it looks like it's been broken. Can you see the damage here?"

Garvan knew he must have looked uncomfortable. He felt a flush of panic. It must have shown.

"Is there something you would like to tell me?"

Garvan thought his best option was honesty. He had known him from the start. The man had proven the perfect docent and guide on his journey. Only the immediacy of this project had brought on this new strict and formal alteration to their relationship.

His knee cracked as he knelt by the alcove cupboard and

removed the tools. "As I was having trouble locating the stone, I think it brought on a bit of anxiety. I was worried about my son, so I took a tiny quantity of shavings," he added earnestly, "It was what I was promised."

Garvan did not look up as he said this.

He should have.

The carpet knife sliced with alacrity and precision. He felt warmth on his neck. Then coldness. All over.

The man stood and watched as Owen Garvan fell to the floor. There was spasming and panic. There was neck clutching and gurgling. He had seen similar before. It was interesting. He took a step to one side to avoid the blood. There was less than there may have been. He realised he must have missed the main arteries when he cut across Garvan's windpipe.

He looked around to see where he had walked and what he had touched. He was confident he had handled nothing but the stone, which he placed in his jeans pocket.

He looked down at Garvan lying at an unnatural angle on the floor. It was a shame. He was useful. Ken Prior had recognised him from a previous job, so he knew Garvan had to go at some stage. Oh, well, today appears to have been the day.

As the man closed the front door behind him, he mumbled, "Shavings. You don't even do it like that."

Paul Casella

30

Lucy joined Eddie at the dining table. "Three mugs. You couldn't wash one up?"

"That's the work of the dishwasher. And good morning to you, too."

"How long have you been up?"

"Since about five. Normal time."

Lucy studied Eddie's red-ringed eyes. "Not normal on a Sunday, Eddie. What have you been doing?"

"I have been trying to work out what this is all about."

"We have been over this. We know what it's all about. George Villiers created a treasure hunt for his best buddy, Charles II."

"That's not what I mean," Eddie sat back and folded his arms. "Other people are trying to retrieve these stones, but we have no idea why."

She shrugged her shoulders. "Yes, but they don't seem to

know where they are. Whereas, we have some pretty easy to decipher clues."

"I know, but that isn't my point. Someone attacked the owner of the house. He died. Someone attacked Jamie, and he could have died. We have also had our wedding money stolen by who knows who? Maybe someone wanted to send us a message."

"What for? You are a heating engineer, and I am an accountant. What reason would anyone have for sending us a message?"

"I know. I don't know. I am just trying to find meaning to all of this."

Eddie rubbed his eyes. "I switched tack this morning. While we've been researching, we have both come across the word 'Rosicrucianism' and learned a man named Malcolm is a practitioner, or whatever they are."

"Go on."

"I started looking into Rosicrucianism, and to be frank, it all sort of flew over my head, to begin with. So, I tried to look at it through the prism of our research."

"The prism of our research?" Lucy laughed.

"Maybe I worded it badly. I tried to find someone else in the seventeenth century scientist crowd that could shed a different perspective on this. We already know the philosopher's stone was about more than turning one material into another, including in a spiritual context. Even the book I found doesn't directly relate to metallurgy or element transmutation."

"Fair enough. What have you come up with?"

"Not what, but who. Although he doesn't appear to be an associate of the great scientific minds of the era, Thomas Vaughan is another character of the period that pops up when reading about alchemy. He was a member of the Society of Unknown Philosophers and appeared to be more into the magic and mystical side."

Lucy looked quizzically at Eddie. "Magic?"

"Maybe. But let's try spiritual instead," Eddie looked down at his scribbled notes. "Vaughan fell out with an alchemical collaborator named Edward Bolnest over money matters, and it ended in litigation. Vaughan was accused as part of this affair of spending, 'Most of his time in the study of Naturall Philosophy and Chimicall Phisick'. He was reported to have confessed that he had, 'long sought and long missed the philosopher's stone'. He was an Anglican rector who began publishing alchemical and magical tracts in 1650. He also wrote under the pseudonym Eugenius Philatheles. Don't forget the evidence we have read suggests chemistry was often identified with subversion of the political and religious order of the time. Hence the pseudonym."

"And where does this lead?"

"The key is Vaughan's wife, Rebecca. She was his collaborator. Even after her death, he included mention of her in his works as his partner. The spiritual side of alchemy is considered the science of everything. This would include a biological component."

Lucy interrupted, "Sex?"

"Yes, could be. There are two possible alchemical paths. Both have counterparts. It can be found in Buddhism: The short path and the long path. It can be found in Tantra: The right-hand path and the left-hand path."

"Are you saying Vaughan and his wife were a seventeenth century Sting and Trudie Styler?"

"It's possible, although they were not pop stars and they did not have tabloid gossip about their sex lives at that time. Vaughan died while practising alchemy. His death was the result of an accident involving mercury which he somehow inhaled. I have read he died in a fire, but also that that he merely died in mysterious circumstances, which could be politeness of the age. It could be historical code for some sort of mystical or spiritual experiment. I read he died while trying to join his wife in the afterlife."

"Okay, so all that is fascinating. But what has it got to do with the stones and Rosicrucians?"

"It's another side of alchemy. As I see it, there are three related parts. One is what most think, turning base metals or whatever, into precious metals. Another is the Alkahest, elixir of life, universal cure, or whatever you want to call it. And the third is this spiritual aspect that relates to religious teachings, mysticism, the occult, and other belief systems of that period. Spiritual alchemy had seven parts. Calcination, dissolution, separation, conjunction, fermentation, distillation, and coagulation. Each part is a metaphor for processing a stone as a path to spiritual enlightenment."

"All right, most of that flew over my head, so what about Rosicrucianism?"

"Vaughan was responsible for publishing the first English translation of the documents of the Rosicrucian Society: *The Fame and Confession of the Fraternity of RC* in 1652. RC is short for Rosie Cross," Eddie tapped on the laptop keyboard and brought up the first-page explainer. "When you type in Rosicrucianism, the definition says this: 'Rosicrucian education combines occultism and theological beliefs and practices, including Hermeticism, Jewish mysticism, and Christian Gnosticism. The main component of Rosicrucianism is the belief that members maintain hidden knowledge and understanding inherited from bygone eras'."

Lucy asked, "How does this associate the seventeenth century with today?"

"I'm not entirely sure, but back then, scientists and learned scholars were often identified with Rosicrucianism. I get the impression that we're talking about a group of intellectuals and polymaths grouping together in secret societies or discussion groups. Don't forget, Charles II pulled together a lot of these people to create the Royal Society. What is most interesting to us is that a lot, if not a majority of, the scientists involved with our stone hunt were Rosicrucians. I found a helpful site which listed a big load of people throughout history that were allegedly Rosicrucians. Loads of people from Walt Disney to George Washington. Victor Hugo to the man that wrote Star Trek, Gene Roddenberry. Napoleon Bonaparte to Barack Obama."

"Seriously?"

"No, I doubt it," Eddie paused. "Actually, I have no idea. There are two points. The first is that many people from the top of professions, societies, and influential groups across the world seem to belong to these secret societies. And the original manifesto, as it was described, was the tale of an alchemist called Christian Rosenkreuz that roamed the world gathering secret knowledge. The follow up was about a secret brotherhood of alchemists that would change the political and religious landscape of Europe."

Lucy asked, "Not religious cranks, then?"

"I would say influential people that got together to accumulate and spread their beliefs and agenda. They were a sort of precursor to the Freemasons and other secretive groups like that."

"I see. So, the next question is, how does that relate to us?"

"I think it's simple. Rosicrucians want their stones back. Well, not their stones, but their antecedents' stones," Eddie paced to the dresser and pulled out the top drawer. He retrieved the *Mutus Liber* book and placed it reverse side up on the table. He said, "Clue one: 'Thomas to Elias Collection'. Clue two: 'The Cross is the Touchstone of Faith'. Clue three: 'Hooke's Folly'. If we start with those three clues, we begin to see the beginning of a pattern."

Lucy asked, "What sort of pattern? I can't see one."

"Rather than look for a motive for George, we should start with the journey Charles would go on. We have to remember he is a king living a rather debauched life in London. For him to visit the places we have visited he would need an incentive or purpose. Especially as they would have been much longer journeys, back then."

Lucy sat in contemplation for a short period. "I think it would be safe to assume both men took their philosopher's stone quest pretty seriously. So, whatever the purpose, I think it's covered. If Charles was convinced George had beaten him to it or was able to help him achieve it, he would have gone to — at the very least — reasonable lengths to follow the clues."

"That's how I see it. I also wonder whether Charles knew George had some of these stones, and it was background noise to the regularity of them falling out."

Lucy said, "Possibly, but more relevant is the timing."

"What do you mean?"

"When do we think George hid the book?"

Eddie said, "Of course. They visited Portsmouth together in 1683. Charles died in 1685, and George died just two years later. It was near the end of their lives, and they were looking for the Alkahest. George might have been teasing his best friend, but it may also have been to help him solve the puzzle by focussing his mind on the hunt. That would mean the incentive was obvious, and the reasons for the quest become less important."

"As there is no way we can know why George sent him on this elaborate chase, except perhaps to channel his king's thoughts, as you describe — which I think is a bit of a stretch — I agree. We need to look at the clues themselves," Lucy looked down at the aged book. "Clue four: 'Invisible Above Myne Owne Crucible'. This is my favourite. It is playful. The stone is hidden in plain sight, but it's right at home. It's pretty obvious where it is. It's almost as if he wants to have a visit with his king halfway through the search."

Eddie rapped his knuckles on the table twice to indicate his approval of the notion.

"And then the Cliveden clue: 'For Anna Maria – The Sceptical Chymist'," Lucy looked up once again, "Did you know that was Robert Boyle?"

"Yes. But there could have been a second stone, apart from the one in Oxford. We had to look."

"And we did have a lovely time."

"As did George with Lady Anna Maria Shrewsbury," Eddie laughed. "Although, to be fair, this is the most romantic of stories. George called it Anna Maria's Lodge, and Robert Boyle was arguably the best connected and most respected chemist of the time. It could be perceived that he had the best chance of achieving the stone. I can't help thinking this clue was George's way of asking Charles to include Lady Shrewsbury if they found the Alkahest. Maybe they could have lived happily ever after. For ever."

"You old romantic."

Eddie blew Lucy a kiss and said, "Which leads us to the last two clues."

"Clue six is a major problem. We haven't discussed it. 'Chancellor Monmouth' then words that are far too faded. Before, it says 'Fire' at the end. She shrugged her shoulders before continuing, "Finally, clue seven: 'My Home from Home – Returned to He Whoe. . .' and it trails off again."

Eddie said, "I've got no idea what either of those mean, but we will work them out in order as before."

"We have seven clues. We have solved five and retrieved the grand sum of one stone. The original one from down the road from where we live."

Eddie said, "That's not strictly true. We only have one, yes, but one was stolen. And we know another is in a builder's fish tank in Westbourne. We also know why we couldn't find one of the stones."

"I think that leads us back to the Rosicrucians. Do you think that tour guide is part of all this?"

"Yes. And not only that, the way the stones were described in his little notebook suggests they have been on their trail for a long time. And ours are obviously not the only stones. These famous scientists, plus others we have not learned about, must have come up with more of these stones during lifetimes of experimentation than we know about."

Lucy stood and paced the living room. "What do you think of this?" she filled an absent gap for an answer, "The bald man."

"Owen Garvan?"

"Yes, him. Maybe he's nothing to do with the tour guide at the Ashmolean."

Eddie pondered this for a short while. "He clearly pursued us and waited for us here to get the stone from the house, but he then took it from Jamie. We haven't seen him since. And James McAllister was a little museum drip. He didn't seem the sort of snob that would mix with a thug like Garvan," Eddie rose to join Lucy in the pacing. "It's possible. We don't know enough, but what we do know is no one is aware that we are chasing these clues. Neither have we seen anyone else wherever we have been looking. When I got the train into London, I considered all sorts of conspiracies and was even looking around the train carriage wondering who could be spying on me."

Lucy grinned. "Really?"

"Oh yes, I even checked behind while I walked through Vauxhall Park. I was thinking about all sorts of nonsense."

"So, what do you think now?"

"I think it's just us looking for the stones, now that Garvan has one — even if it isn't the one he thought he was getting. I have no clue what Malcolm Finlayson was up to, except gathering up museum artefacts. I am concerned about this Rosicrucian thing, though. There could be a group of people after them. Which is where James McAllister might come in. We have to be vigilant."

Lucy asked, "And the wedding money?"

"Once Ian Gale catches up with Owen Garvan, I am confident we will get our wedding money back."

As they knew Garvan did not take the tin, Lucy had her doubts but said nothing.

Eddie added, "I know we have only got three words to go on, but I think we can at least get part of the way to solving clue six."

She raised her eyebrows to question.

"Well, Monmouth was the Duke of Monmouth, the king's son."

Lucy asked, "I thought Charles' brother became king. Did Monmouth die, then?"

"He certainly did. And this has nothing to do with the clue, but it is a good, of-the-times type of story. The Duke of Monmouth was Charles' illegitimate son James Scott, who he had after an affair with a woman called Lucy Walter. She died of venereal disease in Paris, but that's another story. Anyway, Charles accepted his bastard son, made him the Duke of Monmouth, and generally ensured he had a good future. The problem came when Charles died. To cut a long story short, politicians got involved and claimed Charles secretly married Lucy Walter, so the son should be king instead of Charles' brother James."

"The usual sort of stuff that was going on back then?"

"It gets worse. Monmouth became a distinguished soldier with various titles and blah, blah, ended up putting an army together to take his Uncle James on before claiming the throne. He published a," Eddie looked down at his notes, "'Declaration for the defence and vindication of the protestant religion and of the laws, rights and privileges of England from the invasion made upon them, and for delivering the Kingdom from the usurpation and tyranny of us by the name of James, Duke of York'."

"So he died in battle?"

"Again, much worse than that. They went to war all right. The Battle of Sedgemoor was the last open field battle between two armies on British soil, but he was captured."

"Head chopped off?"

"Yes, and again, it gets worse. You'll like this. I have a quote here. When Monmouth was going to the chopping block, he said to his executioner, 'Here are six guineas for you and do not hack me as you did, my Lord Russell. I have heard you struck him four or five times; if you strike me twice, I cannot promise you not to stir'."

"Nice."

Eddie moved the cursor on the laptop to open a page before reading out loud, "An 1861 book called *The History of England from the Accession of James the Second* by James Macauley, has this quote," he turned the laptop, for Lucy to see.

The hangman addressed himself to his office. But he had been disconcerted by what the Duke had said. The first blow inflicted only a slight wound. The Duke struggled, rose from the block, and looked reproachfully at the executioner. Several more inaccurate strikes were delivered, and yells of rage and horror rose from the crowd. Ketch flung down the axe with a curse. 'I cannot do it,' he said; 'my heart fails me.' 'Take up the axe, man,' cried the sheriff. It took two more whacks before the Duke died, and even then, a knife was needed to completely sever the head from the shoulders.

Eddie looked up before grimacing.

Lucy matched his expression. "What a sweet and cuddly tale."

Eddie recaptured his thoughts. "So, that's the Duke of Monmouth, but getting back to the clue, I think the important word here is 'Chancellor' which is where I was before you came in earlier," Eddie clicked on another open page. It was a list of Cambridge University Chancellors from 1215 to the present day. He ran his finger down the list until he reached 1674 to 1682. It read 'The Duke of Monmouth'. He then tapped on the entry above and looked up to Lucy. It read '1671 to 1674, Duke of Buckingham'.

They stared at each other and smiled. Lucy asked, "Something to do with his period as Chancellor at Cambridge and a tie in with George somehow. But what?"

"The only other word we have to go on is 'Fire', so I'll tell you what. How about you make a cup of tea, and I'll do a bit more research.

Lucy left the room. When she returned with two steaming mugs just a few minutes later, she saw Eddie was sitting with his arms crossed, and a wide grin spread across his face.

"I immediately thought of the Great Fire of London again, but that was in 1666. So, I hunted around a bit more, and guess what I found?"

Lucy raised the eyebrow of impatience.

"As we know from our earlier research, Isaac Newton had a laboratory at Trinity College, but what we didn't read at the time was that he experienced a lab fire in 1677, which, and get this, 'destroyed much of his alchemical work'."

31

Ian Gale bounced the knocker on Owen Garvan's front door. He waited patiently as the metallic thudding decreased in volume until it stopped. There was no answer. He saw the curtains were closed and tried again. He pressed the doorbell. Still no answer.

As Gale stepped back from the property, an elderly woman with bright white hair appeared at his side. She said, "I don't think he's in. I knocked yesterday. I keep getting his post."

Gale smiled. "That's unfortunate. I was hoping to catch him."

"Are you a friend?" asked the woman.

"No," Gale reached into his pocket. "My name is Ian. I am with the police," he handed the lady his card.

"Stinks."

Gale asked, "Sorry, what stinks?"

"His flat. I opened the letterbox to put his post in. I think it was a bill. It was in a brown envelope. When I opened the letterbox. I could smell it. Something stinks. It's probably leftover dinner. He gets a lot of takeaways. Mostly foreign food."

"Oh, I see. Thank you very much. I will try again later. Would you be kind enough to call if you see him?"

The lady reached into her bag to retrieve her purse. She placed the card inside before removing it and placing it in an alternative slot. It seemed an age before she eventually disappeared along the road.

Gale moved along to the window once more and took a closer look at the pulled curtains. There was a small gap. He could not be sure, but he thought he might have seen two legs on the floor. He went to the letterbox and pressed the flap. He jerked backwards, and the flap slammed shut with a clang. He had only seen one dead body before, but he would never forget the smell. This was the same smell.

Gale stepped away from the property and made the call.

Within twenty-five minutes, there were flashing lights, a commotion, and officers stretching yellow and black striped tape across the front of the property. Scene of crime officers were quickly in place to secure the property for the investigation. DI Spears was on the scene, and as Gale had not accessed the property, he was operating as the first responder and senior investigator.

Gale had, however, managed to look inside. He had seen enough and did not want to see any more.

Spears called him over to get an update on the earlier visit to Garvan's wife and the conversation with the neighbour. Gale could not offer any more information than the visibly obvious at the scene. There were blood spatter tests to run, photographs to be taken, and reports to be written. The process would be the same in every case. Secure the scene from contamination.

Learn what is suspected or known to have occurred before, during and after the incident. What is known of the persons involved? Record the sequence and timing of events where possible. Assess the nature and characteristics of the items the victim may have come into contact with, including weapons. Was there an opportunity for transfer between the suspect and victim before the incident? In this case, there was no risk of scene contamination. Spears praised Gale for this and asked his opinion of where the investigation should go from here.

This took Gale aback. "At this point, I believe whoever murdered Mr Garvan knew him. There is no evidence of forced entry," Gale said as he looked towards the people congregating at the tape, now stretched several feet from the late Owen Garvan's front door. He considered the neighbour's return from the shops. He thought she would not be pleased if they didn't let her inside her home, and would make sure they were fully aware of her unhappiness.

Spears said, "The wife will need to be informed."

"I can do that, sir. I believe she may know more than she is letting on."

The same woman Gale had visited earlier opened the door.

Gale said, "Hello, Mrs Garvan, DC Gale. We spoke earlier. This is PC Newman. Rachel is a family liaison officer. May we come in?"

Mrs Garvan said, "I told you my husband is not here."

"I'm afraid it's about your husband. I think it would be better if we come inside."

Mrs Garvan slowly walked them through the door and placed a hand on the door jamb. Her left leg trembled. Gale sensed she knew what was coming.

As they entered the living room, Newman asked, "May we take a seat?" as she smiled solemnly.

Gale thought Newman had a pretty smile. It was somehow

both disarming and comforting in a situation like this. He was pleased she was there.

Mrs Garvan regained her composure quickly and said, "Yes, please take a seat. Has he killed himself, then?"

Both the police officers were shocked at the bluntness and visual strength the woman exhibited. It was clear she had experienced difficult times and was hardened to life's worst. Gale wondered whether all armed forces spouses were prepared for these situations. He had not, however, thought of the possibility that Garvan may have committed suicide. He had seen the body lying on the floor. There was no knife visible. Could he have been lying on it? He quickly dismissed the thought. Why would he cut his own throat?

Newman filled the short silence. "The crime scene is still being secured. I am afraid the initial assumption is that he is a victim."

Mrs Garvan lost a little of her composure. "Murdered?"

Gale replied, "We won't know for sure until the examinations have taken place, but it does look that way, I'm afraid. We wanted to start the investigation as quickly as possible, and of course, wanted to inform you immediately."

Mrs Garvan stood. "Hang on a minute," she said as she left the room.

Gale and Newman looked at each other. Both shrugged their shoulders. Gale looked around for the first time and saw it was spotlessly clean. It had all the essential items of furniture, but nothing extra. No ornaments. Nothing on the shelves. There was a pile of pill-boxes on the coffee table, but the room was a sanitary space.

Mrs Garvan returned and placed a small clear pot on the table, somewhat like a contact lens container. "Could it be something to do with this?"

Gale could see it was empty, apart from a couple of dark flecks stuck to the inside of the canister and the residue of a clear liquid around the secure seam.

Mrs Garvan continued, "He came around last night, saying he had a cure for our son. Steven is very ill. He said it was some sort of herbal medicine. It's something to do with these people he's hooked up with. Rosicrucians, or something. He has been going on about how they could cure anything. All he had to do was find something, an ingredient or something. I don't know. Anyway, I chucked him out when he started going on and on about them. I think they might be a cult."

Gale did not want to interrupt. He was surprised at how well Mrs Garvan had taken the news. She had an emotional resilience he had not encountered before. His superiors may want to question her again, but his admittedly limited experience suggested her involvement was highly unlikely.

Mrs Garvan said, "You have no idea what I am talking about, do you?"

Before Gale and Newman could confirm this, Mrs Garvan started to shake before tears came. "I am going to have to tell Steven his dad has died."

Newman said, "Is there someone we can call to sit with you?"

The sobbing stopped as quickly as it started. Mrs Garvan sniffed. "No, I will be all right. Please take that pot and get your analysts to look into it or whatever they do. It might help."

With that, she stood up, and led them from the living room. As the front door closed behind them, Gale considered the irony of Garvan's troubled and broken life ending at a time he believed he had cured his son of an incurable illness.

32

"You know there's a big issue here, don't you?" Lucy asked.

"What is that, my dearest petal?"

"No. Seriously. It's Monday, and I'm taking another day off. You have had over a week without work, and I am going to start eating into the annual leave needed for our next holiday."

Eddie replied, "I know. You are right. I had thought a fortnight on this, and then I'll go back to work next week. I had a text this morning from one of my old customers, who wants a new boiler fitted. So that's helpful. I also thought about your leave. Let's go away over Christmas. A ten-day cruise or something. That way, you can excuse another couple of days."

"A couple of days sounds a bit hopeful to me. Need I remind you we are going to Trinity College at Cambridge University based on the word 'Fire'."

"I have to be honest. Even I think we're on a bit of a wild goose chase with this one."

"Then why are we going? We have spent a lot of money on these," Lucy made air quotes, "little breaks."

Eddie said, "Don't do that. And keep your hands on the wheel."

"See, you've turned me into air quote lady."

"Tell me you are not enjoying this."

"What do you mean, the Jamie getting beaten up bit, or the losing thousands of pounds bit?"

Eddie knew he couldn't keep telling her he wasn't worried about the wedding fund. He didn't know why he wasn't as concerned as he should be, except that there was more to all of this than they were aware of. They just needed to carry on following the clues. Just as it appeared others were.

They had worked their way through the traffic outside Guildford before Lucy resumed the conversation. "Okay. What's the plan?"

"The hotel is a bit far away because I wanted to save money. It'll take around three hours, so we should go straight to the college. Once we've parked, we could grab a bite to eat. We then find Isaac Newton's garden, which I believe is just through the entrance, and then we find a curator or someone that might know about it and ask some questions."

"Well, it's a plan. Not much of one, but at least it's a plan."

Eddie agreed Trinity Street was the most attractive high street he had seen. Of more concern was his experience that the light-coloured stone walls housing chain stores along a narrow, cobbled road was a Lucy playground. "We have research to do," he said as he watched her attention travel.

Lucy followed him past the shops. Eddie pointed to a forlorn-looking tree. Lucy laughed, "Newton's apple tree?"

"Yes, it's supposed to be an offshoot from the original. I would guess they planted it out here so that tourists could take photos of a random tree that had absolutely nothing to do with

Isaac Newton."

Lucy paid the entrance fee and they walked through the Great Gate beneath the statue of Henry VIII. "Why is he holding a stick?" she asked.

"It's a chair leg."

Lucy looked at Eddie with a quizzical expression.

Eddie said, "He beat Catherine of Aragon to death with it."

She shook her head and gazed around the equally impressive Great Court as she emerged from the autumnal shadows cast by the arched entrance and said, "I don't think we're going to take a spade to this lawn."

They continued through to Nevile's Court, past the Wren Library towards the river. Eddie turned around and said, "This isn't going to get us anywhere, is it?"

"There's so much history here I can't see how we can isolate a possibility. I suppose we should start asking around if we want to find Newton's garden."

Five minutes later, they stood at the side of the imposing chapel walls and found a friendly-looking student. As Eddie stared at her youthful acne, and then her torn tights, Lucy interrupted his rudeness and asked, "I don't suppose you know where Isaac Newton's garden might be?"

The young lady exuded effervescence. "I think it would have been around here somewhere," she twirled her hand around her head. "I can find Professor Monkhouse for you. I am heading that way. He knows all about Isaac Newton."

The student walked quickly towards the Wren Library, one arm swinging to her march, the other holding books. "He can usually be found in there," she pointed and went to turn.

"How will we recognise him?" Lucy asked.

"He looks exactly like a Cambridge University professor," the student said as she giggled to herself before walking away.

Eddie looked at Lucy and shrugged his shoulders.

They strolled through the entrance into a black and white

tiled floor space, flanked by imposing dark-wood bookcases, housing thousands of modern and antique books. A blanket of window-cast gloom stretched shade from the ends of the bookcases as if protecting the volumes of reference from the ravages of daylight. Some students were sitting quietly, while others were buzzing around the furnishings. A few tourists were surreptitiously taking photographs.

They saw him straight away. A corduroy jacket with elbow patches, fluffy white beard, large gold wire-rimmed glasses, and a bow tie.

Lucy nudged Eddie. "Stereotype."

"Let's go for a little chat."

"Professor Monkhouse?" Lucy asked.

The man looked over his half-moon glasses to Eddie and Lucy. "Yes, how can I help?"

Eddie introduced them both and said, "A student said we might find you in here and that you could guide us towards the location of Sir Isaac Newton's garden."

The man's beard shook as he laughed. "I am afraid that has long since gone. It was located just inside the Great Gate, but it's now part of the Great Court. We get a lot of people asking about Sir Isaac. You have seen the tree, I presume?"

Eddie replied, "It would be wonderful if it were the original."

"Very good. Very good. I am familiar with Newton's works. Is there is anything else I can help with?"

"We were more interested in his lab fire and the Chancellor at the time, the Duke of Monmouth. Would you be able to tell us about the relationship of the current Chancellor's office and Monmouth's at that time?"

"I see. I see. I am aware of Newton's years, but the Duke of Monmouth was not ever-present. And Newton's fire is well recorded."

Eddie had not thought where he was going with this line of

questioning, but fortunately, Lucy helped him out. "Could you point us in the most likely direction of Newton's lab?"

"There remains conjecture regarding the sites of Newton's labs. The one during the fire was presumed to have overlooked his garden. I am sorry I can not be of more help with that."

Neither knew what else they should ask, so they thanked the professor and left the library without speaking. As they reached the Great Gate once again, Eddie said, "I think we had better go to the hotel and come up with a different strategy. I don't think either of us are likely to win any detective prizes."

They walked past Newton's tree on their left. Leaves fluttered as if waving goodbye to their hopes when another female student approached. This time with a smart dark jacket over a mustard coloured pullover, and matching trousers. Eddie wondered how she could see through her thick-rimmed smudged glasses.

"Professor Monkhouse asked me to apologise on his behalf. He had a rather important issue to assess with a student. He said he would try to make time available for a longer conversation. If you would let me have your phone number, he will call tomorrow."

As they left the university building, Eddie and Lucy agreed things were looking up.

"I must apologise. I was a little busy to call at the weekend. I do, however, have last week's list of people that expressed an interest in Isaac's alchemical pursuits," Professor Monkhouse provided details of two students, a visiting alchemy enthusiast from the United States and a possible distant cousin cum-relative of Newton who was researching their family tree. He added, "There were two more from this week's list earlier today. They seemed particularly interested in one of the Chancellors during Isaac's time, the Duke of Monmouth."

James McAllister asked, "What else did the two from today

say?"

"They seemed rather exercised about Monmouth's office in relation to the current Chancellor's office."

"And their names?"

Monkhouse looked at his notepad, "Eddie Hill and Lucy. Presumably Hill."

James McAllister sucked in air but kept his voice calm.

"Did they perchance mention they were staying in Cambridge."

"They did. The chain hotel on Huntingdon Road. He also left a number if you would like that."

"No, that's okay. I have it."

33

Lucy rifled through her overnight bag once again to make sure. "I haven't packed a toothbrush."

Eddie replied, "Don't worry. We can get one when we go out for dinner."

"It's okay. I saw a supermarket along the road. I will pop out and get one now. I can get a few bits for home while I'm there. For some unknown reason, we haven't been food shopping for over a week."

"Do you want me to come?"

The door closed before Eddie had finished his sentence.

An hour had passed when Eddie looked at his watch for the first time. He paced around the room. Half an hour later, he left it.

Their car was still in the car park. This did not make sense. She took the keys. They were in her jacket pocket, he thought.

The supermarket is down the road, so she wouldn't have walked — not if she wanted to get some shopping to take home.

Eddie left the car and walked to the supermarket, hoping he would meet her on her way back. After walking along the end of each aisle in the shop, Eddie began to panic. He raced back to the hotel, and stopped at the reception desk to ask the woman behind the counter, "Strange question, I know, but did you see my wife leave about two hours ago?"

"Yes, she said she had forgotten her toothbrush. There's a supermarket down the road. She headed for the car park."

Eddie thanked her and walked through the main entrance of the hotel. First, back to the car park and then to the pub connected to the hotel. Lucy was nowhere to be seen. He checked his watch. Two and a half hours had passed.

Eddie returned to their hotel room. He saw Lucy had taken her purse, but her phone was still in her bag. He paced some more. It was now past six o'clock. She would want a shower before going out. It made no sense.

"Is that Ian?" Eddie's hand was shaking while holding his phone.

"Yes. Eddie?"

"Something has happened to Lucy. I think I'm in a bit of trouble here."

In his softest tone, Gale asked, "Can you tell me what has happened?"

Eddie detailed events. It helped settle his nerves.

"It will take me about three hours to get to you, but I will come straight away. Hopefully, she will show up in the meantime. I'm sure there will be a simple explanation."

"You don't need to worry about driving up here."

"It's no problem. I am already outside Portsmouth, and I have plenty to talk to you about, anyway."

Gale did not mention to Eddie that he would call the local hospitals during the drive.

Eddie thanked him and put the phone in his pocket.

Lucy was too busy admonishing herself to be frightened. How had she allowed it to happen? Someone had shoved her from the side and into a van. Maybe she could not have prevented that — the pusher was a big man. But what about the cable tie? Her fists had been yanked in front, and the plastic tie was secured around her wrists while she was fully aware of what was happening. She could have prevented that.

She could make out shapes through what she thought may have been a pillowcase, but all she could see was the back of the passenger's seat and someone with long hair in the driver's seat. Her legs were secured beneath the arms of one person, her head in another's lap, stretched like a retriever over its two owners on the back seat. They were large men. She tried to move once again, but this only increased the pressure of arms keeping her in place. At first, she had concentrated on external noises. She had heard fast-moving traffic. They had travelled over a short series of speed bumps. There was a siren. But there was no hope of remembering a route. She could not even recall how long they had been travelling. After seven minutes, Lucy no longer knew whether she had counted out three hundred and sixty seconds or four hundred and twenty. She did, however, notice that it had been quiet for some time — no outside noise. The only noise inside the van was the muffled sounds of the van changing gear. Nobody was speaking.

It was then that she felt a knot of fear in her stomach.

Eddie could not sit still and wait. He composed himself and went back to the car park to see if there was any sort of sign of Lucy's disappearance. Her purse, anything. If she had been taken, it might have been on the ground somewhere. It was secluded and quiet. He used the car park lamp light to look around their car and then the neighbouring vehicles.

He opened the car door with his spare key and sat on the driver's seat with his legs outside. His eyes welled before a tear burst through an eyelash emboldened dam. He felt limp, weak as if energy had been siphoned from his body. He made himself breathe slowly, but the cycle of emotions continued as the sky darkened further towards night. He felt the wintry coldness descend as his cheeks burned from the rivulet of tears. He swung his legs inside the car and closed the door. He did not know how long he had sat there as he bashed his head against his headrest and squeezed his eyes shut. Not again. Not Lucy. Eddie thought about the circle of grief as his emotions turned to anger. This had now finally gone too far. He wanted to cause severe damage to whoever had taken Lucy and then abandon this stupid game.

He dialled Ian Gale's number once again. Gale answered immediately and explained he was still about an hour away.

Eddie decided it was time to fully explain how they had got to this point. Gale was unsurprised by the revelation about the package and the stone. He was just happy to keep Eddie talking. It would eat up time before he got there. He was amused by the York Gate renovation tale and a little envious of the expensive Champagne. He told Eddie about Garvan, his war record, and his sick son. He even made Eddie laugh a couple of times. The conversation was concluding when Gale pulled into the hotel's parking lot.

It could have been fifteen minutes. It could have been thirty when the journey came to an end on what Lucy assumed was a short gravel track. No one had spoken throughout the trip, and no one spoke now, but Lucy was aware there were three people in the van, two in the back with her, and a driver. She felt a man release her legs, leave the vehicle, and pull her out by the ankles. She was encouraged to sit upright and step down from the van. Someone had their hand on the top of her head.

When all three doors had been closed, she heard a creak of what sounded like a large wooden door. Hands grabbed her under her armpits and led her towards the sound. A small directional light came on, and she instinctively shifted her head towards its beam.

"Did those pillowcases come in a pack of two?" a man's voice asked.

"Yes," said another man's voice.

"Well, I suggest you place the other one over her head. She can see," he added, "And sit her down, there."

The aroma revealed a probable location. Farm animals. She was in a rural building or a barn. She went to move but was brought to a stop. Pressure on her shoulders sat her down on a spiky surface. It was a hay bail — a barn. Someone placed a second pillowcase over the first one.

In as calm a voice as she could muster, Lucy spoke for the first time. "Where am I? What is this about?" she went to stand but was forcibly pushed back onto her seat once again.

The man that had asked about the pillowcases replied, "I am sorry we have had to do this. You are not in any danger. The reason we have covered your face is so that you cannot see us. Someone is coming that wants to ask a few questions. Once you have answered, we will leave and text Eddie to let him know where you are."

Confusion spread across Lucy's face. She did not feel afraid. Maybe because the man's voice was composed and reasonable. Neither was there uncertainty to play with her emotions. He had mentioned Eddie.

It was obvious what they wanted to ask about.

"You just wanted to keep me talking, didn't you?"

Gale held out a hand to shake. "Yes, pretty much, but I like an adventure story. I could tell you were in a bit of a state, so I hope it helped. I saw there was a pub next door. Let's go and have a drink and talk about what we know."

As they walked, Gale added, "At some stage, Lucy will tell them what they want to learn, and they will let her go. It cannot be so serious that they would harm her."

Eddie looked through puffy red eyes at Gale. "It's not as simple as that."

"What do you mean?"

"Lucy won't tell them anything. And she will want to hurt the people that have taken her before she leaves. That could lead to her getting hurt herself."

"I am sure it won't come to that. I think they just want to know what you have been up to. It can't possibly be anything serious," Gale hoped he had struck the right tone to mollify Eddie. He was well aware that whatever it was they were mixed up in, Owen Garvan had been murdered over it. He had hoped he could keep that news from Eddie until Lucy was safe, but he would have to get the local police involved if they left it much longer.

Gale returned from the bar with two pints of lager. He placed one in front of Eddie and took a large gulp of his own.

Eddie looked up from the table at Gale. "I think I have taken this as far as it can go now. I just want to make sure Lucy is safe."

"I understand, but I am afraid this has gone beyond that now. Eddie, I wasn't going to tell you this, but I think we should work together on whatever this is. We need to share everything we know so we can get Lucy back safely. I am a policeman, don't forget. I can make some calls, and Cambridgeshire Constabulary will be straight on this. You have filled me in with what you know, so I should tell you that I was at a murder scene yesterday," Gale paused to make sure he had Eddie's full attention. "It was Owen Garvan. He had his throat slit."

Eddie felt a tingle of sweat flash through his body. He knew the colour had drained from his face.

Gale quickly filled the void. "This can't have anything to do with Lucy."

Eddie stammered, almost inaudibly, "How can you know that?"

"I presume you didn't tell anyone you were coming to Cambridge?"

"No."

"Well, the murder took place in Southsea in the last forty-eight hours or so. Whoever the perpetrator is would be dealing with the aftermath. Deadly assassins with elaborate plans are usually just for the movies. So, if no one knew you were coming to Cambridge, they would have to have an incredible level of clairvoyance, as well as master assassin planning skills."

Eddie said, "I suppose."

"That does not mean to say it is not connected, but even that would mean a network of people involved in something big."

Eddie's attention drifted from Gale to his phone. If he stared at it long enough, Lucy would call. "Was our wedding tin there?"

Gale took a little time to register the question. "The Quality Street tin?"

"Yes."

"I didn't go inside. I could smell the corpse, so I called the station. I did not want to contaminate the crime scene, so I left it for my DI. All I could see was his legs behind the table by the window, which had a pile of books and a Dremel on it."

Eddie asked, "A Dremel?"

"Yes, You know, one of those multi-tool gadgets."

"Did you see what fitting was attached?"

Gale said, "Sorry, I don't know anything about them. I'm not very good at that sort of thing," Gale closed his eyes, "Maybe a small triangular bit. It is a bit, isn't it?"

"Did you see if it had an abrasive surface like sandpaper?"

"Sorry, no. Where are you going with this?"

Eddie replied, "I know why Garvan wanted the stone."

34

After what seemed an eternity of silence, broken only by tapping on phones, muffled shuffling of feet on earthy ground, and the occasional sigh of boredom, Lucy heard another vehicle pull up onto the gravel drive.

The door creaked once again, and she heard a suppressed discussion outside. She tried to rise once more but was pushed down again. The door made its noise. She thought she heard two sets of footsteps on crunching straw.

"I am sorry to do this, Miss Brisley. But it appears your friend and yourself have been obstructing our ambitions."

Lucy cocked her head. The voice sounded familiar.

The voice continued, "We have been researching for several years and have never come across additional pursuers until now. We would like to learn how you know about the stones, and perhaps more importantly, how you knew where to look for them?"

Lucy asked, "James McAllister?"

There was silence for a short period before she heard movement. The door again. More than one person left. Lucy attempted to stand yet again. This time she was unimpeded. She raised her hands above her head, and with one swift movement downward and away from her body, the cable tie snapped. She reached up to pull the pillowcases from her head.

Lucy attempted to assess her surroundings. Quickly. Blurry imagery revealed a large man running towards her from the barn entrance. Instinct took over. Over a decade's worth of training prompted natural movement without thought. Right leg back a few inches, knees flexed. She made a loose fist she would not use. The man approached in the dim light. Although it all happened in a split second, she saw the beam was coming from a phone's torch propped on a hay bale. She also saw the man was thick-set, shaven-headed, and around six feet tall. This was good.

Her height deficit provided the leverage as she strode forward with her right foot and rose from her thigh before thrusting her shoulder through her forearm, delivering it as a blade across the man's throat in an upwards diagonal motion. There was a crunch as she caught the angle of his jaw. The man's head snapped back. She instantly knew she had missed. Not her target — connecting with her target was inevitable. But his throat. He immediately collapsed to his knees and grasped at his misaligned mandible. Lucy did not look back as she raced towards the door, but knew she had not crushed his windpipe. He would live.

She stretched her hands and pushed at the barn door. A shudder burst through her shoulders as she was halted in her tracks. But the door opened sufficiently for her to squeeze through. She saw a second large man falling backwards from the impact. Two other people were standing by a car's bright headlights. Blackness stretched out ahead in the other direction, backlit from the glow — a field.

Lucy set off, and although she could hear rapid footsteps slurping in the muddy and rutted clearing, she had no intention of slowing to look behind. She stumbled in a furrow and found it easier to run in a straight line through the space between the two raised mounds of earth, while pumping her legs as fast as possible. The new route was at an angle rather than directly opposed to the direction she had run, but the wide groove enabled steady footing, and she had covered a reasonable distance before she risked a momentary glance behind.

No one was following.

Slowing to turn, Lucy saw two silhouettes in front of car headlights, including James McAllister. She would recognise him anywhere. Two others, including a chunky woman with her hair tied back, were trudging slowly through the sodden field, towards the two vehicles. Lucy was not struggling for breath. Pleased her fitness was holding up under duress, she set off again.

A tree line appeared ahead. Lucy paused. She did not want to run into woods within which she could get lost. She stopped and turned once more. The four people were still visible, but barely. If they could see her, it would only be from the moonlight flashing in and out of dark clouds. She headed to the trees for sanctuary. This would give her time to decide where to go from there. She looked up to the moon as clouds headed towards it. The darkness would help. She hoped.

As she entered the woods, she stopped to look behind and to the tree to her left. What was she doing? How could she allocate this tree as a marker point? She just had to hope she could walk in a straight line.

She stared ahead for the first time. Was that a light? She tried to focus and took one more glance behind before walking forwards. It was a light. And not too far away.

Less than two minutes later, having stumbled through a

small copse of closely knotted trees rather than the dense woods she had expected, Lucy emerged from the darkness to another road. The light was to her right.

It was a house with an outside lamp glowing brightly. She assessed the distance to be no more than two hundred feet. She looked back again. It was a good job the wooded area did not stretch any further, she could have ended up walking in circles. It was a small farmer's cottage. She looked around and stopped breathing, begging for noise to react to. She assessed her surroundings. There were more outbuildings ahead, and a little further along from that, there appeared to be another two cottages, maybe more.

Lucy deliberated over what she would say, and after banishing hysterical thoughts, she inhaled and pressed the doorbell.

She held her breath until a light illuminated the hallway, and a man approached the door. She could make out grey hair behind the frosted glass panel.

"Who is it? Do you know what time it is?"

Lucy quickly replied, "Yes, I know. I've come out for a run, but I've lost my phone. I don't expect you to open the door, but I was hoping you could call my husband to ask him to pick me up," she held her breath once again. She was not as good at lying as Eddie.

The man stepped away from the door. Lucy's shoulders dropped. She was about to ring the bell again when the man returned. "What's his number?"

Lucy let out a sigh of relief. She slowly told the man Eddie's number as she listened to him tap the keys on his phone. "Can you just tell him the road I am on, please? And I will continue my run. He can pick me up on the way."

The man completed the inaudible call and returned to the door. He opened it to the full stretch of the chain and said, "He sounded very agitated. You must have been out for a long time," he looked at her from feet upwards. "Funny running clothes."

Lucy was wearing muddy trainers, workout leggings and a down jacket.

"It's a bit cold. It's a lightweight running jacket."

"Your husband said he would come straight away," the man closed the door without saying anything further.

Lucy watched as the exterior light dimmed to darkness before walking away from the house and heading towards the outbuildings ahead. She was aware the people from the barn knew where she had headed and wanted to ensure they could not find her. However unlikely it was that the man would answer the door again if they knocked.

35

Eddie pressed the icon on his phone and closed his eyes. "She's safe," he stood and looked down at Ian Gale. "We need to pick her up. You drive. I will look up the road names as we go."

Gale stood as Eddie was already halfway through the pub door.

"Come on, Ian, let's go."

Gale smiled. Eddie knew he was going as fast as he could.

Eddie slowly breathed in and out, sucking in the icy air as he composed himself. "So, getting back to what we were talking about."

"Why Garvan wanted the stone."

"After I told you Garvan had visited Lucy's mum's jewellers in town, she phoned me to say he wanted to get a crevice smoothed out of a stone," he saw the confusion on Gale's face and continued, "I had taken the original stone into the store to see what it was. I thought it was a ruby at first, but although Jean said it wasn't, she didn't know what it was. Anyway, I think he was scraping the stone with the Dremel and wanted it smoothed out. There will be a buffer attachment in the box, but maybe he wasn't confident enough to use it. They are tricky gadgets."

"And why do you think he was scraping the stone?"

"I think he might have bought into the whole eternal life business."

"You are right."

Eddie adopted Gale's earlier confusion. "Am I?"

"Definitely. I saw debris in a small contact lens pot. He must have put the filings from the stone into the pot and filled it with saline solution. His son has an incurable disease, and he must have thought this would treat him. So, the remaining unanswered question is, why would he bother smoothing the stone out?" Gale asked, but knew the answer.

Eddie looked blankly until a switch flicked. "He had promised the stone to someone else."

"I would certainly say something like that," Gale stared at Eddie. "I would guess his murderer would know more."

Ian Gale found the road. The journey had taken less than twenty minutes. It was a long connector, between two A-roads outside Cambridge, on the way to Oxford. There were no other vehicles. They slowed to a crawl to look for Lucy. The sky rewarded them with light and darkness in equal measure as the moon dodged in and out of the clouds, but no one appeared in the headlight glare, even while driving at snail's pace.

Lucy saw the illumination of a vehicle. It was moving slowly towards her, so she ducked beside the wooden structure and watched as it approached. It was not her car — the headlights were different. She peered around the farm outbuilding as it passed. She did not recognise the driver, and she could not see the passenger clearly.

No hang on — there was a spark of recognition, but the car was now well down the road. The red glow of the rear lights could not hide the colour of the car — it was white. The badge revealed the make and model of a car she had previously seen outside her house. She watched as it disappeared around a corner of the field.

"We need to turn back and look again," Eddie sputtered. He was moving his head from side to side, looking out the front and back in quick succession.

Gale slowed to turn at a verge and repeated the same journey. They drove past attached cottages and some farm outbuildings. He saw movement in his rear-view mirror. A woman appeared to be doing jumping jacks in the middle of the road. "There she is."

Eddie swung his head around. He felt adrenaline wash through his body. Gale backed onto a well-worn drive-off area in a gap between some bushes. Before he had come to a complete stop, Eddie had opened the door. He sprinted to Lucy.

Lucy held him tight before releasing and then pushing him away. "I am fuming."

Eddie was about to say something when she continued, "I want to find the bastards and kick the crap out of them."

As Gale walked towards Eddie and Lucy, he asked, "Are you okay?"

Lucy said, "I am fine. I need a shower," she rubbed her sore wrists before adding, "You are the police. I hope you find them before I do."

Lucy left Eddie and Gale standing there as she marched off to the car. She opened the back door, got in and closed it.

Gale said to Eddie, "I don't think she's very happy."

Eddie woke with a start. He turned his head. It was okay —

she was safe. He wrapped his arm over her shoulder and clutched her hands.

"Eddie."

"Yes. What can I get you?"

"Another ten minutes of sleep would be nice."

They showered together as they swapped versions of events. Eddie did not want to stop talking to her. He explained his panic, his full appraisal of proceedings to Ian Gale, the trip to the supermarket, and the journey to the fields.

"Eddie."

"Yes?"

"I am getting dressed."

"Sorry," Eddie turned to pack his bag but took another glance as she fastened her bra.

Gale stood when Eddie and Lucy arrived for breakfast.

Lucy said, "Very gentlemanly of you, Ian. Thank you, and thanks once again for coming."

Gale nodded as he retook his seat. "No problem. Did you see the news this morning?"

Eddie and Lucy looked at each other and smiled. Gale knew what they were smiling about — he was a detective, after all. "Never mind. Anyway, it appears that there was a car accident last night. It said on the local news that a man had died when a car crashed into a farm outbuilding," he added a question, "Guess where?"

Lucy nodded and replied, "On a road very near to where you picked me up from?"

"Yes."

Lucy asked, "Did they provide the name of the victim?"

"No. It was in the traffic and travel bulletin, but I made a couple of calls this morning. The victim's name is James McAllister."

Lucy's expression was impassive. "Good."

Eddie had remained silent during this exchange but then said, "No. Not good. It wasn't an accident, was it, Ian?"

"It has been recorded as an accident."

"What do you think?"

"It seems a little coincidental. There was no traffic, and the road we were on didn't seem to be overrun with large wildlife to avoid. It's just fields in that area. If it was not an accident, I can't say how the crash was manufactured without seeing the report."

Lucy looked at Eddie and then at Ian Gale. "So, what does this mean?"

Eddie replied, "It means it's over. We're out of this now. There have been murders, or at least, very suspicious deaths, and I am not risking anything happening to you again."

Gale looked at them both in turn. His mouth twitched before he spoke. "I'm afraid it's not quite as simple as that. This has escalated beyond what you could have imagined when you started following the clues on that book, and don't forget," he paused before adding, "They, whoever they are, know where you live."

36

Robert Wilson stared at his new Adidas Gazelles in the full-length mirror. The clean white trainers and their three red stripes matched up well with his indigo jeans. He preferred the casual look of this character over the suited version during the hunt for the previous stone.

He pressed the word 'Tower' from his contact list.

The call was answered quickly, despite the late hour. "Do you know what time it is?"

"Yes. I have some news you should hear."

"Go on."

"Earlier today, I received a call from James McAllister at the Ashmolean who wanted me to talk to Eddie Hill."

Wilson continued to explain events accurately but was careful to omit the part where he unlatched McAllister's seatbelt with one hand while simultaneously steering the wheel into the direction of a farm outbuilding. He knew it was risking his own safety, but the priority was to ensure McAllister did not walk away. Neither did he mention the conversation he had earlier enjoyed with his victim that revealed the Cayman Islands account with the freshly deposited three million pounds. From which McAllister was expecting to withdraw a 'scopious and plenitudinous retirement'. He smiled as he recalled using the recently deceased McAllister's finger to access his phone and the account. Seriously, who would leave their bank access details on a piece of paper in their wallet?

There was a short silence at the other end of the line. "That all sounds very convenient for you. You were asked to learn the information we need. How do I know you didn't create this mess?"

"I did not know Lucy Brisley knew James' voice. He was stupid. He is now dead. What difference does it make?"

"James McAllister had provided our organisation with four stones—"

"I instigated the recovery of one of those stones."

"Indeed, you did, but you reported into James, and it was he that revealed its whereabouts, did he not?"

Bravado halted, he said, "Yes, but. . ." he stopped, thinking better of pursuing the matter further.

"You had two tasks in the pursuit of the Buckingham stone, and you have failed at both. I suggest you learn what Mr Hill knows immediately and then come along for a chat about where we go from here."

Before the call ended, he was already considering his options. Leave now with the money or see what he could get for another stone. He smiled once again. He knew it should be easier for him to get the additional stone than most.

The building, made from corrugated steel rather than stone, was erected by cranes and large industrial machinery rather than by craftsmen with bare hands. The space was now completely furnished with all the equipment required. There were flasks, beakers, and dishes, along with the crucible, of course, but these too were machine-made rather than hand blown or crafted by the experts of days long past. The athanor was most similar in construction. Although once made of brick, stone or hand bashed copper, it was now a specifically designed and expensive piece of steel equipment that looked similar to a restaurant range oven.

Elysia Martin closed the door behind her. She stopped to scan her gaze across the mostly idle equipment. It had cost her sponsors a lot of money to put together. It had also taken many years of propagandising — and thousands of well-rehearsed conversations — to reach this point.

She had orchestrated a mysticism around the seventeenth century stones — the world's greatest ever minds assembled at a time, and period of history, to achieve their successes with mutual dedication and application. None before or since had been so successful in joint efforts to achieve the philosopher's stone. Once their journey was complete, they all quickly became aware of the disruption their success could cause, and the stones were hidden from public knowledge. Until now. Martin looked directly at her very own adept, Jason Price. A modern version of one, anyway.

The laboratory felt the encroaching chill of winter as the steel made occasional squeals from contracting panels. Her adept was full-on Arctic with several layers covering his wire-thin frame. She saw the bottom of his full sleeve of tattoos poking from the end of his fleece. The black ink lines were still pristine. Probably from a lack of exposure to the sun. Perhaps he spent most of his time in a snooker hall, avoiding natural light at all costs.

He did not look in her direction but said, "I wasn't expecting you today."

"I like to make unannounced appearances to make sure you

are doing what I have paid for."

"Well, as you can see, I am."

"Did the packaging arrive?"

Price stopped work on the clamp he was tightening between two glass pipes. He wheeled his chair backwards before dragging a cardboard box from beneath a steel preparation table. It was one of six of the same size. He made a show of effort before Martin pushed his hand away and hefted a box onto a clear area of surface.

She looked around and asked for a knife. Price walked over to a makeshift desk that looked out of place amongst the steel and glass of the laboratory. A sheet of chipboard had been positioned on top of aged carved dark wood legs. He pulled a thin yellow paperknife from a stationery filled mug and handed it to Martin.

Martin sliced through the tape to reveal a large polystyrene cube. Price held the box as she slid the interior package from its housing. He shoved the empty box to the floor so Martin could place the cube on the steel surface. She cut through the tape, securing the two polystyrene halves, and gently removed the top section. Additional plastic wrapping secured the small boxes within. While combining with the other boxes, she had a quick tot up. There would be around eight rows and eight columns between them — five hundred and twelve small boxes. She removed one and stroked the red cross inlay on the top of the dark wooden surface. She looked over at the desk and smiled. Each box had been hand-crafted from the desktop. The quality of craftsmanship was extraordinary. Each was a one-inch square cube. She gently prised the two halves apart to reveal padded white silk. "Perfect."

DI Spears took a deep breath and dialled the number.

"This is Bill Gray."

"Yes, hello. This is DI Spears from Hampshire

Constabulary."

"How can I help Detective Inspector?"

Spears replied, "Given your position, I am calling as a courtesy," he paused for recognition of this fact. It was not forthcoming. "I am afraid I have some rather grave news," a further pause, within which Gray still failed to fill the silence, so Spears continued once again, "Following on from our investigation into your former colleague's death. The chief suspect has also been murdered. Name, Owen Garvan. Do you know him?"

Gray slid the wheels of his chair backwards as he sat upright. "No. Sorry. Do you have any suspects?"

"I am afraid I cannot go into details, but our investigation will be thorough. We do not generally experience crimes of this nature in Portsmouth."

"Is Mr Hill a suspect?"

"Not at this stage. Please accept my apologies. I am sure you can appreciate I am unable to discuss the investigation."

Gray replied, "Of course. I understand. But I can assure you that Mr Hill can be eliminated from your investigations and thank you for informing me of Mr Garvan's death. I will let you know if we learn anything here."

After the call ended, Spears wondered why Gray would know anything of Mr Hill? And for that matter, "How did he learn about my investigation?" he said out loud.

Gray replaced the handset and looked towards his colleague John Jackson, "It appears the man that killed Ken is also now dead."

Jackson asked, "From what I could hear of your conversation, I gather they do not have a suspect?"

"No. It also appears that this would rule out Mr Hill, which is good," Gray looked at the Quality Street tin on his desk.

Changing the subject, Jackson asked, "What do you think

he is up to?"

"Hill?"

"Yes."

"You know what? I have been thinking about that. While we have been tracking his movements at a distance and know Hill has visited Oxford, Cambridge, and Windsor over the course of a week, he doesn't seem to be any nearer to visiting us. Despite the invite," Gray rose from his chair and walked over to the small window in the stone wall. He wiped the precipitation from the cold glass.

Jackson asked again, "So, what do you think?"

"The most obvious conclusion is that he is looking into higher education and is buttering up his wife to be with a fancy weekend break."

"Really?"

"Possibly," Gray said, "It could also be that Hill knows something we don't. Which is why I think we should still keep an eye on him. Michael will continue to check on his approximate movements," he continued to stare through the pane. "And if he doesn't come to us for his tin, we will have to prompt him once again."

Gray wiped the water from his hand with a handkerchief and watched as Elysia Martin walked past. She had a large cardboard box in her arms.

37

Ian Gale placed a sandwich and a roll of black sacks on his back seat. He drove from the petrol pump to the small waiting area by the car wash. He returned to the back seat and began scooping up his trash before walking to the recycling section and lifting the lid on the black household rubbish bin. As the blue brushes whirred and clattered against his windscreen, Gale pondered what he had learned. Not the heritage organisations, not Regal Portfolio Properties, but a subsidiary indirectly related to them. It was both tenuous and complicated. But did it matter? He had already eliminated the importance of being involved in the official investigation — someone would soon notice the 'dentist' appointments. What might matter is who was carrying out the refurbishment work. It was the same company involved with similar projects, mainly across south-east England — pubs, hotels, the occasional residential home. All were historic properties. Rose Cross Developments Ltd.

had been trading for eighty-six years, yet its accounts were sporadic. Some years there was nothing filed. This year, the building Eddie and Jamie were working on was its third property.

After researching *Ye Spotted Dogge*, he had learned it was once called *The Greyhound* and was more generally known as Buckingham House. It had enjoyed a variety of owners throughout its near six-hundred-year history, including the man that founded New Hampshire in the United States, but he was unable to find a connection. There was no reason to doubt the house clearance possibility. What was more interesting to Gale was the company Eddie and Jamie were working for featured two names filed as directors with Companies House who had both died in open yet unrelated investigations fourteen months earlier.

He pulled into a space outside Eddie and Lucy's house. He looked around at the cars and homes that he now recognised. He had spent more time sitting outside Eddie Hill's house than inside his own apartment recently. He pulled back the triangular sandwich packaging and picked up his notebook. He had agreed to use the research and database facilities that were unavailable to Eddie to learn about Rosicrucianism. A piece of tomato with bacon attached slid out on a bed of mayonnaise onto his pad. His mum was right — he was a slob. He cleared the mess away and focussed on his notes.

In all, nine people had worked on the project so far. All filed individual accounts as self-employed sole trader businesses. Nothing else stood out. Another dead end. He turned the page, rested the pad on his lap, and opened his crisps. The notes related to James McAllister, the newly deceased tour guide. He lived in Oxford, but his name was on a warehouse lease on an industrial estate in East London and on another property's lease in the City of London. He would have to look into that.

Gale screwed up his now empty crisps bag and threw it on the back seat. He then placed his pad on the passenger seat and got out of the car. He opened the back door and unrolled another black sack. He picked his empty crisps bag up from the floor and included it along with his other empty lunch packaging inside.

He retook his seat in the front — what was he doing here, anyway? It was the wrong house. He had advised Eddie to stay with Jamie.

After driving the short distance via roads he was now all too familiar with, Gale pressed the doorbell. Jamie opened the door. Gale saw he was wearing a baseball cap to cover the stitches.

"Hello, mate. Come in."

"Thank you. How's the head?"

Jamie removed his cap. "Not too bad, but they've ruined my hair," he lowered his head to reveal the stitches and added, "I don't think I thanked you. If it wasn't for you, I don't know how long I might have been lying there."

"No problem. All part of the job."

Jamie offered Gale a mug of tea, which he gratefully accepted.

"Pleased you're getting better. I was going to ask Eddie how you were when I saw him. Is he about?"

"No, I'm on my own and getting bored stiff. There's only so much daytime TV I can put up with. Jamie is working away again, Lucy has gone back to work, and Eddie is getting materials for a boiler fit. I'm going back to work next week. I've had enough of this."

Gale replied, "It's good that everyone is getting back to normal. I want to clear this up so Eddie and Lucy can go back home. I am a bit more answerable now others have been brought in on the case."

"I like having them here. We always have a laugh. What about you? Have you found out anything new?"

"I've learned the company you are working for is called Rose Cross Developments Ltd., and they carry out similar projects to the one you are involved with."

Jamie said, "Yes, I know. My pay gets put in with that as the deposit name," he placed Gale's tea on a mat in front of him.

Gale raised his eyebrows. He could have just asked.

Jamie added, "It's funny. I thought of that when that bald guy came flying at me. He had a gold pinkie ring that had a red cross on it."

"That's interesting. Garvan must have been one of these Rosicrucians," Gale took a sip of the hot tea and stood up. "That's new information for me. It looks like I will have to get back to the station and do some more research. Can you get Eddie to give me a call when he has a minute?"

Eddie asked, "Did you know this is the oldest building in Gunwharf Quays?"

"Yes, it used to be a naval administration building," Lucy replied with a smile. "Don't turn into a history bore, Eddie."

"You wait till I tell you about different rope knots and the period features," he gestured towards the double staircase separating the reception area and spread his arms wide as if opening theatre curtains.

He had an irritating ability to make Lucy laugh at will. While smirking, she said, "I've only got about an hour, so we should order, and you can tell me what's new this morning?"

"Well, I have bought the boiler for that job, and I've got all the pipework and fittings. So I'm ready to go. I will probably pop around there Thursday to start," Eddie pulled his chair out and walked to the bar. He returned and placed a glass in front of Lucy. He supped the top third of his beer before sitting back down. Lucy watched as the bubbles popped to the top of her glass.

"What's up?" Eddie asked.

"I've been thinking about our Cambridge experience," she rubbed her wrists. Slight bruising surrounded the still visible mark by her watch. "It was pointless."

"I know. I was thinking the same. I think we. . . Well I, got carried away with our success. If the stone was still at Cambridge University, it would be in some dusty old archive box or something. Even if someone hid it in a secret compartment of the Chancellor's office, or wherever Isaac Newton's study was, it would have been long gone."

Lucy reached into her bag and placed a stapled four-page document on the table. "I found this on the internet this morning."

Eddie turned it towards him. "What is it?"

"A South African scientific study into the whereabouts of Isaac Newton's lab."

"That's interesting."

"No. It's not. In fact, it highlights what we were up against. They were not allowed to dig up the gardens. We were right by the way — it was where the lawn now runs, inside Trinity Gate. The gardens must be of significance because the researchers were only allowed to take soil samples to guess where his lab might have been."

A waitress placed their food on the table and asked, "Would you like any condiments?"

"No, thanks, this is fine," Eddie replied, eager to continue the conversation. He pushed the sandwich to one side and looked more closely at the document.

Lucy picked up the sheets of paper and folded them in half. "I only printed it to highlight how pointless our visit was. I think we had it right. The stone would have been somewhere related to the Duke of Monmouth and was probably Isaac

Newton's. I even wondered whether our friend George might have been behind the famous lab fire blamed on Newton's dog, but the timeline didn't work."

Eddie adopted Lucy's line of conversation. "I agree, I was thinking the same thing. If the stone did exist, and our clue did lead us to the right place, there's no way we could have found it."

Lucy crunched on her salad leaves and pushed the coated chicken around the plate. "The problem is, Ian is also right. People are aware we are on a trail. They just don't know what trail, so they will want to find out."

"I know we agreed to go back to work and leave this, but apart from collecting heating parts this morning, I have also been doing some thinking."

"And?"

"We need to solve the next clue."

"I agree. Now, pucker up, big boy," Lucy pushed her plate to one side and rose from her chair. Placing her hands on either side of Eddie's face, she kissed him on the lips and picked up her bag.

"Aren't you finishing your lunch?"

"I'm running a bit late. I need to get back to work. And you need to solve that final clue."

Eddie watched as the double doors swung shut. He lifted Lucy's plate onto his and grabbed her fork.

"My Home from Home – Returned to He Whoe. . ." he said to no-one. He heard the munch of salad leaves as he thought. George Villiers' homes included Cliveden, which they had visited, and York House, along with a couple of other long since demolished or replaced London buildings. He switched his focus to Trinity College, Cambridge. That was also a dead-end.

He drained the remaining beer from his glass and zipped his jacket to the top. He left the pub and walked over to the railing overlooking the short canal leading to the Solent. He placed his hands on the steel balustrade before quickly removing them. It was getting colder.

Paris.

George also lived in Paris. Maybe they should go there.

Eddie placed the supermarket bags on the kitchen work surface. "I'll make dinner."

"You don't have to do that," Jamie said as he grabbed the TV remote control and crossed his feet on the coffee table.

Eddie slowly shook his head. "Curry, okay?"

"Yes, hang on. I'll be out to give you a hand in a sec."

Eddie opened the fridge and reached inside. "Beer?"

"I shouldn't really. I'm not even halfway through my antibiotics," Jamie took the bottle opener from Eddie's outstretched hand. He popped the cap off and watched as it flew into the bowl in the centre of the table.

Eddie returned to the kitchen. "It's okay. You sit there. I'm all right out here."

Eddie pulled two onions from the bag and cut both ends off. After cutting them in half, he sliced and chopped.

"So, did you do that research I asked you to do?"

Eddie turned to repeat himself. Jamie was standing at the kitchen's entrance, leaning against the door frame.

"I did, as it happens. Aside from London, George lived in two places in Yorkshire. Fairfax House, which was the home of his father-in-law, where George made his marital home. He was a right rascal, you know."

Eddie said, "I know. George only married the daughter to regain the property that was previously his after it was given to Fairfax during the Civil War."

Jamie said, "So Fairfax House and Helmsley Castle, which was his mum's house. Or, his mum's castle, as it were. Although this was left half-derelict after the Civil War."

"Anywhere else?"

"No. The only other place that could be a possibility is York Cathedral, where George replaced the spire."

"Is it still there?"

"No. The cathedral has undergone a lot of changes over the centuries, and don't forget a fire did a lot of damage a few years ago."

"So, what's your best guess?"

"To be frank, I don't think any of them are of any use. As I said, Helmsley is half derelict, and although it is now a tourist place, the artefacts are few and far between. If anything were hidden, it would be long gone. I thought a better bet would be Fairfax House. It has even been left abandoned by its current owner."

Eddie placed the knife on the chopping board. "Now, that sounds promising."

"Sadly not. I was thinking the same, but I found some old photos, and the property doesn't look anything like it did during George's time. I suppose the stone could be hidden somewhere else in its grounds. Some of the trees appear to be original."

The tin opener slid as Eddie tried to open the tomatoes. Juice seeped out as he struggled. "We could take a metal detector up there, I suppose."

"It's a glass stone, Eddie."

"It looks like glass, but it might have mercury in it which could show up. I've never used a metal detector, but the keyword is metal," Eddie looked over at Jamie as confusion spread across his face. "It doesn't matter anyway. I don't think Lucy would buy the idea of me breaking into an abandoned property and treasure hunting over acres of land until I might or might not find a philosopher's stone," Eddie used a wooden spoon to stir the now sizzling onions. "No, it's not in Yorkshire. I'm missing something."

38

Lucy woke and immediately cupped her forehead. They had to go back home. Jamie would turn every night into a booze-up if they stayed. She elevated herself to see the alarm clock on Eddie's side of the bed. Go home to get another alarm clock for her side of the bed, at least.

As the fug cleared, she saw a folded piece of paper by her water glass. She opened the note. What does he mean? 'Will be back tonight. Have a good day at work'.

Lucy grabbed her phone and called.

No answer.

Jamie was in the kitchen when Lucy strode downstairs. "Jamie, do you know where Eddie is?"

"Morning to you as well, sunshine," he replied as he dropped a teabag onto the kitchen worktop. He handed a mug to Lucy.

"Sorry. Morning Jamie. Do you know where Eddie is?"

"London."

"What do you mean, London?"

"He was creeping out as I got up this morning. I asked where he was going. He said London, and he would be back tonight."

Lucy placed her hands on her hips. "And that was it?"

"Yes, pretty much. He said he left you a note."

Lucy raised her eyebrows. "And what do you think he has gone to London for?"

"Oh. I see what you're getting at. He's following the next clue, isn't he?"

"Do ya think?" Lucy turned abruptly. "Okay. I'm getting dressed. We're going to call Ian Gale, and then we are going to London."

"Are we?"

"Yes, we are. I am not having that idiot get himself into more trouble by trying to keep me out of trouble."

Jamie's phone pinged. "That will be Eddie," he pressed the icon. "No, it's okay. It's just the project manager. He wants to meet up at the site tomorrow to discuss the job."

Lucy clunked the seatbelt in its latch and looked across to Jamie, who was staring back. "So?"

Jamie replied, "So, what?"

"Where are we going?"

"How do I know?"

Lucy leaned back and supported her head on the seat rest.

Jamie said, "It's going to take a couple of hours. We can work it out on the way. I will keep calling him as well."

"Have you heard back from Ian Gale yet?"

"It's just gone seven in the morning, and I only sent the text fifteen minutes ago."

They drove in silence. Jamie was paying more attention to his phone than Lucy was to the road, as she took evasive action to avoid a parked car.

Jamie said, "Your friend George certainly had an interesting life. I am looking at places in London he would have spent some time, whether that would be living or enjoying a period in history where, well, let's just say, anything went."

"What have you found so far?"

"That we are not very good at preserving our history in this country."

Lucy glared at Jamie from the driver's seat.

"Well, there are hardly any buildings remaining from the seventeenth century. And many of those that do still exist have changed. If Eddie is looking for a stone, chances are it's been moved."

Lucy let out a sigh. "Yes, that's pretty much been the experience so far."

"There are a few random houses, shops and pubs, but not many."

"Eliminate them."

"Okay, that leaves us with a few churches, Guildhall and a castle."

"A castle?"

"The Tower of London."

Lucy smiled. "Well, we know George Villiers lived there, don't we?"

"Do we?"

"Yes, he was imprisoned there four times."

A pointer moved on the milometer as Lucy's speed increased. "We'll park near Eddie."

"How will we know where he is if we can't get hold of him?"

"Eddie would walk miles to avoid paying for parking. He would even get a train to avoid paying for parking. Even if the train cost more than the parking."

Jamie laughed. "I know. I've seen him in action. The

problem is there's nowhere to park for miles."

"Okay, where are the cheapest two places to park?"

Jamie scrolled through his phone's browser findings. "There's a car park at St. Katherine's Dock. It looks small. There's also a multi-storey about five minutes from the Tower."

"How much?"

"£3.50 an hour."

Lucy laughed. It was a stone's throw from The Monument. "He won't be happy, but he will park there. He won't stay for more than four hours, and he won't remember the Congestion Charge."

"Even for work vans?"

"Especially for work vans. They don't care about people like you."

"I drove into London the other day, but it was in the middle of the night."

Lucy looked across to Jamie. "It's twenty-four hours. You will get a fine."

"Eddie will get a fine, you mean."

It took an age to work their way through the London traffic, with cyclists and red buses blocking any form of cohesive road use planning. They eventually approached the car park and waited for the red and white barrier to lift.

Lucy drove down the slope and circled until Jamie spotted Eddie's van. They found a space six vehicles along. Jamie unfastened his seatbelt, looked out of his window, and saw someone he recognised. "What the hell is he doing here?"

Eddie checked his watch. It was dead on nine when the large doors opened. A Yeoman Warder wearing a dark blue uniform with what looked like a Morris Dancer's hat turned and marched away. He was holding an oversized set of keys on a large metal ring and was flanked by four Queens Guardsmen.

The keys looked traditional, the rifles were modern.

The autumnal sheen of the cobbles glimmered in the early morning light. The pathway travelled over a grass moat before a second turreted gateway greeted visitors. A plaque declared it was the Byward Tower. Eddie walked through with the other early-birds, in full knowledge that this would be the end of the journey — back to work with a boiler fit the following week.

He had bought a map and quickly circled the accessible areas before joining the first Beefeater tour of the day. It was an amusing and well-rehearsed trip through the memory lane of the castle. The famous executions and prisoners, along with a variety of interesting facts. Eddie let out an audible groan when learning the width of the moat was further than an archer could fire an arrow with accuracy. This brought a firm 'shut up' from his smiling tour guide. He decided not to tell him he looked like a village fete novelty dancer.

The tour moved on to Traitor's Gate. He could not imagine where to start his quest, so chose to continue — the tour was free, after all. The Bloody Tower, formerly known as the Garden Tower, was renamed for 'marketing purposes'. Guffaws.

Eddie was enjoying the spiel but had to learn more. And not just about King Richard III's possible role in the death of the young princes in the Bloody Tower. His ears pricked at the revelation that when the bones of two small children were found, Charles II had them buried at Westminster Abbey. He knew George Villiers was also interred there, along with a variety of the leading scientists and alchemists of the time.

Perhaps he was in the wrong place.

As much as he enjoyed the banter, Eddie ducked out once the Warder began talking about Henry VIII and headed towards another Warder, who was generously answering questions and posing for selfies with a coterie of giggling Asian students with matching hair bands and short tartan skirts.

Eddie pondered how inane some of the questions might be on any given day. He needed to know where a man was imprisoned over three hundred years ago. Was his question inane?

He found a large, once well-built, but now a little portly around the edges, Warder, and asked his questions once again. "Do you know where George Villiers, the Second Duke of Buckingham, was imprisoned?" and, "Are there any parts of the Tower that remain untouched since the seventeenth century?"

Armed with the answers, Eddie approached a similar-looking Warder to double-check. This time, two different answers. Both delivered with cheery confidence. As he walked away, Eddie overheard one of the Warders asked, "Do you mind if we face time, my cat?"

How could he possibly expect to receive proper historical knowledge?

Undeterred, he tried once more.

"Congratulations," said a bespectacled Warder. "You have just asked a question I have not heard before, and one to which I do not know the answer. I would presume the Beauchamp Tower, but perhaps you could ask my colleague by the entrance of the Bloody Tower. He has a binder in the hut that details all of the prisoners incarcerated here over the centuries."

Eddie was grateful to have learned something useful and made his way towards the Bloody Tower. He stopped to look at a wire sculpture of an elephant. He checked his guidebook. The Tower of London had a zoo during Charles II's time, and for centuries after. It was named The Menagerie. The Tower had also been home to the Royal Mint. Its last prisoners were the Kray twins. Fascinating stuff. It would give him something to read about while Jamie was next chatting about a load of old nothing in the pub.

Ian Gale reached around to his back seat to place his chocolate bar wrapper in the carrier bag. He sat back and yawned. It had been an early start. Eddie had asked him to meet at the Tower of London later that day, but first, he needed to watch and wait, to see if anyone entered the lock-up shop, registered in the name of the recently deceased James McAllister. He would get to the warehouse later, but he needed to learn why an Oxford-based tour guide would have anything to do with a City lock-up and an East End warehouse.

A few people wearing business attire walked past — no doubt on their way to the sky encroaching office blocks. The shops, mostly fabric and food stores, were closed with their graffiti-covered shutters pulled down. The shop he was interested in also had metal shutters — locked by new padlocks at their base. There was no name above.

A trader trundled a cart alongside his car. The man tapped on his window, "You can't park there, mate. The market people will be along soon."

Gale acknowledged his instruction and started the engine. There was no benefit to showing his credentials. The morning traffic of people and vehicles was increasing, and he needed to continue his surveillance. Fortunately, he managed to find a space a short walk away. On his return, he saw the shop's shutters were raised, and newspaper covered the windows on the inside. In the morning gloom, he could make out light from inside.

Lucy looked over at Jamie. "What the hell is who doing here?"

Jamie opened the door, and Lucy ducked down to look through Jamie's side window to see who he was talking about. A man was standing next to Eddie's van, peering inside the window.

Jamie shouted, "A bit far from home, aren't we?"

The man turned. Shock instantly stretched across his face. Jamie heard Lucy slam her door. She sprinted around the back of the car and overtook him in an instant. Jamie stood transfixed, confused as to why she was running so quickly, but also, this strange car park coincidence. He jogged after her. Within a blur of seconds, Lucy was standing in front of the man. He was trapped between Jamie on one side and vehicles behind. The man reached inside his leather jacket and pulled out a carpet knife.

Lucy could see he was unsure what to do, so took advantage of the time-lapse and stepped forward with her left foot. His hand moved outwards, ready to swipe. Lucy chopped her left arm across his forearm before she decreased the gap with another stride and swiped down with her right forearm across his bicep, pressing down through the outside, and flattening the flesh. His knees crumbled as his body was thrown off balance. Lucy lifted her left arm as a lever, causing the knife's release before forcing the man to the ground with her right palm. With his hand twisted behind his back, Lucy turned the man and crashed down with her knees.

There was a loud crack. The man screamed in pain as his shoulder popped out of its socket. Lucy did not let go. She stayed there until his skin began to feel clammy, and the gurgling screams slowed.

Jamie grimaced while staring at the events unfolding before him.

Lucy waited until the man was fully incapacitated before loosening her grip and looking up at Jamie, whose expression was now stuck in a blanched wince. He stood still in front of the prostrate man, partly obscured by Lucy, who was kneeling on top of the twisted arm behind his back.

Lucy said, "Do you know him then, Jamie?"

Jamie was motionless. "Yes, that's Rob, the project manager from the job in Portsmouth."

Lucy pressed a little more firmly on her now silent victim with her knee. She pulled his ponytail and leaned to his ear, "This gave you away," she looked up at Jamie. "He is also the bastard that grabbed me in Cambridge."

39

A man arrived to lift the shutters to the shop Gale was leaning against. A van pulled in front of his view. It was getting busy. He decided to take his chance before people asked questions. He walked over to the shop and looked for gaps in the newspaper. There were boxes piled in front of the window covering.

"The light goes on before we get here in the morning, and it's out before Arjun packs up for the night. He leaves last. It's been locked up for months. A couple of decorators went in last week, but the lights have only been switched on since Saturday. We have knocked, but no one answers."

Gale turned to see a man wearing a royal blue Kurta, black trousers, and very shiny shoes. He was also squinting for gaps in the newspaper. Gale snapped upright. "I was just looking around to see if there were any shops available."

"What type of business are you in?"

"It's more for warehousing, to be honest. I scout properties for clients," Gale raised an eyebrow at the contradiction of his likely reply had it been official police work.

Gale politely took his leave and returned as near to his previous watching spot as he could. He pulled his jacket collar up — it was getting colder. After an eternity of pacing and watching, Gale succumbed to a vendor's coffee. He continued his reconnaissance and watched as three more people entered the shop before leaving a short while after. The monotony was broken by the sound of his phone ringing.

"Hello, Ian, it's Lucy."

"Lucy Hill?"

"Well, not yet, but yes. I wanted to let you know before I called the police."

"Sorry. Yes. Brisley. I am the police, Lucy."

"Yes, I know, but I mean the local police. I am in London."

"What's happened? Is it Eddie?"

"I am at Tower Hill Car Park. I am with Jamie, and we have my kidnapper. I have a feeling he is also the murderer you are looking for."

"I will be there in fifteen minutes," Gale turned his phone off and began to run. Before he was in his third stride, he saw a man approach the shop he had been watching. The door opened, and he entered. He looked familiar.

Eddie felt uncomfortable leaving Lucy behind, but he had put both her and Jamie in danger. He was determined get to the bottom of this — whatever this was. He busied himself with the placating excuses he might use as he walked through the arch of the Bloody Tower.

He approached a blue hut. Another friendly Warder held out his hand. Eddie asked his questions, and the Warder moved like a lithe automaton — mechanical routine with the edges smoothed off. The sort of military precision that would ensure crisply turned edges of bedclothes and neatly ironed socks. He retrieved the binder and scanned through to the seventeenth century. George Villiers was mentioned twice, rather than the four times Eddie had learned, but there was no mention of which Tower he was incarcerated within.

"I think they were all used as prisons," the Warder said.

Eddie shook the man's hand again, expressed his gratitude, and watched as the sun disappeared into the dense grey skies. He climbed some steps flanked by two old streetlamps, painted police-box blue. The steps opened to a lawned area surrounded by attractive Tudor houses. It could be a romantic rural hamlet. Instead, it was the village within which the Warders and their families lived inside the gates of the Tower — protected while protecting it.

He continued his walk but paused along Water Lane. He had not been to the Tower of London before and was grateful to bow his head in respect for his family's memories of his great uncle, who had trained with the second battalion of the Scots Guards on the lawn he had just viewed. It was from here that he left for The Great War, not to return. He pondered for a short while, reflecting upon family memories, which this place evoked better than any he had visited before. He thought of Lucy, and the dressing down he would receive when he returned to Jamie's.

He knew he would have to revisit all the towers individually and draw a mental sightline from each opening to see where it led. His impatience grew as the crowds increased. Human hamsters with rotating heads wandered around, staring at the stonework on a relentless trudge in the circle around the battlements that surrounded the White Tower in the centre.

He scribbled rough lines from each tower on his map. All led to the White Tower in the centre but travelled over cobbles, grass, and modern additions, including a snack hut, an ornamental canon, and some more wire sculptures of animals.

If George had a view, the stone could be buried anywhere along one of those lines.

The guidebook told him the Tower of London was once home to twenty-one pubs, but now there was just one, and it wasn't open to visitors. This was not, however, the sort of minor detail that usually stopped him. There was another blue hut. It was empty. Eddie looked around and saw the resident Warder was helping a man unload boxes from a van, so he took the opportunity to step over a black chain fence dividing the public from private areas.

The Tudor stone entrance belied the interior. Named after the famous ceremony, Eddie was surprised *The Keys* was so dated. Given the historic nature of its setting, it seemed rather characterless. The former *Yeoman Warders Club* opened into a white rectangular-shaped hall with light wooden floors, surrounded by red leather seating against the walls. His eye immediately caught the ephemera dotted around, including an autograph by Adolf Hitler's right-hand man Rudolph Hess, who was, he had already learned, one of the last prisoners executed at the Tower.

The only other person in the pub was a tall, stocky man with a misshapen nose, polishing a glass behind the bar.

"I am afraid you are not allowed in here without the personal invitation of a Yeoman Warder."

Eddie replied, "Sorry, sir. I'm carrying out some important research for British Heritage. I have asked a few Warders a couple of questions, but I'm afraid I got very different answers. So, I thought, where better to ask than a pub," Eddie smiled widely. Was 'sir' the right tone?

"I am sure the curators or museum staff could help. I would have thought British Heritage would have a hotline to those people."

Eddie rested a hand on the bar and leaned a little closer. "To be honest, I am looking to refute something British

Heritage have claimed. I don't think my research is too welcome."

The barman pulled his eyebrows together. "I see."

Before the barman could draw a conclusion, Eddie quickly filled the conversation space. "Are you a Yeoman Warder?"

"I am, yes. We all take two-week shifts running the pub."

"Well, couldn't I be your guest for a quick pint and a couple of questions?" Eddie smiled again.

"I am afraid it doesn't quite work like that."

"I am a quick drinker," Eddie said, hopefully.

The friendly barman looked around theatrically to make sure the place was empty and reached for the handpump. "Okay, what will it be?"

"I think I'll have a pint of this Yeoman 1485 Craft Lager, please," Eddie said, cheeks aching from the smiling.

The barman confessed that rather than give him 'tourist's answers', he would own up to not knowing. He admitted he was not surprised the binder did not provide the answers Eddie was searching for. "I'll give John a call. He's probably best with the history of this place."

A short while later, a Yeoman Warder with several stripes on the arm of his blue uniform entered. He did not appear overly pleased to be there but held out a hand. "Hello. My name is John Jackson. I am the Yeoman Jailer here at the Tower."

Still grinning, Eddie replied. "Sounds ominous."

There was no use driving. Traffic would have made it a longer journey than on foot. Ian Gale had run while looking at the map on his phone. It had taken twelve minutes. He leaned on the entry barrier to catch his breath. What floor?

Gale circled the grey concrete interior as it rose upwards until he saw Lucy and Jamie leaning on opposite sides of Lucy's car. There was a man inside. He could see the man was unable to get out without one of them stopping him. He jogged over and leaned against the boot of the car to catch his breath again.

Lucy said, "You're here with Eddie, aren't you?"

He held a finger up. He really did need to get back to the gym. Sunday football was not enough exercise. He gasped a reply, "Sort of, but more importantly, what's going on?"

Lucy explained who the man in the car was. Jamie stared, with murderous intent, through the other window.

Gale said, "Okay, this is good. This is great. I will call the locals and get him picked up. I will also call my DI."

He looked up at first, Jamie, and then Lucy. "Well done for not knocking his block off."

Lucy said, "I might have dislocated his shoulder a bit."

Gale looked through the window. Robert Wilson was clutching his shoulder and was clearly in a great deal of pain. "Don't worry, I'm sure Jamie would like his turn," Gale looked at Jamie, "Would you like to help pop his arm back in?"

Jamie gently touched the brim of his cap. "Thanks. That will help my mood."

Gale turned to Lucy, "I'm not with Eddie, but you appear to have worked out where he is. I was staking out somewhere else that might or might not be related. You should go. I can stay here with Jamie until the police arrive."

Gale and Jamie looked at each other with raised eyebrows. They silently agreed they would not want to be Eddie when Lucy caught up with him.

40

"British Heritage, you say?" John Jackson asked.

"As I explained to your colleague, I am doing it without their knowledge. I don't think they would approve."

"I see. Most people want to know about the Princes in the Tower, Anne Boleyn's beheading, Thomas Blood, or Henry VIII's codpiece."

"Thomas Blood, as in Colonel Blood?"

"Yes. Blood's is my favourite Tower of London story. I can tell you what I say on my tours," Jackson paused before adding, "He also has a connection to The Duke of Buckingham."

"I didn't know that."

Eddie did know that.

Jackson began, "Thomas Blood dressed as a clergyman to gain the confidence of Mr and Mrs Edwards, who looked after the Crown Jewels in Martin Tower. He did this over a period of weeks and eventually asked for their daughter's hand in marriage on behalf of his nephew."

The barman offered Jackson a drink. He held up a hand to indicate he was on duty. "Blood took his son, who was instead a rather nefarious associate, around to visit them along with another accomplice dressed as a clergyman. You know what happens next, don't you?" before Eddie could answer, Jackson, resumed, "They asked to see the Crown Jewels. Eager to please his daughter's future husband and the generous dowry promised, Edwards was glad to show them."

The barman flicked a bottle top into a bin, and poured a glass of cola for Jackson.

"They stabbed poor Mr Edwards and bashed him with a mallet they had brought to flatten the Crown Jewels. Short work was made of the wire meshed cupboard doors behind which the Regalia was kept. Blood flattened the King's State Crown so he could hide it in a bag under his cloak. He hid the Orb in his trousers, and the young man began to file the Sceptre in half," Jackson paused to take a sip of the cola that had arrived while he was talking. "But then it all went a bit pear-shaped. A fourth man — a look-out, rushed in to say that Mr Edwards' son had returned home for his sister's forthcoming nuptials."

Eddie was enjoying the tale and thought Jackson's drink-sipping pauses dramatised the story for full effect.

"The son was on his way up the stairs to visit his parents when he heard his dad shout 'Treason. Murder. The Crown is stolen'. But by this time, Blood and his accomplices were on their toes."

Eddie asked, "They didn't get away, though, did they?"

"They did, yes. Hunt and Halliwell made it through the outer gate. Blood and Perrott made it as far as Water Lane when Edwards junior and a guard gave chase. Edwards shouted at the Yeoman Warder positioned at the drawbridge, but he threw himself to the floor when Blood fired at him. They escaped over the drawbridge and through the Iron Gate."

Eddie asked, "So, what happened to the jewels they did get away with?"

Jackson smiled for the first time. They always get hooked by this one. "Once Blood and Perrott got through, they were hoping to hide in the crowd of the busy wharf, but the soldiers were younger and fitter, and Edwards junior caught up just as the thieves were about to mount their horses," Jackson took a long gulp of his drink before adding, "People were either more honest or more fearful of authority back then because even though some of the jewels scattered in the struggle, street children handed them to the soldiers."

The pub door swung open. A short, round woman, with orange colouring in her otherwise dark hair, wearing a floral dress and Dr Martens boots, entered. Despite the icy air outside, she was not wearing a coat.

Eddie turned back to Jackson. "You mentioned there was a connection to The Duke of Buckingham?"

"And this is the woman to ask."

Jackson beckoned the woman over, "Thanks for coming, Elysia. This gentleman would like to know about Thomas Blood's pardon."

"I'm sorry, I will have to keep this short. I am a little busy," Elysia Martin affected a smile towards Eddie. "Well, briefly, no-one knows why Charles II pardoned Thomas Blood for attempting to steal the Crown Jewels. He was locked up for his crime, but he refused to answer questions from anyone except King Charles. If it was surprising that Charles acceded to this request, what was more surprising was that he not only pardoned Blood but gave him land in Ireland that had an income of £500 a year. He also became a regular at Court from that point onwards."

Eddie asked, "Are there any theories?"

"Three main ones. It could have been that Charles' advisers feared an Irish uprising or that he enjoyed Blood's tale that he once spurned the opportunity to kill the king when he saw him bathing in the Thames."

Eddie said, "That sounds like a bit of a stretch."

"It does. As does the proposition that Charles was merely amused by Blood, who told him his jewels were only worth £6,000 despite being valued at £100,000."

"What do you think?" Eddie asked.

"Blood's most notable previous misdemeanour was just a year earlier than the attempted robbery. He was foiled in a kidnapping attempt of the Duke of Ormonde. Now, Ormonde was The Duke of Buckingham's biggest rival in a political sense, so rumours circulated that Buckingham was Blood's patron. This was not proven, but there was a falling out between the two not long before Blood died. It also adds to the suspicion of Blood's pardon, given how close Buckingham and Charles were."

"I see," Eddie said, quickly pondering what he had learned.

Jackson filled the gap. "Sorry, I didn't get your name sir, this is Elysia Martin, our head curator at the Tower."

Eddie held out his hand. "Sorry, I should have introduced myself. Eddie Hill."

He could have been wrong, but Eddie's hand instinctively moved to provide support as he saw Elysia Martin appear to waver on her feet. He did not see John Jackson's lips curl into a smile.

Martin said, "I hope I have been of help," she turned quickly. "I really must go."

Eddie watched as Martin quickly disappeared through the door.

Jackson said to Eddie, "As must we, Mr Hill. I am sure my colleague has explained, *The Keys* is in a restricted area of the grounds."

Eddie was surprised at Jackson's return to brusqueness but followed him through the door. The pair continued their walk. Jackson looked straight ahead. Eddie was unsure if he should start a new conversation, but it was not long before he was led back to the main entrance.

He knew what was about to happen. He was going to get thrown out. Again.

They reached a wooden door to a turret close to the entrance of the Tower's main gates. The two sides were connected by what appeared to Eddie, to be Tudor offices above the arched access route, with the Beefeater Gift Shop on one side and The Casemates on the other.

"Please follow me, Mr Hill."

The door swung open, revealing a small stone anteroom that opened to a larger area. Eddie entered the hexagonal space and immediately saw the ancient stone walls were adorned with modern pictures, mostly of military personnel. There were grey filing cabinets and desks in the centre with computer screens angled towards each other. Hooks supported a large ornate axe next to the fireplace. He couldn't decide whether it was more junk shop or antique emporium.

On a shelf among some books, he saw a Quality Street tin.

41

John Jackson stood behind his desk and said, "Mr Hill, this is the Chief."

Eddie cautiously held out a hand. "What am I doing here?"

"Billy Gray. Glad to meet you, Mr Hill. Can I call you Eddie?"

Eddie instantly relaxed. He knew something else was going on here. How else would the 'Chief' have known his first name?

Gray looked over at Jackson. "I told you he would come. Ye of little faith."

Eddie saw the two men smile. This was fun and everything, but he needed answers. Now.

Gray saw Eddie was about to speak, so added, "I am very sorry. Please let me explain. We have been watching you. We didn't want to get involved because I am sure you can imagine we have had several false dawns over the centuries, and we can't be seen to be getting involved in" he paused to consider his words, "controversial matters."

Jackson said, "We're excited to hear what you know."

Eddie said as calmly as he could, "I have no idea what you are talking about. As I explained, I am just doing some research into George Villiers, the Second Duke of Buckingham."

Jackson laughed, "Can I ask then, why you are also interested in the parts of the Tower that have not been touched since the seventeenth century?"

Before Eddie could answer, Gray, asked, "And why would you want to visit Cliveden House, Trinity College at Cambridge University and the Ashmolean in Oxford in" he looked at his watch, "less than two weeks?"

Eddie stared at them both, then turned to Gray. "I have a far more important question. What are you doing with my wedding money?"

The door opened.

All three men turned.

Lucy walked towards Eddie.

He could see she was not happy, but she did not give him time to speak, and in a cheerily sarcastic tone, said, "Hello Eddie. Hello, Beefeaters," Lucy turned to Eddie. "May I ask what you are doing here please, darling?"

"It appears that I am here to collect our wedding money," he pointed to the shelf with the sweets tin on it.

As Lucy went to stride around the desk towards Gray, Eddie gently placed his arm across her chest.

Gray said, "I am sorry. Please take a seat, both of you. I will gladly explain."

Eddie and Lucy wheeled two office chairs from beneath the octagonal desk and sat.

Gray said, "Firstly, I would like to apologise sincerely. It was a very rash decision on a friend's behalf, although I inadvertently sanctioned it. He did say he had left a note with our contact information on it. As you have clearly not found it, I can understand your confusion and anger. I hope you can forgive me."

Eddie and Lucy looked at each other and shook their heads before turning back to Gray, who continued, "After poor Ken Prior was murdered, I am sorry to say we suspected you, Eddie. The local police indicated you were a suspect. I intended to return your savings as soon as we learned it was nothing to do with you. I was dealing with Ken's grieving widow, and it slipped my mind for a while."

Gray took a deep breath to continue, but Jackson took up the story. "We were intrigued by your movements and wondered why you were visiting these places so quickly after the incident. Although we knew you were not involved in Ken's death, we did think you knew something."

Eddie said, "That's all very nice, but your apologies won't count for much when I call the police."

Gray said, "I understand. I have never been involved in anything I have regretted as much."

"Are you having a laugh? You tied my wife up and put my best mate in hospital—"

Gray stretched his arms with the palms of his hands facing the couple. "Hang on, hang on. We haven't tied anyone up and have certainly not put anyone in hospital. Let's take a minute. Eddie, please explain. I can assure you we are nothing to do with whatever you are talking about."

Lucy placed her hand on Eddie's arm. She looked at the fading red mark, still visible on her wrist. "It was your boss, Rob, that abducted me, Eddie. Jamie and Ian Gale are with him now in the car park where you parked the van."

Eddie looked at Lucy, confusion spread across his face.

"Once we worked out where you were going. Oh, and," Lucy punched him on the arm, "we saw Rob in the car park looking into your van. I put him in my car and called Ian Gale. Who you obviously thought would be more helpful than me," she added, and punched him on the arm again. "I presume the Metropolitan Police will be with him by now."

Eddie was rubbing his arm as Gray said, "Again, I can't apologise enough about the tin, but I have no idea who or what you are talking about."

Eddie said, "Rosicrucians."

Gray replied, "Rosiwhat?"

Eddie leaned back in his chair and let out a puff-cheeked sigh. He then sat back forward and grinned.

Gray smiled at Eddie. "You know, don't you?"

Lucy looked at Jackson, who shrugged his shoulders.

Eddie said, "I think so. Yes."

As serenely as she could, Lucy said, "Okay. I am normally a very calm, and maybe even, placid, person. However, the past few days have been a bit of a trial. Until today, I had only ever been involved in physical violence in class, but right now, if someone doesn't tell me what the hell is going on, I could very well explode," she looked around at all three men, "And you lot might be in the way of that explosion."

Eddie spun his chair towards Lucy. "It appears these gentlemen are not looking for the philosopher's stone. They are not part of this Rosicrucian group or whatever they are. They are looking for something that went missing in 1670."

Gray grinned and said, "1671."

Eddie resumed, "Yes, 1671."

Lucy stared back with eyes wide open. "Explosion still imminent. Any minute now."

Eddie laughed. "I think they, and their predecessors, have been looking for The Black Prince's Ruby."

Gray asked, "When did you know?"

"I thought something didn't add up while I was following the clues, and when the final clue led me here, I needed to know if you were among these Rosicrucians — who are looking for something completely different — before I could confirm my suspicions," Eddie took Lucy's hand. "I knew I would be walking into the lion's den, and yes, I also know we have had this conversation, but I couldn't risk you getting hurt again when this will be a police matter, anyway. That's why I asked Ian to come along. He said he had something going on in London anyway, so he drove up. I think I only really knew when John started telling me a completely different story to the one I was interested in. I still wasn't sure until this conversation."

Lucy asked, "Would someone mind telling me what The Black Prince's Ruby is?"

"May I?" John Jackson asked.

Billy Gray held his hand out to gesture for him to go ahead.

"The Black Prince's Ruby was originally owned by Prince Abu Sa'id of the Moorish Kingdom of Granada sometime during the fourteenth century. It was mined in what is now known as Tajikistan. King Don Pedro the Cruel had invaded Granada, the last Muslim outpost in Spain, as part of his Christian conquest. Prince Sa'id was planning to surrender to Don Pedro, but Pedro had Sa'id and all his servants killed."

Eddie said, "They had great bad guy names back then."

"Anyway, among his spoils was The Black Prince's Ruby, which it would become known as a short while later. Abu Sa'id's half-brother decided to take Don Pedro on. This forced him to ally with Prince Edward III, who was known as the Black Prince of England. To cut that long story short, Edward demanded The Ruby as payment for helping him win the war."

Gray prompted his colleague, "And the stone itself?"

"Oh yes, Henry V was said to have worn it on his helmet at Agincourt, and Richard III was said to have worn it at Bosworth, where he was killed before being buried under a car park in Leicester," Jackson laughed. "So, the stone itself is a spinel, not a ruby. It was first placed in Henry VIII's crown, where it remained until Cromwell."

Gray interrupted, "Boo."

Jackson added, "Hiss."

These two should be on the stage, thought Eddie.

Jackson continued, "Although The Black Prince's Ruby disappeared during this time, it popped up again as soon as Charles II took his throne. I am sure our curator could confirm this for you, but The Duke of Buckingham quickly regained favour with Charles at this time."

Eddie said, "We researched this period, and it did seem odd that they made up so quickly."

Jackson replied, "Yes, funny that."

Lucy said, "That certainly sounds like the sort of thing George would have plotted."

"Anyway, The Ruby takes pride of place in the Imperial State Crown, or the Crown of State as it is also known, which every monarch since then, exchanges for St Edward's Crown at the end of their coronation."

"Except it isn't The Black Prince's Ruby, is it?" Eddie asked.

Gray stood up. "Would you like a cup of tea?"

Lucy said, "Yes, please. I haven't had anything to eat or drink since seven this morning," as she glared at Eddie, once again.

Gray fussed around with some biscuits and poured four mugs of tea.

"May I continue?" Jackson was enjoying his role as raconteur. "No, it is not The Ruby. It's not glass, but no one that has seen it knows what it is. I say no one, but very few people know about this. The only people to have seen it and are aware, apart from you now, are the jewellers down the centuries, a handful of curators, the odd Constable, Resident Governor, and a few Yeoman Warders. Bill and I only know about it because of boozy gossip with a senior officer one night."

"So, what does this mean?" Lucy asked.

"Well, you see that axe. . ." Jackson pointed to the Jailer's axe on the wall and let loose his hearty laugh once again.

Eddie thought he was nothing like the man he had met in the pub.

Gray took up the conversation from there. "Some of my colleagues throughout the years speculated that among the gems scattered after Thomas Blood's theft of the Crown Jewels was The Black Prince's Ruby. Some believe The Duke of Buckingham masterminded this operation and arranged this as a deliberate act."

Gray looked over at Jackson. "If Buckingham returned the jewel to his king, it would certainly explain Blood's pardon and reward. A favour, if you like."

Jackson replied, "I think Buckingham was there, and the street urchins that conveniently gathered up the jewels handed them to him for a reward."

Gray raised his eyebrows, "That's John's theory, anyway."

Eddie asked, "And yours?"

"Well, something like that, but it's all just conjecture. The burning question now is, where is it?"

It was Eddie's turn to laugh, "I don't know."

Gray sighed.

Eddie said, "The reason I asked if there is anywhere that hasn't been touched is because of this. . ." Eddie reached into his pocket and retrieved a yellow sticky note. He read, "My Home from Home — Returned to He Whoe. . ."

Gray and Jackson leaned over to see the note.

Gray asked, "What does it mean?"

Eddie bent down to remove the *Mutus Liber* book from his backpack. He placed it on the desk. The Warders converged for a closer overview as if examining a rare artefact. Which it was.

Eddie said, "I wrote the clue out because, as you can see, some of the writing has faded too much to read properly. This is one of the clues. I wasn't sure until I realised that George's 'home from home' was perhaps a dig at Charles. He meant where he was imprisoned."

Gray said, "I think we may be missing some context here."

Eddie explained the *Mutus Liber* clues and his theory for them. He told them he believed George and Charles' friendship was extraordinarily louche. And this was the sort of game they played — spoiled rich boy's games.

Gray asked, "Was this in the property in Portsmouth?"

"Not the one I am working on, but possibly the one along the road where George's father was murdered." Eddie saw Gray look down. He knew he was thinking of Ken Prior. It also explained Regal Portfolio Properties, and their interest in these types of buildings.

Jackson interrupted the momentary silence with a more pertinent question, "Why would the king go on a treasure hunt?"

Eddie replied, "I'm not sure he would have, but Villiers did manage to collect these philosopher's stones, which was their lifelong project together. And someone must have replaced The Black Prince's Ruby."

Lucy slumped in her chair.

Gray filled the gap, "So, where would this have started?"

"That's the one thing I can't answer. I think it may be a circular treasure hunt, as it were. There will either be a clue that George provided Charles to kick start him, or once one was found, that would lead to the next, and so on. Until it completed the circle and the full collection, including The Ruby."

"And this clue?" Jackson pointed to the small piece of yellow paper.

"I think you know this. "My Home from Home. Returned

283

to He Whoe. . ."

Jackson asked, "I do?"

"Returned to He Whoe. . ."

Lucy looked up in a daze, "Lost it."

Eddie smiled at her, "Correct."

"Talbot Edwards," Gray said.

"Yes, exactly," Eddie replied.

Jackson said, "He lived in Martin Tower, which is where the Crown Jewels were originally kept."

Gray added the rest for him. "And where Thomas Blood stole them from."

John Jackson said, "Let me call Elysia Martin. She is going to love this. Especially when I tell her we are looking for something in her Tower."

Gray whispered to Lucy, "He's sweet on our curator. He tells her it was named for her. To be honest, I encourage it. He hasn't seen anyone since he lost his wife."

42

Elysia Martin walked towards her office in The Casemates. As she lowered the door lever, she saw her hand was shaking. Although there were more important things to concern herself with, she was unnerved. Of all places, why would Eddie Hill be here? She tried to shake it off — Robert Wilson would take care of Hill. Where was he?

She sat behind her desk. Hill must be here because he is looking for another stone. But how does he know where they are when Rosicrucians have spent so long looking for them? George Villiers, the Second Duke of Buckingham, was the connection. She looked at her shelves of books, papers, archive boxes, and storage tubs. It was a mess. Not that it should concern her. She would be leaving soon. And yet, all minor details were a concern at this stage.

She glanced at the glass block on her desk. The sand-etched quote was by Benjamin Franklin: 'An investment in knowledge pays the best interest'. She had dedicated much of her adult life to the pursuit of learning of and from the past. But to what end? It took a chance encounter with a like-minded soul to set her on the right path, and it was time to claim interest on that knowledge.

She sunk back into her chair, deep in thought. George Villiers, George Villiers, George Villiers. What could it be? The wheels squealed as she pushed the chair back and made for the door. The archive room would be the best place to start.

A modern fire door separated it from the rest of the building. Blue steel racks held hundreds of mostly shoebox-sized cardboard boxes and archive filing tubs. All had labels, and all contained artefacts from the Tower's long history. Martin trawled through the shelving until she found what she was looking for.

She carried the tub to a steel bench and wiped a thin layer of dust from the lid before lifting it. Inside was a smaller air-tight container. She removed this without opening it and peered inside. A book and some papers. It was all George Villiers had left behind at the Tower. She rifled through but could not see how aid could possibly come from inside the container.

Martin carried the tub back to her office. She moved some papers out of the way and placed it on a cluttered side table by her equally untidy desk. She sat back down and shook her head. Priorities. Robert can deal with Hill when he gets here. If he knows where another stone is, Robert can get it. *Where is he?* Not that it mattered, she would soon have enough money not to care. And one of the more important things she had to consider was the telephone call she was about to make.

"Hello, Miss Martin. I am pleased to say that we have had a steady stream of visitors today. All were eager to collect their invitations. Even representatives sent on behalf of others were most animated. I would presume the excitement is infectious."

Martin replied, "That is good news. I have over five

hundred Rewards here and more to collect from the warehouse. How many invitations are left to distribute?"

Mr Fofana replied, "I would say, no more than sixty."

"I see. I will talk to the laboratory to ensure we receive the next batch of Rewards before the end of the week."

"I have now distributed invitations for five days from Saturday as instructed."

"No more than a hundred per evening?" Martin asked.

"Yes, and mixed nationalities as you requested."

"Perfect. I appreciate your help with this, Mr Fofana. After Mr McAllister's untimely death, it has been all hands to the pump. Tell me, have there been any issues that I should be concerned about?"

"Just one, and it was an unforeseen circumstance. These premises are in a rather public area near Petticoat Lane. The irregular arrival of luxury vehicles has been noticed. I don't know whether it is their fervour, but four well known public figures have turned up themselves to collect their invitations rather than send agents on their behalf. Fortunately, I do not think anyone recognised them, but that could change if others appear in person."

"Okay. Once you have distributed the remaining invitations for this batch, will you be able to arrange alternative premises for a potential next batch, if required in a hurry? Something unexpected has occured that could lead to more stones than we had anticipated."

Martin nodded to herself. This is why she was unnerved. This is why she was concerned about Eddie Hill. He knew more and could lead them to additional stones.

Mr Fofana replied, "I already have. I have prepared a similar shop around a mile away. It is a little nearer the apartment."

"That is wonderful. I don't know what I would do without your assistance," Martin ended the conversation and recalled her first meeting with Mr Fofana a lifetime ago at Florence's Uffizi Gallery. They were both admiring *The Birth of Venus* by Botticelli. The afternoon turned into evening, where they discussed their shared passion for the references and teachings of Rosicrucianism. Their joint venture began shortly after that first meeting. Plans were coming to fruition now.

Martin looked over at her dress, hanging on a hook in cellophane. Her attention turned to the silver shoes on the floor below. It would be a relief to rid herself of this uniform and wear proper clothes.

She jumped when the phone on her desk rang. It was John Jackson. The call was short. What on earth does he mean, 'We have found The Ruby'? She would go to meet them as requested, grateful that she would soon be far away from the fool.

Eddie and Lucy listened as Billy Gray revealed that Henry III erected The Martin Tower in the thirteenth century. It was built as a prison but was referred to as the 'Jewel Tower' during Charles II's reign. German spies were imprisoned there during the Great War before their execution.

Elysia Martin's patience was limited. She said to Gray, "The Black Prince's Ruby is unlikely to be hidden there. It would have been discovered during the many renovations that have taken place over the years."

She did not move her gaze from Eddie as she spoke.

The group took the tourist route around the White Tower towards the right side of the current Jewel House. Eddie watched as a bulb flickered in the blue lamp at the entrance of the stairs to the battlements. The group climbed the steps and entered Martin Tower into a hexagonal-shaped room at odds with its exterior. Eddie was disappointed to see the right-hand side of the building had new brickwork and presumed it was the victim of successful German air attacks during the Blitz.

Another blue lamp flickered. Eddie wondered whether there was a Chief Bulb Changer to the Queen.

The entrance led to a carpeted area featuring display cabinets housing jewel-less crowns. Further stairs led to a blocked area above, which he presumed were once bedrooms. It did not matter, the staircase featured visible repairs, freshly painted walls, and even the doors were later additions to the period of history he was concerned with.

John Jackson thought Elysia Martin had changed her hair. He liked it. "I know it's doubtful that we will find anything, but Eddie here found some writing in a book that suggests the Duke of Buckingham hid it during one of his stays."

Elysia Martin looked at Eddie and then back to Jackson. She did not ask about the book.

Twenty minutes later, the group of five had battled through the dwindling number of tourists to scour every inch of the Tower, including the nooks and crannies. If the stone was hidden, it would be within the walls or beneath the floor.

They descended to the Jewel House Shop. Eddie learned it was the original Jewel House where Colonel Blood committed his crime. The mugs, tea towels, and silver-plated knick-knacks were nice, but Eddie could not help but wonder why there was not a mock display of The Jewel House as it was at that time. The castle was all about the great stories of the past, after all.

At this point, Elysia Martin made her excuses and left Gray, Jackson, Hill, and a woman she was not introduced to at the tall squared-off tower entrance.

A book. What did that mean?

If the Duke of Buckingham said The Black Prince's Ruby was returned, could this mean Hill had been looking for that rather than the stones she was interested in? Elysia Martin quickly dismissed doubts and questions from her mind. The answers were only important if they led to additional stones.

There was no indication of that at this stage, and Robert Wilson would find out if there were more stones. What has happened to him?

It was a new problem, and she already had more than enough of those to deal with at this late stage. If there were additional stones, Robert Wilson could take that project on. She was now aware Eddie was working as part of Wilson's team in Portsmouth. It should be easy enough for him to find out if there were further stones. He could also find out what any of this had to do with The Black Prince's Ruby.

She shook the thoughts from her mind once again. These were trivialities. Everything was trivial now. Tonight was the night she visited the apartment Mr Fofana had found for the first time. And she had guests to prepare for.

43

Jamie followed the directions Ian Gale had added to the mapping application on his phone. It was a shame they couldn't go together, but after the arrest was made and congratulations bestowed, Ian had explained there would be lots of paperwork and a long conversation with his boss.

Streetlamps and office blocks now lit the roads. People walked by, but at that time of day, they were going somewhere they wanted to rather than needed to — home. Jamie fell in behind a group of young people in business suits with other ideas. They were heading for an after-work night out. This was their social playground, and it stretched for miles of bars, restaurants, pubs, and entertainment venues.

The blue arrowed dot reached the end of its journey, and he found himself directly outside the destination — a lock-up shop with newspaper plastered to the interior of the windows. Although shielded from view by people walking ahead, he could see the glow of lighting. He spotted a small split in the newspaper and peered inside.

The narrow room was bare, but for crisply painted white walls, floor, and ceiling. There were holes in the walls from shop fixture removal. It had a clinical appearance, and everything had been recently cleaned and decorated. There were two rows of steel pendant lights, trendy coffee shop style. Jamie thought a coffee shop would not work here, a café maybe, but not a hipster coffee shop. Perhaps that's why it was closed. Two thirds through the room, the only active bulbs were adjacent lights above a white Formica covered desk.

There were two men. The one sat on a chair behind the desk had a pile of envelopes in front of him — nothing else. Jamie saw the seated man present an envelope to a well-built man with a closely cropped afro. He turned his back to the shop and withdrew his phone when the door opened. With his back still turned, he heard the door lock and footsteps go in the opposite direction.

At the end of the road, he found a position away from the throng that would operate as a suitable vantage point. As the traders packed away and the street cleared further of people, it left one remaining shop with its lights on. The one he was interested in. He decided the vicinity was clear enough and walked over, checking nobody was around in front and behind. With his back to the shop, he placed one hand on the door handle, and scrolled on his phone with the other hand. He stood in the pose for a few minutes.

Curiosity got the better of him, and he peered through the slit between the newspaper once more. The man behind the desk was not moving. His eyes were closed, his hands were crossed on the desk, and his back was straight. Jamie wondered whether he was meditating. He recreated his pose.

Five minutes later, a black car with darkened windows pulled in front of the shop. Jamie recognised the man that emerged from the rear door instantly. He was favourite for the Christmas number one slot and had already had four chart-toppers that year. Bobby Ross had headlined Glastonbury in the summer, and his world tour was one of the best earners in music history.

Jamie withdrew his hand from the shop door handle. "I can't get hold of my driver. I said I would walk and pick this up. He tapped his jacket where an inside pocket would be. "I don't know where he is," Jamie then raised his head and walked away.

Ross said, "Good luck."

Jamie heard Ross rap six taps on the door window. Three were rapid. The next three were slow but evenly paced.

Jamie was still staring at his phone when the young man re-emerged.

Ross asked, "Any joy?"

Jamie turned his lip up in frustration and shook his head.

"Jump in. I'll give you a lift to my hotel, it will be more comfortable to call from there. We're here for the same thing, after all."

Jamie introduced himself, explaining he was an investment banker. Bobby Ross said who he was.

Jamie laughed. "I know who you are."

The drive took less than ten minutes. They passed the Tower of London, its onion-shaped domes lit against the night sky, and then over Tower Bridge, where both passengers smiled at the incredible Victorian structure and most recognisable river crossing in the world. The car pulled into a narrow entrance to an 'L' shaped building, with a pillared entrance in the centre. Jamie saw a blue plaque that declared the hotel was built on an old grammar school site. The entrance featured black and white marble flooring and had a distinctly colonial feel. Jamie assumed the red brick building was quiet, discrete and away from teenage fans.

Ross said, "I love this place. It reminds me of India. My favourite country."

A concierge rushed towards Bobby Ross from behind the front desk. The pair exchanged a whispered conversation before Jamie, and Ross were ushered into a quiet corner of a large room. There was a bar area at one end, and tables laid with place settings. People were dining at a few. The room had blue coloured vaulted ceilings with giant chandeliers of the same colour. Jamie thought it looked cool and trendy, just right for young professionals and their secret liaisons.

They took their seats, the young pop star with his back to the room.

Bobby Ross said, "Sorry, I couldn't talk in the car. I don't want Phil knowing what this is about. As you know, part of the deal is complete discretion."

Jamie nodded, presuming Phil was the driver.

Ross said, "Do you mind if I ask something personal?"

"Of course not. We're all friends."

"This is very expensive. How sure are you it will work?"

Jamie laughed. He knew what to say. He had been rehearsing since the car park. "I have been studying for nearly a decade. Probably the difference in our age. For centuries there were beliefs, but in recent years the revelation has come to light."

"I have only had money for a couple of years. It still amazes me how much some people have. It's like the venue. The London branch must have some serious funds to be able to afford that."

Jamie did not realise he was looking confused.

Ross added, "I know that sounds tight, but as I said, I haven't had money for long."

Jamie realised he did look confused when Ross added, "Oh, you haven't seen, have you? You were waiting for your driver when I showed up. The new skyscraper next to the Tower of London. We passed it on the way."

With his best impression of nonchalance, Jamie said, "That makes sense."

"What day did the man say your invite was for?"

Jamie was stumped. He had no idea what to say. He took a gamble. "Monday."

Deflated, Ross said, "I'm on Saturday. I was supposed to have a gig, but I cancelled. Who wouldn't, right? It's a shame we're not on the same night. I doubt I will know anyone there."

Jamie did not realise he was holding his breath, but managed to say, "I am sure you will."

"I suppose you're right. I spent a month with a certain film star in Mumbai in the summer. That is where I learned about Amrita. I spend hours studying translated Hindu scriptures most days now. She may be there."

Jamie had no idea about whom, or of what, he was talking, but he did know he had to leave and find out as quickly as possible. The conversation continued for a short while. It was mainly about the pitfalls of fame. Until, abruptly, Jamie's new friend stood up. "I'm going to have to go. Phil will drop you wherever you're staying."

"The Ritz" was the only posh London hotel Jamie could think of.

"It was nice to meet you. And if you want to come along to a gig, just give my manager a call," Bobby Ross handed Jamie a business card.

As Jamie left the hotel and headed to Ross' driver, he cursed himself. If only he had known a closer hotel, he wouldn't have to get a cab from the West End to Lucy's car.

Phil was waiting outside. Jamie jumped in and closed the door. As soon as Jamie slid onto the black leather seat, the locks clicked, and the driver reached behind his seat and grabbed Jamie's phone out of his hand. The dividing panel then elevated between the front and rear seats, which allowed Jamie to see his reflection in the darkened glass.

His baseball cap read, 'J Stuart – Carpenter Extraordinaire'.

Jamie tried the door. It was locked.

44

Billy Gray asked Eddie whether he thought Elysia Martin had acted strangely, but Eddie was not sure he understood the premise of the question. She seemed to rush off quickly, but he did not know her. Gray explained, "She has been acting a little oddly recently. I'm no investigator, but there was the incident with the desk, then the boxes she has been carrying into and out of The Casemates. Not to mention the odd hours she seems to be keeping."

Eddie was none the wiser. "The desk?"

"I asked if it was her own money, and she became a little short with me, but who can afford over a million pounds for a desk? Certainly not Elysia. Not on her salary. I thought she must have been using her expertise on behalf of a rich collector, but I don't know. She was just a bit strange about it all."

Eddie still had no idea what Billy Gray was talking about.

Gray helpfully filled the gap. "It was in the newspapers. It didn't have a verified provenance, but she still paid," Gray turned to John Jackson, "John, how much did Elysia pay for that Isaac Newton desk?"

"One-point-eight-million dollars."

Gray continued to query who she could have been buying it for, especially as there was no definitive proof it was owned by Isaac Newton. He repeated the fact that it made the international press. Eddie and Lucy looked at each other with matching raised eyebrows. Lucy shook her head as Eddie grinned.

Jackson was walking towards The Casemates. Lucy and Eddie were just behind. Gray said, "You carry on. I just need to make a quick call."

Instead, Jackson stopped and stood with Eddie and Lucy. Gray held a finger up as he spoke on his phone. When he re-joined the trio, he looked directly at Jackson. "John, I know you are keen on Elysia, but I think something strange is going on."

As Jackson flushed, Gray continued, "I just called Adrian. I asked him if he had been for his run yet."

Jackson rotated a hand in a forward motion to hurry the Chief up.

"Well, he hadn't, so I asked him to follow Elysia to see where she went."

"To be honest, Bill, I think she has been acting a bit strangely recently as well. I also have to deal with the expenses. Her telephone bill is for as much in the past month as it has been for the past year."

Eddie interrupted the uncomfortable conversation. "This is good news." Gray and Jackson stared as he continued, "It means we can visit her office to find out what she knows that we don't."

Elysia Martin's office looked as Eddie had expected. It was

large. Eddie presumed, as a result of her hierarchical position. There were several desks and tables, most of which were covered in documents, bound folders, books. Lots of books — almost all leather-bound. Those in glass cabinets looked old. Plastic tubs were piled in a corner, in three rows, six high.

Billy Gray walked to the central desk. Martin's work desk. "Her cutlery is as untidy as yours, John."

Jackson whispered to Lucy, "He means her pen cups," he motioned to the row of three pint glasses with stationery spilling over.

Lucy returned Jackson's smile, said, "You are adorable," and gave his arm a gentle squeeze.

There was a desktop computer on the corner of the desk with a closed laptop in front. Gray lifted the lid. It was on its main screen — no password required. "Why don't you three hunt around, and I will see what I can find on here."

Jackson looked at Lucy once again. "He would be better off asking one of you. He's hopeless with tech. Watch his one finger typing speed."

"I heard that," Gray said.

Eddie was already scanning the glass cabinets. Lucy crouched at the plastic tubs while Jackson joined Eddie at the cabinets. "What do you think we are looking for?"

Eddie replied, "Anything to do with the Crown Jewels or The Black Prince's Ruby. Maybe stuff from Charles II's reign, especially George Villiers. Maybe Isaac Newton."

Gray said, "I am looking for recent behavioural changes."

Jackson glanced at Lucy and winked. "He watches CSI."

Without direction, the other three looked in each corner of the room and worked leftwards towards each other's starting point. Lucy moved over to a table. There were papers shoved to the side as if creating a moat around a small plastic tub in the centre. It appeared to have been removed from an adjacent cardboard box with a lid propped askew against it. "Found something."

All four crowded around the box and tub. The box lid had a label, 'Villiers, George. Duke of Buckingham II'. Gray unclipped the four surrounding plastic fasteners. "You will need those," Gray motioned to a pair of white cloth gloves on the side of Martin's desk before looking towards Eddie.

Eddie slipped them over his hands and gently lifted the book from the container. He placed the papers next to it. "Now what?"

Gray held up his hands and wiggled his fingers, "You have the gloves on," before moving back to the laptop.

Jackson and Lucy walked to opposite sides of the office while Eddie studied the spine of the aged book. He could not read the words written on the side clearly, so he opened the first page.

The Sceptical Chymist: or Chymo-Physical Doubts and Paradoxes, touching the experiments whereby vulgar spagirists are wont to endeavour to evince their salt, sulphur and mercury, to be the true principles of things. To which in this edition are subjoyn'd divers Experiments and Notes about the Producibleness of Chymical Principles.

Eddie had identified the book and turned the pages, looking for something out of the ordinary. There was writing on the reverse of a blank page at the front. The ink was once again hard to read. Eddie used his phone to take a photo. He then moved the darkness slider across the image.

Eddie turned his gaze to Lucy. "It looks like we've solved one thing, anyway."

"What's that?"

"How this adventure was supposed to start for King Charles."

The other three walked over, and Eddie added, "We couldn't work out how or why Charles would embark on a weird treasure hunt for philosopher's stones created by the world's leading scientists of the time. Well, this appears to be George's copy of Robert Boyle's *Sceptical Chymist*."

Eddie proceeded to read the inscription aloud, "'My Dearest Sire, Our travails are compleat. Follow the clews from my father's final defeate. In honore, George'."

Lucy said, "This was a gift to Charles, wasn't it?"

"It appears to be," Eddie replied.

Gray glanced at both of them in turn. "I don't know how this was missed and just included in personal effects. He must have had this while incarcerated here. I would guess it is a far more important artefact than our esteemed curator realised."

Jackson said, "Unfortunately, it leads to the start, not the end. It must refer to the property in Portsmouth and his 'father's defeat'. We still don't know where The Ruby is."

Eddie flicked through the gilt-edged pages, aware it wasn't the best way of handling valuable antique books. After realising his mistake. He repeated the process. This time more slowly. He looked up, "Actually, I think it helps a lot. It tells us where The Black Prince's Ruby is."

Eddie stretched the white gloves tightly towards his wrists and flicked through the book once again.

Billy Gray said, "I don't think you should be doing that."

Eddie replied, "Definitely not. This book, especially with this message, will be worth a fortune. No historian or curator would handle an antique book like this. That is why I will only do it once more. Please watch closely," Eddie bent the gold-leafed book edge and flicked through the pages once again. The indentations were not age marks. He saw a message had been written with an inkless quill pen.

Lucy asked, "How did you know?"

"I didn't. I wasn't paying attention. I flicked through part of the book before I realised I shouldn't be handling the book that way. I then established what I was looking at."

"Which is?" Gray asked.

"It's called fore-edge painting. It's an art form created centuries ago. They drew a picture or added writing to the page edges, which can be seen clearly when the pages are curled over. It doesn't show when the book is closed, but it's revealed when opened."

Lucy smiled proudly. She was going to marry a man even smarter than she realised.

"We used to draw dirty pictures on our science books at school using the same principle."

Lucy stopped smiling and shook her head.

Eddie said, "I am going to guess this was a backup plan. If Charles didn't want to go on a philosopher's stone hunt, the side of the book told him where he could find something. I would suspect that whatever went on between George and Charles, he would have known that it was The Black Prince's Ruby."

Gray said, "That makes sense."

Eddie stared directly at the Chief Warder. "So, where is it?"

Gray replied, "Oh."

45

Elysia Martin opened the front door with the nonchalance of someone that knew, in just a few days, they would be able to afford to buy any manner of apartments as impressive as this one. At over three thousand square feet, it was more than three times the size of her current apartment. The furnishings in one of the three living areas alone were worth more than she made in a year. She brushed the back of a couch with her hand as she walked through to the kitchen area and smiled. On the rare occasion the people that lived in a place like this ate at home, staff would prepare the food. Why should the owners care if the kitchen was smaller than four of the five bathrooms? Martin opened the base units. The Champagne was there. She checked the waste bin. No rubbish. Good. Fridge next. Yes, fully stocked. The wall units were full of glass flutes and small plates. The kitchen was equipped and ready for guests. The caterers had done their job. They would repeat the assignment for the next ten and possibly several more days.

The dining area of one of the lounges included a long table. Martin manoeuvred it into position in front of bi-fold patio doors and studied the view. The Tower and adjacent bridge lit the night sky. The outlook was breathtaking. She placed the six associated chairs behind the table in a row and removed the same number of name plaques from her backpack. She tore away the cellophane from each and positioned them in front of the chairs. Mr Fofana, her, and these six people had worked diligently and carefully to carry out the plan. She stepped back to look around. The setting was perfect. She was satisfied she had completed everything required.

Her phone rang. It was one of those six partners. Regular updates regarding the movements of their clients were essential, but while she was coordinating the project, their reliance on her as the central point of contact, even regarding their own clients, was becoming ever more frustrating.

Just a few more days, and it would all be over.

With the Tower now closed to visitors, Eddie saw the moonlit framed entrance to The Chapel of Saint Peter ad Vincula as an invitation to conclude his circular travels. Gray had already explained the inkless quill message, which read, 'The Keepere Talbot Edwards Resting Place' was a problem that would reveal itself as soon as they entered.

The group walked through the aged wooden doors into the small church. Gray lit a nest of candles, and light cast both shadows and luminescence in equal measure throughout a more modern chapel than Eddie had expected.

Jackson took the opportunity to provide another of his history lessons. "Lots of historical figures were baptised, married and buried in the chapel, including several who were executed — Sir Thomas More, Lady Jane Gray, and Thomas Cromwell, to name just three."

Gray pointed towards a sunken altar as Jackson continued, "And over there are the marker stones for Anne Boleyn and Katherine Howard. Although used all the time, the chapel was in a bad way by the mid-nineteenth century. Architect Anthony Salvin oversaw a major programme of works, which sadly saw many seventeenth century additions removed, including the gallery. Because of the number of bodies and bones buried beneath, the chapel's floor was in danger of collapse, so his builders relocated the bones under a new crypt."

Billy Gray led them to the south wall of the chapel. He frowned with disappointment and pointed to the former Crown Jewels guardian's gravestone stuck on the wall.

HERE LIETH Y BODY OF TALBOT EDWARDS GENT LATE KEEPER OF HIS MATS REGALIA WHO DYED YE 30th OF SEPTEMBER 1674 AGED 80 YEARES

"So, what does this mean?" Lucy asked.

Eddie looked at Gray, "I am going to guess Talbot Edwards' grave no longer exists."

Gray nodded solemnly.

Undeterred, Lucy asked, "So where is his body?"

Gray answered, "It could be in the crypt, but I can't say for sure. There are said to be fifteen hundred bodies worth of bones down there. The more famous people are well marked. They even scientifically imagined the human form of the queens from their bones, but I don't think we will find Mr Edwards."

"Not good enough," Lucy turned to Jackson and pointed to the altar. "Was he dug up from here as well?"

Jackson replied, "Yes. The stone tablet on the wall was his gravestone. It, among others, was repurposed to repair the latrines at the Queen's Bench Prison in Southwark."

"I didn't know that," Gray said.

"You know this stuff is my hobby. Anyway, it was returned to the Tower as a paving stone in the Beauchamp Tower before its relocation here."

Although Jackson backed Gray in his assertion that the remains found beneath the chapel floor were behind the wall in the crypt, Lucy was having none of it and marched back through the church doors and out to the frigid night air. The wind picked up as the moon dappled darkness spread a grey chroma across the grass outside. "What about here?" she asked, pointing at the lawn as the three men hastened behind her. "It's outside the front door. There must be bodies buried here."

Gray explained that although the majority were likely to be found in the Chapel's crypt, they would probably find bones buried everywhere within the walls of the Tower if they dug down deep enough.

Lucy then suggested a return to the archives. Someone must have stored the personal effects of the once exhumed but now buried bones somewhere.

Gray provided more bad news. "At that time, if anything of value or interest did exist, it would have been looted or perhaps even mislaid. More likely is it would not have been considered important. There certainly won't be anything useful in the archives."

As Lucy paced the stone path beside the grass, Eddie took Gray to one side to request they dig the lawn next to the chapel. In a variation on a previous theme of expanded truth, he said he had read somewhere while researching that there were bodies below the lawn. Gray admitted that it was a burial ground at one stage but not a graveyard during the period they were discussing.

The group looked to each other in turn, unsure of their next course of action.

Elysia Martin heard someone knocking on the door —
three sharp taps and three with a pause between each.

What now?

Two men were standing in the doorway. One was wearing
a suit, the other, jeans, a leather biker's jacket, and a baseball
cap.

The man in the suit said, "I am very sorry to disturb you."

"And you are?"

"I am one of the drivers assigned to your guests. My name
is Phil."

Martin said calmly, "You appear to be holding a knife in
this man's ribs, Phil. May I ask why you have brought him to
me?"

"We caught him spying on the invitation collection point
near Petticoat Lane. My client asked him some questions. He
knew something but was trying to find out more."

"If your client is English, that would mean he has been
studying with Mr Dear. Why is he not dealing with this?"

"I called, but he said he had been detained and I should
bring him to you, at the venue."

Martin breathed slowly to calm her frustrations.
Coordination between partners and recovery of the stones was
her part of the deal. That was enough. Yet, it appeared she was
expected to take care of everything. "Please come in. I will
wait with you until Mr Dear arrives."

Jamie walked in ahead of Phil the driver. He was not
unduly concerned for his safety. He had watched Lucy disarm
a knife assailant earlier that day. If he couldn't remember the
moves, a knee to the groin would do the trick. He was
confident Phil would not pose a physical threat once disarmed.
He was also distracted by the stunning apartment. He walked
over to see the view. "Wow."

Martin joined him at the window. "Wow, indeed, Mr
Stuart. Now, tell me, what do you and your friend Mr Hill

know about our activities?"

Jamie was thrown off balance by the question. Still facing the patio doors, he closed his eyes before removing his cap. He rolled it and pushed it into his back pocket, and turned to face the woman. "I don't know what you are talking about."

"Oh, I think you do," Martin looked at Jamie's half-bare scalp. "Mr Garvan's work, I presume?"

Her phone rang again. It was Mr Dear. Martin said she would call back in five minutes and directed her attention to Phil, the driver. "Keep him here."

She walked into one of the five bedrooms. There was a bolt across a wardrobe the cleaners and caterers had no reason to open. Martin pulled the door to one side to reveal nine square film-wrapped packages. One batch with five-hundred-and-twelve small boxes. The other with half that number. She knew the total but enjoyed repeating it in her thoughts — a value of one-hundred-and-ninety-two-million. She removed the keys from her bag. The bulky utility knife included a screwdriver. She returned to the living area with the deadbolt and fixings in her hand.

Directing her attention to Phil the driver, she said, "Take him to that bedroom over there. Use whatever kitchen utensils you need to force a hole in the door frame for the bolt and put this on the outside of the door. Lock him in, and then you can leave."

Twenty minutes later, Martin ushered Phil the driver, out of the front door. She tapped another message. Her seventh to Robert Wilson. Where was he? He should be here taking care of these problems. As she pressed send, another call — another client.

It would be a relief when this was over.

Martin made her way to Tower Hill Underground station. She would deal with this minor inconvenience in the morning.

She had a long day ahead which would start with a few questions for Mr Stuart.

If he didn't say anything, his incarceration would be sufficient for Mr Hill to reveal what he knew. And if there were more stones, there would be more days added. The waiting list was long.

She stopped to look around the Underground entrance and wondered how soon her last journey on public transport would be.

46

It was four in the morning when the clear up began. Gray had informed Eddie there were thirty-seven Yeoman Warders at any one time — thirty-six after the murder. With two on leave, that left thirty-four strong and able former servicemen and women. Additional live-in staff included a Resident Governor and Deputy Chief Constable, who were both at overnight events, and a Chief Constable, who was safely tucked in bed and would not welcome a wake-up call. He was not completely sure whether the Chief Constable knew the story, anyway. It was not something that was discussed daily. He did, however, ask three colleagues to join them, one of which, fortunately, knew where the keys to access the garden equipment were.

All were grateful to roll the carefully removed turf back onto the disturbed areas and ensure that no one would be able to tell the difference when the gates re-opened at nine. Apart from the odd yawn during the long day ahead, of course.

They would keep the used shells, the ancient cloth fragments, the buttons, the two clay-pipes, and the single four-hundred-year-old coin for the curatorial team, but The Black Prince's Ruby — which the centuries of dirt had not even clung to — well, it was a quest of the ages, and this generation of Warders would get to invent their own stories one day. Tonight, their job was to return the bones to the ground. Speculating why the stone was not near bones or with fragments of clothing material could wait until another time. There was a lot of back-slapping, and Eddie was hailed a hero. He would be the guest of any one of them whenever he wanted a drink in *The Keys*.

Eddie saw Gray in deep conversation with a Warder in running gear, who he had learned was the guy Gray asked to follow Elysia Martin.

Or did Gray see?

Eddie knew he had to find out and made his way over when Gray was alone. "Where did she go?"

"That's the strange thing," Gray pointed to a skyscraper poking above the Tower's skyline. "Just over there."

"What's that?"

"It's a luxury apartment block called Deliciae. I think it's Latin for luxury, and it costs stupid money to live or rent there, but Adrian said Elysia went in and did not come out. He waited until just before midnight before he had to return."

Eddie asked, "Because the Tower is closed until six in the morning?"

"You have been doing your research, Eddie. Yes, that's right. Thinking of that, I am sure you and Lucy would like some shut-eye. We have a spare room. You can sleep at mine."

"Oh, we couldn't impose like that," Eddie said.

"Well, it's either that, or we do have a few prisons," Gray winked, "but we're waiting for the central heating to be fitted. I don't suppose you know anyone?"

Eddie smiled but thought Gray was going through the motions.

He knew.

Jamie checked the bedside clock. It had been an hour of silence. They had gone. He tried the door handle. The bolt he saw the driver install was strong. Sufficient agitation should wear it loose in time, but the view from the floor to ceiling window drew his gaze. The scene was incredible. He slid the wardrobe doors apart. Handmade. Not bad. One of the hinges was slightly misaligned, and the screws were not dressed. That was shoddy. He was surprised it was not picked up in the snagging before the apartment was sold. He entered the en-suite bathroom via double doors. He saw white marble tiles and a modern slipper bath complete with a floor-standing mixer tap. There was also a double basin vanity with perfect lighting. He opened the two interior doors. One was a shower cubicle, the other a toilet. It was one of those Japanese toilets. Jamie decided he urgently needed to go. He closed the door and laughed. Who would see him?

Having decided the toilet experience was the best of his life — it even had a drier button — he studied the bath. A row of expensive-looking toiletries stood in a tiled inset. Next to this was a second tiled inset, with two robes and a pile of towels neatly folded and arranged.

After his soak, Jamie removed his shower cap — he was not allowed to get his stitches wet. He draped the robe over his shoulders and decided it was fluffy heaven. He could not wait to tell Jamie.

He paced the bedroom a few more times and then decided to see if there was a late-night movie. An array of remote controls greeted him on a console. After pressing for the electric shutters to cover the expanse of windows, he stretched out on the sumptuous bed and began channel hopping.

He would leave in the morning, whoever tried to stop him.

Lucy had gone straight to bed, but Eddie stayed up for a mug of tea with Gray. "You saw, didn't you?"

"I did."

Eddie explained, "I didn't know about the Ruby until our conversation earlier, and I didn't consider that it could be the original stone from Portsmouth until I thought about the message in the Boyle book. We had it the wrong way around. I thought the Portsmouth stone was the first, but it was the last one hidden. Perhaps even the culmination of George's stone hunt — the return of The Black Prince's Ruby to his beloved king, brother, and best friend."

Gray cocked his head and frowned.

Eddie continued, "It wasn't until I saw the date of Talbot Edwards death that I cottoned on. He died in 1674, while George and Charles last visited Portsmouth in 1683, just a couple of years before Charles died. That affected the timeline — it meant the Edwards' clue must have been another philosopher's stone."

Gray asked, "And yet, you dropped the Ruby in the hole you dug."

"I do most of my best thinking when I am working, and it wasn't until the discussion about human bones that I wondered where the stone might be buried. If it was buried at all. I then considered the nature of the stones. They come in powder form, fragments, and jagged rock-like shapes. The penny dropped when I put my hand in my pocket. It was smooth, just like the one John had shown me a picture of earlier. It was only then that I knew I had been carrying it around for nearly a fortnight."

"That doesn't explain why you dropped it in the hole and then walked away, allowing John to find it."

Eddie laughed, "You lot are not as fit and young as you

once were. If you don't mind me saying."

Gray shook his head and looked down at his spreading waistline.

"I knew if I got you all digging up the Tower of London throughout the night, I had to make sure one of you found it. And I'm not sure anyone will care enough to examine burial dates."

"You know you have made my life a misery from this day forth, don't you? He won't stop going on about it. It's a good job Lou-Lou wants me to retire to the seaside."

Gray stood and held out a hand to shake, and promised him Lou-Lou would wake them with the smell of bacon in the morning before he said goodnight.

Gray laughed as he walked the corridor to his bedroom. "That'll teach you."

47

The television was talking to itself when Jamie woke. He looked at the screen. The ITV breakfast programme was on. The presenters were arguing about hair. The icon in the corner said it was 06:49. He stretched, looked around, smiled once again, and decided the more money you have, the better you sleep. He knew it was time to go, but not before another visit to the toilet.

After he dressed, he approached the bedroom door, and pulled the handle down. He did not know how long it would take, but sufficient and repeated pressure would weaken the bolt fixings. He knew this when he saw it being attached the previous night. He heard a noise. A vacuum cleaner? He bashed on the door.

The noise stopped, and he heard the bolt slide across. He positioned himself to charge whoever opened the door.

He saw a dark haired woman. Not the woman from the

previous evening, this one was wearing a cleaner's smock.

"Hello," Jamie said.

"Hello."

Jamie brushed past the woman and asked, "Are you alone?"

"I'm sorry," the woman looked uncomfortable. "My English," she raised her shoulders and smiled.

Jamie looked towards the kitchen. He returned a smile to the woman. "That's okay, I'm a sex slave. That's why I was locked in. I'm just going to pop to the kitchen to grab something to eat, and I will be on my way."

He did not know whether she understood any of that but was grateful when he opened the fridge door to see some cellophane-wrapped crostinis with tiny black, slimy balls perched on top. He didn't care what they were, he would eat anything.

As Jamie made his way to the elevator, he realised how important a mobile phone was to his life. And a wallet. He had no money or cards, and slowed his stride to consider his options.

He exited the building and headed for the car park where he and Lucy had parked the day before. It seemed like a lifetime ago. As he walked up the ramp, he saw Lucy's car straight away. Just along from it was Eddie's van. That's strange, he thought. They must still be here. He walked out of the car park slowly, unsure of a direction to head. Without his phone to call around local hotels, he had no clue how to find them.

He walked to the river and looked back up to the building he had just stayed in for the night. He then saw the domed turrets of the Tower of London. Perhaps they went back there today. Not that he could pay to get in. He needed to speak to Eddie. Everything and nothing raced through his mind, and before he knew it, he had walked to the entrance of the Tower of London.

He made his way to the fenced-off queue line adjacent to the moat. He saw wireframe animals and wondered what they were for. They seemed out of place. Two men in plain black security staff style suits, were scanning tickets near to a Beefeater standing outside a wooden booth. Jamie asked the ticket checkers whether they knew if Eddie Hill was there. They looked at each other and smiled. Jamie admonished himself. How would they know if Eddie was there unless he had introduced himself?

Eddie pushed open the arched door to Beef HQ, as he had now christened it. Billy Gray laughed as he entered, "I bet you're on your own, aren't you?"

Eddie replied sheepishly, "Yes. Lucy will be joining us shortly."

"Let me guess. My dear wife started breakfast at about oh-seven-forty-five-hours. You ate, had a shower, and then, with ear hanging off, you managed to leave, but had to sacrifice Lucy on the way?"

Jackson was sat in his usual place. "She can chat for England, can Lou-Lou."

Both men sat back in their chairs with arms folded.

They really should be on the stage, this pair, Eddie thought.

Gray said, "You won't see your lovely lady for a while, so I think we should put the plan in motion."

"Plan?" Eddie asked.

"Yes, we're going to celebrate finding the stone in the appropriate way at *The Keys* tomorrow night, but for now, we need to solve the other half of your puzzle. If our curator is mixed up in something, we should be the ones that get to the bottom of it."

Eddie had only known about The Black Prince's Ruby for a day. For him, this had always been about the philosopher's stones. With their emphasis and interests aligned, this was good news. He needed all the help he could get, and said, "Well, there's certainly something to get to the bottom of. As you know, my mate Jamie, came to London with Lucy. I have sent him a text and called him but have not heard anything. I have just got off the phone with DC Gale, the policeman I was telling you about, and they are cock-a-hoop back in Portsmouth. I didn't want to say anything yesterday because I didn't want to get your hopes up, but our suspicions were right. Lucy and Jamie caught your colleague's murderer's murderer yesterday."

Gray and Jackson were silenced. Eddie filled in the missing pieces. Jackson turned away, but Eddie and Gray knew he was wiping under his eye with his hand.

"Hello sir, I couldn't help overhearing your conversation. Did you say you were looking for Eddie Hill?" Jamie saw a Beefeater was leaving his hut, to walk towards him.

Unsure of what to say next, Jamie muttered, "Sorry, I'm just looking for a friend."

The Beefeater let loose a hearty chuckle. "Good luck with that. There will be thousands coming in here every day," he smiled and then winked at Jamie, "If, however, you are looking for Eddie. I should imagine he will be with the Chief in that office over there."

As the Beefeater pointed, Jamie became trepidatious. After everything that had happened in the past week or so, the paranoia was taking hold. He shook it off, reminding himself the man was a Beefeater. He must be honest. They are all ex-military.

"Follow me."

As Jamie approached the office, he saw Lucy heading in the same direction. She looked up, smiled, half-sprinted, and wrapped her arms around him. She then punched him on the arm.

"Where the hell have you been? We have been texting and calling non-stop. It's a good job we described a halfwit wearing a stupid baseball cap at the front gate."

Jamie provided the obligatory 'Ow!' and after she led him inside and made the official introductions, he told them of his horrific imprisonment in the luxury apartment block around the corner. He also made Lucy promise she would not download Bobby Ross' new album, even though she 'really liked him'.

When it was Eddie's turn, he briefly outlined the stone hunt, ensuring he did not cross Jamie's boredom threshold. For someone that could spend hours making sure a dovetail joint fitted perfectly, he had a peculiar lack of patience for detail.

Billy Gray told them he had called Elysia Martin, who would not be coming into work today. Jamie was disappointed. He had never hit a woman in the face before. He was also disappointed that he could not see The Black Prince's Ruby again, which was already in the Jewel House for safekeeping. Eddie explained he had seen it before. Jamie replied that he didn't know what it was at the time. Fortunately, Lucy was well-rehearsed at putting a stop to this sort of conversation between the pair.

Gray looked at Eddie and then motioned to John Jackson, who was not paying attention. Eddie realised he did not know that part of the story, so quickly changed the subject. "Which leaves us with a master criminal in a floral dress to catch."

Gray replied, "Don't worry. Alex is parked outside her apartment," he looked at Eddie, "The one with the ginger beard from last night. Anyway, Alex is outside her place. He will follow her movements, and report back regularly."

Jamie said, "You may as well tell him to come back. There's no point catching up with her today when we know she will be at the apartment tomorrow night, hosting a hundred rich and influential people."

319

48

"Okay, what's the plan?" Ian Gale asked as he closed his car door.

Lucy nodded towards Eddie. "This is your project. You heard him."

"Yes, but I like to include my sidekicks in the decision-making process."

Jamie said, "Everyone knows you can only have one sidekick."

"I'm still auditioning,"

Lucy said, "Perhaps you might like to put an advert in the job centre. 'Buffoon, who managed to get his fiancée kidnapped and mate put in the hospital, requires help being an even bigger buffoon'."

Gale said, "I don't want to put a stop to the fun, but I have some bad news. I spoke to my boss about the investigation and the crimes committed, and he said most cases are likely to be closed quickly. Robert Wilson will be charged with murder and abduction. Lucy and I will need to provide witness testimony for that. And I think they might be able to pin the car crash on him. His DNA should be evident in the vehicle. He may name names, but I doubt it. The problem was when I mentioned Elysia Martin, I stumbled."

"What do you mean?" Eddie asked.

"Well, I explained what I knew, but they asked me what the crime was. Apart from conspiracy to commit murder, which Robert Wilson has not confessed to yet, I realised I don't know what the crime is. Except perhaps conspiracy to defraud, which would rely heavily on witness testimony, and which we will need, to have any chance of getting a conviction."

Lucy said to Eddie, "He's right. What do you suggest?"

Eddie detailed a rough sketch of a plan, which led to three shaking heads before him.

Gale said, "I don't think it would be a good idea to put Lucy in harm's way, and it includes some straw clutching and exposure points, but it could work. I should be able to call for support, but I'm not really in a position to launch a strategy to tackle this."

Eddie jumped on the lukewarm response as confirmation of the merits of his proposal. Gale said he needed to get back to work. The others headed to Lucy's car.

Lucy said, "Whatever Ian says, this sounds like a stupid idea. Run it by me again so I can memorise it for your eulogy."

Eddie explained the plan once again. She was the only one of the three Elysia Martin had not spoken to yet. If she put her long hair up and applied some make-up, Eddie claimed it would be unlikely she would be recognised from the Martin Tower stone hunt. He would use his builder's lock-picking tool to get into the apartment. She would hide in one of the bedrooms until the gathering, party, whatever it was, was in full swing. She would then mingle and learn what was going on before leaving.

Jamie laughed before echoing Lucy's view. He was especially amused by the idea of Lucy sitting in a wardrobe for three hours with just her phone for company.

Eddie said, "Billy Gray had a word with the freeholder of the empty apartment next door — he has contacts everywhere. We will stay in there until Lucy knocks."

He turned to Lucy from the passenger seat. "All you have to do is relocate to the bathroom Jamie described, then walk from the bedroom, grab a glass of Champagne, have a quick chat to find out what is going on. Then leave and knock next door. Ian has given me the number of someone from the Metropolitan Police who will be there straight away if there is any sort of problem."

Lucy shook her head. She had half a mind to turn the car around. She also had half a mind to learn what was going on. Especially as she had people to hit. Eddie's grin provided the nudge that tipped the balance towards the half with the cockamamie plan.

Lucy only had time for a brief look at the apartment. And to think, all those bankers that had asked her out. She had even dated a couple of rich men. But no one got under her skin like Eddie Hill. Still, none of them would have her hidden in the bedroom of a luxury apartment in London attempting some sort of spy madness. She shook her head. If her mum was right about him, why couldn't she wipe the grin from her face?

A knock on the door broke her thoughts. "One minute," Lucy said as she slowly opened the bathroom door. "Sorry. I was having trouble with my dress."

A similarly glamorous looking woman in a grey, silky dress said, "American?"

"No, British."

"You must be one of Brian Dear's. You look lovely, Oscar de la Renta?"

"Only if he sells his frocks in TK Maxx," said Lucy, as she nodded.

The woman laughed as if it were the funniest thing she had ever heard. "Have you got yours yet?"

Lucy did not know what the woman was talking about, so she took a leap of faith. "No, not yet."

"I managed to persuade them to allow me four. Although my husband and children are not members of the Society, I paid double. Two-million for four tickets to eternal life is a bargain though don't you think?" before Lucy could speak, she added, "Look, they even come in a box made from Isaac Newton's original desk," the woman stared at the boxes. "I can't believe I am holding the elixir Robert Boyle created."

Lucy's voice faltered a little, but she just about held it together long enough to say, "I am going to collect mine now. May I have a quick peek? It's so exciting."

The woman lifted one of the lids gently. It revealed what appeared to be a glossy red pill resting on a satin white cushion. She then snapped the box shut and laughed as if it was the funniest thing she had ever done, before adding, "You must excuse me, I need to go," she pointed to the toilet cubicle.

Lucy moved from the bathroom doorway to allow the woman inside. She sucked in a deep breath to gather her composure and walked through the living room towards the front door. As she got nearer, a man wearing a Nehru jacket stepped in her way. He held out a hand, "Hello, Dipak. If you can excuse my clumsiness I have to say, you look absolutely lovely. Would you mind if I asked your name?"

Lucy clenched fists, "Do you mind if we speak in a minute, I am eager to collect my box."

"No, of course. I'm sorry. It is why we are here, after all."

The man stepped to one side, allowing Lucy to walk

towards the centre of the room. There were a lot of people —
most in six semi-orderly queues. Others were in small,
animated discussion groups. She recognised a few, including a
Welsh international rugby player, two politicians, three actors,
and a newsreader. She did not see Bobby Ross. Although
desperate to leave with the knowledge she had learned, she also
knew she had to see what was at the head of the queues, so she
joined one. It moved quickly.

She peered around heads and saw six name plaques in front
of six people handing out small boxes, one written in Chinese,
another in Indian. One looked like it was in Dutch or
Afrikaans, or something like that. Three were in English.
'London Rose Cross Society'. 'New York Association of the
Rosy Cross'. 'Rose Cross Society, San Francisco'.

As she moved nearer the front, the queues began to merge
into a group of excited people talking loudly. She did not
recognise the people behind the table, but she saw Elysia
Martin standing to one side. Now was the time to leave. She
made her way through the crowd.

"Leaving so soon?"

It was the woman from the bathroom. Lucy replied quickly,
"I have my box, please excuse me. I am in a rush," she pulled
the handle of the front door and slipped through.

Eddie answered the door a few feet along the corridor. He
was smiling. Lucy was shaking.

She wrapped her arms around him and did not let go until
she calmed. Jamie, Billy Gray, John Jackson, and Ian Gale
stood patiently, watching in silence. She grew aware of the
stares. "I didn't think you were able to get away, Ian?"

"My boss was a bit put out when my new friend at the Met
called him to say he needed my assistance with identifying
suspects, but there was not much he could say, so he had little
choice."

Lucy stared into Eddie's eyes, "I think you will find *you* are the sidekick."

"I am happy to be your sidekick forever, darling. Now, what did you learn?"

After Lucy described events, Jamie asked, "Right, so what does all that mean, then?"

Billy Gray looked at John Jackson and raised his shoulders. He was not alone in ignorance.

Jackson asked, "Anyone want a beer?" as he walked to the fridge in the small kitchen.

Eddie said, "Give me a minute."

Jackson whispered to Lucy, "Does he want one or not?"

As Jackson poured the last bottle into the sixth crystal-cut half-pint tumbler, there was a knock on the door. They all froze in place, except Gale. He looked at Eddie, "Don't worry, Batman, it's back-up."

Gale opened the door and introduced the two detectives as they entered. One explained there were nine vans parked outside the building.

Eddie said, "One might be enough. I think I know what's going on."

"Well, don't keep it to yourself," Jamie said.

"I think the six people Lucy explained were sitting behind the table next door, run Rosicrucian Societies across the world. I believe that Elysia Martin and her associate from the lock-up shop got together with them to create a new narrative about alchemy. Something along the lines of the great scientists *did* achieve the philosopher's stone. I think it might have started with our newly deceased tour guide from the Ashmolean. He had the Robert Boyle stone, and one of them — I am guessing Elysia Martin, came up with the plan to spend several years adjusting Rosicrucian teachings to add weight to the great scientists and their discoveries. A new and re-imagined doctrine, if you like. I doubt very much the organisations Lucy described are genuine. Fast forward to today, and you have some wealthy people buying a box made from Isaac Newton's desk — presumably to add provenance — with a tablet inside made from melted philosopher's stones, that they think will allow them to live forever. Or, as the original studies suggest, cure future illnesses."

The group, including the newly arrived policemen, all looked at each other. Expressions ranged from confusion to admiration. Lucy grinned.

Ian Gale said, "It sounds a bit cult-like, and we all know how that works. You just have to look at how people believe political ideologies," he paused and looked at Eddie. "They are different when it comes to vast sums of money, though."

"I don't think we are talking about vast sums of money. Lucy said the woman she encountered had four boxes, and she paid double. At two million, that means each tablet in a box would ordinarily cost two hundred and fifty thousand."

"That sounds like a lot of money to me," Jackson said.

Eddie replied, "Tech billionaires have persuaded plenty of people to pay hundreds of thousands of dollars to fly an extra fifty miles to the edge of earth in aircraft some wouldn't consider completely reliable yet. I am pretty sure rich people would pay whatever it costs to live forever."

Lucy said, "That's about two-hundred-million."

The group all looked at her in silence. She repeated, "If there were around a hundred people scheduled every day for a week or two, that would be around two-hundred-million. Possibly, a lot more."

At that news, one of Gale's colleagues pressed the button on his radio. He spoke quickly.

The Yeoman Warders, Eddie, Lucy, and Jamie, were told to stay inside as the policemen opened the door.

They could not see events, but the action unfolded swiftly outside. There was a lot of noise.

49

John Jackson tapped his watch. "We need to go, Bill."

Gray said to the others, "You are more than welcome to stay here tonight. Or you can come back with us if you like. Jamie, you could stay with John, and Lou-Lou adores you, Lucy," he looked around at the room. "Just joking. Who would want to pass up a chance to stay a night somewhere like this? Sadly, we have to get back. We need to open up in the morning."

Jackson laughed as he walked. "We have a castle to run."

Jamie saw the two Yeoman Warders out with a, "See you in the morning," before turning to Eddie and Lucy. "I like them."

Jamie also left the apartment for a short period to visit the apartment next door and to leave Eddie and Lucy with some time alone. He quickly learned the police raid did not finish with someone tidying up the broken glasses, returning the overturned chairs to their positions under the table, and quietly closing the door behind them. He returned with two bottles of Champagne and a tray of sandwiches, and all three experienced the luxury the huge apartment had to offer before leaving with great sadness in the morning.

After a quick chat about Japanese toilets, Jamie said, "Morning," to the same cleaner he had seen two days earlier as she walked along the corridor. She yelped when she saw him. She screamed when she opened the door to the apartment.

Ian Gale was waiting for them alongside the two Yeoman Warders at Beef HQ. "I understand you had a free five-star experience last night."

In his poshest voice, Eddie said, "We did indeed."

Jackson boiled the kettle as they swapped personal experiences of the same story.

Gale took a long sip of his tea before he said, "Eddie, you were right. It finished up with eleven arrests. I think there may be more, but they will be minor charges if anything. Elysia Martin even had a fleet of over fifty drivers to take care of all the marks," he took another gulp, "That's what they effectively were, of course. It was a long con, and most of those people at the party were gullible victims. Some will hopefully kick up a fuss. Legal challenges, that sort of thing, but it's more likely that a lot more will want to hush it up. It was most telling that while some raced out of the building, eight people, including Miss Martin, were not in a rush to leave and were very calm and cooperative after arrest."

Jamie asked, "Is that good news?"

"One thing did happen in the panic down the corridor. I might have accidentally tripped up Bobby Ross."

Jamie performed a small air punch. The news made him feel better about his cap. He would wear it again if just to annoy Eddie.

Gale added, "Whoever finds his teeth might do well with them on eBay. The investigation will take some time, but there are a lot of embarrassed rich and powerful people around the world at the minute, that will want this kept as quiet as possible. Some will even still believe what they have learned is true. For most, the sums of money were so small it would be considered pocket change. I was told their contributions could be considered just that, donations. I have a feeling the organisers knew this. Human nature would suggest spending, in some cases, years, learning a truth takes some unravelling to reveal the lie."

Billy Gray rose from his chair and headed towards the shelving behind him. "In all this excitement, I forgot. And again, I am very sorry," he handed Lucy the Quality Street tin before adding, "Most people save coins. I was told this was full of fifty-pound notes."

Lucy said, "We change it up regularly. Otherwise, it wouldn't fit," she glared at Eddie and shook her head. She could see he felt suitably admonished.

Gray said, "Well, I hope you don't mind, but there's just a cheque in it now."

Eddie said, "I don't think we will be keeping that much money in the house again."

"Yes, I really can't apologise enough. I have never been involved in something I've regretted as much. I spoke to Michael, and he confirmed he left a note. I am sure you will find it at some stage, but that doesn't relate to my shame. I hope you don't mind, but we had a whip-round and topped it up a bit."

Eddie looked at the cheque. He knew there was around thirteen thousand pounds in the tin. The cheque read fifteen thousand. He said nothing but held his hand out and shook Gray's. He then walked around the table to John Jackson, who refused his hand and gave him a big bear hug. And then, that laugh again.

Eager to move on, Eddie changed the topic of conversation. "While we're doing our housekeeping, what about The Black Prince's Ruby?"

Gray replied, "Well, the Imperial State Crown will go off for a routine clean tomorrow. The spinel will take its rightful place during that process."

Jamie asked, "Spinel?"

Jackson said, "It's not a ruby. It's a different type of precious stone. Have you got something else to tell them, Bill?"

Gray said, "I had an interesting call from Kensington Palace this morning. They wanted to express their gratitude but don't ask me how they knew. I have no idea. What I do know is some people believe Prince William will be the first king since Charles II."

Jackson saw the visual confusion and took the opportunity. "Charles II didn't have any legitimate children. As you will know, his brother James II took the throne. I won't bore you with all the history at this point, except to say Prince William of Orange was invited over from Holland to become king after they forced James to abdicate. That period was messy, but to be fair, it wasn't the only disruption to the lineage of the throne right through to today."

Lucy asked, "So, where does Prince William fit in?"

"Well, he is, of course, the rightful heir to the throne, but not just as King Charles III's son, but as Diana's son. You see, Diana Spencer was a direct descendant of Charles II, via his bastards, Henry Fitzroy, the first Duke of Grafton, and Charles Lennox, the first Duke of Richmond."

Jamie asked, "Does that mean we haven't had a proper King or Queen since Charles II?"

Eddie and Lucy looked at him and shook their heads. "What?"

Eddie reached for his backpack.

"There is one other thing. I have this book," Eddie removed the copy of *Mutus Liber* and held it out to Gray. "You should probably have this."

Gray put his hands up. "No. We don't want anything to do with that. I should add, just this morning, I removed the dedication page in the book we found in Elysia's office. That went in the bin, and so will that if you leave it here. You best take it home. The only thing I would ask is you sand out, rub out, or whatever you can do to remove that writing on the back. No one needs to know this chapter of The Black Prince's Ruby's legend."

"I think it's probably worth a lot of money, Bill."

"Then let's just call it a souvenir."

As Lucy and Jamie walked out, she saw Eddie grab Billy Gray's arm. She heard the words 'Swap' and 'Stone'.

She asked him what he was trying to swap.

"Did you see that axe?"

Eddie spent the afternoon catching up with the knowledge he needed for the encounter. It took some persuasion, but he managed to convince Lucy and Jamie it was not a good idea for them to accompany him, mostly because they could not be counted on to avoid doing something they might regret.

Eddie followed Ian Gale down the rubberised stairs. They walked along a narrow corridor with terracota coloured epoxy coated flooring. The white-tiled walls appeared to shimmer with wet glaze as they funnelled them towards the penultimate steel door.

Gale said, "I could get into serious trouble bringing you down here. The Police and Criminal Evidence Act means people in custody aren't allowed visitors anymore."

"Ian, I am amazed anyone noticed I was here. You appear to be one of around three policemen on duty."

"It's a football night. It will get busy later, so we can't be long," Gale turned the key and opened the door. The hollow space amplified the metallic clanging sounds.

Elysia Martin looked up from her blue polyurethane bed. "A visitor. I wasn't expecting anyone, Constable."

"Detective Constable."

She ignored Gale and looked straight at Eddie. "How are you, Mr Hill?"

Eddie noticed Martin was not wearing a floral dress but instead a well-tailored suit. It looked expensive. He smiled when he saw a copy of Tatler resting on the padded bed. A woman with expensive tastes.

"How do you like your accommodation?"

"Temporary accommodation," Martin replied.

Eddie looked towards Gale, who nodded.

"I am sure I will sleep soundly in the knowledge that I will be leaving tomorrow."

Although he knew the charges were tenuous, the witnesses almost certainly minimal, and her part in the scheme, virtually impossible to prove, Eddie hid his disappointment. Stretched policing budgets would deny whatever unwitting victims that did want to come forward, any sort of justice. This would certainly explain her confidence. She seemed relaxed.

"I am always content when I can provide a little enlightenment, so let me provide you with the courtesy, Mr Hill. You did, after all, go to extraordinary lengths to disrupt my soirée," Martin turned her lips into a mock-frown. "The process is always the same. A malevolent force will push the appropriate buttons to instil fear within its victim. In our case, we merely provide incentive and reward for the natural human instinct for survival. I am sure you will agree, Mr Hill, survival is the most primordial abstract of fear. We have not, however, chosen to scare anyone. We have educated people with an enlightenment agenda. We provide hope, not fear."

"*Hope.* You are not providing hope. You are conning people."

"We have remained true to Rosicrucian philosophy. Society promotes fear, which reduces the capacity for learning. We provide the opportunity for people to gain power over their potential."

Eddie glared at the woman on the padded seat. "Potential to live forever? You may have lured some gullible rich people into your scam, but you're going to have to get up earlier than that if you think I'm going to buy into your propaganda."

"I have no concern with the hour you get up in the morning, Mr Hill."

Eddie knew she was mocking him but allowed her to continue, while grateful Lucy was not there.

"We are not selling propaganda. We have merely enhanced the value of early science and built on the esoteric truths of the ancient past, which are concealed from the average man, and provide insight into nature, the physical universe, and the spiritual realm."

"I read that exact quote. Lindgren, isn't it?"

"Very good, Mr Hill, but it is nevertheless the truth."

"You can attempt to blind me with claptrap, but I have been reading about Rosicrucianism, and you are replicating previous processes to gain influence, power, and disciples to your cause. Just like the early practitioners, you are taking advantage of human nature by promising spiritual guidance and transformation with the ultimate gift — the elixir of life. A cheap pill that you convince them will enable them to live forever."

"Hardly cheap, Mr Hill. We have spent many years and millions of pounds in pursuit of the gifts provided to future generations by the greatest scientific minds in history."

"Yes, many years spreading your version of an ancient doctrine while undermining a respected organisation. I half believe you have bought into your own nonsense, but then I'm reminded that you are charging many more millions of pounds to your victims for these magic pills."

"Victims. Magic pills. It appears that you are the one using misrepresentative rhetoric Mr Hill. And I am sure I have sufficient funds to reimburse those, that I can assure you will be very few in number," Martin paused to stretch an emotionless smile across her face, "unhappy people."

Eddie replied, "Talking of deceit, I spoke to a representative of the Ancient Mystical Order Rosae Crucis. They provide similar teachings to those you describe, along with charitable works, but as opposed to your scam, they are mostly non-profit in their activities." he did not blink as he stared into her soulless grey eyes. "The funny thing is, they had never heard of the organisations on the little plaques you had made for your event."

"I think that will be all, Mr Hill. Thank you for your visit."

50

Eddie hugged his mum. Her eyes were borderline red and puffy. He shared a knowing glance with his dad — this would not end well for her handkerchief.

Annie Hill said, "I didn't think you would find happiness again. Lucy is so lovely. I can't tell you how happy I am for you."

Eddie turned to his dad, "You know she will be obsessing about her mascara now?"

Eddie's dad moved his cane to his forearm, nodded, and pulled him in for a hug of his own.

Jean Brisley approached and made a beeline for Eddie's mum with outstretched arms. "Anne."

After a short embrace, she kissed Eddie's dad on both cheeks. She then turned to Eddie. "Lucy said you took care of all of this. Is that true?"

Eddie looked around the courtyard with her. The early

summer sun glimmered off the cobbles. The octagonal space had blue and silver ribbons and balloons festooned around doors, windows, and even a cannon. The marquee in the corner was kitted out with matching chair backs, surrounding elaborately decorated tables. "I did my best. Do you like it?"

"Eddie, you have done my daughter proud. Her dad would have loved this," with a whisper, she added, "I can't believe you hired proper Beefeaters."

She then punched him on the arm.

So, that's where she gets it from, Eddie thought.

Eddie saw Billy Gray talking with John Jackson. He left the three parents together and made his way over.

"I can't thank you enough for giving up your time to come. All of you."

Gray shook his hand. "Eddie. The pleasure is ours. To be frank, they all wanted to come. But as you know, we have a castle to run," he said with a wink.

Jackson added, "The ones you don't know are former Warders. As you can see from Charlie over there."

Eddie looked over at a man at odds with a somewhat tight red tunic.

"We had to draw lots for twelve. None of us have been to Southsea Castle before. Henry VIII built it, and he also founded the Yeoman Warders, so some have a special affection for him."

Gray dragged his colleague away. "Don't bore the man on his wedding day, John."

Where did she pop up from? Eddie thought as he saw Lucy's mum by his side. He introduced her to John Jackson. As he left them to acquaint, he said, "Don't forget you owe me a tenner."

"It was a Mulligan."

"No-one that plays off fourteen can claim a Mulligan."

Jackson smiled at Jean as he stretched his arms out in

feigned innocence to Eddie.

Eddie saw the caterer talking to the wedding planner. Now was as good a time as any to get it over with. "Hello, Richard. Hello Lorraine. I wanted to take care of my bills before we left for our honeymoon. I can do it now if you like."

Lorraine replied, "It's all taken care of. We received a cheque. You even wrote a note asking for fireworks afterwards."

Richard laughed. "Don't worry, Eddie, lots of people forget what planet they're on when they're planning a wedding."

Eddie thanked them and walked away. He saw Billy Gray edging away from his mother-in-law to be and rushed over.

"Bill, everything's paid for. Did you have something to do with this?"

Gray smiled and placed his hand on Eddie's arm. "As you know, I pulled some strings to get the castle, but we didn't pay for it. I can't say I'm surprised, though. You may have some new friends in high places."

As Yeoman Warders were ushering people to their seats, Eddie entered the arched chapel. The sun bounced through the dormer windows onto the clean red brickwork. He took a momentary pause to look around before shaking from his daze. He spotted the Jamies.

"Well, don't you two look beautiful. Matching waistcoats, hair, and beards."

Other Jamie grabbed his husband's arm. "We try."

Eddie replied, "Well, you try. He's just trying. But now, I need to relieve you of my best man."

Eddie realised he was probably the millionth new husband around the world, asking, 'Have you got the ring?' that week alone, but it seemed like the right thing to say.

"Yes. Of course. I also collected the fish tank from that guy in Westbourne."

"Contents as well?"

"Yes. Tank. Fish. Cleaning stuff. Red stones at the bottom of the tank. He didn't want anything. I think he was just glad to get rid of it."

Eddie asked, "So, no problems?"

"Nope. It's all set up in your living room. I don't think the son was happy, though. As I finished packing up, he arrived, and they got into an almighty row. I made a sharp exit and left them to it."

Eddie didn't know if he was supposed to turn to look when the music started, but both Lucy's and his mother did. Not that they could see anything through their hankies. Eddie followed their lead. She appeared to glide towards him down the aisle. The ivory coloured dress clung in all the right places. Eddie was fully aware she had the figure of a supermodel, but he had never seen Lucy look more beautiful.

As Lucy turned to face him at the altar, a gentle red glow spread across her face as the sunlight refracted from the large stone hanging from the gold chain around her neck.

Writer's note

I know multi-facetted craggy detectives, sniper trained super-soldiers or world-renowned expert university professors are better equipped for adventures and crime-solving, but I have often wondered what would happen if it was instead an unprepared and ill-equipped man down the road? A man like Eddie Hill. I think he got on okay — admittedly with a bit of help — but perhaps only a genius forensic scientist could say for sure.

You will have noticed Eddie's adventure takes some liberties with historical reference. This is because I wanted to make sure all of Eddie's research material was available for all to read with its authentic inaccuracy on the internet. I, therefore, hope no person, or building, was harmed in the writing of this book. Except for York Gate, for which I apologise on Eddie's behalf. Oh, and George Villiers, the Second Duke of Buckingham, who sounds like a particularly dubious character to me.

I was walking to my brother-in-law's wedding reception in Portsmouth when I passed *Ye Spotted Dogge*. It is a beautiful building, lovingly converted into a small boutique hotel. By the main entrance, a recognition plaque details the death of George Villiers. An army officer named John Felton, who believed he was unfairly denied promotion by Villiers, stabbed the first Duke of Buckingham on 23rd August 1628 at what became known as Buckingham House, 11 High Street, Portsmouth, Hampshire. The hotel includes archival references, including a knife. The accompanying plaque reads: 'Reputed to be the knife with which Felton murdered the Duke of Buckingham'.

This set my imagination racing. I wondered what else builders might have found, which is where the idea for Eddie's unusual discovery came in.

In chapter twelve, I detail a lineage that runs from 1679, and Charles II, to 1840 and the death of Lord William Russell. The inheritance was for my story, but the descendants are accurate. I won't apologise for Eddie's later assertion that the highest level of British society somehow features influential people related to each other.

The blockquote passages are faithful and accurate, except for the relationship between Isaac Newton and Robert Hooke. Another of my meandering considerations was how much further scientific study would have travelled had two of the greatest minds in history been best buddies instead of arch-foes.

While watching the Lord Mayor's Show on television, a presenter repeated an explanation I had ignored many times before. A new Lord Mayor of London has been appointed every year for over three hundred in a lavish ceremony that includes participants from the Great Twelve City Livery Companies: The Mercers, Clothworkers, Drapers, Fishmongers, Goldsmiths, Grocers, Haberdashers, Ironmongers, Merchant Taylors, Salters, Skinners, and Vintners. I wondered what Mercers were and proceeded to look them up. All participants are Worshipful Companies, have elaborate crests, and have been around for centuries. Just as I was about to learn more, an unrelated tangent took me to Rosicrucianism. After the publication of several texts — described as manifestos — Rosicruciansim hit a peak in the seventeenth century. Speculation mounted, and excitement spread at the prospect of a secret society of alchemists and sages preparing to transform the arts and sciences and the religious, political, and intellectual landscapes of Europe. During a period of religious wars and political strife stretching across the continent, it is perhaps unsurprising such a spiritual and cultural movement was considered attractive by so many.

Although my Rosicrucian groups do not exist, organisations operate around the world today. Their teachings are not secretive, and the general public is welcome to learn more about their activities. However, political and ideological truths are very much part of the practice of fringe, new age or even secret societies. Many wish for their affairs to remain private. As this is the case, I think it only fair we get to play with our imaginations. Especially as the pursuit of the philosopher's stone was a serious project for the greatest minds before and during the Restoration period.

It was the most incredible time for political, scientific, and social advancements. One of history's most romantic notions is the idea that a cure-all substance was available to the most ardent experimental enthusiasts. It is not a surprise that many of the most famous minds dedicated their lives to pursuing this universal remedy, or Alkahest. When I stumbled across *Mutus Liber* on a random internet search, I considered it no different from the current study of futurology. *Mutus Liber* is one of the earliest contributions to the study of alchemy in printed literature. It is said to show how to achieve the magnum opus, an alchemical phrase to describe working with the materials required to create the philosopher's stone. As modern-day scientists actively pursue the same goals, I would suggest that the reluctance to accept mortality is humankind's greatest fallibility. The current equivalent could be scientific research into augmentation, Moore's Law, and the potential for downloading consciousness. Something I may have Eddie look into at some stage.

It may be the uniforms. It may be the pomp. It may be the traditions, but Beefeaters have always held a fascination for me. They are very much the best of British, and I look forward to writing about Billy Gray and John Jackson again. The Tower of London is my favourite place in the world, and Yeoman Warders get to live there! It is also home to some fascinating tales and stories. I read the legend of the Black Prince's Ruby as a teenager. I hope its adventure within this book is worthy of its real exploits. The Ashmolean Museum, Cliveden House, Trinity College Cambridge, The Monument, Southsea Castle, and the Tower of London receive around four million visitors a year. They represent a tiny proportion of the incredible sights, monuments, and buildings tourists to the United Kingdom have at their disposal. They may find similarly interesting characters to those Eddie stumbled across, but it's unlikely they will steal their wedding fund tin or have secret offices in broom cupboards (unfortunately).

More importantly, I have people I would like to thank. Mark and Sam Darby were great help with Lucy's fight scenes. I had no idea how intense the learning is to become proficient in *Wing Chun*, but I think it would be fair to say Eddie and Jamie's commitment to the discipline would mirror my own.

Jo Fuller was also very kind to spend time with an unpublished author to answer police procedural questions.

I would also like to thank Tracy, who has been a rock throughout this process. Careful not to disillusion with feedback and ever-patient with me talking about plots and sub-plots.

Finally, I would like to thank you for reading. For any new author, writing a novel features an extravaganza of emotions. For me, most of the experience was enjoyable, but now it's finished, my emotion is gratitude that I managed to get through the process with a similar amount of hair to when I started.

I hope you enjoyed Eddie's diversion from reality. It would be great if you could write a review if you did. It is a tremendous help to new authors and reading kind words about my work would certainly make it all worthwhile.

About the author

Paul Casella is a former sports writer from South London, England. In recent years he has edited a number of websites, including www.chipsandcrisps.com, and is the author of The Wonderful World of Chips & Crisps. You can read more about Paul, his websites and former publications at: www.pcasella.com

If you enjoyed Eddie Hill's first adventure,
this time he's at The Houses of Parliament.
Turn over for a sneak preview of:

The Hegemony Network

He closed the crackle-painted door and made his way to the end of the road, where he flagged down a black taxi. The driver attempted to speak to him. They always do. He wondered how often the question, 'Guess who I had in my cab today?' was asked at dinner tables. He ignored the inevitable chatter ahead and reflected on the space in his archive where a cardboard box should be.

He had stared at the empty shelf for several minutes. It had become a routine. He would stand in the centre of the room and look around to ensure everything else was in its place. Archive boxes with subject matters, dates, and people involved, neatly written on the front of each. He would then refocus on the space. It needed filling. He knew it existed, but its whereabouts remained a mystery. He had tried tracing back to before 1812 — the period of origin. He had learned of the men and women involved and of their descendants. Their homes, buildings, anywhere their records might be stored, kept, lost, hidden. He had spent over a decade checking everywhere he could think of.

As the car fought its way through the London traffic, he recalled the time he inherited the role from his mentor and first love. The start of a journey that led him here. A place where everything was in order, except this one small section. He had removed the extensive records from Lord Neville's home and relocated them to the house he used for storage, his office, and his home. Everything had to be collated in date order and archived to his exacting standards. Patience was key. It was more than a labour of love. It was his life. And now, everything was finally in order, apart from the missing records.

The one place left was Parliament itself. He had walked every corridor looking for potential hiding places and tapped every wall for hollow sections. He was a constant source of irritation for the maintenance staff. It had taken some time, but the works to renovate the hidden bowels of the Palace of Westminster were well underway. It was a monumental job that would continue for many years. Papers, files, documents, old newspapers — all discovered, all discarded. He had always known there was only a slim chance the records would be among all the potentially promising discoveries. Especially as he presumed it would be a reasonably sized stack, at the very least. It did prevent disillusionment, though, even as each search avenue was exhausted.

But finally, an untouched area.

He interrupted his melancholic reflections and clapped his hands with excitement. The taxi driver looked up, saw his fare was deep in thought and turned his attention back to the road.

Could they be there?

An intuitive ability to compartmentalise his thought process allowed him to switch instantly to his diaries. He kept two. The work diary, which staff took care of, and a private journal he kept himself. His assistants changed regularly, but they were consistently grateful that he always seemed to know when dates and times were available for work-related meetings and obligations.

His private diary reminded him of the Scotland trip the following week. The Americans were also due over, which would almost certainly mean a trip to Portsmouth for Alex. He would need to leave plenty of time free from parliamentary responsibilities. The time he spent in surgery was often remarked upon. Always the end of the week, even if it meant missing important matters of state. Few Members of his stature and standing spent so much time working so diligently for constituents. Or so, they thought.

He stared at his hand-written 'To Do' list.

Prison, Alex, Progress.

Edinburgh, Angus, President.
Portsmouth, Dawn, Progress and Detail. Possibly Alex.
France, Germany, Russia x 2, China x 4.

He sat back as the taxi bumped along the A40 and glanced at a road sign for RAF Northolt. He was nearly home, but where would home be for his successor? The future could see so many Chinese projects it could mean relocation. He smiled at the thought. That would never happen. Irrespective of The Club's global reach, its home would always be England. He knew his time at the helm was almost up, though. He no longer had the energy that took him to the front benches within two years of being elected. A period in his personal history that seemed a lifetime ago. He momentarily drifted to that other lifetime. The one before the one everyone knew about.

He nodded his head. The Club would be in safe hands — if only Alex could keep his urges in check. There was a time and place. Strategy was the most vital lesson he had to pass on. He would ensure he provided a method, procedures, and a personal blueprint before he concluded his career with the inevitable.

He had never wanted to be Prime Minister, but who better to steer his country clear of the disarray once he arranged for Scotland's independence? A unique legacy that none of his predecessors could match. No, he had no choice but to run the country. Despite the public profile and intrusion, he had accepted he was the best man for the job. It was the least he could do.

He studied the list again. Detail and explanation omitted, he knew the implication of each simple notation. Regular phone calls to Club members — rarely text messages — were prioritised. Immediate updates were critical. Predecessors would have written letters. It was a miracle they got anything done. The smooth running of projects and affairs was imperative if all were to reap the full benefit of their Club membership. This was the most important lesson he needed to pass on to his successor.

The crunch of gravel was etched in his consciousness. As soon as he heard it, he was home, whatever he was doing or concentrating upon. He estimated the driveway to his door was around a hundred, maybe a hundred and fifty metres, but it was always long enough for a brief friendly chat with his driver of the day. Although he ignored them entirely during the hour-long drive, sometimes much longer in rush hour, this short period provided the opportunity for that dinner table conversation. He always hoped, no, he knew, a phrase along the lines of, 'Lovely fella. He would make a good Prime Minister', would follow. He had the gift, irrespective of the walk of life, the recipient of his charm trod.

He opened the door, scanned his expenses card on the reader, and said, "Thanks, geezer."

The out of presumed-character simplicity always threw them. This one would definitely be a 'lovely fella'.

He watched and waved — he always waved them off — as the taxi driver reversed to return the way he came. He then looked up at the imposing Gothic structure he called home, a ten-bedroom country house and former hunting lodge of a Victorian newspaper proprietor, who seemed to require more servants' quarters than 'upstairs' rooms. These days, apart from a gardener, an occasional cook, and a daily cleaner, he only needed Stevens. He never took it for granted, although it was no more than he deserved, of course. He would have had more were it not for his father. He shifted his back and felt the marks of that other life scrape against his shirt.

Sir Richard Plume entered his home, handed his jacket to Stevens and turned left towards his office. It was where he did his best thinking. This evening, the first agenda item — did Dawn Thatcher make a mistake telling the attractive young tradesman to dispose of the 'junk'?

Made in United States
Troutdale, OR
07/06/2023

11009484R00195